COURTNEY MILAN

Trial by Desire

Recycling programs
for this product may
not exist in your area.

ISBN-13: 978-0-373-77485-2

TRIAL BY DESIRE

Copyright © 2010 by Courtney Milan

This edition published by arrangement with Harlequin Books S.A.

For questions and comments about the quality of this book
please contact us at Customer_eCare@Harlequin.ca.

www.HQNBooks.com

Printed in U.S.A.

Acknowledgments

I've heard before that second books are hard. This one was…very hard. I am first and foremost grateful for all the readers who contacted me demanding Ned's story. Without your encouragement and enthusiasm, I might have given up on this.

As always, I am deeply grateful for Tessa and Amy, who offered support, encouragement and advice. Elyssa Papa and Kris Kennedy gave valuable feedback on various drafts. Franzeca Drouin saved me from about a billion errors. Nancy, my mother-in-law, answered a thousand questions about horses for me. And Kim Castillo truly is an author's best friend.

Kristin Nelson, my awesome agent, and all the Nelson Agency staff—Sara Megibow, Julie Kerlin, Anita Mumm, and Lindsay Mergens—provided the absolute best support an author could want.

A great many people who put up with my whining about this book: the Pixie Chicks, the Vanettes, the Bon Bons, and my favorite debut loop ever.

Margo Lipschultz, my wonderful editor, provided the proper balance of encouragement and gentle prodding, and Ann Leslie Tuttle let me know when I was going off the rails. I wish I had space to thank everyone on the entire team at Harlequin by name for the amazing job they have all done launching my career—from the extraordinary sales force, to the marketing department, to the editorial enthusiasm at HQN Books— but that would take pages and pages.

And last but never least, there's my husband, who never once complained about my writing while he did the dishes, made me dinner and took care of the dog.

Trial
by
Desire

For Teej. Because when I had to make Ned a hero, I gave him a little bit of you.

PROLOGUE

London, 1838

LADY KATHLEEN CARHART had a secret.

Truth be told, she had more than one—but the secret she had in mind as she sat across from her husband at breakfast had arrived only today. It was wrapped in paper and had been set carefully atop her chest of drawers. And if her husband knew what it was…

She suppressed a faint smile.

Across the table from her, he set the paper down and fixed his gaze on her. His eyes were a liquid brown, three shades beyond her breakfast chocolate. They stood out, uncannily dark against the sandy brown of his hair. He had no notion what it did to her when he looked at her like that. Her toes curled. Her hands clasped together. All he had to do was look at her, and she found herself wishing—wanting—no, *desiring.* And therein lay the root of her problem.

"I had a talk with my cousin a few days ago," he said.

Around London, a thousand couples might have been having a similarly prosaic conversation. Kate's mother had cautioned her to be practical about marriage, to accept that she and her husband would share a genteel, friendly politeness.

But then, Kate hadn't married the average London gentleman. Mr. Edward Carhart did nothing properly or politely—nothing, that was, except his newly acquired wife.

"What did Blakely have to say?" Kate asked.

"You know that some of our holdings are in the East India Company?"

"Aren't everyone's? It's a good investment. They trade in tea and silk and saltpetre...." Her voice trailed off into roughness.

If he'd known what flitted through her mind when she said the word *silk,* he'd not sit there so sanguine. Because she'd purchased a filmy night rail on Bond Street. It was made of imported silk and fastened together in front by means of lavender ribbons. Those scraps of opaque fabric were perhaps the garment's only concession to modesty. It lay on her chest of drawers, simply beseeching Kate to wear it one evening.

"Silk," Ned said, looking off into the distance without seeing her lean forward, "and other things. Like opium."

"Opium was not on my shopping list."

He didn't smile. Instead he glanced away as if uncomfortable. "In any case, Blakely and I were talking about the recent events in China." Ned shook his paper at her. "And we decided it would behoove someone to personally inquire into what was going on over there."

For once, he sounded serious. Kate frowned at him.

"By *someone,* you mean Mr. White, and by *over there,* you mean the office on—"

"By *someone,*" Ned said distinctly, "I mean *me,* and by *over there,* I mean China."

He set the newspaper down and bit his lip. The morning sun suddenly seemed too bright. It blasted in from the window behind him, casting his features into shadow. She couldn't make out his eyes. He had to be joking. At any moment, he was going to grin at her.

She gingerly relinquished her hold on her teacup and essayed a small smile. "Have a lovely journey. Will you be home in time for tea?"

"No. The *Peerless* is leaving St. Katharine's at noon, and I intend to be on it."

Not just the light was blinding. She raised her eyes to him, and his sincerity finally penetrated. "Oh, God. You really meant it. You're leaving? But I thought—"

She'd thought she had time for that silk night rail, folded carefully in paper.

He shook his head. "Kate, we've been married three months. We both know that the only reason we wed was because people found us alone together and imagined more had happened. We married to stave off the scandal."

Put so baldly, her impractical hopes sounded even more foolish than she'd supposed.

"The truth is," he continued, "neither of us is ready to be married, not really."

Neither of them?

He stood and pushed back his chair. "I've never had the

chance to prove myself to anyone. And…" He trailed off, his hand scrubbing through his hair. "And I want to."

He set his serviette atop his plate and turned around. The world swirled around Kate.

He was walking away, as if this had been normal breakfast conversation on a regular day.

"Ned!" Kate vaulted to her feet. The word seemed as like to hold back the breaking floodwaters of her marriage as the insubstantial silk gown waiting upstairs.

His shoulders tensed, two sharp blades beneath the wool of his coat. He stopped in the doorway on the verge of escape.

She didn't have the words to capture the cold tremor that ran through her. She settled on "I wish you wouldn't. I wish you would stay."

He tilted his head, just enough to see her over his shoulder. For just that one second, he looked at her the way she'd dreamed about: with a deep hunger, an almost open yearning, as if she were more to him than a name written under his on their marriage license. He exhaled and shook his head.

"I wish," he said quietly, "I *could,* too." And then he turned and left.

She wanted to run after him, to say something, *anything.* But what rooted her in place was a realization. He was as restless as she'd once been.

And she knew well enough that she couldn't fill that up, not with any number of silken gowns.

At least this way he could imagine her quiet and practical, not hurt in the slightest by his leaving. She'd kept the secret of her attraction all too well, wrapped up in paper.

She'd kept *all* her secrets, and it was too late to explain.

CHAPTER ONE

Berkshire, three years later

A SHOULDER-HIGH WALL hugged the dirt road that wound its way up the hill Kate was climbing. Last night, when she and the nursemaid had crept by on foot, the dark stones of the wall had seemed menacing, hunched things. She'd imagined Eustace Paxton, the Earl of Harcroft, crouching behind every rock, ready to spit vile curses at her.

But through the diffuse morning fog, she could see little yellow-headed wildflowers growing between the rocks. Even this aging edifice had become friendly and bright. And Harcroft was thirty miles away, in London, unaware of her involvement in his latest misfortunes. She'd won a respite, and for the first time in two weeks, she breathed easily.

As if to belie her certainty, the plod of horse hooves carried to her on a breeze. She turned, her heart accelerating. Despite the flush of heat that rose in her, Kate clutched her heavy cloak about her. She'd been discovered. He was here...

There was nothing behind her but morning mist. She was imagining things, to think that Harcroft would have uncovered her secret so quickly. She let out a covert breath—and then gulped it back as the creak of wooden wheels sounded once more. This time, though, it was evident that the noise came from up the road. As she peered ahead of her, the dark form of a cart lumbering up the hill resolved in the mist.

The sight was as calming as it was familiar. A blanket of fog had obscured the sound's origin. The cart moved slowly, drawn by a single animal. As Kate trudged up the hill, her calves burning with the exertion, she made out more details. The conveyance was filled with heavy wooden kegs, marked with a sigil she could not make out from here. The animal that pulled this cargo seemed some nondescript color, unidentifiable in the mist. From this distance, its coat appeared to be both spotted and striped with light gray. It strained uphill, bone and muscle rippling underneath that oddly colored pelt.

Kate sighed with relief. The man was a common laborer. Not Harcroft; therefore, not someone who posed a threat if he discovered the role she'd played last night. Still, Kate pulled her hood up to shield her face. The scratchy wool was the only disguise she had.

As if in reminder of the nightmare that Louisa had escaped, a whip-crack sounded in front of her. Kate gritted her teeth and continued up the hill. Half a minute later, and a number of yards closer, the whip cracked again. She bit her tongue.

She had to be practical. Lady Kathleen Carhart might have had sharp words for the man. But right now Kate was wrapped in an ill-fitting cloak, and the servant she was pretending to be would keep her eyes downcast. A servant would never speak up, not to a man with a horse and a whip. He would never believe her the lady of the manor, not dressed as she was.

And besides, the last thing Kate needed if she intended to keep her secrets was for society to hear that she'd been skulking about, dressed as a servant. As she climbed the hill, the lash continued to fall. She gritted her teeth in fury as she drew abreast of the cart. Perhaps that was why, at first, she didn't hear it.

Above the complaining rumble of the cart wheels, the noise had been at first indiscernible. But the wind shifted, and with it brought the rhythmic sound of a gentle canter to her ears.

Kate glanced behind her. A horseman was coming up the hill.

A simple carter might once have caught a glimpse of Lady Kathleen at a harvest festival—a close enough look to boast, over a tankard of ale, perhaps, about seeing a duke's daughter. He wouldn't recognize her when she was swathed in a heavy cloak and a working woman's bonnet.

But a man on horseback could be a gentleman. He might, in fact, be the Earl of Harcroft, come looking for his missing wife. And if Harcroft came upon Kate dressed in this fashion—if he *recognized* her—he might guess the role she'd played in his wife's disappearance.

All he would have to do was trace her path back a few miles. That shepherd's cottage wasn't so very far away.

Kate pulled the hood of her cloak farther over her eyes and slunk closer to the wall. Her hand brushed against grit on its uneven surface. Even though she huddled in her cloak, she set her chin. She was not about to surrender Louisa to her husband. No matter what he said or did.

The man on horseback came into view through the mist just as Kate crested the hill. Shreds of fog splashed around his horse's hooves, like gray, slow-moving seawater. The horse was a gentleman's beast: a slim mare, gray as the wisps of vapor that clung to its legs. *Not* Harcroft's chestnut stallion, then. Reassured, Kate studied the gentleman himself.

He wore a tall hat and a long coat; the tails flapped behind him in rhythmic counterpoint to the fall of his mare's hooves. Whoever he was, his shoulders were too broad to belong to Harcroft. Besides, this man's face was covered by a sandy beard. *Definitely* not Harcroft, then. Not any man she recognized.

That didn't mean he wouldn't recognize her, or that he wouldn't carry stories.

Slowly she let out her breath and turned to look forward. If she didn't draw attention to herself, he wouldn't notice her. She looked like a servant; she would be virtually invisible to a man of his class.

The mare's light hoofbeats pattered up the hill. It moved in effortless contrast to the other poor animal, which was still dragging its Sisyphean burden to the summit. But Kate had her own burden to concentrate on. Out of the corner of her eye she saw the horseman pull ahead of the cart. The tails of his coat flapped briefly across the beast's blinkered vision. A foot or so of fabric; nothing more.

The horse pulling the cart, however, stopped and shied, pinning its ears against its head in a gesture of

equine distress. Kate pressed against the wall as the cart's
wooden shafts creaked. Another flap of the coattails in
the wind; when the whip cracked again, Kate winced.
The carter's horse did more than that: it let out a frightened cry and reared up on its hind legs. The cart tilted
precariously; the hooves thundered down. Kate heard the
crashing splinter of wood, and she whirled to face the
animal.

One of the cart shafts had split down the middle. The
horse was tangled in halter and traces, and no matter how
it strained, it could not escape. When frightened, horses
ran; and when they couldn't run—

Kate caught a glimpse of a dark eye rolled back, ears
flattened against the long head. The horse's blinkered
gaze momentarily fixed on hers. *Crack* went the whip,
and the horse reared in response. It was so close, Kate
could see its iron shoes as it pawed the air above her
head. She felt frozen in that moment, as useless as a rabbit
cowering in the grass with a hawk plummeting down. Her
hands went cold. Her mind moved sluggishly. She might
have counted the horse's ribs, every prominent ridge, as
the hooves descended toward her.

And then the moment of fear passed, and practical
considerations overtook her disbelief.

She dropped to the ground in a crouch, just as those
massive hooves hit the crumbling wall where her head
had been. Once, and bits of stone and crumbling grout
rained on her head; twice, and flying chips of rock struck
her cheek. The animal whinnied and reared again.

Before the hooves could land a third time, someone
stepped in front of her. Whoever it was jerked her to her

feet—the sockets of her arms twinged in protest. His body pressed against hers momentarily, a brief imprint of hard muscle fitting against her curves. He turned his back to the beast, shielding her from those iron-clad hooves. It was the horseman—the gentleman with the gray mare. He must have dismounted and come to offer assistance.

She had no chance to protest, even had she wanted to, no opportunity to pull away. His hands clasped her waist, and he lifted her up, up, until her palms scrabbled along the top of the wall behind her. She pulled herself atop it, heart thumping, and glanced down. The horseman was looking up at her. His eyes, liquid brown pools, sparkled at her over that shaggy beard, as if this were the best excitement he'd come upon in weeks. For one instant, she felt a sick thrill of recognition.

I know this man.

But he turned away, and that feeling of familiarity slipped through her fingers, as hard to contain as the gritty pebbles on the wall she clung to.

Whoever he was, he had no notion of fear. He turned back to the careening beast. He moved on his toes with a graceful economy of motion. It was almost as if he were leading the horse in a waltz. The man sidestepped another furious stamp of those hooves.

"There now, Champion." His voice was quiet but carrying. "I don't *want* to crowd you so closely, but you'll never calm down if I can't cut the traces."

"Cut the traces!" protested the carter, clutching the handle of his whip. "What the devil do you mean, *cut the traces?*"

The gentleman paid him no mind. Instead, he made a half turn, and stepped behind the animal.

The carter held his whip back, his mouth pursed in ugly disapproval. "What in blazes do you think you're doing?"

The gentleman turned his back on the furious driver. He was talking—murmuring, actually. Kate couldn't hear his words, but she could catch the tone of his voice, soft and soothing. The beast pawed the air once more, and then danced from hoof to hoof. It whipped its head to the side, trying to keep its eyes on the gentleman behind it. A swipe with his knife, then another; one final adjustment of leather, and the animal came free of the cart.

"What the devil are you doing? That's my animal you're freeing, it is!"

The horse surged forward. The carter still held the reins in one hand, and so it couldn't bolt far. But without the bits of cart swinging around it—and more important, with the carter left to impotently clutch his whip now that the beast was out of range—the horse pranced, pawed the ground in distress once and then, eyeing the people around it, lapsed into a restive silence.

"There," the gentleman said, "that's better, isn't it?"

And like that, it *was* better. All the other sounds of the autumn morning seemed to resume with his words: the thump of Kate's heart, the horse's uneasy stamp on the dust road below her, the impatient sound of the carter beating the handle of his whip against his other hand. She clutched the wall beneath her.

"You gentlemen are all alike. You're coddling it," the carter complained. "Stupid animal."

The last was directed at the horse, which still trembled despite the so-called coddling, its ears flat against the sides of its head. The bearded gentleman—and by the cultured drawl of his voice and the fashionable cut of his coat, he was surely a gentleman—turned to face the carter. He walked toward him and then reached down and gathered the animal's reins in his hand. The carter relinquished them, staring in front of him in stupefaction.

"Coddling?" the fellow said gently. "Champion here is an animal, not an egg. Besides, I make it a point to be kind to beasts that are large enough to stomp me to bits. Particularly when they are frightened enough to do so. I've always thought it foolish to stand on principle, when the principle is about to trample you to death."

That evanescent sense of familiarity came to her again, troubling as an unidentified smell on the wind. Something in his voice reminded her of something, *someone*—but no, she would remember that tone of quiet command if ever she'd heard it.

Kate took another deep breath—and froze. She'd seen the beast only in sidelong glances up until now. In the fog, that strange coloration, those odd white spots, had seemed as if they were some curious form of natural marking. But from her vantage point atop the wall, she could see the marks for what they were: scars. Scars where a whip had drawn blood; scars where an ill-fitting harness had rubbed over the course of who knew how many years.

No wonder the poor animal had rebelled.

The carter was holding his hands out. "Here now," he complained. "It don't hurt him. My mam always used to say that tribulation was sent to make you stronger. It's in the Bible. I think." The carter trailed off, giving the horseman a hapless shrug.

"How curious." The fellow smiled disarmingly; even through that thick beard, his grin was infectious, and the carter echoed it with a gap-toothed smile. "I cannot recall the commandment to beat animals. But then, I disagree with the premise. In my experience, tribulation doesn't strengthen you. It's more like to leave you with a bron-chial inflammation that lingers for years."

"Pardon?"

The gentleman waved a hand and turned back to the animal. "Never trust aphorisms. Any sentiment short enough to be memorable is undoubtedly wrong."

Kate suppressed a smile. As if the gentleman could see her, his lips twitched upward. Of course, focused as he was on the trembling cart-horse, she doubted he even knew she was still here. Slowly, she slid from the top of the wall to the ground.

The gentleman fished in his pockets and pulled out an apple. The animal's nostrils widened; its ears came forward slightly. Kate could see its ribs. They were not prominent enough to indicate starvation, but neither were they covered with a healthy amount of skin and muscle. Underneath those healed lacerations, its coat might once have been chestnut. But coal dust and road mud, stretched over scarred skin, had robbed the pelt of any hint of gloss.

"Oh, don't *feed* it, for the love of all that is precious," the carter protested. "The beast is useless. I've had it for three months, and no matter how I beat it, still it shies away from every last mother-loving noise."

"That," said the gentleman, "sounds like an explanation, rather than an excuse. Doesn't it, Champion?" He tossed the apple on the ground next to the horse and then looked away into the distance.

He seemed good with the beast. Gentle. Kind. Not that it mattered, because whoever he was, she couldn't speak to him. No matter how kind he was, he couldn't know what Lady Kathleen had been doing, not if she intended to keep her secrets safe. Kate began to sidle away from the scene.

"Champion? Who're you calling Champion?"

"Well, has he got another name?" The man had made no move to get closer to the horse. He stood, a rein's distance from the beast, looking away from the valley. Toward Berkswift, actually. Kate's home, just beyond one last rise and a row of trees.

"Name?" The carter frowned, as if the very concept were foreign. "I've been calling it *Meat*."

"Meet?" The gentleman frowned down at the reins gathered in his hands. "As in a championship meet? A tourney?"

"No. *Meat*. As in *Horse Meat*. As in I could get a ha'penny per stringy pound from the butcher."

The gentleman's fingers curled about the reins. "I'll give you ten pounds for the whole animal."

"Ten pounds? Why, that's barely what the knacker—"

"If *Meat* here panics on the way to the knacker, you'll be out far more than that in property damage." The man glanced at Kate, where she'd been sneaking away from the battered cart.

It was the first time he'd looked at her directly, and

Kate felt his gaze settle against her, disturbing and familiar all at once. She pressed against the wall.

The gentleman simply shook his head and looked away. "You should be brought up on criminal charges, for endangerment." He reached into his pocket, produced a small purse, and began to count coins.

"Here, now. I haven't agreed. How am I supposed to move my cart?"

The gentleman shrugged. "With that shaft broken? I don't imagine a horse would prove much help." But as he spoke, he added a few more coins from his purse and then dropped them on the cart driver's seat. "There's a village yonder."

The carter shook his head and collected the pile. Then he stood and left his cart, trudging on toward the village. The gentleman watched him go.

While the man was still distracted, Kate began to walk away. The horse was safe, and if she left now, her secret— *Louisa's* secret—was safe, too. Whoever this man was, he couldn't have recognized her. No doubt he thought her some servant, off on her mistress's errands. An unimportant thing, as nondescript as the beast he'd rescued.

He touched his hat at her, and then turned back to his own manicured steed, which waited in nonchalant obedience ten yards down the track.

Kate had supposed the newly purchased beast would follow docilely in the gentleman's footsteps, beaten-down specimen that it was. But it did not hang its head; instead as the fellow led it back to where he'd loosely tossed the reins of his steed, Horse Meat tossed its ragged mane.

It lifted one lip in disdain and stamped its bone-thin, lacerated legs.

The gray mare ducked its head and backed away a step.

"Do you suppose they'll walk calmly together?" the gentleman asked.

With the carter gone, there was nobody else around. He had to be addressing her.

Kate glanced at him, in the midst of her escape. She didn't dare speak. Her voice would betray her as a lady, even if her clothing hadn't. She shook her head.

Horse Meat curled its lips at the mare, showing teeth. It could not have communicated more clearly, had it spoken: *Stay away from me. I am a dangerous stallion!*

The gentleman looked from animal to animal. "I suppose not." A soft smile of bemusement passed over his lips, and he turned to meet Kate's eyes, once again halting her forward progress.

There was a restless vitality about those eyes that resonated with her. Something about him—his voice, his easy confidence—set her skin humming in recognition. She knew him.

Or maybe she just wanted to know him, and she'd invented this subtle sense of familiarity. She would have remembered a man like him.

Unlike other gentlemen, underneath his hat, his skin was sun-warmed gold. His shoulders were broad, and not by any artifice of padding. He was walking away from his steed, toward Kate.

No, she couldn't *possibly* have forgotten a man like

him. His gaze on her made her feel uneasy, as if he knew all her secrets. As if he were laughing at every last one.

"Well," he said, "this is a pretty pickle, my lady."

My lady? Ladies did not wear itchy gray cloaks. They didn't cower under shapeless bonnets. Had he seen the fine walking dress she wore underneath when he lifted her up? Or did he know who she was?

His eyes flicked up and down, once, an automatic male survey of her figure, before returning to her face.

Kate was not fool enough to wish he'd let the horse trample her. Still, she wished he'd been on his way earlier. At least he didn't remark on her outlandish garb. Instead…

"This," he told her, gesturing with the reins of the animal he'd just acquired, "puts me in mind of one of those damnable logic puzzles a friend of mine used to pose when we were at Cambridge. 'A shepherd, three sheep and a wolf must cross a river in a boat that fits at most two.…'"

Understanding—and disappointment—took root. No wonder he wasn't courting her ire by asking inconvenient questions about her cloak and her lack of companionship. He was one of *those* men. He addressed her with easy intimacy. A tone of expectation warmed his voice, entirely at odds with his formal "my lady." She recalled his hands on her waist, that brief flash of heated contact, body to body. At the time, she'd noticed nothing more than a fleeting impression of hard muscle pushing her out of harm's way. Now her skin prickled where he'd touched her, as if his gaze had sparked her flesh to life.

If he knew her well enough to attempt to win that

wager, then he knew her well enough to gossip. He knew her well enough to spread the word in town, and well enough for that word to travel round until it reached Harcroft's ears. It was no longer a question of *if* Harcroft would hear about this episode; it was a matter of *what* and *when*.

Kate didn't dare panic, not now. She took a deep breath. She needed to make sure that the crux of his story had nothing to do with the clothing in which he found her.

"This isn't the time for games of logic," she said. "You know who I am."

He stared at her in befuddlement. One hand rose to touch his chin, and he shook his head. "Of course I know who you are. I knew who you were the instant I set my hands on your hips."

No true gentleman would have alluded to that uncouth contact. But then, no true gentleman would make her want to wrap her arms around her own waist, to press her palms where his had been before.

She cast him a brilliant smile, and after a moment he responded with a like expression. She crooked her index finger at him, and he took a step toward her.

"You're thinking about that bet, aren't you?"

He stopped in his tracks and shook his head stupidly—but all that false bewilderment could not fool Kate. She'd seen too many variants upon it over the years.

"It's been on the book for two years now," Kate said. "Of *course* you're thinking of it. And you—" here she extended her gloved hand to point playfully at his chest "—*you* have convinced yourself that you will be the one to claim the five thousand pounds."

His brows drew down.

"Oh," Kate said with false charity, "I *know*. A lady ought not to mention a gentleman's wager. But then, you can hardly be deserving of the term *gentleman* if you've entered into that pact to seduce me."

That brought his shoulders straight up and wiped all expression from his face. "Seduce you? But—"

"Am I making you uncomfortable?" Kate asked with pretend solicitousness. "Are you perhaps feeling as if your privacy has been violated by my inquiry? Now, perhaps, you can imagine how it feels for me to have my virtue discussed all over London."

"Actually—"

"Don't bother protesting. Tell the truth. Did you linger here, thinking you would have me in bed?"

"No!" he said in injured tones. Then he pressed his lips together, as if tasting something bitter. "To be perfectly truthful," he said in a subdued tone, "and come to think of it, *yes,* but—"

"My answer is 'no, thank you.' I already have everything a lady could wish for."

"Really?"

He was watching her intently now. She could imagine him reporting this speech to his friends. If he did, the sum of the gossip would be her words, not her clothing. Harcroft would hear, but he'd think nothing of it. Just the story of another man who failed to collect. Kate counted items off on her fingers. "I have a fulfilling life filled with charitable work. A doting father. Virtually unlimited pin money." She tapped her little finger and shot him another disarming smile. "Oh, yes. And my husband lives six thousand miles away. Now why in heaven's name do all you fools believe I should want to complicate my life with a messy, illicit love affair?"

He froze, then recovered enough to reach up and rub the tawny bristle on his chin. "Would you know," he said softly, "my solicitor was right. I should have shaved first."

"I assure you, your slovenly appearance makes not one iota of difference."

"It's not the beard." His hand clenched briefly into a fist at his side, and then relaxed.

She felt a grim delight at that sign of confusion. It wasn't fair to take all men to task for her husband's failings—but then, this one *had* set out to seduce her, and she was not in the mood to be kind. "You seem out of sorts," she said, imbuing her voice with a false charity. "And foolish. And bumbling. Are you quite sure you're not my errant husband?"

"Well, that's the thing." He glanced at her almost apologetically. And then he took another step toward her.

This close, she could see his chest expand on an inhale. He reached for her hand. She had time to pull away. She *ought* to pull away. His thumb and forefinger caught her wrist, as gently as if he were catching a dried leaf as it fell from a tree. His fingers found the precise spot where her glove ended and her flesh began. She might have been that leaf, ready to combust in one heated moment.

She desperately needed to escape, to reconstruct the feeling of success that had been so rudely taken from her. He smiled at her again, and his eyes twinkled ruefully. And suddenly, horribly, she knew what he was going to say. She knew why his eyes had seemed so unnaturally familiar.

She *did* know this man. She had imagined meeting him a thousand ways in the past years. Sometimes she had said nothing. Other times she'd delivered cutting speeches. She always brought him to his knees, eventually, in apology, while she looked on regally.

There was nothing regal about her now. In all of her imaginings, not once had she met him wearing an ill-fitting servant's cloak, with smudges on her face.

Her wrist still burned where he touched her, and Kate jerked her hand away.

"You see," he said dryly, "I'm quite sure that I *am* your husband. And I'm not six thousand miles away any longer."

CHAPTER TWO

SIX THOUSAND MILES. Three years. Ned Carhart had convinced himself that when he returned, everything would be different.

But no. Nothing had changed—least of all, his wife.

She stared at him, her lips parted in shock, as if he had announced that he had a penchant for playing *vingt-et-un* with ravens. She drew her cloak about her. No doubt she wanted to shield herself from his gaze. And like that, it all came back—all the ragged danger of that old intensity— burning into the palms of his hands.

Her cloak was dusty all over and, thank God, falling about her as it did, it hid the curves of her waist. After all these years of careful control, the check he performed was almost perfunctory. Yes. He still controlled his own emotions; they did not jerk him around, like a dog on a chain.

But then, it had been a long while since he'd felt these particular emotions. Ten minutes in his wife's presence, and already she'd begun to befuddle him again.

"You really didn't recognize me," he said.

She stared at him, suddenly mute and uneasy.

No, of course not. All that easy conversation? That, she'd produced for a stranger. A stranger who she believed had intended to seduce her, no less. Ned scrubbed his hand through his hair.

"Two years? There's been a wager running for two years to seduce you?"

"What did you suppose would happen? You left me three months after our wedding." Kate turned away. She took two breaths. He could see the rigid line of her shoulder even under all that wool. And he waited, waited for an outpouring of some kind. A diatribe; an accusation. For anything.

But when she turned back, only the clutch of her gloved hand on her cloak betrayed any unease.

That smile—that damnably enchanting smile—peeked out again. "And here I supposed your departure was the masculine equivalent of sounding the bugle to presage the hunt for your fellow gentlemen. You could not have declared it hunting season on Lady Kathleen Carhart any more effectively if you'd taken out an advertisement in the gossip circulars."

"That's certainly not what I intended."

No. His thinking had taken a different cast altogether. When he'd left for China, he'd been young and idiotic; old enough to insist that he was an adult, and not wise enough to realize how far he was from the truth. He'd spent his early years playing the dissolute and useless spare to his cousin's rigid, rule-bound heir.

He'd made himself sick on the uselessness of himself. When he'd married, he had hungered to prove that he wasn't a child. That he could take on any task, no matter how difficult, and demonstrate that he had grown into a strong and dependable man.

He'd done it, too.

One woman—one who had already sworn to honor and obey him—shouldn't have seemed so insurmountable a prospect.

Ned shook his head and looked at Kate. "No," he repeated. "When I left, I wasn't trying to send any message. It didn't have anything to do with you at all."

"Oh." Her lips whitened and she looked ahead. "Well. Then. I suppose that's good to know."

She turned around and began to walk away. Ned felt the pit of his stomach sink, as if he'd said something utterly stupid. He couldn't think what it was.

"Kate," he called. She stopped. She did not look at him, but there was something—perhaps the line of her profile—that suggested a certain wariness.

He swallowed. "That wager. Did anyone succeed?"

She stiffened slightly, and then her shoulders lowered in defeat. Now she did turn around.

"Oh, Mr. Carhart." It was the first time she had spoken his name since he'd returned, and she imbued those few syllables with all the starch of sad formality. "As I recall, I vowed to forsake all others, keeping only unto you, for as long as we both should live."

He winced. "I wasn't questioning your honor."

"No." She put her hands on her waist and then looked up at him. "I merely wish to remind you that it was not *I* who forgot our wedding vows."

And with those words, she glanced up the packed dirt of the path to where his gray mare stood. She let out a deep sigh and turned away once more. For a second, Ned imagined grabbing her wrist again, imagined himself swiveling her around to face him. She wouldn't look at him with sadness or that wary distance. In fact, distance was the last thing he wanted between them—

She cast him one final glance and then crossed to his mare, which was cropping grass by the side of the road. "One solution to your logical dilemma?" she said. "Get another boat."

She took his horse's reins and wrapped them around her wrist. And before he could say another word, she set off down the track.

Champion's reaction to Ned's mare meant that he could not walk close to Kate, not without risking a repeat of that skittish rearing and bolting. He perforce trailed after her, feeling rather like a clumsy duckling to her elegant swan.

The English countryside smelled like dust and autumn sunshine. His wife walked ten yards ahead of him. She strode as if she might outrun his existence entirely, if only she put one foot in front of the other quickly enough. Maybe it was madness, that he imagined he could catch the scent of her on the breeze—that half remembered smell of fine-milled soap and lilac. It was even more foolish to watch her retreating backside and wonder what *else* might have changed about her while he wasn't looking.

Her hair, or what he could see of it from under that floppy gray bonnet, was still such a pale blond as to appear almost platinum. Her eyes still snapped gray when angry. As for her waist… He hadn't lied when he said he recognized her by the feel of her waist in his hands. He hadn't touched her often, but it had been enough. She was delicate, with that fine, elegant figure and those pale gray eyes ringed by impossibly long lashes.

When he'd married her, she had seemed like some bright creature. A butterfly, perhaps, its wings vibrant and shimmering in the sunlight. When she had smiled at him, Ned felt himself wanting to believe that it would be June forever, all warmth and blue skies. Instinctively, he'd shied away from that promise of eternal summer. After all, one didn't talk to a butterfly about the coming snow, no matter how bright its wings appeared to be.

Fewer than twenty-four hours back in England, and he'd rediscovered how much of a threat his wife still posed to his equanimity. A man in control of himself wouldn't have wanted to press her against that damned gritty stone wall, in broad daylight. A man in control of himself enjoyed his wife within the careful, pleasant confines of marriage.

Well. Ned had faced down a captain in Her Majesty's Navy. He'd issued orders to an officer in the East India Company. He wasn't the foolish boy who had left England, eager to prove himself. And he wasn't about to let a little desire get the best of his discipline now.

The road ran on, and a fine sheen of dust gathered on the wool of his coat. They turned off the track and onto a wide, tree-lined way. Ned knew the road well. They were approaching Berkswift, his childhood country home. He supposed it was her home now, too; odd, that their lives had intertwined so, even in his absence.

As he walked down the lane, the lazy smell of cultivated earth recently turned in preparation for winter wheat, wafted to him. Even before they broke through the line of trees that shielded the estate from the road, Ned could conjure up the image of the manor in his mind—the golden-rose of the stone facade, the three long wings, the graveled half ring out front for carriages. At this time of the morning, the yard would stand empty, waiting to be filled by the day's activities.

But as they came through the final copse of young birches, they did not find quiet. Instead, the drive was busy: positively boiling with servants. The cause of their work was clear. Three heavy black carriages stood on that circular drive before the house. Ned could make out a coat-of-arms, picked out in blue and silver, on the one standing nearest him.

In front of him, Kate stopped. Her entire body froze, her posture as rigid as a duelist poised at thirty paces. As he came abreast of her, she cut her eyes toward him.

"Did you invite him?" She gestured toward the coat of arms. "Did you invite him here?" She had not raised her voice, but her pitch had risen a note or two.

"I just arrived in England myself."

"That's not an answer. Did you invite the Earl of Harcroft?"

That would be Eustace Paxton, the Earl of Harcroft. Most of the *ton* was related in some twisted fashion. Harcroft was Ned's third cousin, twice-removed, on his father's side. They'd been friends, of a sort, for years. He'd married even younger than Ned had. And just before Ned had left London, Lord and Lady Harcroft had done Ned a favor.

Kate was still watching him, her lips compressed in sudden wariness.

"No," he said slowly. "The only one I've spoken to so far was my solicitor." And even if word of his return had traveled, as no doubt it would, Ned didn't see how Harcroft could have mustered himself out of bed in time to actually *beat* Ned to Berkswift, and traveling by heavy carriage no less.

Beside him, Kate frowned, as if he'd committed some egregious breach of manners. Maybe he had. Eight months aboard ship and a man forgot a great many things.

"I think that's Jenny and Gareth's carriage in front. Maybe they've come with Harcroft?" Gareth was his cousin, Gareth Carhart, the Marquess of Blakely; Jenny, his marchioness.

Kate smoothed her skirts with her hands, brushing them away from Ned subtly, as if whatever disease of gaucherie he carried might be catching.

"Lord and Lady Blakely," she said primly, "are welcome here." She stared forward fixedly and let out her breath.

She said nothing of Louisa or her husband. Kate and Louisa had seemed on their way toward friendship when Ned had left. Clearly, a great deal had transpired in Ned's absence.

When Kate inhaled again, she straightened. It was as if she'd taken in a lungful of sunshine. Her face lifted, her eyes relaxed, her shoulders lost their rigid cast. If he hadn't seen her unease just seconds before, he might have believed her expression genuine. "Unexpected house-guests," she said. "What a pleasure this will be."

And, handing the horse she had been leading to a groom, she walked in.

CHAPTER THREE

KATE HAD DRESSED FOR BATTLE, donning her finest pink muslin morning dress. With lace at her wrists and mother-of-pearl buttons at her throat, instead of that itchy servant's cloak, she felt capable of matching wits with anyone.

And yet she could not make out the conversation coming from the morning room a few yards distant, where the guests had been ensconced. She only heard the low murmur of voices, echoing down the wood of the hall. Her company was waiting, and the sound they made reminded her of thunder lurking on the horizon.

It was a good thing she was wearing her mother's pearls. With those clasping her neck, she felt as if she could conquer anything. Harcroft would mock her, no doubt, if he knew her thoughts. He'd dismiss her attire as frills and furbelows—a woman's only armor. Idiocy on his part.

There were a great many problems that could be solved with a visit to the mantua-maker. And fine gowns or no, this meeting promised to be a war, however politely and subtly it was joined.

Kate took a deep breath and readied herself to enter the room.

"Kate."

The voice behind her—that deep, now too-recognizable voice—pierced through her gathering sureness. She whirled around. She felt a strand of hair fall out of her carefully pinned coiffure as she did so, to dangle in untidy fashion against her neck.

"Ned." Not even his name; the nickname his intimates gave him escaped her in a breathless rush. She'd meant to use a careful, distancing surname. Kate cursed that betraying slip. He could probably hear her heart hitting her ribs in staccato emphasis, revealing every last emotion she wanted hidden. Likely he was taking note of the blanch of her cheeks, the pinch of her lips.

"I thought you'd gone ahead." She'd intended the words to come out an accusation. But to her ear they sounded unfortunately breathy. "I was sure you would hurry to greet the Marquess and the Marchioness of Blakely, if not Harcroft himself."

"I *did* hurry." If he had, though, his breath came evenly. Kate felt as if she were gasping for air.

He didn't seem the least out of sorts to find her here. In fact, he smiled at her, almost as if he knew a joke that she did not. "But I had to shave."

"I see that."

It was half the reason her heart had accelerated to this unsustainable pace. With his beard shorn, Kate could see every last feature—chin, lips and, worst of all, that assured smile. She could find only the roughest sketch of the man she had married. The man Kate had married had been scrawny, a youngster barely out of adolescence. That youthfulness had made him seem sweet.

The intervening time had washed the youth from her

husband's features. His jaw was no longer set in awkward apology; now it was square, and he looked at her in clear command. His nose no longer seemed too sharp, too piercing. It fit the look of canny awareness he'd developed.

Once, he'd seemed clumsy, constantly tripping over feet that were too large for the rest of his body. But over the past years, he'd grown into those feet. What had once seemed a surfeit of bumbling motion had transmuted into a restless economy, a sheer vitality highlighted by the sun-darkened gold of his skin.

Her husband had stopped being safe.

"Shall we go in together?" he asked, holding out his elbow.

Even that slight motion tweaked her perverse memory. Where once he'd apologetically claimed the space he needed, constantly pulling his elbows into his side, now he seemed to fill an area far beyond his skin. It seemed an act of bravery to reach out and set her fingers in the crook of his elbow. He radiated an unconscious aura now—as if he were more dangerous, more intense. *Give this man a wide berth,* her senses shouted.

Instead, she closed her hand about his finely woven wool coat. She could feel the strength of the arm underneath.

"I don't think we'll fool any of them, coming in together." She forced herself to look up, to meet the intensity of his gaze. "If anyone knows the truth about our marriage, it's the people in the room in front of us."

His head tilted to one side. "You tell me, Kate. What *is* the truth of our marriage?"

He did not smile at her, nor did he waggle his eyebrows.

His question was seriously meant. As if somehow, he did not know. His ignorance, Kate supposed, must have been bliss for him. For her, however, it sparked a deep ache beneath her breastbone.

"Our marriage lasted a few months. Once you left, what remained faded faster than the ink on the license. And what's left…well, it could blow away in one tiny puff of wind."

"Well, then." He spoke with an air of certainty. "I'll try not to exhale."

"Don't bother. I stopped holding my breath years before."

Even when he'd been a young, deferential boy, he hadn't truly been safe. He'd hurt her when he left. Now she felt a stupid surge of hope at his words. A damnable, irrepressible whisper of a thought, suggesting that something might yet come of her marriage.

The real danger wasn't the strong line of his jaw or the powerful curve of his biceps under her fingers. No; as always, the real dangers were her own hopes and desires. It was that whisper of longing, a list that started with, *step one: find a night rail.…*

Those old girlish wants would return unbidden if she gave them the least encouragement. It wouldn't matter how lightly he breathed.

And nowadays, she had far more important secrets to occupy her worries than a little scrap of silk.

"Well," he said, "let's give it a go anyway. Our guests expect us." Without waiting for an answer, he set his hand over her fingers, clasping them to the crook of his arm. The gesture was strong and confident. He didn't know what awaited them. Kate ignored the queasiness in her stomach and walked with him into the room.

After the dimness of the hall, blinding white morning light filled her vision. All sound ceased, swallowed up by an immense shocked silence. Then fabric rustled; a flurry of lavender blurred across Kate's vision, and before she could blink and get her bearings, a silk-clad form cannoned into Ned beside her, breaking Kate's contact with her husband.

"Ned," the woman said, "you ridiculous man. Not a word of warning, not one hint that you'd arrived. When were you planning to *tell* us?"

"I just landed," Ned said. "Late last night. You'll find the missive on your return."

The woman was Jennifer Carhart, the Marchioness of Blakely. She was Ned's cousin's wife, and as he'd explained to Kate after their marriage, also one of Ned's dearest friends. "I missed you," Lady Blakely was saying.

Lady Blakely was pretty and dark-haired and clever, and Kate felt a prickle of unworthy resentment arise inside her. Not jealousy, at least not of *that* sort. But she envied the easy friendship Lady Blakely had with her husband.

When the marchioness pulled away, her husband, the marquess, took her place. "Ned."

"Gareth." Ned clasped the offered hand. "Congratulations on the birth of your daughter. I know my good wishes are much delayed, but I only just had the news from the solicitor this morning."

"My thanks." The marquess glanced at Kate, briefly,

and then looked away without meeting her eyes. "Lady Kathleen."

Naturally, Ned did not notice that little dismissal. Instead, he clapped his cousin on the shoulders. "I do wish you'd hurry up and spit out an heir, though. It's uncomfortable dangling on your hook."

"No." Lord Blakely spoke directly, almost curtly. But his gaze cut to his wife, who poked him. "No," he amended with a sigh. "But thank you for the sentiment. I'd much rather have children than an heir. I'll keep my girl—you and yours can have the damned marquessate when I'm gone." His gaze flicked to Kate again, as if it were somehow *her* fault she hadn't burst forth with twin sons, with her husband half the world away.

Kate should have been playing the hostess here, setting everyone at ease. Instead, she felt as if she were an interloper in her own home, as if she were the one returning after a bewildering absence of three years. And perhaps her feelings had something to do with the precariousness of Louisa's situation. But this gap, this feeling of *not belonging,* had arisen long before she had even known the danger Louisa was in.

It had happened so gradually, on her husband's disappearance from England. Kate had blamed Blakely for sending her husband to China. Foolish; she'd known Ned had volunteered, that he'd wanted to leave as much as she had wanted him to stay. She'd blamed the marchioness, out of a deep envy for the woman's easy friendship with her husband. Kate had known the response was neither reasonable nor rational, but her resentment at being left behind had been too large to direct at only one person.

Over the years, the familial relationship had quietly strained. A different woman might have made some attempt to mend what had frayed; instead, Kate had excused herself. She had her own set of friends. She didn't need to add her cousins by marriage to that number.

And so it had come to this: everyone in the room, if they knew what she had done, would see her as the enemy.

Her greatest enemy stood next in line to greet her husband. The Earl of Harcroft was slim and tall. He was Ned's age, but he looked as if he were still eighteen, his face unlined by worries or age. The earl, Kate thought bitterly, appeared to be quite the golden child. He was a master at cricket, a veritable genius at chess and an expert when it came to appraising Flemish paintings of goat-girls. He gave to charity, never swore and attended church, where he sang hymns in a delightful baritone.

He also beat his wife, taking care to hit her only where the bruises wouldn't show. It was his legal right, as Louisa's husband, and if he discovered that Kate had hidden her away, he could compel her at solicitor-point to give her up.

Kate wasn't about to give him the chance.

Ned relinquished Harcroft's hand and looked expectantly around the room. "Where's Louisa?" he asked brightly. "Is she lying in, finally? I certainly hope she hasn't taken ill again."

Silence fell. The three guests exchanged glances. Kate's spine straightened; Lady Blakely subsided into her chair and spread her hands carefully down the light purple of her gown. She did not meet Ned's eyes. Instead, she glanced at her husband, who by a shake of his head clearly delegated the task of divulging the truth back to her.

"We don't know where she is," Lady Blakely said simply. "But you've just returned. Don't concern yourself with it."

Of course. They'd come to talk with *Kate*. Not a good sign, then, that nobody in the room was looking at her.

"Jenny," Ned said carefully. "Are you trying to *protect* me?"

The smile on Lady Blakely's face wavered.

"I should think that if I've earned anything over the last years, I've earned the right to the truth. I've proven to you by now that I can help."

"Ned, that's not what I meant. I simply thought—"

Ned held up a hand. "Well, stop thinking simply." He spoke lightly, but again something passed between them, and Lady Blakely nodded.

Oh, it was irrational to feel that stab of jealousy. And it was *not* because she suspected that anything untoward could happen between them. Lady Blakely was devoted to her husband. Still, that exchange of glances bespoke a trust, a *friendship* between them that Kate had never had a chance to develop with her husband. All she'd had was a handful of breakfasts, and a smaller handful of nights that had more to do with marital expectation than ardor. She'd had three months to raise her hopes, and years to watch them dwindle into nothing.

"If anyone has the right to the truth," Kate said with some asperity, "it is *I*. Louisa is one of my dearest friends. I thought, after she gave birth three weeks ago, the danger had passed. Has something happened to her?" Kate didn't have to pretend her concern for her friend. "Is she well? And did you come to fetch me to her side?"

Harcroft's cold gaze fell on her as she delivered this speech. But as much as she quaked inside, she did not let herself show more than natural worry.

Lady Blakely must not have seen anything amiss in her expression, either. She let out a sigh. "There's no easy way to say this. Louisa's gone."

"Gone?" Ned asked, his shoulders drawing together, his head snapping up.

"Do you mean she's *passed on?*" Kate echoed in perfidious concern.

"I mean," Lady Blakely clarified, "she is *missing.* She was last seen yesterday shortly before noon, and we are absolutely frantic trying to locate her."

"Was she taken by ruffians?" Kate asked. "Have you received some sort of a demand letter from abductors?"

Ned turned to Harcroft. "Harcroft. You used to find misplaced books in the Bodleian Library for amusement. How could you be so careless as to misplace your own wife?"

Harcroft scrubbed his hands through his hair. He made a fine picture of a distraught husband, Kate thought bitterly. "You know," Harcroft said softly, "about the illness she's suffered. The problems she had conceiving. Well, after she got with child… The physician said some women don't take to childbirth. Something about too much excitement laid upon the feminine sensibility. She wasn't herself afterward. The female mind is delicate as it is, you know. She changed during her confinement. She was less biddable, more excitable. More given to hysterics."

Harcroft shrugged. The gesture conveyed helplessness, and Kate's lip curled. Helpless, Harcroft was not. Kate suppressed the urge to lift the nearby oil lamp with her delicate, female hands. She felt excited and unbiddable right now; why, she might slip and use her own delicate, female sensibility to bash all that heavy brass into his head.

However satisfying that exercise might prove, it wouldn't help Louisa.

"And no," Harcroft continued, turning to Kate, "we've had no notes of ransom. Whoever it was that took her—" his voice took on a sour note, and he tilted his head to look Kate directly in the eyes "—whoever it was, packed a valise for Louisa and clothes for the child. *They* took my son, without his uttering a cry to alert the nursemaid."

"Oh, no," Kate said. She froze her face into a mask of perfect sympathy and met Harcroft's eyes. "Not little Jeremy. What sort of wicked, depraved, *awful* person would hurt that little angel?"

Her words might have been half lies, but the emotion that crept out during that speech was all real. She only hoped that everyone understood it as sympathy for Harcroft instead of the painful accusation that it was.

He couldn't know what was in her mind, but his own thoughts could not have been comfortable. The skin around his mouth crinkled and he looked away.

"As I said," he muttered, "there have been neither threats nor demands."

"How can I help?" Ned asked. "I assume that's why

you came, right? As soon as you heard I'd arrived? Because—" He stopped and looked at the carefully schooled faces surrounding him. "But no. None of you even knew I'd returned here."

"They've come to speak with me," Kate said into the intervening silence. "To see if Louisa divulged anything of importance."

The Marquess of Blakely stepped closer. He was tall, and Kate had never seen him flinch at anything. He was damnably intimidating, and she leaned away despite herself. "And has she?"

Kate shook her head as if trying to recall. "We had planned to see each other again at the Hathaway's house party in November, if the roads were passable. She made no mention to me of any other plans."

True enough; Kate had been the one to coax her into action. Kate had laid the plans; Louisa had only agreed.

Kate continued, "She had not spoken of any desire to see anything else. Or—excuse my plain speaking on the subject, but under the circumstances, it seems necessary—*anyone* else. Louisa isn't the sort to stray."

A disappointed silence followed this.

"Perhaps," Harcroft offered, "you might trouble yourself to recall anything she might have said about Berkswift's environs. Yesterday evening, a woman alone, answering Louisa's description, alighted from a hack in Haverton, just five miles from here. The hack had been hired in London, and so the occurrence was much talked about."

"A woman alone? She didn't have a child? Where did she go?"

"No child. But an auburn-haired woman with deep blue eyes—it couldn't have been anyone else."

"It must be." Kate shook her head. "Louisa would never leave Jeremy, not for any reason." It had, in fact, been a sticking point of their plan—convincing Louisa to allow Kate to take her child in London, so that when Louisa traveled she would not be so easily identified. A red-haired woman with a newborn was too memorable, and looking as Louisa did would only have made her shine, like a lighthouse set on the shore.

"Perhaps," Kate ventured, "you might tell me if there is anything that happened that might have precipitated her flight. It might help my memory."

She didn't want to be the only one telling lies here. Let Harcroft announce that he'd hit her in the stomach, and promised to break her infant son's arm if she told anyone.

"I can think of other ways to jog your memory." Harcroft stepped closer.

For a second, Kate shrank from him. She, of all people, knew the violence he was capable of. Then Ned moved to stand beside Kate. It was foolish to feel more secure because of a man who had abandoned her years ago. But she did.

"For instance," Harcroft said smoothly, as if he had not just uttered a threat, "you might allow yourself time to think about the matter. You could report to me if you recall anything important."

"Of course. I will send a messenger the instant anything comes to mind."

Harcroft shook his head. "No need for that. Ned, my friend, you asked me if you could help. A hired hack left my wife a mere stone's throw from here, and no accounts yet have that woman leaving the district. I'm convinced she's nearby."

A prickle ran up Kate's neck. Harcroft lifted his cold, unfeeling gaze to Kate, as if he knew the substance of her thoughts, as if he traced every hair standing on end to its inexorable conclusion. "I ask only," he said, "that I be allowed to impose upon your hospitality while I investigate."

This was not good. It was very not good. Kate curled her lips up into the semblance of a smile while she tried to arrange her muddled thoughts. "Of course," she said. "I'll ring for tea, and you can tell me how I can help."

CHAPTER FOUR

"JENNY," NED SAID as Kate stepped outside the room, "before we begin to discuss Louisa, there is something I must ask you."

Jenny, who had sat next to her husband on an embroidered sofa, smiled up at Ned and motioned him to sit. Ned slipped into a nearby chair and leaned forward. What he had to say next was something that had bothered him for the past hour. Under the circumstances, it seemed unfair to confront her with the question. And yet…

"Why didn't you write me that the gentlemen of the *ton* were conspiring to seduce my wife?"

Jennifer Carhart had never, in Ned's experience, been a coward. Yet she looked away at this, biting her lip. "Letters took so long to cross the ocean," she finally assayed, not meeting his eyes. "And Lady Kathleen—Kate, I mean—dealt with the wager so matter-of-factly. I didn't suppose she needed my assistance, and to be quite honest, I suspect she wouldn't have appreciated my interference. Besides, you…" She trailed off, her finger tracing circles against her palm.

"I what?"

"You needed time to sort through matters." Jenny reached over and adjusted his lapels in some invisible manner.

"Christ," Ned swore.

All those years ago, Jenny had been the one to observe the sum total of his youthful foibles. When he'd made a hash of his life, she had helped him pick up the pieces. She was like a sister to him, and one who had quite literally saved his life. Perhaps that was why she sat here, protecting him, as if he were still that fragile child in need of mollycoddling.

"Next time," he said quietly, "tell me."

"Tell you what?" Harcroft's voice boomed behind Ned, and he turned reluctantly. "Are you telling us that you had great success in your venture abroad?"

"If by 'success,' you mean, did I discover the truth? Yes."

Gareth looked up and leaned forward. "That bad, was it?"

"Worse than even the discussions in Parliament indicated. If matters have not changed, John Company is currently shelling villages at the mouth of the Pearl River, all because China refuses the privilege of purchasing India's opium. This is not Britain's finest hour. When we've resolved this other matter, we'll have to have a discussion about what can be done in the Lords. I've made notes."

"And did you find it easy to take those notes?"

"Easy enough." Ned smiled briefly. "Once I stopped letting the officers push me about."

Harcroft waved a hand. "We can speak more of that later. For now, we'll need a plan. The first thing that we must organize is—"

"I thought we were going to wait for Kate to return," Ned interrupted in surprise. He'd never known Harcroft to be downright rude before. And imposing on Kate's hospitality, while starting the conversation without her, seemed the height of rudeness.

Harcroft made a disparaging sound in return. "Why bother? What do you suppose she could do to assist us? Go shopping?" He shook his head. "If my wife were hidden on Bond Street, I might turn to Lady Kathleen for assistance."

Ned's hands balled at that implied insult.

"Yes, yes." Harcroft waved a dismissive hand in Ned's direction. "I know. You feel duty bound to complain. But do be serious. Some women just don't have the head for anything except frivolity. She's good at a great many things, I'll give you. Planning parties. Purchasing of a great many hats and gloves. Trust me, Ned. We'll all be happiest if Lady Kathleen restricts her assistance in this matter to choosing the menu."

At that precise moment, Kate came back into the room, followed by a servant with a tea-tray. She didn't meet Ned's eyes. She didn't meet anyone's eyes. She didn't say anything about the conversation. She didn't say anything at all. But Ned could tell, by the careful way that she concentrated on the distribution of delicate, gold-edged cups and cucumber sandwiches, that she'd overheard those last few words. And they'd hurt.

Worse, nobody had leapt to defend her. Not even him. And by the way she fixed her gaze on the teapot, she knew that.

When she sat down, she took the chair farthest from their company, as if she were outside the enterprise. Harcroft began outlining his plans for questioning villagers and hiring searchers, and Kate sat in silence, staring into her teacup. Ned could put no words to the prickle of unease he felt watching her. She was dignified and pleasant, every inch the duke's daughter he'd married.

She was also hurt. And looking at her, he could not help but feel as if…as if, perhaps, he'd forgotten something.

Not her; he'd never forgotten Kate. Not their vows; he'd struggled long and hard with how to both cherish Kate and keep her safe from the darkness he knew lurked inside him.

No. After what she'd said in the hall, he was certain he'd not done well by her, and he was not sure how to patch matters up. If he could even do so. She had said their marriage might blow away with one gust of wind; he had no idea how to bring it to life. He wasn't sure if he *could* do so, without also resurrecting his own dark demons alongside. But what he did know was that if he kept silent now, if he did nothing to try to mend the hurt she'd just been given, he wouldn't be able to look himself in the mirror any longer.

He stood and walked to her. Behind him, Harcroft was still nattering on. "These days," he was growling, "nobody gives a fig about the husband's rights. Too many newfangled notions interfering."

Standing above his wife, Ned could see the fair lines of her eyelashes. She didn't darken them, and as she gazed down into her teacup, those fine, delicate hairs fluttered. Without lifting her eyes to Ned—he wasn't sure if she was even aware of how close he stood—Kate blew out her breath and added another spoonful of sugar to her tea, followed by another.

The time they had together had been damnably short. But those days spent breaking fast with Kate had been time enough for Ned to know that his wife never took sugar in her tea.

"In fact," Harcroft was saying behind them, "the very *notion* of Britain is founded on the rights of a husband."

"Husbands' rights," Kate muttered. "In a pig's eye."

"Kate?"

Kate jumped, her teacup clattering in its saucer. "That is the second time you've come up behind me in as many hours. Are you trying to do me an injury?"

From her private reaction, she didn't think much of marriage—either Lady Harcroft's or her own. Perhaps they had compared notes. He didn't know what to do, except to try to make her smile.

"Am I interrupting a private conversation between you and your teacup?"

Kate stared down. Even Ned could see the liquid was practically viscous with dissolved sugar. How many spoonfuls had she dumped into it? But she said nothing.

"I must be," Ned continued. "No doubt you and your tea have a great deal to converse about. Can I call it merely tea?" She looked up at him in surprise. "I'd hate to insult your efforts to transform it into a syrup, after all."

A reluctant smile touched her lips, and she set down her worthless, oversweetened beverage. And oh, he didn't know why, but he reached out and laid his hand atop the fingers she had freed. The delicate bones of her hand felt just right against his skin.

"Let me guess," Ned said. "I've mucked up the forms of address. You'll have to excuse me. I haven't thought about etiquette and precedence in years. You're a duke's daughter, and furthermore, you are the tea's only natural predator. According to Debrett, that means—"

"I am not!" she said. But she hadn't lost that shine in her eyes. Maybe, if he made her laugh again, he could resume where they'd left off. Maybe he could bridge the gap between them with humor.

"You're not a duke's daughter?" He looked about the room in exaggerated confusion. "Does anyone else here know that? Because I shan't tell if you won't."

Her hand shifted under his, and he won another reluctant smile from her. This, too, Ned remembered—his attempts, at breakfast, to make her choke on her toast and reprimand him for making her cough. It had seemed a dangerous endeavor then, even in the bright light of day.

"Don't be foolish," she admonished.

"Why not?" He reached out and tapped her chin.

She tilted her head. And then, he remembered why conversing with her had always seemed so dangerous. Because she looked up at him. The years washed away. And for one second, the look she gave him was as old and complicated as the look Delilah had once given to Samson. It was a look that said Kate had seen inside his skin, had seen through the veneer of his humor to the very unamusing truth of why he'd left. She might have seen how desperately he needed to retain a shred of control over himself…and how close she came to taking it all away.

His wife had been a threat when he'd married her. She'd been a confusing mix of directness and obfuscation, a mystery that had dangerously engrossed him. He'd found himself entertaining all sorts of lofty daydreams. He'd wanted to slay all her dragons—he'd have invented them, if she lacked sufficient reptilian foes. In short, he'd found himself slipping back into the youthful foolishness he had forsworn.

He'd run away. He'd left England, ostensibly to look into Blakely investments in the East. It had been a rational, hardheaded endeavor, and he'd proven that he, too, could be rational and hardheaded. He'd come home, certain that this time, he would leave off his youthful imaginings.

"Are you planning to play the fool for me?" And in her face, turned up to his, he saw every last threat writ large. He saw the sadness he'd left in her, and felt his own desperate desire to tamp it down. And he saw something more: something stronger and harder than the woman he'd left behind.

He had come back to England, planning to treat his wife with gentlemanly care. He would prove once and for all that he was deserving of their trust, that he was not some stupid, foolish boy, careening off on some impossible quest.

Kate made him want to take on the impossible.

When she smiled, the warmth of her expression traveled right through his spine like a heated shiver. It lodged somewhere in the vicinity of his breastbone, a hook planted in his ribs, pulling him forward.

For one desperate second, he wanted to be laid bare before her. He wanted her to see everything: his struggle for stability, the hard-fought battle he'd won. He wanted to find out why she sat as if she were not a part of this group.

And that was real foolishness. Because he'd worked too long to gain control over himself, and he wasn't about to relinquish it at the first opportunity to a pretty smile. Not even one that belonged to his wife.

"No," he said finally. "You're quite right. I'm done playing the fool. Not even for you, Kate. Not even for you."

THE SMELL OF HAY and manure wafted to Ned as soon as he stepped inside the stables. The aisle running down the stalls was clean and dry, though, and he walked carefully down the layer of fresh straw. The mare he had pulled from the mews in London for the journey here put her dark nose out over the stall, and Ned reached into his pocket for a small circle of orange carrot. He offered it, palm up; the horse snuffled it up.

"If you're looking for that new devil of a horse, he's not in here."

Ned turned at the sound of this ancient voice. "You're talking about Champion, then?"

Richard Plum scrubbed a callused hand against an old and wrinkled cheek. It was the only commentary Ned expected the old stable-master would make on the name he'd chosen. Ned could almost hear the man's voice echo from his childhood. *Animals don't need fancy names. They don't know what they mean. Names are nothing but lies for us two-legged types.*

"I've seen a great many horses," the man offered.

Ned waited. Plum spent so much time around animals—from the horses in the stables to Berkswift's small kennel of dogs—that he sometimes forgot that ordinary human conversation had an ebb and flow to it, a certain natural order of statement and response. Plum seemed to think all conversations had only one side, which he provided. But if left unprompted, he usually recollected himself and continued.

"This one, he's not the worst I've seen. Not the best, neither. Conformation leaves a lot to be desired, and even after we've put some flesh on his bones, he'll likely always be weak-chested. But his temperament... He's as wary as if the devil himself were pissing in his grain. I don't trust him near my mares."

Technically, they were *Ned's* mares, but Ned wasn't about to correct the man. He'd hoped this morning's equine tantrum had been nothing more than an after-effect of Champion's earlier mistreatment.

"That sounds bad."

"Hmm." Mr. Plum seemed to think that bare monosyllable constituted sufficient answer, because he put his hands in his pockets and looked at Ned. "An animal needs to know some kindness in its first years of life, Mr. Carhart. If your, ah, your *horse*—" Ned noticed that Plum carefully eschewed the name of Champion "—has never known good from people, that's the end of it. It can't be fixed, not with a day of work. Or a week. Or a year. And if that's the case, there's nothing to be done for it."

"When you say 'nothing,'" Ned ventured gently, "you don't literally mean *nothing* can be done. Do you?"

"Of course not." Plum shook his head. "Always something to be done, eh? In this case, you load the pistol and pull the trigger. It's a mercy, doing away with a one such as that. What an animal doesn't learn when young, it can't find in maturity."

Ned turned away, his hands clenching. His stomach felt queasy. He hadn't saved Champion only to have him put down out of some sense of wrong-headed mercy. An image flashed through his head: a pistol, tooled in silver, the sun glinting off it from every direction.

No.

He'd not wish that end on anyone, not even a scraggly, weak-chested horse.

"How far gone is he?"

Mr. Plum shrugged. "No way to know, unless someone gives it a try. Have to make the decision out of rational thought, sir. Me? I doubt the animal's worth the effort."

He paused again, another one of those too-long halts. Ned began to drum his fingers against the leg of his trousers, an impatient ditty born out of an excess of energy. Another bad sign.

"Very little use in him, sir."

"Use." Ned pressed his palms together. "No need for an animal to be useful, is there?"

Plum met his gaze. "Use is what animals are for, Mr. Carhart. Useless animals have no place."

Ned knew what it was like to feel useless. He had been

the expendable grandchild, the non-heir. He'd been the fool, the idiot, the one who could be counted on to muck up anything worth doing. His grandfather had expected nothing of Ned, and Ned, young idiot that he had been, had delivered spectacularly.

But he *had* learned. He *had* changed himself, and it had not been too late.

"Where have you put him?"

"Old sheep corral. It's empty, this time of autumn, what with the sheep all brought to the lower fields."

"He'll come around."

"Hmm." It was a versatile syllable, that. Plum might have delivered an essay on his disbelief with that single sound. "In all those heart-felt do-gooding stories, some child rescues an animal and it then proceeds to take the cup at the Ascot. And the knock-kneed beast does so, just because it's fed a decent measure of corn and lavished with kind words. But be realistic, Mr. Carhart. This is a barrel-chested animal that's down on its strength. Even if you do somehow calm the thing enough to toss a harness on it, and convince it to pull in tandem with another animal, it'll be skittish all its life."

"Skittish," Ned said, "I can live with."

Plum stared at him a moment, before giving his head a dismissive shake. "Hope so, then. There's still hay out in that field," he finally said. "We'd been planning to bring it in soon, before the rains come. I'll pull a pair of men from the home farm this afternoon and see to it."

"Don't bother," Ned volunteered. "I'll do it."

This was met with a longer pause.

"You'll do it," Plum finally repeated, looking off at a

speck of dirt on the ground. He said the words as if Ned had just announced that not only did he plan to save a useless horse, he had five heads.

And no wonder. Gentlemen offered to pitch hay approximately as often as they sported five heads. And a marquess's heir was no common day-laborer to dirty himself with a pitchfork. But then, Ned wasn't precisely a common marquess's heir, either. He needed to do *something* to bleed off the excess energy he felt. It was beginning to come out in fidgets; if he didn't do something about it, it would never dissipate.

Instead, it would go careening off at the first opportune moment. Or, more like, the first inopportune one, as he'd learned by experience.

"This is a joke?" Plum asked, bewildered. "You always were one for jokes, when you were a child."

Oh, the inopportune moments of his childhood.

"I'm perfectly serious. I'll manage it."

Over the past few years he'd learned he could contain the restiveness, his simple inability to just *stop*. All he had to do was channel that excess energy into physical tasks. The more mundane, the more repetitive, the greater the strain on his muscles, the better it worked.

Plum simply shook his head, no doubt washing his hands of his master's madness. "Cart's already in the field," he said.

Ned found the cart in question half an hour later. Champion watched him, his eyes lowered, yards away at the fence. Pitching hay into a cart was excellent work—back-straining and tiring. Ned could feel his muscles protest with every lift of the fork. His back ached in pain—the *good* sort of pain. He worked through it.

One hayrick. Two. The sun moved a good slice in the sky, until Ned was past the point of tiredness, past the point of shoulder pain, until his muscles burned and he wanted nothing more than to set down the pitchfork and leave the work to the men Plum would undoubtedly send.

But he didn't. Because not only did this bleed off all that extra intensity, this was good practice. While there were days like today, when he felt vigorous and invincible, there also came times when he wanted nothing more than to simply come to a halt.

Those were the poles of his life: too much energy, almost uncontainable, followed by too little. When the next pole came riding 'round, he'd be ready for it again.

For now, though, he pitched hay.

CHAPTER FIVE

KATE FOUND her husband's coat carelessly tossed across a fence rail. She'd trudged down a muddy footpath in search of him. The trail meandered behind a short scrubby line of trees, past an old, weathered line of fence. In the distance, ducks gabbled peacefully.

By the time she found him, her dress, once pristine, had picked up a band of mud at the hem. The starch of her collar had become limp against her skin. Not quite the way she'd wanted to confront her husband.

He, on the other hand… Ned had stripped to his shirt-sleeves. His dark waistcoat hung open. He was wielding a pitchfork with the deft efficiency of a farmhand. Beneath the unbuttoned waistcoat, she could see the loose folds of his shirt swinging in time to his work. He had no cravat. A moment's search found that white length of cloth draped near his coat.

The other gentlemen of her acquaintance would have looked foolish, without the armor of their clothing to hide thin shoulders, or the bulge of their bellies. But Ned had an air about him, not of disorder, but of casual confidence. Perhaps it was the self-assured rhythm he'd adopted. That uncivilized swagger suited him.

He had never seemed dangerous before he left, and she felt no fear now. And yet there was something different about him. Too casual to seem arrogant; too controlled to come off as happy-go-lucky. He'd changed.

He had a touch of the carefree ruffian about him even now, when he thought nobody was watching but a solitary, skittish horse. Champion huddled on the opposite end of the pasture, ears plastered against his head.

Ned was friends with Harcroft. He'd been the one to introduce the man to Lord Blakely and his wife. Anything he discovered—and as her husband, Ned had the legal right to discover a great deal from Kate—would ruin all of her carefully laid plans.

He was *already* ruining her plans. He had unquestioningly taken the side of Lord and Lady Blakely. He had ushered Harcroft in with hospitality. And he would want to know—quite reasonably, he would think—how his wife spent her time. His presence would impede Kate's ability to communicate with Louisa. How could she see to her friend's safety if she couldn't even visit her?

No. Even if he didn't know it himself, her husband was a danger to her. The slightest word to him, carelessly spoken, could be repeated. In the blink of an eye, Louisa could be exposed.

He was dangerous in a more subtle way, too.

Five minutes of conversation, and she could still feel the mark his finger had left on her chin. Her hand bore an invisible imprint, where he'd laid his atop it. Five minutes, and he'd stirred her to laughter.

He had not heard her approach, and so she had the chance to watch him. He finished moving the last of the hay into the cart and set the pitchfork down slowly. He stripped off his leather gloves, one by one, then pulled off the waistcoat and laid it on the tongue of the cart, next to the gloves and his cravat. Then he stretched and took a clay jug off the cart. Instead of drinking from it, though, he held it above himself and poured a thin stream of water over his head.

His hair, already glistening from exertion, matted to the sides of his head. His white shirt turned translucent and clung to his chest.

Oh, heavens. Kate's breath stopped. The intervening years had been very kind to him. Fabric adhered to defined muscles—not thick, like a laborer's, but lean and rangy, like a fencer's.

It was abominably unfair that he should leave for years and come back looking like that.

She felt the glorious unfairness of it bite deep in her chest.

Kate was not the only one watching. Some twenty yards distant stood the animal he had impetuously purchased today. The servants must have seen to it, because someone had transformed the beast from bedraggled to…slightly less bedraggled. The harness had been removed, and its dull coat had been brushed. Those small hints at grooming underscored how far the animal had yet to come. There were hollows where the animal should have sported muscle and worn spots where the ill-fitting harness had rubbed skin bare.

Ned was not talking to the animal, not even in the low, gentle tones he'd used earlier that morning. For that matter, he didn't act as if he was even aware that it stood so many yards distant. Instead, he picked up his discarded waistcoat and patted its pockets, as if searching for something. He plucked out a little sack and walked away.

The horse—Champion, Ned had called the beast— watched him warily, turning sidelong to keep one eye on him as he walked. Ned whistled tunelessly and peered off into the distance, out at the short, scrubby stretch of trees that blanketed the nearby hill. Just as casually, he began tossing a tiny object from hand to hand. Kate caught a glimpse of white as it danced back and forth a few times, before he lobbed it off into the yellowing grass. He threw it with a sidelong motion, as if he were skipping a stone on the sea of shorn stubble.

Kate took two steps closer, her hands closing on the fence rail.

Champion's nostrils flared at Ned's sudden movement. He backed away, hastily. Ned turned from the horse. As he did, he caught sight of Kate. He stopped dead, and the small smile he'd been wearing slipped away. He didn't say a word. Instead, he walked back to the cart. Once there, he donned his waistcoat and then his cravat, pulling the cloth around his neck. He tied the knot with grave finality. Then he advanced on her.

Behind him, Champion laid his ears back in dire warning to any predators that might attack. He stamped his feet—once, twice. Then he trotted forward, lowered his head, and lipped up whatever Ned had thrown at him.

Ned still hadn't said anything. But as he came upon her, he put his hand in that sack again. He set another object on the fence post in front of him. In the sunlight, the thumb-sized object gleamed like a lump of white porcelain.

"Come," he said to Kate. "Walk with me."

Kate's corset seemed to tighten. Hot lines of whalebone pressed into her ribs while she tried to draw in a pained breath. Some trick of the light made his eyes appear darker, almost black; by contrast, the afternoon sunlight tinted his brown hair halfway to gold.

Shaving had revealed the strong line of his jaw. But he could still have used a valet's services to trim his hair. The ends, still dripping water, curled into his eyes. Slowly, he lifted one hand and brushed those strands back.

It struck her as monstrously unfair. When Kate's hair fell into her eyes, it looked blowsy. On her husband, the untidiness seemed nonchalant and approachable. And yet, if she were to approach him with the truth of what she'd done…

When they'd married, she'd thought he had an essential sweetness to him, a kindness. Perhaps that was why she had agreed to marry him. Marriage was a frightening business for a woman; one never knew what one's husband might do. The man she'd married would never have condoned what Harcroft had done to his wife.

But this man? It had looked as if he had left a white rock atop the post. But as she walked up to it, the object he'd left shone innocently up at her. Her husband might have been careless and thoughtless, but he had never been cruel. A man who fed a wary horse—she sniffed the air delicately—peppermints was not the sort of man to make her fear for her safety.

So he was still sweet. But back then, he'd been sweet like a meringue—all froth and sugar, no substance. Now…

She walked after him, her fingers tapping a worried percussion against the rough wood rail of the fence. He stopped ten yards away, on the opposite side of the fence. A few thin strips of wood. Not really much of a barrier.

Kate took a deep breath. "I see you're coddling the horse again."

He let out an amused snort of air. "Someone has to."

She couldn't look at him. If she did, she might stare at the way his shirt plastered to his biceps, might think of that wet fabric under his waistcoat, clinging to his abdomen.

She might imagine—oh, *drat*. She *was*. Kate turned into the wind, hoping the breeze would cool her flaming cheeks.

She sniffed and set her foot on the wooden stile that traversed the fence. It was composed of an ingenious set of narrow, wooden steps, placed so that humans, but not cattle, could clamber across on agile feet. Still, she felt as graceless climbing those narrow strips of wood as if she were an ox. A well-laced corset and heeled half boots, set with jet buttons, were all well and good in a drawing room. They weren't made for scaling fences.

When she reached the top, she glanced down at her husband. His gaze was not fixed on her face, as would have been proper. He stood too straight, his eyes caught on that bare strip of ankle revealed by her movement. The moment lasted just long enough for him to blink and look up. He offered her his arm; she took it.

As if he hadn't looked at her legs. As if *she* hadn't looked at him, either. When her heels wobbled on the last step, he steadied her; and when she stood beside him, he looked away. So did she. Her gaze settled on the horse. It lifted its head and stared at her, its ears tilting forward. Some women of her acquaintance had practically grown up on horseback; Kate had been thrown once when she was younger, and the broken leg she'd nursed had left her somewhat shy of the animals. Her father had once explained to her what that particular tilt of the ears meant. It was either horse language for *I am very hungry,* or the equine equivalent of *Help, a wolf!* Now, which one was it?

"Don't look at him." Ned's voice was deep, right beside her.

"Why ever not?" She kept her voice light, to disguise the flutter in her stomach.

"Because he's nervous."

Help, a wolf! it was. She looked away—but her eyes caught on her husband, and she felt her stomach contracting. She quickly looked back to Champion. Twenty yards away, the horse peeled his lips back. She caught a glimpse of yellowing teeth.

"He's going to think you're challenging him." Ned sounded amused. But the alternative to looking at Champion was looking at her husband.

"Maybe I am," she teased. "I should like to be lady of this pasture. I should reign over the goats in spring, and the straw in winter." *And I would command you to move piles of hay in your shirtsleeves. Daily.*

"You may reign over as many goats as you wish, if you just—oh, damn."

Across the field, Champion stamped. Kate had only a second to realize how serious the situation was before the animal charged toward them. Hooves pounded against turf. She didn't think he would actually trample her, but before she could turn and scramble over the stile, Ned had picked her up for the second time that day, and swung her over the fence. She landed, awkwardly, and grasped the fence rail to keep from crumpling to the ground.

He vaulted lightly after her, and then turned to face her.

Champion's charge came up short, and the horse let out what sounded to Kate's ear like a very self-satisfied whinny.

"I take it back," Kate said, catching her breath. "He may rule *all* the goats."

When Ned had swung her over, she'd twisted to face away from the pasture. Her husband had landed catlike next to her, and as Champion came close, he stepped nearer, his body pressing her against the fence rail. He didn't seem angry; he merely smiled at her.

"I suppose you think I'm very foolish." She spoke softly; Champion was just behind her.

"What? Because you challenged a creature twice as strong as you and five times as fast?"

Kate flushed.

"Not foolish in the least," he said, peering into her eyes.

"No?"

"You weren't in any danger. I was there. I wouldn't have let anything happen to you."

Kate froze, unable to breathe. He stood so close to her, scarcely six inches away. Every breath she took narrowed that distance between them by a finger's breadth.

His gaze dropped to her bodice, to the high neck of her ivory walking dress. She felt as if he could see through the lace collar, as if she were the one wearing translucent fabric.

Help. A wolf.

He was impossibly close. To him, she'd always been a *wife*. And she'd learned all too well what it meant to be a wife. She was to engage in delicate charity and complex embroidery. She was a figure to be trussed up in a corset and petticoats, to be protected when necessary and indulged when not. A lady did not get her hands dirty. Kate had learned that all too well from her parents.

She wondered what Ned would say if she told him she'd arranged Louisa's escape. If he would even believe her capable of that much, or if he imagined that she was as frivolous—as *superfluous*—as Harcroft had said.

She could hear the animal's breath behind her. She had never realized that a solitary horse could breathe so loudly.

"Why isn't he going?" She pitched her voice low, but even she could hear the desperation in her words.

Ned did not move his eyes from her. "I don't know. I think he can smell the peppermints in my pocket. Here."

He moved his hand slowly, slowly to his waistcoat pocket; then, just as agonizingly slowly, he pulled it away. His hand was close enough to brush her cheek.

He tossed another candy, throwing it far off into the grass.

She could not see the horse. She heard only its breathing. No tentative footfalls signaling its departure. Nothing.

She could imagine Champion, warily scenting the wind, considering whether to put its back to its enemies.

Ned winked at Kate, and her toes curled.

"I don't dare move," she confessed.

"Really?" He gave her a naughty smile. "I can think of a dozen ways in which I might use that to my benefit."

Kate swallowed. If she'd been reluctant to move before, his words rooted her in place now. Her half boots seemed to be made of thick iron. Her arms were bound at her side. Her mind filled with all the wicked things he might do to her. He might kiss her. He might run his hand down her side. He might undo those mother-of-pearl buttons at her neck and peel back the lace at her bodice.

He looked in her eyes. That old, heady desire swirled through her. A breeze eddied between their bodies, and she felt its caress as if it were his. His eyes narrowed, oh so subtly. He leaned forward.

Maybe this was why she had come here, danger or no danger, plan or no plan. She needed to assure herself that on some basic, primeval level, Edward Carhart still thought of her as his wife. To see if he would treat her as carefully, as *gentlemanly,* as before.

Champion moved away. Kate felt an elusive brush of wind against the nape of her neck, a wisp of air turning to nothing. Then, the clop of hooves.

"There," Ned said. He had not dropped his gaze. Her lips tingled; her skin seemed too tight. He was going to kiss her. And foolishly, after three years of absence, she still wanted him to try. She wanted to believe he would attempt to revitalize their phantom marriage. She wanted to put her hands on the rough, wet fabric of his shirt, to feel the skin beneath. She wanted a taste of his carefree casualness, some indication that he thought of her as more than a delicate duke's daughter. She wanted to believe he felt something for her, even if it was an emotion as evanescent and fleeting as desire. She bit her lip in an agony, waiting for him to move forward.

Instead he pulled away. "There," he declared again. "Now you're free to leave."

Leave. She could *leave?* She stared at his profile in disbelief. After he'd practically pinned her to a fence post and joked he could use her twelve ways—after all that, he thought she could leave before he tried even *one* of them?

She bit her lip, hard. She could taste copper salt on her tongue. She could finally breathe now—and her breath seemed heated to fury.

"I can *leave?*"

He didn't look back at her. His hands were balled at his sides.

"I can leave? And here I thought that was what *you* were best at."

He flinched and looked back at her. "I was trying to be a gentleman."

"I think," Kate said, "you are the most obtuse man in all of Christendom."

"Possible, but unlikely." He gave her an apologetic shrug. "There are a great many Christians, and a good number of them are idiots. If there were not, Britain would never have gotten into a war with China over the importation of opium."

She kicked at his boot—not hard, but enough to vent

her frustration in physical form. "If I want to speak in hyperbole, I am going to do it. And don't believe you can stop me with irrelevant political analysis. It's neither sporting nor gentlemanly."

"Trust me," he said wryly, "right now, all I can think about is being a gentleman. It taxes my brain to think of anything except my gentlemanly duties."

He swallowed and glanced down her neck. It was almost as if he'd never left, as if they were three months into their marriage. As if she were the one yearning forward, while he held himself back in polite denial.

"I retract my statement." Her voice shook. "You are not the most obtuse man in all of Christendom."

"No, no. You were perfectly right. The lady of the pasture always retains the right to hyperbole. Use it with my blessing."

"There's no need," Kate said. "I've realized that *I* am the most obtuse woman."

That finally brought his gaze flying from her bodice to her eyes.

She'd come out here to see if there was any substance to this marriage of theirs, to ascertain if he could accept a wife who took on unladylike pursuits. But she was still susceptible to him after all these years. And despite his informal attire, he still treated her as if he were the consummate gentleman.

"Here I am," she continued, her voice still shaking, "practically *begging* you to kiss me. That you haven't done so…well. I'm not so innocent that I miss the import of that. Men are creatures of lust, and if you haven't given in to yours, you probably haven't got any. At least not for me."

His mouth dropped open.

"Just say so." She looked up into his eyes. "Make this simple for both of us, if you will. Tell me you have no interest in me. Tell me, so I can stop standing in the middle of a field, believing you might kiss me. It's been three years, Ned, and I am sick to death of waiting for you."

He turned to her; his eyebrows drew down. He stared at her for a few seconds, and then he shook his head.

"Speak already." She felt on the edge of desperation. "Tell me. What have *you* to fear? I can't hurt you. And you can't possibly hurt me more than you already have."

"Women are the most curious creatures." He reached out and caught a strand of her hair against her cheek.

That bare contact froze her. "Oh?"

"That's what you think, is it? That I haven't kissed you for lack of interest?"

"If you really wanted me, you wouldn't be able to hold back. I understand how these things work."

"Someone has been telling you lies. You must think all men are beasts by nature. That we see a thing, and like Champion, we charge unthinking across the field."

He leaned toward her, and Kate moved back. The wood of the fence post pressed against her.

"You must think we have no semblance of control, that we can do nothing except obey our baser urges."

That had rather been the import of the furtive discussions she'd conducted with her married friends. It was, after all, why men took mistresses—because they could not control their urges. So she'd been told.

"You're half right," he continued. "We *are* all beasts. And we do have base urges—deep, dark thoughts that you would shrink from, Kate, if you heard what they whispered. We have wants, and trust me, I *want*."

She swallowed and looked up at him. He looked no different than before. He had that carefree, casual smile on his face, and for all that he loomed over her, his stance was easy. But she saw something in his expression—a tightening of his brow, the unbidden press of his lips— some quiet, unexplainable thing that suggested gray clouds lurked behind the casual sunrise of his smile.

"Right now," Ned said, lifting a hand toward her, "I am thinking about taking you against that post."

Her lungs contracted.

"Trust me when I say I am a beast."

His fingers brushed down the rough lace at her neck. He found the line of her collarbone through the fabric. The gentleness of his touch belied the harshness of his tone; his hands were warm against her skin. He ran his finger down the seam of her bodice, down her ribs. The trail burned a line down her body. And then his palm cupped her waist and he pulled her closer. She tilted her head up to look in his face. His eyes were hot and unforgiving, and she could almost see the beast that he claimed he was reflected in them. And then his head dipped down—oh so slowly, so gently.

She might have escaped if she had simply turned her head. But she tasted the heat of his breath; she could still feel his words searing into her lips. *I am thinking about taking you against that post.*

In the back of her mind a voice called out in warning.

He would kiss her and be done; he might even have her against that post. It was his prerogative as her husband. And when he was done, he would walk away. As always, she would be the one left wanting upon his departure. She had to protect herself. She had to turn—

But she was already wanting, and it would serve nobody to send him away. And the truth was, women were beasts, too. She could feel the desire in her, crouched like some dark panther, ready to strike if he backed away.

He didn't. Instead, his lips touched hers. They were gentle for only that first blessed second of searing contact. Then his hands came behind her and he lifted her up, pressing her against the post. His body imprinted itself against hers. His mouth opened, and he took the kiss she had so desperately wanted. His lips were not kind or polite or gentlemanly; his kiss was dark and deep and desperate, and Kate could have drowned in it. He tasted incongruously of peppermint. She gave back, because she wanted, and she had not stopped wanting.

She was not sure how long they kissed. It might have been a minute; it could have been an hour. But when he pulled his head away, she felt the sunshine on the back of her neck, heard a lark calling in some sad minor key from the faraway forest. Every nerve in her body had come to life; every sense was heightened.

"You see," Ned said, "men are beasts. But the difference is, I control my beast. It doesn't control me. Don't think my control means anything other than…my control. Because right now the beast wants. It wants to ravage you, out here in the open where anyone can see. It wants to take you, and it will be damned if you're not ready."

"I've always been ready." She heard the confession slip from her mouth, so clear and crystalline.

"Really?" His tone was dry. "'I think our marriage might dry up and blow away,'" he paraphrased at her, "'with one good gust of wind.' Kate, you don't even *trust* me. I would be a monster if I came back after a three-year absence and expected everything to resume, just like that."

"You don't need *trust* to consummate a marriage, Ned." She shook her head. "I am nothing if not practical." But her heart was beating in impractical little thumps.

"Would you tell me why Harcroft made you so uneasy today? I know he can sometimes be a bit exacting, a bit *too* perfect. But I've known him since the two of us were in short pants. He means well. He was—*is* a friend of mine, you know."

Everyone thought Harcroft meant well. It was the hell of the situation, that anyone she told would run to Harcroft, seeking confirmation of her tale. The man seemed reasonable. Nobody would give credence to a week-old collection of bruises, not when Harcroft explained them away so capably. And besides, she'd promised Louisa to keep silent.

As for Kate's own wants and desires—the substance of her marriage, the yearning of her flesh for his—set on the scale opposite Louisa's life, they balanced to nothing.

Ned thought Harcroft meant well. They had been not only friends, but best friends. When Ned had asked, Harcroft had welcomed Lady Blakely into society despite her lack of provenance. His support had made the difference between a grudging acceptance and a complete denial.

He had smoothed over a situation that might otherwise have proven difficult. They *all* owed Harcroft. Nobody even asked whether Louisa might have been prudent to run away.

She backed away, but the post prevented her retreat. "No. You're right. I don't trust you, yet. If you had left your new wife to the depredations of the *ton,* exposed her to jokes and uncouth wagers, would *you* trust yourself?"

"Kate, I—"

She set her hands against his chest and shoved. She had hoped he would stagger away; instead, he moved back, gracefully, as if her push had been nothing more than a gentle reminder.

He scrubbed one hand through his drying hair, which had fallen into his eyes again. "I left England to prove something to myself. I suppose…I suppose I still have a great deal to prove to you." He said it in a tone of surprise, as if he were somehow just discovering he had a wife and responsibilities.

Hardly reassuring. He hadn't needed a reminder of what he owed *Harcroft.*

CHAPTER SIX

NED'S DAY HAD NOT improved. Supper conversation had been blighted; nobody had wanted to act as if this were a typical house party, where the men would consume a quantity of port before meeting the women for a companionable game of charades. Bare civility, it seemed, was charade enough.

Instead, after the evening meal, Ned's houseguests had disappeared, and Ned had made his own way to the library. He'd gone there because the room seemed safe— an empty cavern of bookshelves and shadowed furniture, lit only by a lamp on a low table and the orange light of a fire.

But as he stepped inside, he realized he wasn't alone.

"Carhart."

Ned heard the deep voice before he made out the dark silhouette slouching in a chair before the fire. The boughs had burned almost to coal; only a dim glow came from the grate. A glass of port, filled knuckle-high, sat on a little table beside Harcroft. Knowing the man, he'd likely scarcely touched it.

"Come," Harcroft said. "Join me in a glass."

Not a chance. His lip curled in awkward distaste.

Even though Ned hadn't said a word, Harcroft must have caught his meaning. The man swiveled in his chair to look Ned in the eyes. The look they exchanged was rooted in a years-old memory, dredged from their respective youths. They'd both been at Cambridge. One evening they'd shared one too many bottles of claret. It had been during one of Ned's bad periods—just before he was sent down for sheer listlessness. The spirits he'd imbibed that night hadn't cured whatever it was that ailed him. Instead, on that evening, he and Harcroft had ended up getting bloody drunk.

After what Ned was sure was only the fourth bottle of wine, and Harcroft insisted was the sixth, they'd engaged in an activity that no self-respecting men would ever admit to—they had talked about their feelings.

At *length*.

Ned still got the shivers just thinking about that night.

"A very tiny glass," he said, holding up his fingers. "Just to hold."

"Just so." Harcroft's lip quirked in understanding—and possibly in memory. He stood and walked to the decanter on the sideboard and poured Ned the barest slug of tawny liquid.

Ned took the glass and seated himself in the chair opposite Harcroft. They stared into the fire.

It was easier than looking Harcroft in the eye. Even drunk, they'd instinctively avoided direct discussion of any topics so squishy and laden with emotion as the ones that had most bothered Ned. But aside from the Marchioness of Blakely, Harcroft was the only person who knew even a hint about what ailed Ned.

That night, he'd made his veiled, maudlin confession.

He had told Harcroft that he feared there was something wrong with him, something irretrievably different. Harcroft, who had been similarly drunk, had admitted the same was true for him. They'd talked around the issue, of course; even soused, Ned was not so stupid as to complain about a bewildering and inexplicable sadness that sometimes came over him. Harcroft, too, hadn't described what happened. Instead, they'd called it a *thing,* an accident. That night, it had seemed a separate beast. They had drunk to its demise.

Drinking hadn't killed it.

Instead, Ned remembered the conversation as a dim, drunken mistake. Mutual confession hadn't brought them closer; instead, Ned had wanted to scrub all memory of that conversation from his mind. Harcroft had been a good friend, before; after, Ned had wanted to stay very, very far from the man, as if he had been the source of contagion. As if speaking about the thing that afflicted him had somehow made it more real.

The fire crackled in front of them, and Ned shook his head.

"What was it like?" Harcroft fingered his glass of port. If he'd done more than wet his lips tonight, the level of liquid in the glass didn't show it. Since the evening of the mawkish confessions, Harcroft, too, had scarcely touched spirits. He'd barely sipped his wedding toast.

"What was what like?" Ned asked uneasily.

"China."

A safe enough topic. So it might have seemed, were Ned's journey not so inextricably bound with the subject of their conversation on that night. He set his own glass aside and shut his eyes. Images flashed through his head—high green hills rising steeply out of the clear blue glass of the ocean, vegetation choking every inch of land; humid heat and the overpowering stench of human waste; the glint of water off polished steel, the sun hot overhead; and then, once he'd left Hong Kong, the delta of the Pearl River, obscured by the acrid smoke of cannon fire.

This evening, Ned had no desire to delve into those feelings. Not at any length at all.

Hot was finally the word Ned settled upon. "So hot you sweat buckets, and so damned humid those buckets never evaporate. I was wringing sweat from my coat half the time."

"Ha. Sounds uncivilized." Harcroft stretched out and hooked his feet on another chair, pulling it closer to use as a footrest. The fire snapped again, and a small draft brought the smell of woodsmoke to Ned. The faint scent seemed an echo of those sulfurous clouds of gunpowder in Ned's memory.

"If civilization is waltzes and twelve-piece orchestras playing in gilt-edged drawing rooms, then, yes. It was uncivilized." With his eyes still closed, Ned could feel the soft swell of water rising underneath his feet. A small smile played across his lips.

"What else might civilization be?" Harcroft's voice was amused.

In Ned's mind, a ragged breath of low mist obscured the mouth of the river—no mere cloud of water vapor, but smoke, acrid and sulfurous. Shredded remnants of cannon fire.

"I think we carry our civilization inside us," Ned said

carefully. "And our savagery. I suspect it takes very little for anyone to switch from one to the other. Whether you happen to be British or Chinese."

"Blasphemy," Harcroft said with very little heat. "Treason, at least."

"Truth." Ned opened his eyes and glanced at Harcroft.

The man had folded his hands around his glass. He stared into the liquid, as if he could discern all civilization in its golden depths. When he finally spoke, his voice was low. "Is your savagery so close to the surface, then?"

This was coming rather too close to that drunken conversation.

As for savagery… Before he'd trekked halfway round the world, the word *savage* had connoted all kinds of strange and different things: cannibalism and half-clothed women. After, he thought more of Captain Adams. Or that acrid bank of mist, rising over rubble. Or the dens where the opium-eaters retreated, to escape a world they did not dare remember.

"My savagery?" Ned asked. "That's rather the wrong word for it." Savagery also entailed *action,* and for Ned, the dark times that visited him were quite the opposite of action. He'd never wanted to eat anyone's flesh or murder anyone's mother. At his very worst, what he'd wanted more than anything was simply to…stop. Sometimes he still wanted to stop; the only difference was, now he'd learned not to.

Ned blinked, and the firelight caught his port, the light glinting off it like steel, flashing the hot sun against water.

Harcroft simply stared into the fire. "It's not savagery to teach someone a lesson. To show someone his rightful place in the world. Sometimes you need a show of strength to demonstrate that rules are not to be trifled with. You may call desire for order and dominance in yourself *savagery,* but we both know the truth. It's the way of the world."

"But one can go too far," Ned interjected. "We're the ones who continue to insist on our right to poison the Chinese with opium. We've killed women and children. One doesn't need to commit savagery to show strength."

"Sometimes these things happen by...by accident." There was something strangely earnest about Harcroft's tone, and he looked away, an oddly rigid set to his jaw.

"You call those things accidents?"

"Sometimes, you know—I suppose I can understand how it all starts. The beast just grabs you by the throat, and before you know it..." Harcroft looked up and met Ned's eyes. "Well. *You* know."

Ned *did* know—at least, he knew how it happened for himself. But he had learned how to control his responses, how to pretend that he was like everyone else. But then, neither of them was soused enough to tell the full truth, and so Ned had no idea what Harcroft intended.

"I know that you need to be ready," Ned said. "You need to be stronger, better than it, so that the next time it reaches out with cold fingers, you are faster than it, and it can't touch you."

Harcroft looked into Ned's eyes for a very long time. Finally he looked away. "Yes," he said. "That's it. Of course." The wood on the fire crackled, and a log fell. Sparks flew up.

"As we're done talking about China, how do you find England, by comparison?"

Gray. Rainy. Even the *birds* sounded different. He had come home, but every aspect of that home had been rendered foreign in his absence. Even his wife. *Especially* his wife.

"I find England cold," Ned finally said. "Damnably cold."

THE NIGHT HAD BECOME even colder by the time Ned waved his valet away. After the servants left, he carefully snuffed the fire they'd started in the grate. He didn't want the warmth. The chill kept his mind sharp.

Only a single candle on a chest of drawers cast a little light. Now yellow light fell on the door that connected his room to the room where his wife slept. Without asking, the servants had put him up in the master's quarters; even the architecture seemed to think a marital visit was a foregone conclusion.

Any other man would not have needed to think any farther than that. Kate was his wife; and she was willing—if grudgingly so. She was also damnably arousing. There was no reason not to take her, then—no reason that would have signified for any other man.

Ned set his jaw and walked to the connecting door. He had been expecting a rusty squeak—some resistance to signify that this door had remained closed for years. But it opened easily. Some servant with no sense of the symbolic had kept the hinges well-oiled during the years

of his absence, as if their marital life had merely been
cast into temporary abeyance.

Her curtains were pulled back, and the moon cast a
shimmery light along the floor, highlighting a path that
led to her bed. Her seated silhouette was outlined in silvered clarity. Her slender limbs were drawn up in front of
her; her arms were clasped about her knees. He could see
the delicate arch of her foot, peeking out from underneath
a white chemise.

She turned abruptly at the sound of the door. "My God,
Ned. You nearly scared me out of my skin."

Aside from that long fall of muslin, it appeared that
skin was essentially all she was wearing. His mouth
dried.

It had been a *long* time. And damn, he wanted her.
He wanted to claim the curves that lay under that fabric.
He wanted to cross the room in one bound and press
her against the feather tick. Desire coursed through him,
pounding in his ears as powerfully as a flooding river,
pulling all his good intentions downstream.

She pushed her legs out in front of her, exposing a
smooth curve from foot to calf. Her feet flexed, pointed,
and then she stood in one graceful movement. The moonlight rendered the white stuff of her shift translucent. He
could see the curve of her waist through that thin fabric.
His hands yearned to touch her.

She's yours. You might as well take her.

She frowned at him. "You're wearing a surprising
amount of clothing."

"I am? I hadn't realized." The thick fabric of his trousers was the only protection he had, the armor behind

which he could hide the truth of his physical response. He'd been erect since he'd walked in the room.

He didn't move forward. Instead, he concentrated on the rise and fall of his breath. *He* was in control, not his pounding desire. Not his fevered imagination. *He* was in control. He *wasn't* a savage.

But then she moved toward him. The gown rippled about her, fading into translucence where the light from the moon shone through. She set her hands on her hips—a movement that only cinched the fabric about that gentle curve. The material slid against her skin in a soft whisper. It was a challenge she issued him, even if she didn't know it yet.

"Really, Ned. How hard can this be?"

"Excruciatingly hard." And long. And thick.

"Well," Kate said, "I'm your wife. We both know how to proceed from here." She let out a hard-put-upon sigh. "Can we just get this over with? I won't protest."

She promised not to protest in the ill-used tones of a servant, agreeing to shovel manure. But even with so little encouragement, Ned went from hard to rigid. His rationality was shredding around him. "It doesn't work like that."

"*It* doesn't work?" She glanced down in surprise. "I see. Your years abroad *did* change you. *It* never had a problem working before."

It stiffened upon being so directly addressed. For a second, he berated himself for not changing from trousers to a loose robe, one that would hide *it*. "*It* works. Trust me. If you waved your hand about, you could verify that *it* is working right now."

She reached out, and he caught her fingers before they could explore the depth—or rather, the length—of his attraction.

"That was a rhetorical device." Her hand fluttered in his. "Not an invitation. Not twelve hours ago, you were telling me you didn't need anything as complicated as a love affair."

"Goodness." She pulled her hand from his grip and shook her fingers. "We're married. It would hardly be a love affair. It's not as if you need to seduce me. No other man has such scruples."

No doubt. Most of Ned's peers thought that "scruples" meant that a man took pains to keep his mistress far from his wife. One demonstrated scruples by taking out subscriptions to charity, by supporting the parish's poor. Scruples were inconveniences, to be set aside in the dark of night when a woman whispered that she was willing.

"That's the thing." The words scraped harshly in Ned's throat. "You see, I don't want to be just any man. I intend to be better."

She rolled her eyes. "Yes, I'm quite sure of it. You're better. And longer. You forget, I've spent three years here, with gentlemen clamoring to seduce me. It's just your luck that I don't need sweet nothings to succumb tonight."

"Kate, I know I've made mistakes these last years. Hell, the only reason we *married* was because I made a mistake."

Her chin lifted at that. "You arrogant…arrogant…" Her mouth worked.

No doubt, Ned thought, the phrase she was searching for was *son of a bitch*. He wanted to hear those vulgar syllables delivered in the perfect tones of a duke's daughter. But alas. Her ladylike vocabulary failed her.

"Arrogant cad," she finished. "We married because I said yes."

"I convinced you to meet me alone. We were caught together because I—"

"I met you alone, Ned. Why on earth do you suppose I did that?"

A sense of unease grew in him. He shook his head, starting over. "It was a marriage of convenience, and—"

"Oh, do be quiet," she snapped. "I was raised to be practical about marriage, Ned. I don't need a declaration of love. I don't *want* you to swear your undying affection, and if you did, I wouldn't believe it, anyway. I just want—" She cut herself off, and then turned around. Her hair spun with her, pale gold decorating her shoulders.

"You want what?"

She looked at him over her shoulder. In that instant— even with the dark of night shielding her expression from his eyes—he guessed at the truth. He didn't want her to answer. He didn't want to hear whatever it was she was about to say.

"You," she said quietly. "I just want you."

He could hear three years of hurt echo in her voice, and he shifted from one foot to the next.

"It wasn't all about convenience," she said softly. "I married—"

"You married a scrawny little mister," Ned said dryly. "An arrogant cad." And, apparently, a bigger son of a bitch than Ned had realized.

She smiled faintly at that.

"Well. Yes."

"You've never asked me for much." The only time she'd ever asked him for anything was when she had asked him not to leave. He hadn't listened then.

Matters had become bad around here. She accepted Harcroft's slights so easily. She was willing to submit to Ned—and God, what an image the thought of her sweet submission still made—even though he'd hurt her. She accepted that she was to have nothing from this marriage but dry dust.

Had he made them that bad?

Ned was afraid he had.

"Just come to my bed," she said with an exhale.

If he had been any other man, he might have done so. He wanted the taste of her badly enough to do it. But then, even though she'd never asked him for anything, he could hear the entreaty in her voice. No matter what she said, she didn't deserve an emotionless coupling in the dark.

Other men might set their scruples aside after nightfall and then take them up again in the morning. But Ned was laboring under another burden. When he let his control lapse, he'd found himself slipping down into darkness.

No. He couldn't be just any man. He had to be better, stronger and more in control. After he'd hurt her, he owed her more than a few minutes with his trousers bunched at his ankles.

"When I take you again, Kate, you won't be offering yourself to me out of a sense of *duty* or obligation or whatever this happens to be." He slid a finger under her chin.

She shivered under his touch and took a step back.

"You won't flinch when I touch you. And you won't tell me it's not a love affair. You won't ever tell me that."

More important, he would have control over himself—control over the inexorable wants that she brought up in him. He would be able to trust himself around her, trust that this time, he would not go careening off into the abyss again.

She looked up at him, the gray of her eyes silver in the moonlight. Her lips were parted. She didn't say a word; she just stared at him, a strange combination of innocence and seduction, desire and hurt wafting off her. She drew him as strongly as any siren would have, and without any notion of the rocks that waited to dash him to pieces if he were to give in.

He pulled his finger from her chin and rubbed it surreptitiously against his trousers. "You told me earlier that our marriage might dry up and blow away in one great gust. If a little wind could do us in, what do you suppose would happen if I just *used* you?"

Her tongue darted out to touch her lips. "Then you'd have the use of me." Her voice was low and husky.

He could have her flat on her back in the bed, her ankles wrapped around his thighs, in two seconds. He would hold her down and pour himself into her, would let go of all the rigid strictures that held him in place. His blood thumped insistently in his ears—not loudly, but a quiet beat, as unstoppable as the sea creeping up the strand. As impossible to ignore.

Ned had become an expert on turning back tides as they came in. "I won't do that."

Her eyes glittered, and he reached out one hand and touched her cheek. She shut her eyes under his touch. He wanted to take her, hard and dark and desperately, her body fitting around his. Instead, he forced himself to skim his hand over her face, a gentle brush. His thumb found her lips and he traced the path of a kiss against that pink softness.

She didn't open her mouth, but he could smell her—lavender water overlaying the faint scent of rose soap. He traced that almost-kiss into her skin.

Before he could think better of it, he leaned down and touched his lips to hers. She was soft, and for all the murky complications of his own lust, the kiss he gave her was as simple and unshadowed as a summer noon. She tasted of warm sunshine and soft breezes. By contrast, he felt dark and wanting. He pulled away, the touch of her incandescent against his own mouth, before his wants could overwhelm him. He'd given her more the promise of a kiss than the actual delivery of one. He straightened while she was just beginning to reach up on her toes.

And then, before his own baser urges could be enlarged on, before he could put his hands on her waist and push her against the wall as he desired, he turned and left.

CHAPTER SEVEN

A FLUTTER OF COLD AIR. Kate's nightgown swirled around her—she opened her eyes after that delicate dream of a kiss, to see her husband retreating.

His leaving, *now,* was even worse than it had been before. He'd touched her, and she'd felt as if her heart had cracked right open. Her hands had spread; her fingers still tingled; her lips still yearned for his.

She'd been raised to be sensible about marriage. Marriage was an alliance, and Ned had been quite eligible— heir to a marquess, wealthy, handsome and without any truly horrendous shortcomings.

That kiss hung between them, like a thought half spoken. Her whole marriage hung before her like a sentence waiting to be finished.

He'd been calmly, politely, *completely* in control. She was the one who burned, who seethed. She was the one who'd made a fool of herself over a man—and apparently she'd not stopped fooling herself. This time she'd only needed the cheapest of excuses to hop into his bed—and he'd dismissed that excuse, threadbare as it was, and had sent her running with a mere pat on her head. He'd kissed her as if she were a child.

It was as if nothing had changed.

But it had.

Last time he'd been in England, when she was a new, naive bride, he'd commanded only her body—her scorching response, her searing desire. But now he wanted more than her body's compliance. What had he said? He wanted her to come to him as if they were engaged in a love affair. He wanted not only willingness, but *trust*. He wanted every ounce of lonely strength she'd built for herself during his long absence. He didn't just want her naked; he wanted her vulnerable and weak. Easy to hurt. He wanted *her,* and damn it, she'd worked too hard for herself to give it over to him for the asking.

No. He might wish for her compliance with all his carefully controlled might, but he wasn't going to get it. Quite the contrary.

She'd seen one spark in his eyes, one hint that her failed seduction had been something to him other than an eye-rolling display. He'd leaned toward her. He'd kissed her. And when she'd reached for him, he'd grabbed her hand before she could touch him.

His armor had flaws.

Kate could hear the floor creak in his room. What was he doing in there? Taking off the rest of that clothing? She gave the door between them a baleful, jealous glare.

He wanted to win her without giving himself up in return. He wanted to conquer her, not win her regard in exchange for his own. He wanted to hold back.

But this time Kate wouldn't be the one left behind with her burning desires. She was going to crack his control. This time he would burn. He would want. He would desire her beyond all reason. And once she had him, desperate and pitiful, begging on his knees…

Kate sighed, her practical side taking over. If she ever brought her husband to his knees, she would likely feel as confused as she was now. She wouldn't know what to do with him.

Rage had a place and a purpose, but even anger left her vulnerable. What had her furious imaginings been but hope in another form? Already she'd reverted to girlish dreams, involving declarations of love, delivered on one knee. But she didn't need revenge. She had no use for petty scorn. She just didn't want to be hurt.

She shut her eyes and breathed deeply. No hope. No longing. No desire. If she could just excise her wants, he could never cause her pain again.

KATE REMOVED THE EGGS, one by one, from her pockets and set them on the rickety table in front of her. Motes of dust tangled in the pale morning sunshine, filtering through the thick glass windows of the little shepherd's shack.

"I cannot say when I'll be back," she said, pulling the last egg from her cloak pocket. "I had thought I might come out here with greater regularity, but there have been complications."

Louisa sat in her chair, her arms folded about her swaddled infant. She looked as ladylike as ever, even though the serviceable green wool she wore was no match for the delicate silks and sprigged muslins that had made up her wardrobe in London. Her face grew long at these words, and she pulled her child closer to her chest.

"Complications," she said quietly. "I detest complications."

Kate began heaping provisions from her basket onto the table. Her shoulders ached, having carted the load five miles here. "There's a cured ham and some carrots and a bunch of greens. You know there are already potatoes and turnips in the shelter. But I've brought some scallions from the garden, such as they are. I might not return for a week. The fare will likely be monotonous."

She trailed off, feeling useless. Louisa shook her head.

"What sort of complications could keep you away for a week?"

Kate glanced away and pulled another cloth napkin from the basket.

The cottage where Louisa was hidden lay five miles to the west of Berkswift. It had once been little better than a shepherd's shelter, four walls and a makeshift fireplace. But over the decades, it had grown into a tiny three-room affair—an open room for cooking and eating, furnished with a rough-hewn table and trestles, a sleeping room and a storage shed.

Louisa and the Yorkshire nursemaid Kate had hired fit compactly in the space, packed together like common passengers shoved into a stagecoach.

Kate reached into the basket one last time. Her hands closed on metal, cold and deadly. "I brought you—"

"News, Kate. I want *news.*"

"This." Kate set the silver-tooled pistol next to the ham.

The clink it made as she laid the weapon on wood seemed somehow too soft, to demure, to have been made by a gun. She'd found it that morning in a cabinet. It had been a grim sort of serendipity. Under the circumstances, bringing it had seemeed like a good idea.

"Do you know how to shoot?" Kate asked.

Louisa's face shuttered. "Not really. One—one simply points and squeezes, I suppose?"

"Harcroft is staying at Berkswift." Kate spoke quickly, as if saying the words faster would make them less painful. "He caught wind of a rumor about a woman looking like you disembarking from a cart. He flew out here in a rage."

"He knows." Louisa's face froze. Her hand curled around her sleeping baby in quiet protectiveness. Her eyes pinched to narrowness. But by the slump in her spine, that show of strength was little more than bravado.

"He doesn't, not yet. But I'd like to keep it that way. He's furious. And—unfortunately—he is staying in my house."

"I see." Louisa let out a breath and then smiled. It was a brave expression, somewhat belied by the nervous dart of her eyes. "Well, at least worry will keep me from boredom. I never thought I would miss those dreadful meetings that the Ladies' Beneficial Tea Society insisted on holding, but right now I would give anything for a heated argument about the merits of embroidering handkerchiefs versus the knitting of socks and scarves." She smiled lazily. "Right now I have nothing to do but watch over Jeremy. And he sleeps a shocking amount of the time."

Over the course of Kate's less-than-ladylike secret career, spent stealing women away from husbands who didn't deserve them, she'd seen many different responses.

One woman had escaped her husband—but after two days she'd begged to return, insisting that the man could not survive without her, that he *loved* her. That he wouldn't hit her again. Another had cowered for three weeks in this cottage, unable to lift her head. Yet another had grabbed hold of the chance and scampered for freedom as soon as it was offered. Louisa had landed somewhere in between those extremes.

She had argued her duty as wife for months, when Kate had first found out what was happening to her. Then Louisa had given birth to her first child, and whatever she felt her dry duty as *wife* had been, her duty as mother had overwhelmed her with a ferocious passion. There were not many women in Louisa's situation who would joke about boredom, with their husbands off raging in the distance.

"He'll stay a few days," Kate predicted. "He'll uncover no trail, no clues—just that rumor of an auburn-haired lady who paid a merchant for a ride in his cart, and then disappeared. In a week, he'll have moved on."

Louisa nodded.

"But while he's here, he mustn't suspect me. Not even a little bit. He thinks I'm a frivolous, foolish sort of female, forever shopping and planning parties. I want him to continue to think so. For the next few days I shall devote myself to my guests' entertainment. I'll plan meals. I'll protest when Blakely refuses to participate in my musical evenings."

"*Blakely's* keeping him company? Harcroft must be calling in all his old favors. I gather he trotted Blakely out to frighten you into divulging my secret plans. That *is* a complication."

"It's even more complicated," Kate confessed. "You see, my husband is back."

"Carhart? When did he return?"

"Yesterday. Can you believe it? Of course his vessel could not have been blown off course by two weeks. And now he's here, and instead of having Harcroft ignore me, Ned will be following me around, bothering me. Last night—"

She shut her mouth ruthlessly. It didn't seem right to disclose what her husband had told her. His promise had seemed so real in the moonlight, as sacred as a wedding vow. It seemed almost a violation to share it.

Be practical, she reminded herself.

But before she could answer, Louisa took her hand. "I know it's been a great while since…your last time. Did he hurt you?"

If there was one thing worse than spilling marital secrets, it was *Louisa* offering Kate comfort because Kate's husband—the man who fed peppermints to ill-tempered horses—might have hurt her.

"There, there," Louisa soothed. "I promise, if he shows his nose around here, I'll shoot him for you."

Kate choked back a laugh. "That won't be necessary. He was never *that* bad. In fact, he is…" Different. Dangerous. "Gentle," she finished awkwardly. "He always has been. You've met him. Do you suppose you might…well. Tell him?"

Kate felt a sudden sense of vulnerability at the thought. She had no idea how he would respond, if he knew. Her own father had flared up at the slightest intimation that Kate intended to take on an interesting project—as if it somehow reflected poorly on his capabilities as a father if she did. His had been a prickly, cloying sort of love— the kind that did everything difficult for her, so that she might sit in peace.

And boredom.

She loved her father, but hiding her work had been a necessity.

"No." Louisa stood and turned away abruptly, patting the swaddling firmly. "He's friends with Harcroft, for goodness' sake."

"We'll need someone to help obtain a divorce. You might have options, besides fleeing to America. And it would be better than *this*." Kate spread her hands to encompass the tiny room and all it implied—a life spent hiding from a man who had the legal right to compel her presence; her son, growing up without the natural advantages that were his birthright. "It's a radical process, but surely you could obtain a petition on grounds of extreme cruelty."

Louisa's hands fluttered uncertainly. "Would he help? Do you know? How much influence do you have over him?"

Not even enough to get him in bed.

If she'd had any influence over her husband, he would never have left. And he'd come back more frightening, more *mysterious* than ever.

Louisa slumped into her chair again, and Jeremy, in her arms, gave a small, sleepy hiccough. "Even that's no solution. Even assuming your husband was willing to defy mine, it would end with Harcroft having Jeremy. I won't abandon him." A fierce note entered her voice. "Not to him. Not to *that*. I would rather *die*."

An extreme pronouncement, although by the fierce light shining in Louisa's eyes, the sentiment was heartfelt. A thread of uneasiness curled around Kate's spine. She'd given Louisa a gun.

But it was rather too late to rip the pistol from her hands, and it would have made no difference in any event.

"The weapon." Kate licked her lips. "It is to be used only as a threat, understand?"

"Oh," said Louisa bitterly. "I understand. This is as much my fault as anyone's. I let this happen to me. I didn't say anything for years. No complaints. No protests. I accepted it. I dare say I deserved it."

"Nobody deserves to be hit in the stomach with a fire poker."

"But I didn't stop it." Louisa's gaze abstracted. "Until he threatened Jeremy, I didn't stop it."

Kate had discovered the truth of her friend's mysterious illnesses a year before. In that time, she'd urged her to leave, to do *something*. It had taken Louisa thirteen months to act. It was impossible not to feel sorry for her, after what she had survived. She understood that her friend had been damaged in more ways than by just her husband's physical betrayal. Still, it was impossible not to feel a hint of frustration.

"Don't speak that way," Kate said. "You *did* stop it, eventually. You're here. You're safe. Nobody will ever find you."

Kate looked out the window. Before them, dying grass covered the hill, stretching down into the autumn-brown of the valley below. A spiral of smoke rose from a village miles distant. Kate counted to ten, pulling her own confused emotions in line, until that plume of smoke had disappeared and reformed again, before she answered.

"I think you underestimate your own strength."

"And you always assumed too much of me," Louisa said simply. "I'm not strong, not the way you are."

Kate kept her gaze on the waving field of grass. Through the uneven glass, she could not make out individual blades. Instead, they passed back and forth, rippling like a sea. If Louisa could see into Kate's heart right now, Louisa would not call her *strong*. She feared Harcroft. The terror of discovery filled her almost to panic. Her own husband might betray her at any moment, and still she wished he had taken her last night.

She wasn't strong.

No; Kate was afraid. But she had become an expert at hiding her emotion behind a veneer of practicality. And now her husband was threatening even that.

She waited for practicality to win out before speaking. "There's nothing to fear." She raised her chin and caught a glimpse of motion cresting the hill. Her blood ran cold; practicality disappeared in a flap of brown fabric. In the space of time it took Kate to gulp breath into her seizing lungs, she saw men on horseback.

She *knew* these horses. It was Harcroft and her husband. While they'd broken their fast this morning, they had talked of visiting a few nearby hamlets, of making a few inquiries. Kate just hadn't expected them to take this tiny path to the west.

"Get down," she hissed.

Louisa dropped to a crouch—quickly enough that Jeremy opened his eyes, blinking in confusion. They huddled on the floor.

So long as they were very still…

Jeremy began to cry. He didn't start with little sobs, either; instead, he screwed up his nose and screamed. Kate hadn't realized that a bundle of cloth scarcely larger than a large cabbage could generate so much noise. She stared at Louisa in appalled horror. There was nothing to do about it. Louisa patted him ineffectually on the back, and cast a worried glance at Kate.

There was still no reason the men would come up to this cabin. The track they were on passed a quarter mile from here, leading over the ridge to a village eight miles away. Even if they came near, unless they passed close enough to peer in the window, they would see nothing but a shepherd's cottage, abandoned in the autumn. And loud as Jeremy was, they would still have to come very close to hear his wails.

Wouldn't they?

Kate's hands were cold. She wasn't sure if she trembled, or if it was Louisa; their shoulders were pressed together so that their shivers merged into one. Kate could not let herself be overtaken by fear. If the men came close—if they came by—she would need to act quickly, to forestall their inevitable questions. The pistol, after all, would be of no use.

Jeremy's wails paused, as he gulped breath. For a brief

instant she could hear the wind in the weeds, the entirely inappropriate happy trill of a blackbird outside. He started again, but his startled screams were dying down, trickling into a few minute sobs. Still, she imagined she could feel the vibration of horses' hooves drawing closer and closer, across the field. She waited, her fingers clenching.

But no, that cantering was only the wild beat of her own heart. There was nothing.

No sound, except the last gurgle of Jeremy's outburst. They were safe.

"You see?" she breathed with a shaky a smile. "Nothing to worry about. I'll just pop up and check—"

She drew up into a crouch, and then pulled herself up to the window.

Not two hundred yards away, Harcroft and Ned were racing across the fields. They were traversing the meadow parallel to the cottage. Headed away, but that would change if they saw a woman standing at the window. Kate froze with fear.

A sudden movement would attract more attention. Slowly she stepped back into the shadows. She watched them, her heart pounding, as they spurred their horses onward. They passed by, and then took the hill behind the cottage at a trot.

Halfway up, Ned turned in the saddle. She could not see his face, but from his stance, he could have been looking straight at her. It was unlikely he could see into the room, dimly lit as it was. It was impossible that he could make out her features through the poorly made glass. It was inconceivable that he would somehow comprehend what was happening. Kate repeated these things to herself, in fervent supplication.

Perhaps those desperate prayers were heard, because he turned away. She watched his form, wavy and distorted by the glass, until the rise of the hill swallowed him.

Only then did Kate draw breath into her aching lungs. "They're gone," she croaked, her tone as cheerful as she could manage. "You were right under Harcroft's nose, dear, and he didn't suspect a thing. You see, there's nothing to worry about."

"Yes," Louisa said, sounding equally unconvinced. She looked down into Jeremy's face. "You see?" she told him. "We're perfectly safe."

CHAPTER EIGHT

KATE DIDN'T DARE RETURN to Berkswift by way of the well-used road that led straight there. Visiting Louisa had been risk enough. But if she met Harcroft along that dusty track, his suspicions, never quiet, would leap up.

Instead, she took a route that cut circuitously along fence boundaries, dipping through a small scrub forest. It lengthened her journey from two hours to three. Shadows stretched as she walked. The path led over a small stream, its waters crossable only by means of a few slippery rocks, dotting the trail. She started across, balancing her empty basket on her arm. The stream was shielded on both sides from the sun by a small copse of trees, which dropped yellowing leaves into the mulch underfoot. The walk had calmed her fears. The fields had been quiet, and this little stream presented the perfect picture of solitude: quiet, but for the burble of the water, and hidden from view. She stepped on the last rock, green with moss, almost at the far bank.

At that moment, her husband stepped out from behind a tree.

Kate let out a shriek and stumbled backward. For a second, she teetered on the slippery stone, desperately flinging her arms behind her for balance. The basket went flying. Then he stepped close. His arms came about her, and he hauled her against his frame.

He was solid and strong. Her heart thumped against his solid chest; his breaths pushed against her breast. Even after her feet were planted on solid ground, he did not let her go.

"Ned. You surprised me. You were so quiet."

He looked down at her, his hands on her arms. "How terrible of me. Maybe I should wear a bell, like a cow."

She pulled away from him—just far enough to look back into his eyes. In the overshadowing trees, they seemed dark, impenetrable pools. There was nothing bovine about him; the shadows rendered him rather more wolfish. Her heart pounded. "Or like a goat," she said. "You may recall I have aspirations in that direction."

But he was not distracted. "Where were you just now?"

No. Definitely nothing of the cow about him. That question bordered on dangerous, desolate territory.

"Walking." Kate twisted the tie of her cloak. "And delivering food to the tenants, actually. We've had a good run of eggs of late." She did not dare drop her eyes from his, did not dare let him see how much his question discomfited her. "Besides, walking is healthful, my physician says, and I haven't the opportunity to do much of it in London. London is a dirty, smoky place, and the parks are overrun by other people. I don't much get the chance to be alone." She was talking too much.

He let go of her waist. "*Were* you alone?"

"Of course. With whom could I possibly have been walking?"

"I don't know. I ask only because you jumped from me like a guilty thing."

"Like a frightened thing, you beast." She tapped his chest in a pretense of playfulness, but he did not respond. "And what were you doing, lurking behind that tree?"

"I wasn't *lurking*," he said. "I was waiting for you. I caught a glimpse of you when you crossed the upper field. And yes, Mrs. Evans told me you'd gone to deliver some goods to the tenants. But who lives out west?"

A cold awareness seeped into Kate's hands. It trickled down the back of her neck, trailed along her spine until it lodged in an icy indigestible mass in her belly. Her father had always taken her statements as truth, never questioning them. She'd never imagined Ned would *think* about what she said.

"Oh," she said. "Only Mrs. Alcot. She's getting on in years. I did take a rather roundabout route home."

He glanced at her. Maybe it was her imagination, but she caught a hint of suspicion in the set of his lips.

"If you must know, I wanted some time alone to think. Much has changed in the last few days."

"But the Alcots live in the village," Ned said.

"Not anymore, they don't." Kate spoke with some asperity, but it was either that, or let a hint of fear invade her voice. These days, it seemed that all conversations led back to Louisa.

He raised one eyebrow at this. His gaze fixed upon her; she imagined clockwork in his head working as he followed the evidence to the inexorable conclusion. *Had* he seen her in the cottage? He couldn't have.

"Is there something you'd like to tell me?" His words

seemed so kind, so solicitous; Kate shivered. Tell him? She would have to trust him, first. And that lay a long way off. Even the story of Mrs. Alcot proved dangerous.

Once he had heard it, he might begin to put together all the strange, unexplained events. After all, Kate was the reason Mrs. Alcot was no longer living with her husband in the village.

"Is there something I should know?" Ned repeated.

"Yes," she said, and stood up on tiptoes. It wasn't lust that drove her to place her lips against his, but splintering dismay. She needed *time*. He reacted with a scalded hiss. His hands came around her waist. And yet when she touched his chest, his mouth opened to her. His tongue met hers. She could feel his body, the outline of his shoulders, the swell of his thigh brushing hers. And then he gathered her up in his arms and pulled her against him. He was hot to the touch, and his heat did nothing to dispel her growing sense of panic. The hard expanse of his chest pushed into her breasts; her legs fell against his thighs. She reached up to touch his face, and a half-day's worth of stubble prickled the palms of her hand.

It had started as a kiss given out of panic—the easiest way to put off his questions; the best way to garner time to think. But thinking was the last thing she could do with his mouth on hers. What had started as panic became more. Her lips traced the sum of her fears against his; her tongue met his in sheer desperation. He tasted bittersweet. She could not kiss him, not without remembering the secret, sad certainty of his abandonment. She could not feel the warm promise of his arms around her without knowing that she had to push him away from her secrets.

Her kiss spoke of years of loneliness, and his body had no answer.

She could have poured all her shattered marital hopes into that one kiss, if he had let her continue. But he did not. Those strong arms about her held her in place. He lifted his head and looked into her eyes. She doubted he could make out any truth in the shadowed light dancing through the leaves overhead.

"That was very nice," he said, his voice low, "but it was not an answer."

Drat.

"Mrs. Alcot's husband lives in the village," Kate said quietly. "Mrs. Alcot herself lives in the old Leary place. She has, these last two years."

"Why the devil would she do that?"

"Because her husband was beating her black and blue," Kate snapped, "and now that she's coming up in years, he might have broken bones."

"He agreed to the separation?"

He would find the truth of the matter; all he had to do was poke about the village. Kate lowered her eyes reluctantly. "He did after I decreed it." Mrs. Alcot had been one of the few women she'd been able to help openly. Kate had been the lady of the manor; in her husband's absence, her word had not precisely been law, but it had been very, very persuasive.

"You decreed it," Ned repeated. "Why did *you* decree it?"

"Because *you* were not here."

He was silent, rubbing his chin. He shook his head, as if clearing it of preconceptions. "I hadn't realized I left you with so much responsibility. It seems a serious matter to have been placed upon your shoulders."

She *wanted* him to underestimate her. She wanted him to overlook her, for Louisa's sake.

But for her own sake, she could have happily shoved him into the mud of the stream bank for the solicitous tone in his voice. "You may notice that I failed to shatter under the strain."

"Of course, I didn't mean to imply you were unequal to the task," he said, practically tripping over himself to reassure her. "No doubt you dealt with the matter magnificently. I merely meant that you shouldn't have *needed* to do so."

Heaven forfend that she take time from her schedule of frivolity to think of matters of substance.

"Indeed," she responded. "The matter took valuable *days* from my last trip to Bond Street. Why, that season, I had to go to the opera with ready-made gloves on opening night. You can imagine my shame."

What she wanted to say was *I've been doing more than that since I was sixteen.*

"Are you angry about something?" he asked in bewilderment.

"Of course I'm angry. There was a shortage of peacock feathers that year, and because I was late to town, I had to settle for diamond pins instead."

He frowned at her. "Did I say something wrong?"

It was a form of kindness he practiced. She'd felt one like it most of her life. No doubt her father had intended to keep her as every woman ought to be kept, safe and out of harm's way. Women were supposed to plan parties, after all, not escapes. Ned wouldn't understand that she wanted more than that. She imagined herself trying to tell him anyway.

I wanted more responsibility, and so I started stealing wives. Did you know Louisa is number seven?

No. That clearly wouldn't work.

"I did say something," he said, staring at her. "You *are* angry."

"I'm *furious* just thinking about those diamonds," Kate said with a sigh. "Remember, if you love a woman—buy her sapphires."

Ned simply stared at her, as if she'd announced her intention to give birth to kittens.

"I will never," he finally said slowly, "*never,* in my entire life, *ever* understand women."

No, he wouldn't. And Kate wasn't sure whether she should thank the Lord for that, or burst into tears.

NED HAD NO MORE OPPORTUNITY to talk to his wife that evening, and in any event, he very much doubted she would say anything he comprehended.

After the evening meal, Kate had cheerfully asked if anyone wanted to play at hide-and-seek. She'd spoken with a bright smile, her hair glinting in the lamplight. If it had been a *real* house party, her suggestion might not have been taken amiss.

As it was, Harcroft had stared at her for a very long time before shaking his head and leaving the brightly lit dining room without a word. Jenny had made polite excuses for herself and her husband. And when they'd all left, Ned had caught that look on her face again—that curious combination of self-satisfaction and hurt, all mixed into one.

He couldn't shake the feeling that she was already hiding. He wasn't sure what role she'd assigned him in the game, but he felt uneasy. Nobody else seemed to notice, and Ned was left to his own devices.

There was more to all of this than appeared on the surface.

He had gone in search of Jenny, who had a keen eye for seeing hidden things. He'd stopped at the downstairs study. A little sullen light shone from beneath the door, which stood ajar.

Ned eased it open.

Harcroft turned as he entered. "Ah, Ned. Your wife told me I could sit in this room. I hope you're not accustomed to making use of it."

"No, no. I have a desk in an alcove in my upstairs chambers."

Harcroft had laid a heavy sheet of paper on the wooden table. As Ned drew nearer, he realized it was a rough hand-drawn map of the area, roads and villages sketched in by the wavering marks of pencil. Wood shavings—and the aforementioned pencil—decorated the edge of the table.

A single spot of red ink in the center marked the point where gossip had placed the woman who looked like Louisa. Two straight-pins pierced the villages Ned had conducted Harcroft to earlier in the day.

"You're being quite thorough," Ned said. For some reason, those two pins, bristling out of the map like the spines of a hedgehog, made him feel uneasy.

"I dare not let anything slip by. Not so much as a single cottager, who might otherwise have useful knowledge."

The man's hair shone almost copper in the orange lamplight; he frowned and shifted, staring at those pins until Ned thought they might reduce to slag in the heat of his gaze.

Ned had known Harcroft for years. The ferocity of his expression was nothing new. Harcroft looked like a ruffled angel, with his gold hair and his tired slouch. He had always seemed perfect—so damned perfect. But for his confession on that long-ago night, Ned would have believed him to be truly without fault.

Harcroft had poured himself a finger's breadth of sherry, but as usual, the liquid sat untouched in a tumbler by his map. He leaned back and sighed, scrubbing his hands through his hair.

"I can help with your sojourns," Ned said. "I spent enough time hereabouts in my youth that I know the environs quite well." He reached for the pencil and sketched a little X between two hills. "There are five farmers' cottages in this valley. Not truly a village, but the houses are built within shouting range of each other, the lands radiating out from that point. And here…"

Harcroft nodded as Ned talked. It was good to feel *useful,* to know that someone was willing to speak with him. Ned discussed the area within a day's ride from Berkswift slowly, starting from the north and then filling in details in a clockwise sweep. It was only until they got to the southeast quadrant of the map that Ned paused to sharpen the pencil with a penknife.

"There's very little out west," he said. "It's all sheep

pasture now." He tapped the map at the old Leary place, remembering Kate's words that afternoon. "Mrs. Alcot, apparently, lives alone here." He sketched in an obligatory squiggle. "The house she is staying in is rather out of the way."

Now that he was looking at the rough map, he was re-minded of precisely how out of the way the house was—a good thirty minutes on horseback. On foot? Kate's trek must have taken considerably longer. Over an hour. Another two or three to come back, by the roundabout route she'd taken. She could have made it back to the point where he'd met her in the time allotted. If she'd walked very quickly, and spent no time visiting with Mrs. Alcot.

"Something doesn't add up," he said aloud.

"I know that feeling." Harcroft rubbed his eyes. "I feel as if I'm missing something right in front of my nose, and if I could only draw back, I would see it."

"There's another cottage." Ned moved his pencil a few inches north. "It should be abandoned—the shepherds use it in spring and summer. It's right here, along the ridge. We passed it this morning. But it's empty this time of year."

"Perhaps I'll go knock these two dots off, tomorrow morning," Harcroft said, watching as Ned inscribed a second squiggle to represent the shepherd's cottage.

Ned had scared Kate this afternoon. By the tempo of her breath and the pallor of her skin, she'd seemed terri-fied to see him at first. And it hadn't just been his abrupt appearance. His questions had discomfited her enough that she'd thrown herself at him in that frightened parody of a kiss. And he hadn't even done anything—just asked after Mrs. Alcot.

"Kate spoke with Mrs. Alcot this afternoon," Ned said slowly. "She would have spoken up if the woman had seen anything." He reached for a straight-pin, to puncture that dot on the map.

Harcroft reached forward and blocked his hand. "No. I think not."

"Kate is friends with Lady Harcroft. I know she wants to help."

"She's a woman. She'll be rather too kind in her questioning. I've seen your wife with mine for three years, Ned. If there's a thought in her head beyond the latest fashions in head gear, I've yet to see evidence of it."

That seemed too much an echo of Kate's own words this afternoon. Ned felt another prickle of unease travel through him. He was *definitely* missing something.

"Well," he said, "then I'll do it myself tomorrow. I know Mrs. Alcot, and if what Kate said is true, she'll be more likely to talk to me than a stranger. You go here." Ned tapped east on the map. "Concentrate on the towns with significant populations—it's the best use of your time, in any event. I'll handle these two."

That sense that something was eluding him intensified.

Harcroft shook his head. "Well. That decides that. I suppose I should turn in if I'm to have an early start tomorrow." He stood and stretched.

Ned stared at the map a while longer. "I was just wondering one thing, Harcroft. Jenny and Gareth spent all their time today searching out news of any ruffians who might have absconded with your wife. But this afternoon, you asked after gossip about a woman and child alone. Do you think she left of her own free will?"

Harcroft froze, his arms still above his head. "I cannot afford to discount any possibility."

"But why might she have done that?"

"Why does any woman do anything?" He shrugged, as if all feminine foibles could be reduced to whim. "Honestly, I simply cannot comprehend those women who claim that they should be granted the right to vote or own property. If they could vote, they would choose the fellow with the prettiest moustache. Or the one who promised to usher in a new fashion."

"That's a rather harsh assessment."

"Hardly. In my experience, if a woman thinks she is capable of deciding an issue of importance, it should be taken as presumptive evidence of her incapacity. Too foolish to know what she cannot do."

Ned shut his mouth. Harcroft was overset. Unhappy. It was inevitable that he feel a bit embittered toward womankind, under the circumstances.

But Harcroft was looking at him with a disbelieving glower. "Surely you don't believe that women deserve *more* rights? That they are competent to handle men's affairs?"

Ned's father had died in a hunting accident. His mother had raised him practically on her own—choosing his tutors, making sure that he learned the fundamentals of hunting and boxing from uncles and cousins, and the principles of estate management from his grandfather. In his later youth, he'd watched Jenny, the marchioness, handle situations that would have brought lesser men to their knees. Ned knew the prevailing sentiment was that women needed to be protected from the world, but in his personal life, the women he'd known most closely hadn't had much male protection. They'd still triumphed.

Perhaps that was why he found it difficult to become exercised, as many of his compatriots did, at the thought of women gaining traditionally male prerogatives. In his life, women had *always* had those prerogatives.

"If you're worried about how Lady Harcroft will fare on her own," he suggested gently, "it's been my experience that women are capable of more than we give them credit for. I am sure she might surprise you with what she has done."

But Harcroft appeared not to hear what Ned said. Instead, he smacked his fist into his hand. "In fact," he said, "we should just declare them incompetent as a rule—incompetent to own property, to divest themselves of it, to testify in court against the men who protect them, to avail themselves of any sort of divorce."

"Married women already can't own property at law," Ned said. "They already can't testify in court against their husbands. And divorce is available to married women only in extreme cases of spousal cruelty."

Harcroft coughed gently. "Listen to yourself. Don't tell me you're a follower of Bentham. How is it that *you* can recite that pale litany of female complaints?"

Those same points had all been listed in the newspapers, the subject of a handful of political discussions. Ned shook his head wearily.

"Yes," Harcroft said bitterly. "I should like to see all

women declared feeble-minded, as a matter of principle. Then they wouldn't even be able to dispose of property. They wouldn't be able to threaten to testify in court at all. They wouldn't ever leave their husbands, because there would be no recourse for them if they did."

Ned couldn't take the sentiment seriously. That spiteful mouthful was just bitter emotion. Harcroft would have warmer feelings, no doubt, once he'd recovered his wife.

He'd met Lady Harcroft shortly after her marriage. She'd been married on the young side of things—at fifteen, if he recalled correctly. She had always seemed a small, timid soul—ready to jump at a single word uttered by her husband, devoted to his comfort—except for the days when she took to her bed with whatever illness afflicted her.

She had often been ill.

But when she had been well, she had fawned over her husband. Harcroft had only to think of crooking his finger, and she would respond. Once her husband had her safely back, he would remember how well his wife looked after his comfort.

But looking at the man—sitting in a chair, staring at the map as if he could flush his wife from her hiding spot with the intensity of his gaze—Ned couldn't quite make himself believe it. No, he was missing something. He felt as if he'd added columns and columns of numbers, and come up with an answer that he knew must be incorrect.

If only he could ferret out the error.

"Have you had the honor of meeting my mother?"

Ned asked gently. "Or the Marchioness of Blakely?"
Ned would have added his own wife, if he hadn't already
known that Harcroft was set against the woman. "Neither
of them are precisely examples of feeble-mindedness."

"Perhaps." Harcroft waved this attempt at reason away.
"Perhaps. Well. I'm to bed."

Ned waved him off and studied the map in front of
him. That sense of unease remained even after Harcroft
had taken himself off. In the dim light, the pencil marks
seemed child's sketches, failing to capture some basic
truth of reality. The numbers still didn't cast up into a
proper sum in his head. Two and two came together, but
they only managed to whisper dark intimations amongst
themselves, hinting at the possibility of a distant four.

He gave up trying to make sense of it all when his head
began to ache.

NED HAD GONE PAST the small shepherd's cottage on the
ridge—a tidy construction of stone and mortar—a thousand times without ever attaching any particular signifi-
cance to it. There had never been any reason to do so,
after all. Sometimes shepherds were in residence. Often
they were not. When he was twelve, he'd once crept inside
on a wager and found himself disappointed by the tidy,
prosaic interior. He'd had no reason to think about the
structure since.

Now he eyed the thing warily. His gray mare sensed
his unease and shifted beneath him. This visit should have
required a matter-of-fact glance inside, prerequisite to
ticking an item off of Harcroft's list. The hut itself looked
preposterously harmless in the morning light. Picturesque

vines crept halfway up the doorframe, and a tiny wisp of smoke slipped out the chimney, before being smudged by the wind into insubstantiality. The cottage seemed small, cozy and eminently unworthy of his attention.

Except for one small thing. The place was supposed to be unoccupied, and someone had lit a fire. That, coupled with Kate's behavior last afternoon, Harcroft's strangeness in the evening…

Well. He dismounted and looped his mare's reins on a post near the entry. It was inconceivable that Harcroft's fancies might have come true, that his wife might be here, on Ned's property. But there was that smudge of smoke. Maybe it had been taken over by ruffians, after all.

In the cold light of an autumn day, last night's fears seemed truly ridiculous.

Ned shook his head. His imagination, always fertile, had a tendency to run amok, if he let it. There were a few points to keep in mind. One, it was a drafty shepherd's cottage; ruffians generally preferred easy access to ale. And women. And future victims. Two, it was on Ned's property. Ned was not precisely an expert on the subject, but he suspected madwomen were more likely to wander the moors, tearing their hair out, than they were to build boring little fires in tiny buildings.

It was probably just one of the shepherds, come to inspect the land in preparation for winter. No doubt they intended to do some final cleaning before winter set in. To patch the roof. There was undoubtedly a simple explanation. Anything was more likely than the possibility that he would encounter a band of unknown brigands stealing

Harcroft's wife and secreting themselves in a shepherd's hut on Harcroft's friend's property.

He strode to the door and knocked loudly.

Inside he heard nothing. No footsteps. No hasty, frightened shouts. No bugle, sounding a piratical call to arms.

Even the wind seemed to hold its breath.

He glanced up, to make sure he hadn't imagined that sign of habitation. That stream of smoke still purled from the chimney; waves of heat distorted the air above the capstones. There had to be someone inside; no shepherd would leave a fire alone and untended, not during these dry days of autumn.

"Draven?" he tried.

No answer.

"Stevens? Darrow?" He cudgeled his brain, trying to remember more of the shepherds who worked this land. "Dobbin?" he tried at last. Desperation, that; Dobbin was a sheep dog. Still no answer, neither from canine nor human compatriot. Whoever had once been inside had undoubtedly wandered off for a few minutes. Ned would have sharp words for the fellow, leaving a fire burning with the fields so dry.

But there was no reason not to have fun until the man returned.

Ned set his fingers on the handle of the door.

"Well, then, Lady Harcroft." He spoke loudly, pitching his voice to deepness, a grin on his face. It helped to mock his own fancies, to show how ridiculous they were. "You are exposed. I have found you all. Ruffians, prepare to be brought to justice! Ha!"

If this had been a story, and Ned a Bow Street Runner—or a knight of old—he would have kicked the door in dramatically. Of course, that would have necessitated an embarrassing explanation, when he shamefacedly asked his estate manager to repair the damage. Ned settled for swinging the door inward.

He expected to see the tiny front room of the cottage—barely large enough to contain a trestle table and the fireplace. He was a little taken aback to find the floor of the room piled with lumpy sacks that might have been potatoes or turnips, and another smaller sack of flour. The only reason he knew he wasn't dreaming was the rope, strung from one side of the room to another. A multitude of damp cloths had been strung to dry. He never would have dreamed of anything so prosaic.

And when he moved his eyes from that curiosity, he was astonished to see Lady Harcroft herself, standing as far from the door as she could. Her auburn hair was braided and pinned to her head; she wore a deep brown gown, bereft of embellishment. He was so surprised to see her, after all his self-mockery, that it took him a moment to comprehend what she held in her hands.

It was a silver-tooled pistol. The stuff of his nightmares. And she was aiming it at Ned's midsection with hands that seemed surprisingly steady.

His good humor evaporated. That sense of unease he'd entertained last night returned, this time in full-blown panic.

"Damn me." His lips seemed to move of their own accord. He let go of the door handle.

Lady Harcroft didn't respond. Her lips pressed together.

"Of all the—Lady Harcroft, *you're* the gang of ruffians?"

She didn't seem to be hearing what he said, which was just as well, because his world had narrowed to the ice-cold beat of his pulse. Her shoulders squared, and she brought the barrel up to point directly at Ned's chest.

"You realize that was a joke. About bringing you to justice." It didn't seem funny anymore. It didn't even seem embarrassing. It was just absurdly frightening.

"Mr. Carhart." Lady Harcroft's voice trembled, where her hands had not. "I am sorry. Truly."

"Wait. No."

But she'd already squeezed her eyes shut, and before Ned could throw himself out of the way, she pulled the trigger.

CHAPTER NINE

THE HAMMER HIT THE PISTOL with a metallic, percussive click. The sound echoed about Ned—but it was quieter than the explosion of black powder he'd expected.

She stared at him down the barrel of the firearm, her eyes widening. "Damn you, Kate." Her voice was low. "Don't come any closer, Mr. Carhart. Or I'll—" She grimaced. "I have a knife." Her voice quavered up on the final syllable, as if she were on the brink of asking a question.

Ned was not so distracted by his unexpected survival as to overlook the singular fact that Lady Harcroft had cursed his wife.

"This is not what it seems," he said.

She glanced across the room—no doubt searching out a grubby knife she could use on him.

"I'm here to help," Ned continued. He stepped into the room, brushing aside the cloths that hung from the line. They were an infant's napkins, he realized. By the state of their dampness, they'd no doubt been cleaned down at the stream a half mile away in the early morning.

"Did Kate send you? She promised not to tell."

"Kate…" Ned glanced at the firearm she clutched. Come to think of it, that was *his* pistol. He'd brought it back with him from China and had tossed it in a cabinet. He'd hoped never to see it again.

"Kate," Ned continued dryly, "has been sending you assistance, courtesy of me, for a very long while."

Lady Harcroft met his eyes. "Tell your wife that *next* time, she needs to load the gun."

Ned stepped forward. He'd only seen Lady Harcroft before in her husband's company. This woman—short but stately—did not seem anything like the pale, sickly shadow he'd met at Harcroft's side.

Now, as he walked toward her, her knuckles whitened on the pistol. She hadn't lowered it yet. Instead, she clutched it wildly, as if she might wring some use out of it, even after she'd fired.

"Are you planning to bludgeon me with that?" He smiled to show he was joking.

She hesitated, which meant that she might have been.

Ned shook his head and reached to pluck the weapon from her hands before she embarrassed them both. He'd meant to make a joke about her shoulders becoming weary. But as he extended his hand, she flinched backward, her arm flying between them. He froze, midreach; she looked up into his eyes in horror.

She must have seen the shock in his own eyes.

He'd not wanted to think of it. In the frozen aftermath of nearly being shot, he'd not sorted out the implications of her presence. Lady Harcroft wasn't *insane*. She hadn't been abducted. But she was frightened. And when he'd reached for her, she had brought up her hand to protect her face.

Kate was involved. Kate had separated Mrs. Alcot from her husband. Lady Harcroft was here, on Ned's property—on *Kate's* property—flinching from him as if she expected a blow.

Oh.

God.

It made an awful, horrific sense out of everything— Harcroft's comments last night, Kate's reaction at meeting Ned last afternoon.

Lady Harcroft's flinch betrayed more than a thousand bruises. Someone had hit her, and often enough that even friendly gestures now seemed menacing. Ned moved back, giving her room.

"God," Louisa choked, letting the firearm finally fall. "I am so *stupid*." And she burst into tears.

Ned had no idea what to say in response. He didn't dare come forward and comfort her, not when a mere reach toward her gave her such a start. Instead, he could do nothing but slip a handkerchief from his pocket and slide it down the table toward her. She sat down and cried in the most ladylike manner, choking back her obvious sobs, dabbing at her eyes with the cloth he'd given her. Ned waited in uncomfortable silence.

"If I weren't such a wretch, I would not be here. If only I hadn't let it come to this. If I'd had the strength to… to…" She gave a quiet hiccough and winced again.

"To what?" Ned enquired mildly.

"To *stop* this whole thing, before it even started." She set her jaw. "If I were not such a weakling, none of this would ever have happened. You knew me. I was such a timid, foolish—"

Ned held up one hand, interrupting the flow of self-berating before it could get started. "You've used the word *this* a great deal here. By *this,* are you referring to Harcroft's treatment of you?"

She sniffed once, and nodded. "That would be it."

"And by *it,* you mean…" The world slowed, and Ned swallowed. It didn't clear the damnable dryness in his throat. "You mean the fact that he hit you."

It was not a question, but she nodded anyway.

"How long?"

"Never more than fifteen minutes at any one time," she replied earnestly. "I know. It could have been much worse."

Ned met her gaze, unable to look away. "That wasn't what I meant. Has this been going on since I first met you?"

"Oh. It started after our first year of marriage. It wouldn't have if I had been a better wife. You see, there was a gentleman—a friend, only, but…"

She trailed off, and Ned shook his head. She'd been sixteen then, for God's sake, and newly married. Harcroft had shaped her entire adult existence. He must have tried to do so forcibly.

He would have flinched himself. He understood all too well how her thinking went.

How many times had he wondered that about himself? What if he had been different? If he had been better? If he hadn't been betrayed by his own weaknesses? Those doubts would debilitate him if he ever gave them full sway. It had taken him years to learn to discard them, to keep going in the face of his own fears. He could imagine all too well how Lady Harcroft must have felt.

Her husband had been Ned's friend—and it was unsurprising how quickly that sentence properly became phrased in the past tense. But Harcroft could not have understood the degree to which Ned would find himself in sympathy with his wife.

He knew what it was like to feel powerless, at the mercy of others. And he didn't like seeing it in anyone else.

It was a sentiment as idiotic as kicking her door down would have been. After all that, he still saw himself as some sort of a hero—a strange and useless one, no doubt. He was no Bow Street Runner, no knight in shining armor. If he'd had chain mail, it would all have rusted at sea. But Ned wasn't the sort of knight who perished in glorious battle for the sake of a poetic ending.

He had prevailed. He'd beaten back those doubts. He'd found his place and he'd learned to stand on his own two feet, free from that cloying hint of bitter dependence.

It looked as if Lady Harcroft—and by extension, Ned's own wife—needed a hero. If he could bring Lady Harcroft the kind of peace he'd found, it would prove once and for all that his victory had not been temporary. It would be proof that he'd truly won, that he'd tamed his own response. It would be like a medieval tourney, his very own trial.

She looked at him with quiet eyes. "I should have been different."

"Hold that thought." Ned couldn't touch her, not without risking another flinch. Instead, he knelt before her, making himself seem small and harmless. He looked up in her eyes from his vantage point on the floor. "Hold that thought tightly, with both hands. Can you feel it?"

She clasped her hands together.

"I believe what you just said was that if you had been a different person, your husband might not have hit you."

She gave a second jerky nod.

"Well, let me show you something I've learned. Now, are you still holding on to that thought? Gather it all up in your hands—don't leave any of it out. Have it? Good. Now stand up."

She stared at him suspiciously. "Is this some sort of trick?"

"Lady Harcroft, if I wanted to betray you, I wouldn't *need* any tricks. I would have come here with twelve men and your husband. I'll stay here with my knee on the floor for now—you stand up."

Warily she clambered to her feet; as she did, she started to drop her hands to her waist.

"Careful," Ned warned teasingly. "You'll drop the thought, and I specifically told you to hold it with both hands."

"But there's nothing there."

"Nonsense. You can feel that thought in your hands, even if you can't see it. You're holding it, all one great weight. It's bowing your shoulders. And if you run your thumbs over it, you can feel the surface. What does it feel like?"

Lady Harcroft glanced down at her empty hands. "It's a harsh, spiked thing," she said softly, "full of bitterness and recrimination."

"I'm going to stand up now." Ned did, and then, giving her a wide berth, he walked to the door and threw it open. He took three steps back, so that she could stand in the doorway without coming too close to him. Then he motioned her forward.

She crossed over to him.

"Now this is the hard part. Draw back your arm—yes, like that—and throw the thought as far away as you can."

"But—"

"Just toss whatever you were thinking right out the door, like the slimy piece of refuse that it is. That sort of thinking has no place in your life. It wasn't your fault. It's never your fault if a man hits you."

She glanced at him in hesitation.

"Go on. Throw it."

"But I'm not holding on to anything."

"Then it shouldn't bother you to discard it."

Tenuous logic, but then, doubts that wormed into his own heart had little truck with logic. Ned had discovered a thousand ways to cast out that legion on his own.

Louisa drew in a tremulous breath, and then looked out the door. Her gaze sharpened, and she focused on the valley that lay below. Slowly she raised her hands to her waist. Then she mimed a throw—a girl's throw, halfhearted and tentative, the sort that would have made him toss up his hands in outrage if she had been bowling in cricket—but a throw nonetheless. And then she turned and gave him a faltering smile. It was the first smile he'd seen on her since he'd arrived.

"There. Now don't you feel better?"

"That," she said, stepping backward, "should not have worked. It was entirely irrational."

Ned shut the door behind her. "It helped, didn't it?"

"You're a black magician, Mr. Carhart. How did you *know?* Did Kate send you to cheer me up?"

Ned shrugged. He knew because…he *knew*. He'd known doubt and uncertainty. He'd grappled with fear. And he'd won, damn it. Eventually.

It shouldn't have mattered that he needed to employ such cheap tricks to claim his own triumph. It shouldn't have mattered that in the worst of times he still needed every scrap of dark magic he could conjure, just to maintain his illusions. All that mattered was that he won, every damned time.

"It's my job to know irrationality," Ned replied with more airiness than he felt. "As for my wife…" He looked around the cabin and a second truth struck him. Someone had thought of everything. There were provisions. A little washtub stood to the side—no doubt where the infant's napkins had been cleaned this morning, something Ned would never have thought of in a million years. She'd planned for this as carefully as for a siege. Now that he glanced into the small adjoining room, he could see the shadowed form of a nursemaid, holding a child in her arms.

And he'd thought Kate was delicate. He felt as if he'd glanced into a room, expecting to see a china tea set, and found instead an intricate mass of gears, silently running the clock tower to which every man set his watch.

"My wife," Ned said, "will handle the eggs."

Lady Harcroft raised her chin. "Tell Kate thank you, then. This was as good as eggs for breakfast."

THE MILES BACK to Berkswift blurred in Ned's mind, dust and the scent of burning leaves commingling into a confusion in his mind. The slow trot of his horse seemed to drum the important points into his mind.

Lady Harcroft had escaped her husband.

Kate had helped. And she'd not said a word of it to Ned—or, as far as Ned could tell, to anyone else.

She didn't trust him. She didn't trust *anyone,* so far as he could tell. And it was probably partially Ned's own fault.

Whatever their marriage might have been, he'd destroyed those nascent seeds of hope when he had left. Their marriage had been a convenience, an *accident.* It had only seemed polite to leave her alone, to not inflict on her the worst of his faults. He hadn't wanted to burden her.

But now he wanted to be more than a burden.

It was in this mood that he arrived at home and handed his horse off to Plum. He headed round to Champion's pasture, armed with a bag of peppermints. Easier, perhaps, to talk to a horse than to carry on a conversation with his wife. Anything he could imagine saying to her came out in his mind as a confrontation. And the last thing he wanted to do at this point was engage in recriminations.

But it was not Kate who found him as he leaned against the railing. It was Harcroft. Ned had not had time to sort his thoughts about his wife into place. He wasn't ready to think of Harcroft. He strode through the thick grass, his boots gleaming as if even the cow shards made way before his shining magnificence.

He walked up to Ned and stared through the fence rails. "That's the most flea-bitten, mange-ridden, hollow-chested mongrel of a horse I've ever seen. Why was it never gelded?"

"His name," Ned said in abstraction, "is Champion."

Harcroft sighed. "You always did have an odd sense of humor, Carhart." He spoke those words as if he were hurling insults.

Ned shrugged. "You always didn't."

Once, Harcroft's epithets might have stung Ned, along with the implication that Ned was too frivolous, too ready to make a joke. If Ned had just pledged himself to knighthood, Harcroft was his enemy. He was the dark knight across the field.

He didn't look much like a villain.

A pause.

"Any luck?" Harcroft finally asked.

"Nothing." Ned had gone on to visit Mrs. Alcot after he saw Lady Harcroft. "Just an ancient widow, who insisted on talking my ear off. She was delighted to answer my questions—and to tell me about the health of her pigs, her ducks and Kevin."

Harcroft frowned in puzzlement. "Her grandson?"

A point to Ned. He smiled grimly. "Her rooster."

"Ah." Harcroft's lip curled. "*Women.* Always talking. Naming things."

Harcroft's wife had surely kept her silence long enough.

Years and years. And all this time, Ned had known the man and never guessed. It made him feel queasy.

What he finally said was, "And your day?"

Harcroft didn't answer. "Where did you get this horse?"

"I bought him for ten pounds." If Ned were a knight in rusted armor, Champion—mangy, distrustful Champion—might have made an appropriate steed.

"So the story I heard today was true. You happened upon a carter struggling to control a vicious animal, and you intervened to save the brute from a beating."

Ned nodded. "Talking about that in the village, are they?"

"You always were too soft-hearted." Harcroft spoke in smoldering disdain.

"It's true. I'm funny and modest. I really shouldn't be kind, too—it makes life difficult for the rest of you fellows, who never will measure up."

Harcroft's eyes narrowed, and his face scrunched up. He peered at Ned in confusion. Slowly his expression cleared. "Oh," he said flatly. "You're joking again."

Go ahead and believe that. "We'll talk tonight," Ned said. "I'm more than willing to help you continue the search. The faster we work, the less likely that any trail will grow cold. I want to make sure you finish what needs to be done here, as quickly as possible." And *that* last was no joke.

Harcroft stared at Champion one last time. Finally he shook his head. "Was Lady Kathleen with you when you purchased this beast?"

Ned put his head to one side, unsure how to respond.

The truth seemed innocent enough, though, and if he were caught in a lie, Harcroft might begin to suspect that Ned knew something. "Yes," he finally said.

"Thought so. Trying to impress her?" He snorted. "Women. They'll make you weak, Carhart, if you allow them to sway your actions. Be careful of her."

"And here I thought she did nothing but shop."

Harcroft shrugged. "Well, there's that wager about her. You might have heard. Whoever seduces her, and produces one of her undergarments as proof, will win five thousand pounds."

Ned felt his sense of humor rapidly evaporating. "Nobody's collected."

"Where there's smoke…" Harcroft trailed off, spreading his hands suggestively.

"Where there's smoke, there's arson." Ned's hands gripped the rail. "And arsonists *will* be dealt with. Let me assure you, Harcroft—for all my humor and kindness, I'm not weak. Just slow to anger. I won't brook any insults. Not even from you."

Especially not from you.

Harcroft paused thoughtfully. "Well. Don't say I didn't warn you. And you know the old saying. Speak of the devil…"

Ned glanced toward the house. Kate was picking her way across the field. She could see that he was talking to Harcroft, and Ned felt a sudden urge to push the man away and disclaim all knowledge of him. Harcroft had made no effort to modulate his tone; she might even have heard him. But her expression did not change, not even in the slightest, and Ned was struck again by what an exquisite, complicated thing she had accomplished. To have had Lady Harcroft brought here, with only a hint of a whisper of talk—and even that, evanescent—was a tremendous thing. To not show her natural revulsion—to welcome Harcroft into her home with so little reaction… Well. She was playing a tremendous role indeed.

Behind that seemingly fragile femininity stood something strong and indomitable.

She walked toward them, sure-footed through the ankle-high grass. She was wearing a sober high-necked walking dress, in a purple so bruised she could have been in half-mourning. The fabric shone subtly in the afternoon sun; the lower hem was darkened with dew.

Ned reached into his bag and pulled out a handful of candies.

"Peppermint, Harcroft?" The man stared at the white blob. His nose wrinkled and he took one, popping it into his mouth.

"Lady Kathleen?"

His wife glanced at him distrustfully, and then reached out and took the candy. She tossed it back and forth, from gloved hand to gloved hand. Then, without once looking at Harcroft, who crunched his treat noisily, she said, "I assume Champion's licked the peppermints in this batch, as well?"

All crunching stopped. Harcroft froze, a pained expression on his face. Too polite to spit; too fastidious to swallow. Instead, he turned bright red and choked.

Ned swallowed a delighted chortle. Champion hadn't come close enough to Ned to lick anything, but the look on the earl's face was too precious to interrupt.

Kate threw her peppermint into the field.

"Excuse me," Harcroft choked out, his words garbled around the candy in his mouth. "I have to—I have to—" He pointed vaguely, desperately, in the direction of the house.

"Horses have clean mouths," Ned intoned innocently. "Harcroft, where are you— Ah. Well." He turned to his wife. "There he goes."

A slight, satisfied curl to her lips was the only indication she gave that she'd intended to drive the man off. The signs were all there, for anyone to see.

"You," Ned said, "are..."

"He *did* speak of the devil," Kate said. "A little taste of the diabolical, I believe, would do him good."

"Oh, yes. I have it. 'Speak of the devil, and he licks your peppermints.'"

Kate snickered. "Something like that."

"Also, thank you."

"For driving off your friend?" She looked surprised.

"No. The more I discover about what transpired in my absence, the more responsibility I realize you've taken on. I had assumed that Gareth would take on much of it—that was our agreement when I left, you know. But then, responsible as Gareth always has been, he would never have noticed the little things. The human touches. Like Mrs. Alcot."

Like Louisa Paxton, Lady Harcroft.

Kate nodded regally and held out her hand again. For a tiny instant, he contemplated taking those delicate fingers in his. Stripping off her glove, baring that soft skin to the sun and his touch.

But she wasn't asking for importunity. He put another peppermint in her palm instead. She didn't throw this one, though; instead, she weighed it from hand to hand, as carefully as if it were an ingot of metal whose worth she had yet to judge.

Finally, she looked up at him. "What does Harcroft matter to you?" Her eyes were almost silver with refracted light. They seemed to cut through Ned.

He had been so much in sympathy with her, he'd forgotten. She didn't trust him. She didn't *know* he knew. The question wasn't idle. She wanted to know if he might betray her.

Ned swallowed.

She'd never trusted him with the truth of her competence. He wanted her to tell him the truth, let him into her life. He wanted her to judge him worthy of knowing her—the *true* Kate, the one she hid away.

"Harcroft is a distant cousin," Ned said softly. "We were friends, long before, when we were younger. I think we're rather too dissimilar now to be more than acquaintances."

"But he's your family."

"Half of polite society is my family, if I must count him my relation," Ned said dryly. "If you must know, my main obligation to Harcroft is that he assisted me with the people I think of as my *true* family. When Jenny and Gareth married, Harcroft and his wife welcomed Jenny—Lady Blakely—into society. It wasn't clear at the time that she would take. With his assistance, she did. I am not insensible of my obligations to him. But he's not true family."

"True family," Kate mused quietly. "Those are the people who ask, and on whose say-so, you go halfway round the world? People like Lord Blakely, then."

She looked up at him.

"Rather like oxygen," Ned agreed, "inhaled into lungs that burn with exertion. Family consists of the people who are vital, even though sometimes they hurt. But if you're worried that I feel some obligation to Harcroft that would make me reveal that little trick you played on him with the peppermints, or, um, anything else—worry no more."

She glanced at him, and then looked away once again. "And who do you include in this category of true family, then?"

"Jenny," Ned said instantly. "Gareth. My mother. Laura—that's Gareth's half sister. She and I were practically raised together. It's not a large group, Kate."

Still she didn't say anything. Her lips pressed whitely together.

He'd wanted her to know that the people who could command his loyalty were few, that she could rely on him. Obviously, that hadn't worked.

She was looking at him still. Not one muscle had shifted in her face, and yet he could see that the glitter in her eyes was not hatred or even mistrust. He'd completely misunderstood; this wasn't about Harcroft, somehow. He was never going to understand women. By the furrow in her forehead, he guessed he'd said something truly awful. He'd misread that silver glint all along. She wasn't angry with him. She was devastated.

"Christ," he swore in confusion. "What did I say? I didn't mean to hurt your feelings."

She shook her head. "Wrong question. It's what you didn't say."

"Very well, then. What didn't I say?"

"Nothing I didn't already know." Her words were bitter, and now she looked down. "And nothing that I couldn't have expected. It doesn't matter."

The edge of the sunlight caught the smallest reflection of moisture in her eyes. She was doing a valiant job of not crying. Her nostrils flared. She took in a deep breath, no doubt intending it to be calming.

"It *does*. Kate, I don't actually want to cause you pain, you know. If you would just tell me—"

"Jenny," she counted softly. "Gareth. Laura. Your mother. I don't question your allegiance to any of them, or the sincerity of the connection. It's foolish of me. We're not that kind of husband and wife. But Ned, you are married to me."

Oxygen? It was as if suddenly there were too much of it, as if his every breath counted for twice as much. Ned felt himself gasping—as if he were a salmon cast upon the sand.

"That's not what I meant."

"It never does seem to be. You vowed to cherish me," Kate said quietly. "You vowed to love me and honor me. When I spoke my vows, *I* meant them. I intended to cleave unto you for the rest of my life, but you disappeared for years. To you, that ceremony was nothing but words," Kate said bitterly. She held up her hand, index finger pointed. And then she touched his chest—as if she were tallying up his mistakes on his ribs. Her finger swished along him as if making an accusatory notch: *One*.

Ned had nothing to say in response.

"That's all you've ever given me—words."

"No. You can trust me."

She clenched her hands and faced him. "Who do you suppose I am?"

Kate was the impossibly attractive woman he'd married, and if he'd craved her before today, he hungered for her now.

She raised her chin. "I was the one who waited at home while you strolled the world. I withstood the questions. I endured years of the betting books, and I held on to fidelity through all the long years of your absence."

"I—I may not have acted as well as I could with regards to you. But that's going to change, Kate. It's already changing. Listen—"

"If you had really wanted to stay—if you had really wanted to keep company with your new wife, you would have found a trusted minion to take your place. I think you wanted to go. I think," she said, "that like all young men, you wanted to sow your wild oats. And having lost your chance to do so here in England, by virtue of your unfortunate marriage, you decided to take the matter abroad."

She raised her hand again, to tally that second accusation against his chest. Ned reached out and grabbed her fingers. "No," he said. He could barely recognize his own voice. "No. That wasn't it. That wasn't why."

"How many women? You were gone three years. In all that time, how many women did you kiss?"

"One," he replied. "And she was you."

She waited. The silence that followed was cold with her disbelief.

"I was young, Kate. Young and determined to prove I was more than a useless fribble. I've made mistakes. I wanted to show everyone that my mistakes hadn't made me. That I was rational. Sober. Reliable."

"And what did you want to show *me?*"

"You?" He glanced at her and understood innately why he'd left. She flummoxed him. Even now, peering into the gray of her eyes, he could feel a tide of want and desire rising. He'd had a million reasons to go. But primary among them, he'd fled England because when he was around her, that sober, rational, reliable part of him faded into nothingness. It left behind this dark beast, this needful thing. When she stood near him, he sure as hell didn't want to *honor* her. He hadn't wanted to keep any of the gentle vows required by the Anglican ceremony. No, standing this close to her, he yearned to possess her. He wanted to own the curve of her waist with his hands. He wanted to claim her for his own. And he was unable to suppress that longing, no matter how ferociously he tried. He'd hoped that proving to himself that he was steady and reliable would alleviate that want.

"I left to *find* control, not to dispense with it. I didn't sow any oats, Kate. It would have defeated the purpose."

He *could* hold his wants in check. He was the master, not his lust, not his cavernous want and not his deep, dark fears.

Unfortunately, three years of intimacy with his own

palm had done nothing to alleviate his physical longings. Where Kate was concerned, he'd not become more sober. He'd become less.

But she didn't understand that. She stood next to him without the least bit of concern for her person. His hand was still wrapped around her fingers, and she looked up at him, not understanding the danger she was in.

Instead, she sighed. "I thought not," she said. "When you left, you weren't thinking of me at all."

"I thought of you." The words sounded hoarse and guttural in his ears. "I thought of you…often."

Her lips pursed, but still she looked at him, her head tilted to one side.

"You're wondering if you can trust me," Ned said. "You can." She didn't know that he knew her secret. And he wanted to win her trust, not force his knowledge upon her. He waited.

"I trust you," she said calmly. "I trusted you enough to marry you. I trusted you wouldn't abscond with the portion of my fortune over which you were granted free rein. I trusted you wouldn't hit me." Her voice dropped on that. "I trust you enough to do my duty, should you require such a thing again. I trust you to put your own comfort first. But you told me that we had a marriage of convenience. Why should I trust you with anything *more?*"

"Because…" Ned began, and then ran smack into the hard truth of it.

He had no reasons. She was right. He'd left, thinking selfishly of himself and what he could prove. When he'd thought of her, it had only been to imagine what she might do for him. To him.

Even now, he was putting her in his bed.

Oh, why bother to travel so far? His dark selfishness was undressing her here. He was imagining peeling the gown from her shoulders. He would kiss his way down each rib. He was on the edge of forfeiting every shred of control he'd ever fought for. He was still holding her hand, crumpled up like a handkerchief. Her fingers trembled in his.

And yes, he was—and he had been—a selfish cad. He leaned forward. The motion pulled her skirts against his trousers. For one glorious second, he held her—her body, her sweet curves, sliding against him. He could smell the faint scent of her rose soap. One last inch, and he could possess her as he'd always wanted.

For one glorious, lightless second, he thought of giving in to his selfishness. But no. He was still in control of himself. Once she trusted him…

Slowly, he released her hand. She flexed her fingers in the air. She had no idea how close she had come to being ravaged in broad daylight.

"You're right," Ned heard himself say. "You're completely right. If I were you, I wouldn't trust me, either."

Her eyes rounded.

He sketched her a half bow, and turned to go. But before he could complete that turn—before he could give her his back, one last strand of selfishness caught in his chest. And he checked that movement and stepped toward her.

"You're right," he said. "I haven't given you much

reason to trust me. But Kate…" Ned let his index finger draw near to her. She did not draw back, not even when he placed it on the edge of her lips. "Kate," he repeated, "I will. I promise."

Ned handed her his bag of peppermints and walked away, swiftly, before he changed his mind.

He had never given any thought to what it meant to be a husband. The duties, he'd supposed, were spelled out by the marriage ceremony: endow her with worldly goods and, when necessary, father children. He had only to look at Harcroft to find a husband who had done substantially worse.

But when the best thing your wife could say of you was that you didn't beat her, you weren't doing very well.

As for Kate herself, Ned knew he'd left England too soon after their marriage. He'd been as fooled by her delicate demeanor and her fine clothing as Harcroft.

He wondered how often he'd looked at her, not seeing anything except the exquisiteness of her features. There was more to her than he'd imagined.

A second realization struck him as he turned down the path that led to the barn.

She'd wanted him once. What would it be like, to don a mask all your life? To hide what you could accomplish behind layers of silk and lace? To do all that, knowing that no one—not your husband nor your family—knew the truth of who you were?

Kate was complicated. She was strong. And she was very much alone. He might do something for her besides meet the bare necessity of their physical needs. He could mean something to someone besides being a mere provider of things. He wasn't much of a knight, and he'd just left Kate with the closest thing he had to a war stallion.

Still, he might be the rock she could stand on. He could be the arm she leaned upon. She wanted proof? He could start, for once, by letting her know what she could mean to him.

Ned swallowed again and clenched his fist. For a long time he stared at his fingers, wrapped in a ball. He thought of strength, of power. He let himself feel all the fear of failure that had once entangled him. He imagined it, a dark solid ball in his hand, all those fearful thoughts holding him back. And then, slowly, he pulled back his arm. He threw his fears as far from him as he could. He imagined them soaring above the barn, high over the house in front of him, before plummeting to the ground and bursting apart like dry, baked clay.

Black magic, for sure; but he'd been crippled by doubts before. He didn't have time for them any longer.

It was time to start becoming the husband he could be.

CHAPTER TEN

"I KNOW WHAT YOU'RE DOING."

That harsh voice echoed in the marble entry as Kate entered the manor. She had stared at Champion for a few minutes after her husband had left her, and then, confused and heartsick, had returned home. Now, she paused on the threshold, her eyes still adjusting to the dark of the interior, before she located Harcroft. He stood in the comparative shadow of the hallway, watching her. His expression was shrouded in darkness. Then he walked forward and the light caught his features. A half-mocking smile curved his lips.

Kate's silk stockings were still damp about her ankles where the grass had brushed her feet. He looked her over; instinctively, she pulled up the black stole that she'd looped around her arms, covering herself.

He had changed into soft slippers and loose trousers. Smoke curled from the pipe he held in one hand—he must have just come in off the verandah—and he put his other hand up and leaned, negligently, against the wall. It would be foolish to draw back in fear, as she wished; it was doubly foolish to wish her husband present, to step between them.

But Ned wasn't here. He'd walked away from her again.

Kate took a deep breath. Harcroft *couldn't* know what she was doing. He couldn't possibly have any idea. She'd do best to keep up her ruse.

"Good heavens, my lord," she said warmly. "However did you guess? Was it the wet shoes? Or the damp hem of my gown?" She tried to keep her smile friendly; it was like trying to smile at an Egyptian crocodile without noticing the sharpness of its teeth.

Harcroft took a step toward her.

"Perhaps the hour of the day, just before supper." She reluctantly pulled the stole from her shoulders and folded it; the action gave her an excuse to step away and set the garment down on a table. "Whatever it was, you *must* tell me how it is you figured out that I was just about to change my clothing. I had thought to wear my blue satin tonight. Do you think my mother's pearl necklace would suit? Now, if you'll pardon me—"

"Pardon?" He spoke in a low growl. "There is no pardon for what you've done."

She stared at him, feigning blankness. "You feel strongly about the pearls, then."

"You think yourself very clever, don't you? All those backhanded comments, every last word spoken in front of the group. I haven't forgotten a word of them, you witless woman."

Kate let her eyes widen in shock. "Oh, dear. How inexcusably rude you are being, Harcroft. I know your delicate emotions are overset by recent events, but I must insist that in my own home, you treat me with respect."

If he heard her, he didn't acknowledge it. "No doubt you talked to my wife about marital affairs that ought to stay between husband and wife. No doubt she offered you her own female version of events, calculated in typical feminine fashion to make me appear as awful as possible." He spat the words *female* and *feminine* as if they were the foulest curses imaginable.

If he thought she'd restricted herself only to *talk,* he really hadn't the faintest idea what she'd done.

Still, Kate blushed. "Ooh." She let her eyes drop. "You mean…you knew about that? But how humiliating for you. And no wonder you are rude. All married ladies talk about the marital bed. How else are we to have a point of comparison? Infidelity is gauche. One must rely upon gossip instead."

"Gossip about the marital bed? But I was speaking of—"

"If you must know," Kate continued, "it happened years ago. Louisa was curious, and I had questions. We described our respective experiences and asked for advice. When it was Louisa's turn, it was Lady Moncrieff who made the indelicate comparison to an undersized carrot. I never mentioned it. I *promise* you."

That froze him in his spot. He licked his lips carefully, and then looked around, as if to ascertain that nobody else had heard. "An—an *undersized* carrot?"

"I would never have participated in such an indelicate conversation, I assure you. A lady should not speak about a gentleman's vegetables. But you are entirely right to reprimand me, my lord. I sincerely apologize for listening. Sometimes, when ladies get in very large groups, our feminine nature takes over. And we do say some indiscreet things."

"A *very large* group of ladies had a discussion about… about…"

All his bravado, all that masculine intent, had shriveled up—smaller than carrot size, Kate judged. He looked about the entry wildly, as if expecting a bevy of ladies to leap from the woodwork, all laughing at him.

"Don't look so abashed. We only spoke of vegetables for a few minutes. I'm positive nobody else recalls the conversation."

He looked slightly mollified.

"After all," Kate mused on, "*that* comparison was rather eclipsed by Lady Lannister's comment about a maid—"

"A *maid!*"

"—beating laundry against a metal washboard."

He had nothing to say to that. His mouth gaped. He stepped back. "It wasn't—no—have *all* the ladies been thinking that, all these years, when they see me?"

"Thinking what? About a very tiny root vegetable?" Kate held up her thumb and forefinger, slightly more than an inch apart.

Harcroft blanched.

"No," Kate said, imbuing her voice with all the reassurance she felt. "Not at all."

He let out a breath.

"There were other descriptions," she said cheerily. "All equally memorable."

He stared, appalled, at the inch-and-a-half gap between her fingers. "Well. This is what you've done with your… groundless speculation. You helped lay the groundwork for a good woman—an *obedient* woman—to question her marriage. You raised doubts in her, about her lawful husband. And no doubt it was the uncertainty that *you* engendered that fevered her mind." This track, apparently, took his mind off vegetables. Once removed from the horrifing thought of his inadequacy, he remembered his tirade. "You women, with your disgusting analogies—*you* caused her to forsake me."

"Analogies! Oh, not at all, sir! They were more in the nature of metaphors."

He was still underestimating her, and inside, Kate felt faint with relief. He imagined only that she'd encouraged Louisa's complaints. If he knew that Kate had planned every step of the journey that had stolen his wife from her home in broad daylight, he would have used a stronger word than *disgusting*.

"Stop looking at me, for God's sake," he snapped. "That's just—it's just *obscene*."

What was truly obscene was what he'd done to his wife. But Kate couldn't let Harcroft suspect she was capable of actual cogitation—not that he was likely to attribute such a thing to a woman.

"Harcroft, I know you're upset. But do try to see reason. I never participated in that conversation. You and I have perhaps not been the best of friends, but I'm Louisa's friend. I want to help her." All true; she *hadn't* participated in the conversation. At the time, she'd been laughing too hard.

He glanced up at her, warily. But before he could respond, footsteps sounded in the hallway behind them.

"Harcroft?" Lord Blakely appeared behind the man. "Good. I've been looking for you. In the latest dispatch from London, there's some rather interesting news. White has uncovered a woman—a nursemaid—who was hired from her home in Chelsea and spirited away."

Harcroft looked down at Kate, a confused look on his face. "Chelsea? But I was so sure..." He trailed off. "I thought—well. Never mind."

Kate couldn't smile now, or they might wonder. And Kate could hardly disclose that she'd hired a nursemaid and a parlor maid answering to Louisa's description, to take a paid tour of the Peak district. A nice bit of misdirection; now, if only the men would oblige her by being otherwise directed.

"It's a very interesting report," Lord Blakely repeated, "and we must decide what to do about it." He turned back down the corridor.

Harcroft cast one glance backward at Kate. "I apologize," Kate said in a low voice. "The laundry maid comparison was most unfair. I should never have repeated it."

He nodded, jerkily, once. "Apology accepted."

Kate held her tongue until the two men left, until their steps receded down the polished corridor and a door closed softly on their conference.

"A most unfair comparison," she said to the empty hall. "After all, a scullery maid beats her laundry for longer than two minutes."

"WHAT DO WE DO NOW? Do Jenny and I go to Chelsea, while you stay here, Harcroft?"

As his cousin spoke, Ned shifted uncomfortably in his chair. The council had convened fifteen minutes prior, right after Ned had come in from the field. Jenny, Harcroft and Gareth had all taken places at the long wooden table.

Notably missing from the conversation was Ned's own wife. Harcroft hadn't spoken of inviting her, and given what Ned now knew, he was happier not to have her present.

Across the table from him, Jenny shifted on her seat, her lips pressing together. She glanced down the table where Harcroft sat. Harcroft was—*had been*—Ned's friend, not Jenny's and Gareth's. Ned had made the introduction. At his request, Harcroft had welcomed Gareth and his new wife into polite society. What might otherwise have been a difficult matter for them had turned into a few months of discomfort, forgotten once the gossip had been eclipsed by the newest scandal. Still, for that, Jenny was *obligated* to Harcroft, and no doubt thought her assistance on this matter would even out that old score.

But it was just obligation.

And perhaps that was why Jenny shook her head. "Gareth," she said quietly, "it has been several days. If we venture into Chelsea…"

In front of them, papers lay piled. Reports from Gareth's man of business were stacked neatly to the side of Harcroft's map, complete with its prickle of straight-pins.

Gareth glanced at her. He had a more rigid sense of duty and obligation, and naturally, the thought that he might shirk either would not sit well with him.

"Someone has to go to Chelsea," Gareth said. "Someone we can trust."

Harcroft nodded.

Jenny's hands played along the tabletop, and she said nothing.

She didn't need to complete her thoughts—at least, not to Ned. Some women of the *ton* would never balk at leaving their young children to a nursemaid for weeks on end. But Jenny had been abandoned by her own mother, and even a hint of doing the same would doubtless bring up her hackles. A few weeks—with her first child just over a year old—would not have sat well with her.

"I could go on alone," Gareth offered. He bit his lip. "But making people comfortable enough to divulge details is not precisely one of my strengths."

If Ned were to talk of honor and obligation—and true affection—a great deal of his lay here. He owed Jenny for her long-ago friendship. He owed Gareth for tugging him out of his own youthful mistakes. And he loved them both, and could not countenance sending them off to chase down wild poultry, when he knew precisely how futile the hunt would be.

"Are we truly worried about a little thing like a few weeks' absence, when my wife's well-being might be at stake?" Harcroft demanded.

Jenny looked away once more.

Oh, yes. And there was the fact that Ned couldn't blurt out the truth with Harcroft close by. He'd gotten his cousin and his wife entangled with the earl; it was his responsibility to untwine them. If he could arrange this, nobody would ever be able to say he was useless again. Least of all himself.

"You're quite right, Harcroft," Ned heard himself say.

All three turned to him—Jenny, Gareth and the earl himself. "This matter is too important to bungle. Harcroft, *you* should go to Chelsea." He turned to his cousin. "The two of you should return to Blakely manor—it's closer to London, and it's centrally located. That way, if any new information is discovered, you could easily move on to where you are needed."

Harcroft paused contemplatively, then shook his head. "No good. I have to stay here, to finish the canvas of the district. If that woman we heard of on that first day turned out to be Louisa, we might lose her trail. I can't risk that."

"I spent my summers here when I was younger. I know the residents. And—" Ned felt a little dirty, but under these circumstances, the lie was better than the truth coming out "—you know you can trust me to pursue *all* your interests."

Jenny's eyes narrowed as Ned spoke, and he looked away from her to contemplate the pins on the map. He wasn't any good at lying to Jenny—he never had been. Jenny was damnably observant. And he could *not* have this conversation with her—at least not with Harcroft looking on. But all he had to do was convince Harcroft.

So he added the coup de grâce. "And besides, Harcroft, you know Lady Blakely will be distracted by her own feminine concerns. This matter needs the best attention that you can give."

Even Gareth raised his head at that phenomenal stinker of a falsehood.

"Ned, are you trying to goad me into acting?" Jenny's voice had taken on a dangerous note.

"Take me to task later." He spoke to Jenny, but looked at Harcroft still.

Harcroft met his gaze. One benefit of the man having no sense of humor was that he had little sense of sarcasm, either. He showed no sign that he heard anything amiss in Ned's treasonous speech. Finally, he gave a short, sharp nod. And like that, there was nothing more to do but divide the tasks, and try not to let the relief he felt show. Gareth left the room to order the packing to start. Jenny sat, stiff and silent, throughout the remainder of the conversation. Ned felt her eyes on him.

"Ha." Harcroft rubbed his hands bitterly as he watched the man leave.

The room wasn't cold, but Ned felt a chilling prickle under his collar.

Harcroft leaned close anyway and whispered, "Watch your wife, Ned. I know you don't want to hear my warnings. But I've talked to the servants. She's gone on walks—long walks—twice in the last week. And before any of us arrived, she spent a night away from the house."

"Harcroft, this isn't the time to speculate on—"

"No." Harcroft stood and dry-washed his hands. "A gentleman doesn't speculate on a lady's proclivities. A duke's daughter is not some…some laundry maid, to be exposed to the world's censure." His lip pulled back bitterly. "But Ned—do spare a moment, while looking for my wife, to keep your guard up around yours."

"I'm not worried about Kate. I trust her."

"Well." Harcroft strode to the door. "To each their own. I suppose I'll be ready to leave in the morning. Lady Blakely?"

"If we're off in the next few hours, we'll arrive home tonight." There was that look in Jenny's eyes, though, the way she dropped them so quickly, that suggested she had something else in mind. She remained seated, watching Ned as Harcroft walked out. She said nothing, long after his footsteps echoed down the hall.

And this was the true test. Ned could fool Harcroft. He could bamboozle Gareth. But Jenny had spent the years before her marriage watching for reactions, looking for the tiny, betraying clues that would suggest hidden motivations. Even if his heart had been in the deception, Jenny would have been difficult to lie to.

"We've not talked about Kate much," she finally said. "I know she and I have not been the best of friends. But are things well between you?"

"Well enough."

"If that's an answer, I'll eat my hat." She tossed her unclad head, and Ned found himself grinning.

"You're not wearing one."

Her mouth curved up in brief appreciation, but she was not to be misdirected by levity. "What a mess this has been. I just want to know that someone here has a chance of happiness in the next week, Ned. It might as well be you. It's your turn, after all." She turned a hand over in her lap and inspected her nails.

"Really?" Ned asked. "That's all you wanted to say?"

"Of course. I care for your welfare. You know that."

"What I meant was that you did not use to be so obvious when you were trying to persuade me to divulge my secrets."

She glanced up sharply, then smiled. "You *have* grown up, I see. Very well. Are you going to tell me why you are trying to rid yourself of Harcroft and my husband?"

Ned considered this briefly. "No."

She smiled. "Are you going to share any of your suspicions?" She spoke lightly, as if his suspicions were inconsequential fears that could be divulged in a sentence or two. If he told her everything, she would help him. She would insist on it—she and her husband both. And as much as Ned cared for them, he didn't want their help. He didn't want them meddling, interfering in his relationship with his wife.

And he still wanted to prove himself.

Besides, Jenny wanted to go home.

"Suspicions?" Ned parroted.

She cocked her head. Ned forced himself to remain calm under that examination. He took regular breaths, relaxed his shoulders.

"My suspicions," Ned said, "are mine. And the instant I have information beyond what I possess in the moment, I'll share with you. You can be sure of that."

True; everything he knew now, every certain scrap of knowledge, was *his*. It would take some vast new piece of knowledge to get him to betray what he knew.

"You know," Jenny said too casually, "before you arrived in this room, Harcroft said he suspected Kate was maligning him. That she might have precipitated his wife's flight."

Any answer—or no answer—would betray too much. Ned rubbed his chin, as if he could scrub off the weight of her attention. He couldn't, though; she watched him, as clear-eyed as before. Finally, he met her gaze head-on. "And does that arouse your suspicions as to Kate or Harcroft?"

"You also didn't use to answer my little prompts with questions. I should have liked to ask you the same thing, as it turns out. And as it turns out…I don't know. Neither. Both. Maybe. Harcroft is a moody fellow. I can't quite put my finger on him."

Saying Harcroft was moody seemed a bit like saying that an unexpected winter storm was a mild inconvenience.

"He'll never admit it, as he's one of *those* men, but this ordeal has left him completely overwrought. If he were a woman, everyone would say he was on the verge of hysterics. I don't know what else to say, but I am sure that he loves Louisa. He wept when he told us she was missing. He *wept,* Ned. Imagine what that must mean to a man stuffed as full of pride as he. There have been times I could have happily slapped him—he constantly drops these unthinking little insults to his wife. But he *wept*."

"And you?"

"I have not known Louisa—or her husband—well enough to weep. If this information from Chelsea comes to nothing…we must simply wait and hope that Louisa has not come to any harm." She cocked her head and looked at him. "Or must we?"

Jenny had always been able to ferret out his secrets. But now…

Ned simply looked at her and shook his head. "Trust me."

Jenny sighed. "Ned, I know you want to help. But this is too important for you to handle on your own."

He felt a familiar clutch in his stomach. He might have been fourteen years old again, overhearing his grandfather disparage him. To have Jenny, of all people, do it…

"What?" His voice dropped. "Are you saying I can only be trusted with responsibility over *unimportant* matters?"

"That's not it. It's just that this is a very complicated situation. Repaying this debt we owe means a great deal to both Gareth and me. And—"

"Yes. That's precisely what you're saying. You can't claim to trust me in words, and then not actually trust me. What you're saying now is akin to, 'Thank you, Ned, for blundering into a situation you can't handle. Now step aside and let the adults take care of it.'"

Jenny put one hand to her forehead and exhaled.

"This may come as a surprise to you, Jenny, but I *am* an adult. I *do* understand how complex and dangerous this situation is. I could not have possibly missed the fact that you feel an obligation to Harcroft—and that I am the one responsible for the obligation in the first place. I am not telling you that I wish to make a training exercise of this matter. I am saying this situation is more delicate than you can possibly imagine, and if you keep poking about, *you* are the one who will blunder." His hands were shaking.

Jenny's eyes widened at that outburst and she leaned back, folding her arms over her chest.

"And when I say *trust me,*" Ned continued, "I do not mean that you should don a blindfold and repose your unthinking faith in a foolish youth. When in the last few years have I exaggerated? When have I made you a promise and not kept it? When have I broken faith with you?"

"You haven't." Her voice was hoarse. "I'm sorry, Ned. I thought only to save you from the trouble and heartache of this affair. It's only because I care for you."

"You can take that sentiment and stuff it. This time, Jenny, I'm going to save you. And you are going to sit quietly and *let me do it*." As he spoke, Ned leaned over the table, until he was glaring into her eyes.

Jenny lurched back.

He was already regretting the harshness of his tone. Jenny cared for him, as a sister for a brother—literally— but all that sisterly concern left him feeling uselessly swaddled about, covered in cotton wool. She'd already spent too much time caring for him.

Jenny's eyes dropped from his in similar regret. "I suppose," she said weakly, "I should like to see Rosa again. It has been more than a week, and we both miss her."

Ned let out a breath.

"Very well, Ned. Save me." She rolled her eyes as she said the words, as if to indicate precisely how much weight she put on them. "But if you muck this up because you were too proud to ask for help when you needed it, I shall smack you."

A wave of relief washed over him. "Don't worry," he said. "You won't need to." He gave her an assured smile. "Prepare to be saved."

CHAPTER ELEVEN

"I HAVE SOMETHING to tell you."

Kate looked up from her contemplation of the tree-lined horizon through the sitting room window and turned to the doorway. Her hands clenched around the useless pillow she had been pretending to embroider. Ned stood there, nonchalantly leaning against the doorframe. He smiled at her, carefree.

So she was to be told about what had been decided in the meeting, after all. She hadn't been sure whether she was glad to have been left out, or wounded that she was seen as so useless. She was not sure whether her husband's presence intensified the feeling of isolation that had enveloped her or alleviated it. But that smile he gave her—that bright smile—seemed to cut through the depressing blue of her thoughts.

Silly impulse, that. Just looking at him tugged at her heart, made her remember how inadequate everything was between them. She looked away and out the window again. Just this morning, she'd traversed the path she saw in front of her, looking for her husband. Now, with the autumn sunset dipping toward the horizon, painting brown fields gold, she wanted no reminder of what she'd learned.

His care for her was a perfunctory thing, a matter of

duty. And no matter what else transpired she was alone. Now more than ever.

Behind her, he let out a small sigh. "Gareth and Jenny will be off in half an hour. Harcroft will be leaving for Chelsea in the morning."

She turned around and looked at him in surprise. "How did that come about?"

Ned stepped into the room and shut the door behind him. "I suggested it."

"And how, precisely, did you go about suggesting it?" Kate felt her hands trembling. More important, *why?* And why had he come to her with such news? "Has someone found Louisa?"

"No, Kate." His voice sounded patient. "Actually, I promised I would search for her here myself. I'm familiar with the area. I promised to send regular reports with my findings."

Even worse. She'd have to avoid him assiduously, and mislead him. Lying to Harcroft seemed a kind of a civic virtue. To her husband, however, it was another matter.

"And will you?"

"I'll look until she's found." His voice was mild. "But is there anything you wish to say to me on the matter?"

Nothing. She could say nothing.

He came to stand beside her. The red rays of the sunset painted his face in warm tones.

"If there is anything you wish to tell me in confidence, you have my word it would go no further."

His word? She wanted to trust him. She did. But…

"That would be the same word you gave me at our wedding ceremony?" She spoke primarily to remind herself.

Because she was a fool to even consider speaking to him. A true fool to want to believe she could trust him. She heard his intake of breath. "You're furious now, because I'm questioning you."

"Furious?" His voice sounded amused. "Not particularly." He touched the back of the sofa near her shoulder, his hand falling so close to her she could have kissed it. She looked up into his eyes and found nothing there but trusting brown. No anger. No fury. "I don't think I really understood how much I hurt you until we spoke this afternoon."

Kate couldn't bear to look in his eyes any longer. His words were too close to her dreams, too close to her own wants. She was like to put an unfortunate complexion on them, and she had nobody but herself to hurt. She'd learned, all too well, that her marriage was a *practical* thing, something to suffer through and survive. Anger she could manage. But kindness led to hope, and hope would break her down.

"Is that what you see when you look at me, then? You see a frightened, wounded creature, one to whom you must speak softly?"

He didn't say anything in response. Instead, he walked round the sofa and looked at her straight on. And now that he was in front of her, she could not look away. If she bowed her head, he would understand that she *was* afraid. That even now he could shatter her. And so she looked back. He reached down and took her arm and gently pulled her to her feet. He did not relinquish her hand, though, when she stood.

He was far taller than she, and as close as he stood, she suddenly felt small.

She should *never* have even mentioned her fear. She could see the knowledge reflected in his eyes. She could feel it in the strong grasp of his fingers about her wrist. And now that she'd let slip that unfortunate truth, what else would she admit? That standing this close to him, she could smell the strong, masculine scent of his soap? That some unfortunate part of her longed to lean against him, to open herself once again to the heated touch of his hands on her bare skin?

Perhaps she would say that the primary thing that held her back was the fear that once again, he would be the one to walk away.

She pulled her hand in his grasp. But his hand was as steadfast and gentle as a velvet manacle.

"You must see me as the most pitiful, ineffectual, cringing little *rabbit*." She pulled again.

In response, he set his hand on her shoulder and turned her to the right. "Look straight ahead," he suggested. "I think I may be seeing you for the first time."

Kate looked across the room. The fire burned low. The cavernous maw of the fireplace was framed by a simple mantel. Above that hung a looking glass.

She could see their reflections in that expanse of silvered glass—Ned, tall and strong, vitality wafting off him. In the mirror it seemed as if he were barely touching her—his hand on her wrist, his arm lightly overlaying her shoulder. Two simple points of contact. The mirror could not show how his touch seared her skin.

She shuddered. Looking at the two of them framed in

the mirror seemed even more intimate than their wedding night had been. She could feel the warmth of his body behind her. She could imagine him taking one step in, enfolding her in those strong arms of his. She could feel the warmth of his breath against the back of her neck. And yet there was nothing anonymous about his touch, because she could not escape his eyes in the looking glass.

They sparkled with deceptive friendliness.

"No," he said, giving her shoulder a squeeze. "Don't look at me. Look at *yourself*."

Her hair was so light it was almost colorless. Her skin seemed wan; her dress fitted to her form, bound and corseted and drawn in on itself, as if she were so insubstantial that she needed whalebone to prop her up. She looked like a dainty, breakable lady.

"I've seen you before," Ned said quietly. "But I think it's high time I look again." His hand came up; she could see it in the reflection, before the callus of his thumb swept alongside her face. "First, there's the line of your jaw. A perfect curve, held high. It's one triumphant, resolute sweep. This line—" his finger traced it back again, and the hairs on Kate's arm stood up "—this line says you are a woman who will brook no nonsense. I believe I have discovered that before."

Kate swallowed. In the mirror her neck contracted.

His hand slid down that smooth expanse of skin.

"Then there are your shoulders." His thumb spread along her collarbone. "I have never seen them bowed by fear or drawn together in weariness. You carry your shoulders high, and no matter the weight that is set upon them, you do not falter." His voice dropped.

As he spoke, his hand traveled down her spine. She could feel the heat of him through the layers of muslin and whalebone as that hand traversed the curve of her back. When he reached her waist, he slid his hand around her front to grasp her own. His fingers entwined with hers, briefly; then he turned her hand palm up, in his.

"I've heard," he said dryly, "that fortune-tellers can see your future in the palm of your hand. What do you suppose I see in yours?"

Her hand was dwarfed by his, her fingers seeming wan next to his. The color of his hands made her think of long days aboard ship, of adventurous treks with strange beasts cavorting nearby and strong men with sharp cutlasses. She could feel the heat of him, as if all the sun absorbed in that golden brown skin were emanating from him now.

Next to him…

"I look small," she said. And fragile. The kind of woman to be set to side, for fear that she would shatter. That was all anyone had even seen in her.

"I think you look delicate," he corrected. "Delicate and indomitable, all at once. I see no tremor in your hands, Kate, no fear, no smallness of character."

"But I—"

"And when I look into your eyes," he said, "I think you are as implacable as an archangel."

He closed his hand around hers; her fingers curled into a loose fist, cradled in his. "Your feelings," he said, "are your own. And if you hold them tight to your chest, nobody need ever see beneath the surface."

As he spoke, he leaned into her. His words brushed her skin in little puffs of breath.

"Nobody need see a thing. But *I* want to," he breathed.

She turned her head to look up into his eyes. And that, assuredly, was a mistake, because if her stomach had been in knots before, the knot clenched into a tangle of Gordian proportions when she looked in his face. She could not have unraveled herself from his gaze, and when she tried—when she glanced away—her eyes alighted upon his lips. Strong and smooth, powerful and gentle.

It left her with the most curious fluttering feeling in her belly. Not that he was going to kiss her—but that he had already done so. Her lips already burned with the impression that his words had left on her. Her skin flamed with the possibility of his nearness. And no matter how practical she told herself to be, rational thought fled before his words.

When Kate parted her lips and stood on her tiptoes, turning in his embrace, it seemed she was merely bringing the words he had spoken to their physical conclusion.

She kissed him, not because she wanted to bring him to his knees, but because he had lifted her off hers. She tasted him, and he tasted of salt and man and the power that the right woman could wield in the right place. And he kissed her back, giving no quarter.

He pulled away. "No, Kate," he said quietly. "I don't want to intimidate you. I don't want you to fear me. I want to look at you and finally see what I've been missing these long years. You're a damned Valkyrie."

He turned her back to the mirror. Kate felt almost on the edge of tears.

She didn't want this—didn't want her secret dreams to come true, didn't want to hope again. But it was too late. She was already yearning for this. She was already yearning for him.

"It's not quite true. I *am* afraid," she stated baldly. "If I were a Valkyrie, I would not be. I wouldn't feel a thing."

"In the stories," he said, his voice a dark rasp against her skin, "the heroine always slays the dragon and lops off his head. The villagers rejoice and build a bonfire, and darkness never again falls on the land."

She could feel his hands at her side, warm and powerful. "But those," Ned continued, "are only fairy stories. In *reality...*"

He smiled at her in the mirror, a lopsided smile. There was something faintly wicked about that expression, as if he were about to impart to her a great secret, one that had been closely guarded by a centuries-old society. She swayed unwittingly against him.

"In reality," he whispered, "the dragons never die, and the big sword-wielding buffoons in unwieldy armor cannot slay them. Real heroes tame their dragons. Your fear, my—" He cut himself off, and that sad half smile burst into an incandescent grin. If she had not been awake to the flitting expressions that passed his face, she wouldn't have noticed the suddenness of the change.

"Your what?" she prompted.

"I went to China to slay dragons. Instead, I tamed them."

"I thought you went to China to examine the Blakely holdings in the East India Company, to see if the rumors you had heard were true."

He shrugged, and in that instant she remembered what

he'd said. *Your feelings are yours.* And what were his feelings in all of this?

"Does it matter why I went?" he asked. And he must have intended the question rhetorically, because before she could answer, he continued. "I can't change the past. All I can do, Kate, is try to make up for it. And that means that if you still flinch from me—if the memory of the pain I've caused you is still too strong—I won't get angry. You deserve my patience."

"And where will you be?" Kate's voice shook. "All this time, while you're waiting in patience for me to trust you. Where will you be?"

"Where will I be?" She could feel his breath whispered against her. "I'll be right where I should have been this whole time. When you think your castle walls will fall, I will shore them up. When you are afraid you cannot stand, I will hold you upright. I ought never have left. And when you understand that you need do nothing but lean…"

His hands clasped her waist, strong and gentle, holding her up without restraining her. She might have leaned back then.

She didn't.

"When you lean," he whispered into her ear, "this time, I will catch you."

Oh, she was as dangerously vulnerable as ever, and as like to fall against him.

And that she believed him, that she believed he would be there to catch her, believed that this time he wouldn't leave her…that, perhaps, was the greatest danger of all.

THAT, NED DECIDED after Kate left, had been idiotic.

It hadn't been idiotic to look at her. It hadn't been stupid to pledge himself to her. And the kiss had been every kind of clever, even if it had been her idea to begin with.

No, the foolishness had been when he'd forgotten himself so far as to let that admission slide off his tongue.

Your fear, my—

He'd cut himself off, not out of intelligence, but for want of an adequate word. He'd been saved by his lack of vocabulary, not any sense of propriety or self-preservation. Her fear, his… What was it, then, that dark thing that belonged to him? He thought of it more as that moment, sun striking metal, with him feeling bereft of every other option. He carried it with him even now. Not anything she needed to know about.

Foolishness might have done. *Stupidity,* as well. But neither of those words captured the height and breadth of the beast that Ned had tamed. And neither conveyed the sheer darkness that resided in him.

It *was* foolish. It *was* stupid. But then, he'd learned that if he held the leash on his own reactions tightly, they could do him no harm. It was his own private madness, his own hidden dragon. Kate had single-handedly stymied the Earl of Harcroft. She would never trust Ned if she knew the extent of the beast he'd kept hidden from her. She had no idea how useless he had once been. But he would prove to every one of them that it didn't matter any longer.

But so long as he remained in control, nobody else would ever need to learn about it.

CHAPTER TWELVE

IT WAS AN ODD little evening, Kate thought after her maid had undressed her and left her to her own bed.

With Lord and Lady Blakely departed, Berkswift seemed even emptier than it had when Kate had the manor to herself. Perhaps it was because Kate was the only lady in residence, and she had spent the remainder of the evening in isolation. Perhaps she felt alone because she knew that for one night longer, Harcroft was still in her home, and he had spent the last hours before retiring browbeating Ned with the details of his irrelevant search.

Perhaps it was because Kate could still feel her husband's hands about her waist, his fingers hot against the base of her spine. Perhaps it was because, even through the soft wool of her dressing gown, she could feel the heat of his breath on her neck.

This time, he had said, *I will catch you.*

No mere gentlemanly politeness, that; she'd heard the ring of truth as he spoke, the hoarse acceptance in the timbre of his voice. It had been real, every last scrap of it.

Every scrap? No. There was one last scrap remaining, and it was jagged enough to slice through that nascent trust.

She had no notion what he would do if she told him

the truth about Lady Harcroft. If Ned knew that Kate was the cause of his hours of search, would he still look at her with that same light in his eyes?

Maybe he would take her side. Support her. Congratulate her ingenuity.

Kate sighed. *Be practical.*

No. The practical answer was that he would shrink from her. That he would turn Louisa over to her husband. That he would shake his head at her, and the dragon-tamer would disappear. Because for all the apparent kindness of his words, his actions bespoke a rather different sort of trust.

It was night, and Kate *was* alone. Again. After all that heated talk this afternoon of trust, their marriage was still a mere token of what it could have been. Kisses—and no more. The absence left her hollow, as if she'd been burned to a shell by some dark fire.

And as to that last little thing, she was still as much a coward as ever.

Because this afternoon, as he'd held her, she had stood still and unmoving under his touch, content to simply soak in the feel of his hands against her. She'd been as passive as a lily-of-the-valley, tracking the path of the sun across the sky.

With time, all ink faded. If she did nothing, this memory—like the ink on their marriage license—would eventually bleach into nothingness. All that support, all his help—all that controlled anguish she'd felt in his hands on her—and still, he wasn't coming to her.

Perhaps it was *because* of that controlled anguish that he wasn't coming.

Everything Kate knew about the marital act, she had gleaned from her own limited experience, years prior, and the whispered discussions conducted among married ladies—which tended toward metaphor. Sly innuendo to Harcroft notwithstanding, she imagined she had a pretty good grasp of the process—from both the male and the female point of view.

Men, she had been told, required fairly regular release. They obtained this either through their wives, or through access to mistresses. Without that…well, the consequences hadn't been spelled out to her, but any time the matter came up, every lady had nodded in concert. If there was one thing the ladies of the *ton* had agreed upon, it was that consequences attached under such unfortunate circumstances. And for the men, they were Exceedingly Dire.

Fever? Perhaps. Excruciating pain? Probably. Irrational behavior? Well, that would explain a great deal about gentlemen.

Ned had claimed that he'd honored their wedding vows. That assertion had seemed simply inconceivable to her at the time, given what she'd been told by her friends. But if he was telling the truth, he was suffering. It would, perhaps, underscore the fundamental irrationality that had kept him from visiting her bed, when she was obviously willing to do her duty.

Yes. Irrational behavior, resulting from deprivation, would explain a great deal about her husband—and so many other men.

Besides, if she offered him relief from that one condition, perhaps he would not judge her so harshly when he discovered what she had been doing.

Before her mind could go over the reasons why she didn't dare do it, she stood and walked to her chest of drawers. Long ago, her maid had brought that night rail to Berkswift. *That* one—the one she'd planned to use when their marriage was young and innocent. It was nothing but flimsy silk and ribbons. Better yet, it spoke what she wanted without her ever having to say anything aloud. Near-nakedness spoke louder than words.

She took off the modest nightdress her maid had left for her and slipped the silk gown over her shoulders, her hands trembling slightly as she fastened it in front. Even with the fire burning in her room, she felt a chill in the air.

The temperature wouldn't matter much longer.

She walked briskly to the door connecting their rooms and threw it open. She was struck by a blast of cold air. Her skin pebbled and she felt her nipples contract in protest.

For some reason, he had built no fire in his room.

A branch of candles on a chest of drawers cast a pale and unforgiving light. The wood posters of his bed threw ominous shadows at her. Her eyes adjusted to the light as she brought her arms about her for what little warmth they would give—and she saw Ned.

He was seated on the edge of his bed. His mouth had fallen open in surprise.

And—oh, God, Kate stopped breathing again—he was naked. Completely, utterly, gloriously naked in all this cold air. The light painted his skin bronze all over—as if he were a cold, hard statue of a god, frozen in place, instead of a man made of warm flesh and blood.

But what flesh. She sighed in appreciation. What had seemed an imposing breadth of shoulders when covered in wet linen was an impossible expanse of chest, hard and corded. The muscles of his arms were tensed and contracted, almost as if he were in pain.

Almost? The way he looked at her, his lips caught in a surprised half grimace, he must have felt a great deal of pain. It could not have been even a second before her gaze dropped from his lightly furred chest to his navel. It might as well have been an eternity, though, for the blankness that enveloped her mind.

Her husband was not only naked; he was erect. And his hand was clasped around his member.

Luckily, she did not say the first idiotic thing that popped into her mind. Unluckily for her, she did say the second. "Ned. It's really cold in here."

"Ah." His voice seemed casually companionable, in sharp juxtaposition to the muscled rigor of his body. "Kate. This is not the most convenient time to talk."

No? Her mouth went completely dry, and she was bereft of speech. He was touching himself—there—and oh, God, they'd had marital relations before, but so long ago, and always in the dark. She'd never even *seen* him. She just had the memory of her hands, her flesh; the feel of him inside her; the flash of his skin illuminated in moonlight. That feeling of *want,* never quite satisfied, and hidden behind the necessity of procreation.

On those long-ago nights, he'd never even lit a candle. What a crying shame that had been. She stepped inside his room and pulled the door shut behind her. It was even colder than she'd believed. One hard swallow, and she banished the dryness in her throat. "On the contrary." She was unable to take her eyes off him. "This is very convenient. I didn't come here to talk."

He let out a shaky breath, a puff of white in the chilled room. His eyes slipped down her form. "Oh? I—I suppose I can see that."

That—and by the way his eyes lingered, a great deal else. Marriage wasn't a matter of love, but of bringing together families and estates and producing children. Intercourse could be enjoyable, just as it was enjoyable when she touched herself. But it was not a matter for easy discourse. Despite whispered conversations with the other married ladies, all of that practicality had left her damnably bereft of improper vocabulary. Her husband stared at her, frozen in the act of…the act of… Kate's internal lexicon, built up of proper words used by proper women, deserted her on this point. Even among married women, lurid discussions were composed of circumspect euphemism. One offered *comfort* to one's husband, or perhaps one engaged in intercourse. Their discourse ranged to washing women and carrots precisely because proper ladies didn't *use* those other words.

Whatever those other words might have been.

It seemed simply criminal to Kate that she'd learned one hundred words to describe the weather in French, and not one that would encompass the stroke of a man's hand down his own penis.

But she didn't need a dictionary to instinctively grasp the import of what he'd been doing. She certainly didn't need a primer to comprehend that jealous desire that rose up inside her. Whatever the word for it, she had caught him in the act of doing to himself every improper thing Kate longed to do to him. She swallowed back hysterical, inappropriate laughter.

"Didn't you think to build a fire before…um… before?"

"Before I what?"

"You know." Kate gestured helplessly, her hands inscribing a wide circle.

Perhaps her circle was too wide—or perhaps he wanted to make her uneasy—because he simply shrugged. "You'll have to be more specific."

She shook her head in embarrassment.

"Before I took off my clothing?"

She nodded. "Yes. And took… Took the matter…"

"Before I took the matter in hand?" he finished with a wry smile.

"Yes. That."

"To answer your question, tonight I needed it cold. If not, I would have wallowed in the luxury of this too completely. Cold sharpens the senses. Heat dulls them."

"Oh." Her eyes fell on his body—her husband's body—naked, spread out before her. He was hard; his body was so clearly willing to oblige her in this particular point of their marriage. She had a thousand questions. *Does that feel good? Does the cold help with your release?*

Could we build a fire now?

What she settled on was, "Can you do that to me?"

He shook his head. "Pardon?"

She stepped forward into the lamplight. "You're my

husband." Her gaze fell again to that thick, rigid rod between his legs. Maybe he hadn't wanted *her*. Maybe he'd just wanted the privacy of…of the thing. He reached for a silk banyan that lay across the bed linens.

"Oh, no," she said quietly. "Please don't cover yourself."

He looked up at her, his hand clenching on the cloth. "Kate, I have no right to make demands of you."

"Why not? You're my husband. Men who don't exercise their marital rights become irrational."

He frowned at that.

"Or feverish, or they have headaches or some such. I never did find out. But I have some idea how these things work."

"You do, do you?" His lips twitched.

"I am only thinking of your health," she said piously. But her gaze strayed again to impious territory, and she bit back a sigh.

"Why? I left you. I have not been as good to you as you deserve. I—"

"You," Kate said quietly, "are an *idiot*. If you have need of me, do you suppose I would flinch away? Do you think me so weak that you cannot lean on me on occasion? Don't you understand—you aren't the only one who can make demands. I'm your wife, and I wish to God you would treat me like one. In every way."

"As you may recall, I can be a terrible beast." He didn't move. "And you still don't trust me."

Kate crossed over to him and sat down on the bed. The cotton batting of his mattress gave way under her weight. It sagged; as a consequence, his body canted toward her.

Ned didn't pull away. But he didn't move closer, either. Instead, he looked at her, his eyes dark and dilated.

"I'm freezing."

He didn't pull her close, as she'd hoped. Instead, he watched her warily. "I don't like to lose control."

Kate inched her fingers across the coverlet toward his now free hand. His knuckles were heated, even though he'd been sitting in the cold. "Ned," she whispered, "let me inside your control."

A shiver passed through him, from his shoulders on down. The transparent silk that covered her offered scant protection from the chilled air. She fumbled with the knot of ribbons in front. It was awkward to try to remove the garment one-handed, but it felt right to keep her fingers pressed on top of his. The material slid past her shoulders.

His eyes fell to see what she had bared. Beneath the nightgown, her breasts were peaked, the nipples poking into the fabric, her skin pebbled.

"Don't pretend you don't desire me," she said. "And I won't pretend, either. Let me inside. You're not the only one who will descend into irrationality if we continue on this path of abstinence."

His member twitched in what appeared to be happy agreement. But he stared at her for a long while before speaking. "I thought you'd take lovers," he finally said. His voice was low and hoarse. "I assumed you would, when I left."

After all that had happened, after all that had passed between them this past week, she hadn't thought that he could still hurt her. But it stung. His words stung so badly—his casual assumption that she would give herself to another, and the even more casual assumption that he would have simply accepted that outcome instead of fighting to keep her his—that she almost turned away. But she'd asked him to let her inside.

He'd left her. She wasn't going to like everything he had to say. And as much as the possibility frightened her, if she never risked hurt again, she'd never have happiness, either.

Kate pulled his hand close. "It's not about my honor. It's… Well, I thought about infidelity at first. It would have been easy enough. I wanted to make you really and truly sorry for abandoning me. I imagined that Lady Blakely would send you word, and you'd come rushing back to me, all hotheaded anger."

"Ah," he said slowly. "When you imagined me rushing back, did I challenge your lover to a duel?"

"On bad days," she said with some asperity, "you lost." But she drew a circle on the back of his hand with her thumb.

That little scene was so much supposition—a fanciful drama, to contain the shape of her own tortured desires. Because what she'd really imagined was that her husband had cared about her, enough to come rushing to her side.

"I *did* think about what I would do if I returned to find you'd taken a lover."

"And did you think about challenging my hypothetical lover to a duel?"

"No." He raised his eyes from their joined hands to look her in the face. "In my imagination, I was given the chance I squandered when first we married. This time, I would court you. I would seduce you. I would show patience and care and I would convince you that this time, you would choose *me*—not have me foisted upon you by some happenstance of fate. I wanted to earn your regard, not have it handed to me by default."

"Well. You're seducing me now."

He ran his thumb along her wrist. Such a tiny point of contact, to send such a jolt through her. "No, blast it. You're seducing me, which I have to say is rather unfair of you. I want to prove that you can rely on me, that I'm not some foolish man driven only by irrational lust. I want—I *need* you to know I'm not Harcroft, to be swept up in a surfeit of emotion."

It was the first criticism she'd ever heard him utter of his friend. She wasn't sure how to respond. But if there was a surer way to bring this conversation to a halt than to discuss Harcroft, Kate didn't know it. She looked up at him in cool regard. "Are you saying it's irrational to want me? Is this going to run along the lines of the reasons why you refuse to light a fire?"

He walked his fingers up her wrist, up the curve of her arm to the crook of her elbow. And now he leaned in until his face was inches from her.

"Hardly." His voice was dark; his breath came hot against her lips. "I'm fairly certain I don't deserve you." She could actually see the mist his breath made in the cold.

"Naturally." Her voice seemed calm, but her heart was racing. "Luckily for you, I've decided to take you as my lover anyway."

He peered into her eyes. "You seem to have forgotten my many flaws. That's not like you. Are you *sure* you're my wife?"

His naked chest brushed her breasts as he leaned toward her. She could feel the heady weight of him poised above her. His flesh, so warm, was in sharp contrast with the cold air. Her own skin quivered in anticipation. He brought his hand up to touch the side of her cheek, and he brushed her jawline. A shiver went through her, a sweet portent of pleasures to come.

She could taste his kiss before he touched her lips—a mingling riot of mint and sherry. His other hand came to her shoulder and he guided her down, down until her spine met the mattress. For an instant, he looked into her eyes. He held himself above her, the muscles in his arms corded to support his weight. And then he lowered his whole body atop her, from the hard planes of his chest to the weight of his thighs. She could feel his erection pressing into her belly. His mouth found hers, and her mind emptied of everything except desire.

She wanted his kiss, and his mouth opened to hers. His lips were warm against hers; they moved slowly, yet firmly. His hand slid down her side; she could feel his touch through the thin fabric of her half-discarded nightgown, trailing down her ribs. There was nothing between them but a scant layer of silk, and even that seemed too much.

No wonder he'd not started a fire. He was a blast-furnace himself, his body searing hers.

He pulled back for breath. "Feeling feverish?"

Her blood was pounding in her head; her own breath

came only in short pants. And she was hot all over, from the palms of her hands to the core of her body. She nodded shortly.

"Do you have a headache?" His tone was solicitous. "Or any pain? Or do you find that you are thinking irrationally? Women who don't find release often do, you know. I'm only thinking of your health."

She stared up at him, her mind completely blank for a bare instant. Then she remembered what she'd told him when she came in—her worries about the symptoms of male abstinence. She smacked his shoulder with her fist. "Are you mocking me, at a time like this?"

"Are you laughing?"

She was; her breath froze around him.

"Then it worked," he said. "You definitely *are* irrational. That's what I was waiting for."

His hand crept up to encircle the swell of her breast. Hot and cold warred against her skin, the frigid temperature of the room contrasting with the heat of his fingers. Her nipples tingled in anticipation.

"It would be wrong for me to take advantage of you in such a state," he intoned piously.

"It would be more wrong if you didn't."

He drew a figure eight atop her breast; his thumb feathered briefly over her aching nipple.

"Ned," Kate said, "stop playing and *do* it."

He was still looking her in the eye. He smiled again and raised one eyebrow. "If you insist."

And then he leaned down and closed his mouth around her nipple. She had a moment to feel the warmth of his breath. It enfolded her, like that instant of silence between

the stab of lightning and the rumble of thunder. Not the
particular *it* she had meant but, oh, she wouldn't stop
him, and the cry she let out was the farthest thing from a
protest. The heat of his tongue around her nipple overtook
her. She felt the sweetness of the connection clear from
the bottoms of her feet to the palms of her hands, a powerful tingling net cast about her. Her thighs parted; she
pressed up against him in unspoken longing, in years-old
desire.

This was *supposed* to be practical. But there was nothing practical about her want, about the deep well of longing that overtook her.

And still he held back from her. When she arched
her back, one of his hands slipped behind her; when she
pushed up at him, his tongue inscribed a circle, a wet,
heated kiss, about her breast. He lifted his head to nuzzle
her ear, and cool air washed over her.

"You're going to undo me," he growled against her
neck.

"Hurry up and be undone."

His fingers pressed into her back. "Do you know what
I was doing when you walked in?"

Even the thought of it left her awash in further longing.
She still had no verbs to describe that action. Only the
one pitiful word, a mere noun: onanism. And that word
described a sin, not the near sanctity of her husband's
body.

"The only words I know are proper and stilted." Not
hot and needful. Not a match for what she felt.

His mouth covered hers again. There was a rough ur-
gency to his kiss, as if she would fade away if he let her

go. But she was positively alive with light. She felt her blood pulsing through her, in time with the rhythm of his caress. She angled her head back and he kissed his way down her chin, her collarbone.

"There are only improper ones," he said.

"Don't treat me like a flimsy thing. Don't pawn me with kind assurances and excuses of propriety."

He didn't. Instead, he pulled away from her an inch and looked into her eyes. When he realized she was serious, he sighed. "I was, as the schoolboys say, frigging myself senseless."

A wave of longing passed through her. *Yes.* She wanted to know that. She didn't want to be shielded from her own desire with ignorance. She wanted to be able to describe her thoughts, her wants. Her husband.

As if he sensed that tumultuous passion, he touched his nose to hers. "But it's not the words that matter. What I was doing when you walked in—I want to watch you do it to yourself."

"What?" The suggestion was more fraught with peril than merely succumbing to his touch. Admit to him the depth of her longing? Be something other than a passive recipient?

He pulled away from her, rolling onto his side next to her. He gulped in breath and met her eyes. "I want you to do it to yourself." His hand engulfed hers. He was warm around her. His other hand slid up her leg. She could feel the night air, cold against her thigh. Her skin leapt under his touch. Surely his pulse beat in time with hers. Surely he could feel that harsh thump in his wrist echoing deep inside her.

His right hand joined with hers. He brought their linked fingers down. "Here," he said. "Touch yourself *here*." And he placed their hands between her legs. She met his gaze. His pupils dilated. She was touching her own slippery wetness. No—better yet—they were touching it. Intimately. Slowly, he moved, slipping between the folds of her skin. His fingers explored her, sliding down her flesh, rubbing her in her most forbidden place.

It was so deliciously *right*—and yet even then, she could feel that his touch was...not wrong, but incorrect. He should have touched her *there,* not there; he was off a hairbreadth there, misplaced his fingers ever so slightly there. Her hand met his, touching. And then she was teaching him, showing him that she needed pressure *there,* that she wanted the rhythm like *that,* that he trace a pattern that she had never before felt, but that she knew with a sure, stubborn instinct.

There.

He slipped one digit inside her. She couldn't have said where his skin left off and hers began. There was nothing but that slide, that pressure, nothing but sheer unadulterated white-hot need.

There, again. He bent his head to kiss her breast, and a sweetness consumed her. She could still feel the cold air against her skin, but he was right—it did sharpen the senses. The temperature heightened the pleasure, made the heat building inside her all the more painful. Her release built with savage intensity. Every inch of her skin caught fire. She gasped as ecstasy passed through her, raging in its brilliance. When it had gone, she lay back, reaching for breath. Her lungs drew in only cold air.

Slowly he pulled his hands away from her. Her breath returned, and with his withdrawal she felt doubly chilled.

"There," he said. "That's what I was doing when you came in." There was a hint of ragged satisfaction in his voice.

Her breath returned to her slowly. "Oh, my. And I interrupted."

"Even if you hadn't come through my door, you'd have interrupted in spirit. I was thinking about you." He smiled at her. "I want you to trust me. Not just with your body, but with everything else." He brushed her hair from her face. "You see, when I take you, I want to have *all* of you. Not just one portion."

"I don't understand what you mean. You could have me now."

He smiled wryly. "I'll be thinking about doing it— every damned stroke. If I can do this…" He trailed off, shaking his head.

Rationality was returning to her with each breath. She'd come to give her husband release. Instead, he'd led her to her own. He was still erect, and by the uncomfortable way he shifted next to her, she hadn't helped matters at all.

And yet…

"Ned."

He must have heard the hint of longing she imbued in that syllable, because he smiled at her. "Don't. I was just congratulating myself for not swiving you like the rutting beast that I long to be."

Kate's pulse pounded in her throat. Her skin tingled.

Her throat ached. She could *hear* the roughness of the beast he claimed to be in his words, in the husky rasp in his voice when he'd looked in her eyes and said those words. Every. Damned. Stroke.

"You're not going to, then. You're not going to—swive me."

"No. Not tonight. Apparently." He looked heavenward. "Damn it."

"Are you going to…to take up where you left off?"

She'd come here tonight thinking only of her own vulnerability. She'd never imagined she would discover his. But it was there, in the touch of his hands on hers. In the slight tremble of his arm.

"Yes." His quiet exhalation sounded like a surrender.

"May I stay and watch?" she finally asked.

His eyes widened. "It's not that interesting."

"Well. Then. I'll try to contain my boredom."

He met her eyes and nodded once, jerkily. He did not look away from her; instead, he slowly reached out and touched himself again. His hand slid up his member, then down, a curiously staccato movement that sent an unexplainable thrill down her spine.

He made her feel vulnerable in ways that she could not avoid.

The room was silent, except for the slap of his palm against his member; every last stroke seemed a palpable thrill, as if it were she who he touched, instead of his own eager flesh, as if it were her hands that encompassed him, her body that enveloped his waiting erection. She was cold and warm all at once, alone and yet joined with him. She wanted his eagerness, his vivacity, the hard press of his manhood inside of her.

She couldn't excise him from her life. She couldn't even set him to one side.

If she'd been vulnerable before this evening, she was achingly exposed now.

These sensations in her veins—they were nothing new. She'd always bottled them up, tamping them down into the farthest recesses of her soul as if they belonged to some wild and dangerous creature. Today, though, she thought of Ned's hand on his member, that heated slide of flesh on flesh.

It was the height of foolishness to imagine her husband's body crouching over hers. It was complete idiocy to fantasize about his mouth finding hers. And when she imagined that hot, firm erection she'd watched pushing inside her, filling her up, she should have flinched away.

But she did not. She was more vulnerable than ever— but for the first time, with his eyes on her, she realized that in this, for all of his jokes and casual airs, they were evenly matched. He wanted her. He wanted her so desperately that he feared his own response, so powerfully that he'd fled to China and stayed there for three years.

When he came, she felt it clear to her toes. He met her gaze afterward. They didn't touch. He stood and walked away to a basin of water that stood on the other side of the room. Slowly, the heat dissipated again, and she was left with nothing but a thin layer of silk and the frigid temperature of the room.

IT HAD BEEN A FEAT of impossible proportions, what
Ned had accomplished, knowing that Kate was holding
a secret back from him. He had yet to earn her complete
trust and so he'd kept himself from the final consumma-
tion, no matter what his body had desired.

But *he* had been in charge. He had been in control—not
his body, nor his own foolish wants. It had been proof of
the sort he'd longed for.

*See? I'm not some boy, to be led about by my desires
any longer.*

He set the towel down and turned back to Kate. As he
did so, all his fine self-congratulations faded. She was
laid out on his bed, the thin film of her gown displaying
rather than hiding the lines of her body—sweet, enticing
curves, all the more appealing because he could still feel
the echo of her skin against his hands.

She lay on his bed, the embodiment of everything
warm and comforting.

There was a reason he hadn't lit a fire. Some men might
relax their guard, might simply forget about their troubles.
Ned, however, had learned that there was always danger.
He heard a siren song of home and heart, of comfort and
no further need for strife. What she didn't understand was
that he could dash himself on the rocks of complacency
as easily as on darker shoals.

He knew. He'd done it before.

She smiled at him. "Ned. Are you going to have someone lay a fire?"

He wasn't quite sure what he'd hoped to accomplish
these last few moments, but he suddenly realized what

he'd managed to give her. Satiety without satisfaction; the illusion of closeness, without any actual penetration.

And now, when it was over, she was beginning to realize there was nothing left but the cold. It had won out again. In the mirror above the basin, he saw a little shiver go through her.

"No," he said quietly. "I don't sleep with a fire."

She sat up in bed and stared at him. "Some people go without comforts. Usually it is because they cannot afford them."

True. He couldn't afford himself too much comfort—any more than he could give up the regimen of physical exercise he engaged in. Comfort was the enemy. Comfort was complacency. Comfort lulled him into believing that he did not need to worry about the future.

She huffed. "You don't sleep with a fire? Well, I do."

Her import was obvious. She wanted to stay the night, wanted to lie down next to him in bed and tempt him all night with the brush of her limbs against his, the scent of lilac on her skin. It would be so easy to succumb to her, to wallow in the warmth of her. It would be easy, right up until the moment when it was not.

But it would be weakness to light a fire just because the air was a little cold. Just as it was weakness to indulge in one's desire for intercourse, merely because a woman was willing.

She looked at him levelly. "You're not saying anything. Does that mean you want me to go?"

"Not exactly."

She gathered the shreds of her gown about her. "Well. That hurts."

She had confessed her hurt to him so easily, without worrying what he might think of her. Ned felt a twinge of oh-so-unworthy jealousy.

Just before he'd left for China, he had once sat in on a set of meetings that his solicitor had arranged, so that he might hire an estate manager. He had not known what sort of questions to put to the candidates, beyond requesting letters attesting to their character and competence.

His solicitor, however, had filled the time. The man hadn't interrogated the potential workers on their views about agriculture or animal husbandry—questions that Ned might have found relevant. Instead, he'd concentrated on questions that seemed irredeemably useless.

"What," the man had asked each fellow earnestly, "is your greatest weakness?"

It was a stupid question because it was nothing but an invitation to spout falsehoods. No man had ever answered with, "I drink to excess and beat my children." Instead, the vast majority of them had come up with answers that were carefully crafted to avoid any appearance of weakness at all.

"I am so eager to serve my masters," one fellow had said, "that I must sometimes take extra precautions so as not to work on the Sabbath day, in violation of God's commandments."

Another man's greatest weakness had ostensibly been a proclivity for boiled sweets.

It hardly seemed a surprise. Only an idiot or a very brave man would confess his true feelings. Ned kept his greatest weakness lodged deep inside him, hidden from common view. It was a deep, frightening chasm of inadequacy, which he had learned to hide behind a veneer of humor. He'd papered over that chasm these past years, but he kept it in check with what Lady Harcroft had called black magic tricks. Cold at night. Exercise in the morning. Tricks designed to keep him firmly in control of himself.

Everyone lied about weakness. Everyone, that was, except Kate. She admitted fear and hurt without pausing at all.

It was not just that she owned *up* to her weakness. She *owned* her weakness; it did not own her.

She did not need to tiptoe around it. She did not need to grab control and hold on, unwilling to let go. She just said it aloud.

She stared at him, and he realized he'd been silent all along.

He wanted her to stay. He wanted to own not just her body, but her easy self-possession. To feel the strength of her seep into him as she slept beside him at night. All he would have to do was light a spill from the oil lamp and start the kindling going with a little bit of fire.

She wouldn't understand what that bit of warmth would mean to him. She would see it as light and heat, not another aspect of his control, ceded to someone else. She had no way to know what he feared, had no need to fight the encroaching darkness.

"Right." She stood and gathered her night rail about her. Even cloaked in that filmy material, she seemed as regal as a queen. "Well, then. I suppose I should go."

She started to walk away from him.

He stood, took three strides across the room and grabbed her arm.

She looked up at him, her eyes implacable in the reflected lamplight. "What is it?"

He couldn't say what he meant, so instead he simply hugged her to him. She was soft and lovely, and she smelled like lilac in summer. "It's not you," he muttered into her hair. "It's the fire."

She pulled away and raised one eyebrow. "That's comforting," she said in a tone that suggested she was anything but comforted. And before he could damn himself with faint explanations, she left the room.

CHAPTER THIRTEEN

THE MORNING WAS STILL GRAY and misty, the sun not yet over the horizon when Ned arose to say his farewells to Harcroft. The man had dressed and breakfasted by the time Ned's boots crunched the gravel on the drive. Harcroft's carriage waited, the boot loaded with the trunks the man had brought.

Ned put out his hand. "Best of luck to you," he said. "And Godspeed." The latter he meant; he couldn't wait until Harcroft had put miles between him and Kate. The former sentiment was about as insincere as he could manage.

The earl clasped his arm briefly and then looked around. "Think on what I told you the other night. Think on it carefully. Because if you *do* find Louisa here, you'll have to act in my stead."

God forbid. Ned shook his head. "I thank you for your concern. You'd best be off. You've a long journey ahead of you, and you'll need every hour of daylight." He glanced behind him.

"Looking for your wife?" Harcroft asked dryly. "Still nervous about her, eh? Still asking for her permission for every touch, and cringing like a child if she says no?"

"Not quite." Ned saw no reason to share the complicated details of his life with a man who believed that intimacy ought to be conducted with fists and blows. He looked away in exasperation.

But Harcroft must have read agreement into his averted gaze because the man clapped him on the shoulders. "There. If that doesn't motivate you, nothing will. Trust me. True men don't *ask*. They *take*."

In Ned's estimation, real men didn't throw tantrums if their whim was thwarted.

"Quite right," he said. "And, oh, do look at the time! You really should be on your way."

"Come, Carhart. Tell me you'll rein your wife in."

"She's my wife." He glanced over at the man. *And it really is none of your concern.* "Why does it matter so much?"

Harcroft chewed his lip before leaning in close to impart his secret. "Because I think she may have instigated whatever happened with Louisa. I've been thinking it over, and Louisa didn't start truly questioning my authority until she and Kate became friends. In fact, I'm sure of it. Your wife set her against me in some female fashion. I'm certain of it, although I can't prove how—although with women, one has to just trust one's instincts."

"My instincts differ," Ned said carefully.

Harcroft straightened, brushing his coat down. "If you won't rein your wife in, I'll do it for you."

Ned's hands cramped with the effort of not clenching into fists. He stepped forward, squaring his shoulders. "What, precisely, are you threatening my wife with?" he asked.

Harcroft glanced at Ned's shoulders once, and then smiled uneasily. "Oh, don't be so melodramatic. When I find Louisa again, I'll need to make sure she's not exposed to unsavory influences. I'd hate for you to be considered one of those."

Harcroft had fenced as long as Ned had known him. He was good with a rapier and quick on his feet. In all those years that Ned had known him, that confidence had made Ned believe the man was taller than he was. But standing shoulder-to-shoulder with the earl, Ned realized for the first time that he was actually taller. And after months aboard ship, where he'd labored alongside common seamen, Ned was stronger, too.

No amount of expertise with a rapier could save Harcroft from someone who had two stone on him. It helped alleviate some of Ned's wariness.

"Don't worry," Ned replied, as carefully airy as Harcroft. "I'm not about to engage in anything untoward, and you can rely on my promise to free my wife from all unsavory influences." *Such as you.*

"Good man." Harcroft smiled. "I knew I could depend upon you." And then he paused, as if waiting for Ned to return the compliment.

Ned ought to have done so. One little lie would put distance between Harcroft and his wife. But the words choked in his throat, as bitter and cutting as cinder. "I'll take care of matters here," he finally managed.

Harcroft smiled again. Even though Ned had washed just ten minutes before, and brushed with tooth powder, that smile made Ned's mouth taste foul. He should have protested. He should have told the man to take himself off for good. But if he had, Harcroft's suspicions would have been roused. They were already on point, and while it would have been satisfying to smash the man's face in, it wouldn't have been particularly wise. His own wants gave way to cold clarity.

"I knew you'd see it my way," Harcroft said with a smirk. "You'll see it with your wife—soon enough, mark my words. Perhaps I shall even be the one to show you."

That self-satisfied expression was too much to bear. Clarity abandoned Ned, and he leaned in. "I'll conduct your search for you. I will tell you what I unearth. As soon as you leave, I'll canvass the county on your behalf. But, Harcroft—there's one thing you need to know."

Harcroft screwed up his mouth quizzically.

"You are never to threaten my wife again." As Ned said this, he brought himself up to his full height. Harcroft looked up at him, as if realizing for the first time just how much larger Ned was than he. "She's *mine* to contend with."

She's mine. It was not the most settling thought, but after last night it had begun to be true. She'd done precisely as she'd said; she'd gotten inside the hard confines of his control. Perhaps she was his, but he was ceding a portion of himself to her. And that scared him more than any smirk that passed over Harcroft's face.

Harcroft met his eyes. And then, slowly, he jerked his chin in a nod. Just as slowly, he got into the carriage. Ned contented himself with the thought that the earl was going away. The footman shut the door and clambered up onto the seat behind the carriage. The reins shuffled, and Harcroft's horses pulled in their traces.

Ned listened to the rattle of wheels over gravel as the carriage pulled away.

For now, they'd earned a respite from all outside cares. And Ned intended to use it very, very well.

Now it was time to talk to his wife. After what had happened last night, he had no idea what she thought of him. The possibilities ranged everywhere from very excellent to very bad. He looked around him at the dreary autumn morning.

How terrible could matters be, with Harcroft gone?

For the first time since he'd woken that morning, a true smile curled his lips.

KATE WOKE when her door creaked open.

The person who entered wasn't her maid. Kate could tell, because the air against her face was warm. Someone had already laid the morning fire. But the curtains were still drawn shut, and the light that seeped around their edges was pale and insubstantial.

In other words, it was not yet time to rise. Waking would mean thinking. It would mean greeting her husband—and how she was to do that after the confusion of last night, Kate couldn't say. She was too sleepy to even contemplate humiliation, and so she closed her eyes again.

Sadly, footsteps had the temerity to approach her bed. She glanced up through slitted eyes.

Of course it was Ned. And of course he was carefully groomed, his hair curling about his ears in entrancing little waves. Kate didn't even want to think about what her own hair looked like. After last night, she didn't want to see him until she was clad in her favorite dress. Perhaps the aquamarine silk—the one everyone always said made her eyes look blue.

"Oh, good," he said in a tone far too cheerful for a morning that had not even properly started. "You're awake."

No. She wasn't. This was a bad dream. "Mmm," she croaked in protest, and pulled the covers to her chin.

He clicked his tongue at her. "Aren't you going to rise? There's something I want to show you."

She blinked up at him in bleary-eyed horror. "You want me to get out of bed? Isn't it enough that you sleep in the cold? Why in heaven's name would you want to arise? It's barely dawn."

But she could see at least one benefit—it was too early for her to work herself into embarrassment about what they had done together last night.

"You could join me," she added, before her sense of shame woke properly.

Ned's grin broadened and he held out one hand. "Right now I think I would lose my head entirely if I tried anything beyond holding your hand. I want to savor you."

The way he said that word—*savor*—made Kate think of all the word's meanings. To dwell on; to enjoy; to *taste*…

"You," she said shaking a finger at him from the warm cocoon she'd made of the covers, "are an evil, evil man. Particularly if you expect me to get out of bed."

He shrugged. "My natural modesty requires me to disclaim the description of evil until you've seen what I can do. I've done nothing truly wicked yet. Right now I must insist on labeling my behavior up until this point as merely tormenting."

He walked to the bed and leaned over her. He set his hands on either side of her head, gripping the covers around her. "Kissing you," he murmured, "now, that would be mischievous."

"Yes." She inhaled his breath. Her lips tingled.

"Touching you all over—that would be rather sinful."

"Indeed," she breathed as she felt her body react sinfully to his words.

"Bringing you to release, I suppose, might count as truly wicked."

"It would be almost as good on a morning as a cup of tea."

He leaned down, his eyes meeting hers. They had that sinful sparkle in them, as if he were planning something truly diabolical; his voice was low, and she shivered in expectation. Maybe he'd held back last night because he planned to touch her this morning. Given the pleasure she'd experienced last night, whatever he had planned was sure to be decadent. She could anticipate the languorous slide of his hands down her sides. He would touch her, soon. He had to, or she would lose her sanity.

"Do you want to know what might be classified as truly, darkly, unforgivably evil?"

"Yes." Her assent was quick and breathy. "Oh, yes."

He smiled broadly. "This."

His hands fisted in the covers and then he yanked them away from her—everything from the muslin sheets to the warm wool coverlet.

Cold morning air hit Kate's skin and she yelped in protest, curling up involuntarily. "Ned, you beast! You led me to expect—"

He laughed. "You wanted me to be evil, didn't you? Well. This is all the evil you are going to get for now. I've rung for your maid. I'll see you downstairs in ten minutes."

"Ten minutes? You expect me to be ready in ten minutes? You've truly lost your mind."

Something flitted across his expression at those words—a hint of wariness, perhaps, in the tweak of his mouth—but he shook his head at her. "Ten minutes," he warned her. "Trust me. It will be worth it."

She managed to ready herself in half an hour by forgoing the usual four layers of petticoats, and settling for a tidy pink walking dress—the kind she might wear for a visit to a tenant farm. Not quite in fashion, but easy to travel in. Her maid twisted her hair up into a simple knot and handed her a wool shawl, and Kate dashed downstairs. It was a measure of how evil he truly was that she didn't even consider taking longer.

He was as good as his word—which was to say, when he met her coming down the stairs, he handed her a thick clay mug filled with tea, and then gestured for her to follow him out of the front doors, which had been thrown wide. His hand fit warmly into the small of her back.

Outside, mist clung to the trees that lined the road, sifting hanks of white wool out over the world. It stifled all sound. Kate inhaled; her lungs filled with cool air.

"There. You see?"

"It's a misty morning."

"Sensible Kate." He tucked her hand into the crook of his elbow. "It's far more than that."

He set off at a slow pace, and she followed. "There." He pointed with his free arm up into a tree as they walked under it. She looked up into a mess of leaves and branches. In the quiet, windless morning, the limbs of the tree stood still; she could see clear through them into the blue of the sky.

"There. In the crook formed by those top branches. It's a nest. At this point, the fledglings have all grown up and flown away. The parents, perhaps, might still be around, although it's rather late in the year for that."

She blinked up at the little structure of twigs. "How did you ever see that through all this fog?"

"Oh, I've walked this way before. I spotted it several days before." He shrugged and they kept walking.

A little while later, he paused and pointed out a red-breasted bird on a faraway oak. It pecked the tree trunk smartly once, twice and then flew away. A little bit farther, and he flipped a rock over and showed her the creepy things underneath.

Kate shuddered and looked away. "Centipedes? Ned, did you wake me up to show me centipedes?"

"It's all part of an autumn morning. This early, humanity—we people with our speech and the noise of our industry—we're holding our breath and giving nature a chance. Flip over any rock," he said with a smile, "and no matter how lovely the bird that was perched on top, you'll find a bug underneath. During summer, the world is warm. But that warmth is just a moment at apogee. The rest of the time, we're all just hurtling toward winter. It's not pretty, but it's real. And in some ways, it's a bit more fun."

"Is this supposed to be some sort of oblique commentary on last night?"

He cast her a sidelong glance. "Maybe."

Kate's feet were beginning to ache in her half boots. They had been walking for close to an hour, and they were approaching the small village in the valley near Berkswift. "What a depressing way of looking at the world."

Ned shrugged, but she felt his arm stiffen under hers. "It's not depressing. That's the way things work. Seasons come and go. There's a certain beauty to that, too. During summer, you see, we humans are not so different from the birds or the squirrels. We store up foodstuffs so that we'll make it through the cold. The birds eat up every last crawling thing they can find, in preparation for a great flight south. We all find our ways to prepare for winter." He didn't look at her as he spoke.

Kate shook her head in confusion. "And this is what you wanted me to see?" She had the feeling that something was passing her by, something great and momentous. She didn't understand, and she could no longer blame her muzzy head on a lack of coffee.

"I know. This explanation has been a bit elliptical. I'm a bit too fanciful this morning."

"Dragons are never killed, only tamed to do your bidding. You tend toward the fantastical in your speech no matter the time of day."

He shrugged again and lapsed into silence. It was in silence they walked through the main thoroughfare of the village. It was not a wealthy place, but neither was it

beaten down by poverty. The little touches—the mari-
golds growing in a riotous mass in a box, the woodwork
on the outside beams of the carpenter's shop—suggested
that this was a place that was well-loved. Ned, likely, had
taken in those details instantly. But it seemed as if this
were the first time Kate was noticing them.

"It *is* a beautiful morning," she said as they passed
the inn. The door was open several inches; inside, she
could hear the rumbling voice of the innkeeper, ordering his lackeys to wrangle someone's luggage and ready
some room for the coming day. Aside from those gruff
orders, the silence held. Perhaps, later this morning, the
taproom would come alive with noise. Now, maybe one
or two people breakfasted inside. They might glance outside and see Kate and Ned pass through, arm in arm, in
companionable silence.

She wondered what they would make of the sight.
Would they see a happily married couple, strolling arm
in arm?

Would they be wrong?

"I hope I haven't given offense. I intended no insult. In
truth…" She looked up at him. "In truth, I think you're
good for me in that way. You're fanciful without ever
crossing the line into foolishness. I can be…practical."
She swallowed and stared straight ahead.

This was the want she'd held deep inside her, suspended all those years. This rush of vulnerability. She
wanted to be swept away. She wanted to be safe.

She wanted to shut her eyes and let her hopes carry
her, like the rising floodwaters coming from some tor-
rential downpour. She wanted to believe that if she ever

did falter, he would be there to catch her. She wanted to tell him about Louisa.

And she didn't know if it was her own hopes she trusted in, or the real strength of her husband.

"I can be as practical as I must about our marriage," Kate finished. "But Ned…I don't *want* to be."

He stopped and looked down at her. "And here I was thinking I couldn't be any luckier. I was strolling about on a fine morning, with the loveliest woman in all of England on my arm. I was positive everyone about me would be overcome with jealousy at my good fortune." He fitted his hand to her cheek. His touch was cool, for an instant, before her skin heated his palm.

"Ned. We're in full view of the taproom. We can't see through the darkened windows doesn't mean they can't see us—"

"Hang the taproom," he said, "and indulge my fancy." And then he leaned down and kissed her. It was a very public kiss—discreet enough to only be one shade darker than was proper. His lips touched hers for a bare instant. Still, he laid claim to her in public. Her toes curled in her half boots; her feet stopped aching.

And when he pulled away, he looked at her without smiling. "Hang practicality," he told her.

"Ned," Kate said carefully, as they resumed their walk, "would you dare throw me out of your room two nights in a row?"

They passed the inn before he answered. "No," he finally said, his voice low. "No. I don't believe I would."

CHAPTER FOURTEEN

THE MUCH-ANTICIPATED EVENING approached with all the weight of a coach-and-four. Still, to Kate's mind, it moved forward at the speed of an incoming snail.

After they returned from their walk, Ned retired to the library to review some papers that had been sent up from London; Kate took the time to talk with the housekeeper and the bailiff about some of the tenant farms. In the afternoon, Ned left to spend time with Champion.

What Ned hadn't done was search for Louisa, as he'd promised Harcroft. Kate pondered this conundrum through the hours that passed.

Did Ned know more than he'd admitted? Had he gathered from Kate's reticence that she wished Harcroft's venture ill? And would he truly choose her over his friend? She almost believed he would—and yet she couldn't quite banish that last flutter of fear from her belly. Maybe after this evening, she would trust him enough to speak. After she'd cunsulted with Louisa on the morrow.

Time crawled, and Kate struggled to fill it, with the awareness that evening was hours and hours away. She found herself walking the halls, pacing between the parlor and the entry. On her fifth pass back, her wandering was interrupted.

"Ah. Lady Kathleen. There you are." The voice was

deep and masculine—but it wasn't Ned's. Kate whirled around and gasped in surprise.

Harcroft was standing in front of her. He blocked the hallway, his arms folded cavalierly. He seemed like some sort of sinister angel, with all that blond hair and those bright blue eyes. He tapped his lips and watched her, as keenly as a cat watching a moth flutter against the wall.

"You know where she is." It was a flat pronouncement, not a question.

Kate tamped down the fear that trickled into her belly. He couldn't know what she knew. If he did, he wouldn't be here. He'd be five miles from here, out threatening his own wife. But he had to know *something,* or he'd be halfway to Chelsea by now.

"Harcroft. What are you doing here? Did you forget something? Has something happened to your carriage? Can I be of service?"

His lips pressed together, and he looked into Kate's eyes. A cold shiver of fear ran down her spine. He didn't look at her with sexual desire; however unclean that might have made her feel, it was an emotion she could have understood. No, she grew cold because he looked at her as if she were not anything at all. For all the clarity in his piercing eyes, for all the sparkling and malevolent intelligence directed toward her, he didn't see any worth in her. Not an object to be desired, not a person to be reasoned with. Perhaps he saw her as a piece of furniture he might make use of—or break, if she failed to suit his needs.

"She has a young child," he said. "She needs me. She needs her husband, her family. What she doesn't need is to be off, gallivanting on some stupid adventure. She needs protection and direction." He scowled into the distance.

"Harcroft," Kate said, "you must know I love your wife as I would a sister. I would never want anything that was bad for her. If she needs you, why would I keep her from you?"

It was a dangerous tack to sail into, that line of questioning. He let out a breath, and then—she was watching his eyes—his pupils contracted, slowly but surely, until all that malevolent attention focused on Kate. If his lack of attention had made her shiver, that focus froze her to the bone.

"Yes," he said quietly. "Why *would* you keep her from me?"

He took a step toward her, and Kate flattened herself against the wall.

"Why would you keep her from her lawful husband?" Harcroft asked. "Why would you think she needed to stay away from me? Do you imagine she has anything to fear from me?"

He took another step. Kate made to sidle away from him, but he rammed his hand into her shoulder, slamming her into the wall. The force of the blow pushed her against one of the carved cornices that decorated the doorway. The wood embellishment bit into her back. Kate stifled a cry of pain.

"Because surely, any obedient wife would know she need feel no fear of me right now. That's what you feel, isn't it? Fear?" His hand clenched on her shoulder. "Louisa would want for nothing at all, so long as she followed the commands of her husband. Any God-fearing woman would never set a foot outside the path dictated to her by the man she'd made a sacred vow to honor."

"Get your hands off me." Kate set her hands on Harcroft's chest and pushed, but the man didn't move. "I don't know what you're speaking about."

"But then, what would you understand of God-fearing women?" Harcroft pushed close into her. She choked on the angry smell of smoke on his clothing. Taproom smoke. "A God-fearing woman wouldn't lead her husband astray. When I left Ned this morning, he had promised to start canvassing immediately. Yet not a few hours later, he was traipsing about the village, gazing into your eyes. Why would you distract him from his duty, if you weren't afraid of what he might uncover?"

"You've lost your senses." She pitched her voice to carry. Any second now, a footman would hear them. He would intervene, and then Harcroft would have to let her go.

"Have I? God-fearing women don't steal other men's wives away. Do they, Kathleen?"

Maybe the servants wouldn't come. But Kate wasn't the sort to cower and wait. She was tired of feeling scared, of cowering and waiting for help. She grasped the ends of his cravat and twisted, hard. The cloth scraped against her hands. He choked, and pulled his hands away from her involuntarily. He scrabbled at his neck, grabbed the ends of the cloth she'd ripped loose and pulled it off.

Kate skittered sideways.

He glared at her. "You goddamned bitch."

"I told you to get your hands off me." Kate's heart was pounding.

He raised his arm in threat.

What she said next wouldn't matter—not to him, she didn't think, because a man who would hit a woman didn't need an excuse. But it mattered to *her* that she not placate him, that she not give him even that much power over her. She balled her hands. "Get out of my house."

His fist flew. She just had time to turn away, to keep from getting the brunt of the blow against her mouth. His hand smashed against her neck as she turned. For one second, she was so numb, so surprised that he'd actually done it, that she didn't even feel anything. Then she felt the stinging ache of it.

He grabbed her elbow and tried to pull her around. Kate ground the heel of her shoe into his boot. He yelped—a decidedly unmasculine sound—but wrenched her arm. A shooting pain traveled up her shoulder, and she bit her lip.

"Where is my wife, Kathleen?"

His breath felt clammy against her ear, and she shook her head.

He only yanked her arm again, harder. "I said, where is my wife, Kathleen?"

Kate pressed her lips together in defiance. There was nothing Harcroft could do to make her divulge that information. Every violent impulse he indulged now he would visit on Louisa a thousandfold if he found her. Harcroft would eventually have to leave her house. But if Kate spoke now, Louisa would be stuck with her husband for the rest of her life, however long—or short—that might be. Kate would not speak. Harcroft pulled harder, and the shooting pain burst into stars.

"You think you understand," Harcroft ground out into her ear. "You don't know *anything.* I love my wife. You're completely wrong. I just want to keep her safe."

"You should be careful," Kate said as distinctly as she could manage with her cheek planted against the wall. "I'm a woman. I'm quite delicate, and I think I might faint if you continue."

"Some women," he spat, "have delicate sensibilities. Then there are women like you—false serpents in human form, who tempt real women to go astray. Where in God's name is my wife?"

His fingers gripped her arm; Kate could feel his nails press into her skin, cutting through the fabric at her wrist. She took a deep breath and shoved ineffectually at him with her free elbow, but he didn't move.

"If I pull back your arm," he said cruelly, "eventually, it will pop out of its socket. In the process, it will cause you excruciating pain. I should hate to cause pain to anyone."

"Even if 'anyone' happens to be a serpent in human form?"

"I am," he said, "essentially a gentle, unassuming creature."

He sounded as if he really meant it. She held her breath and stared at the wall he'd pressed her cheek into. And then she laughed. She laughed even though she knew it would enrage him. She laughed, even though she knew he would follow through on his threat and wrench her arm from its socket.

She laughed so that Harcroft would know that no matter how hard he hit, or how badly he hurt her, he could not win. That she would not be the weak, sniveling creature who waited on help to arrive, who dithered before obstacles until it was too late.

And he needed to know that now, because if she scraped and begged before him, sniveling for mercy, he would just visit his wrath upon her all the harder.

"You aren't stronger than me," she said. "Not with all your muscles. No matter how hard you strike me, you aren't stronger than me. And that must make you furious."

His eyes glittered with all the fury she'd anticipated. His hand tightened on her wrist; she rose on her toes as he turned her arm. She kept that smile on her face, flattened against the wall, her eyes clenched tightly shut. She didn't dare let him see how much he hurt her.

And then Harcroft gave a pained cry of his own, and that wrenching pressure on her arm vanished. Kate turned in time to see Ned lift him by the lapels of his coat and slam him against the wall.

"I told you," Ned said, his voice gravelly, "I told you to leave my wife alone. But no. You didn't listen."

Harcroft waved his legs furiously in the air, but he was as ineffective as a beetle overturned on the pavement, struggling to right itself. "No, *I* told *you,*" he squeaked. The whine of his voice seemed impotent against Ned's dark anger. "I told you I would find my wife by any means necessary."

"Oh, I see how it is," Ned said in a dark voice. "You've driven away the woman you believe you deserve, and so, in the absence of having your own wife to do violence to, you've chosen mine."

"I—"

"To think," Ned continued, "there was a time when I actually respected you. When I first came back to England, I took pity on you. When you told me Louisa was missing, I felt sorrow. I have no idea when or how your wife disappeared. I was out of England, as you know. But as matters stand, if my wife helped Louisa escape you, she has my full, unmitigated support. If I had been here, I would have stolen her away myself."

Oh.

Even with her arm tingling, Kate felt a sudden rush of warmth and safety at those words. He meant them. He did.

"You can't mean that. You can't mean to foster such suborning. It will lead to chaos, if women make decisions—"

"I should hardly think so," Ned said. He didn't seem to be getting tired, holding Harcroft against the wall with one hand, but he gave the man a shake for good measure. "I don't see the fabric of *my* life eroding, just because my wife happens to have a brain in her head. In fact, it's actually one of her most attractive qualities. If you'd allowed your wife to make a few decisions of her own, instead of trying to control her with blows, perhaps you wouldn't be here."

Harcroft didn't say anything. He'd stopped struggling against Ned's inexorable hold. But his lips compressed to a hard line, and his eyes blazed with fury. His breathing was ragged; by contrast, Ned's chest rose and fell as if he were not doing anything more strenuous than sipping tea.

It was in that moment that Kate realized something quite startling. Her husband was magnificent. It was not just the contour of his arm, that hidden strength that held the man who'd threatened her against the wall. It was not just the ease with which he defended her.

It was that assumption he made, without even glancing at her, that she was doing the right thing, that she was strong rather than weak, decisive rather than dithering. It was as if he had turned everything everyone saw of her upside down.

"Kate," he said, without taking his eyes off Harcroft, "what should we do with this carrion-eater?"

"We've sent him home once. I suppose we can do it again." Kate shook her head and gingerly touched her wrist. "We haven't any use for him here."

"Shall I decorate his face for him, before he takes his leave of our fine hospitality?"

"I should think there has been enough decoration for now." Kate thought of the fine network of bruises she'd seen on Louisa's arm. She thought about the spreading ache from her fingers on up to her shoulder. "The last thing we need at this point is violence. Isn't that the case, Harcroft? I say that because I am, in fact, a gentle creature."

"There," Ned said. "Now you see why I turn to my wife for consideration in these important decisions. Because if it were up to me, I would break every bone in your body before I tossed you in the water trough to cool off. What do you think, Kate? May I break one rib? Please?"

Kate smiled. "If he comes back, break everything."

"There. Mercy and justice, all in one delightful

package. I shall put you down now, and you will walk out the door."

Harcroft licked his lips and turned to them as Ned let him down. "You will regret this," he said. "You will both regret this."

"I know," Ned said, shaking his head sadly. "I already do. I shall have to make do with envisioning your body bloodied and in need of a physician. But we all suffer disappointments."

"I won't give up. You can't send me away."

"And I—" here Ned stepped forward "—I am not going to let you hurt my wife. Not for any reason, and certainly not for no reason at all, which is what you appear to have. You are not welcome here any longer, Harcroft, and you'd damned better crawl off and lick your wounds. You have some nerve, threatening my wife just because you can't beat your own any longer. Now scramble away."

Harcroft took one step toward Ned, his hands clenched into fists. And then he turned—and he scrambled.

Kate watched Harcroft scamper down the hall. Beside her, Ned's chest heaved. He flexed out his hand. He stared at the empty hall, his eyes focused unseeingly on nothing. His head bowed, finally, and he scrubbed that hand through his hair.

"Hell," he said. "I think I might have finally said too much. What have I done?"

Saved me, she thought, before the rest of his speech caught up to her.

"You mean—you knew?"

He looked away. "Um. If you mean, did I happen on

Lady Harcroft in the shepherd's cottage a few days prior? Well. Perhaps."

Oh, God. Kate's stomach fluttered. "Are you dreadfully angry with me for not disclosing it earlier? Do you want me to stop?"

"I am ablaze with curiosity as to how you managed such a tremendous feat in secret. But angry?" He looked in her eyes. "It took me years to trust myself. You're allowed to wait at least a week. Now, if you had actually *loaded* the pistol Lady Harcroft pulled on me, *then* I would have been wounded by your mistrust."

"She didn't." Kate's hand covered her mouth.

"She did." He smiled faintly. "But you needn't worry. We saw eye-to-eye shortly after."

He let out a sigh. "Damn me. I had it all under control—Harcroft actually *believed* I was on his side. I had allayed all his suspicions. One little setback and the next thing I know, I've ruined it all."

"Ned. Are you joking?"

"If I had been in control of myself—"

Kate held a finger up to his lips. "I have had it up to here with your control," she said, her voice shaking. "There is a time and a place for control. And that time and place is not when a man is threatening to rip your wife's arm out of its socket. That is the moment when you are allowed to lose control and crush him like the worm that he is. You think too much of your control."

He looked down at her, the afternoon light catching his eyelashes in gold. "Do I?"

"Yes." Kate shook the last of the smarting pain out of her wrist and looked up at Ned in return. If she said the word, he might run after Harcroft and pound the man to a delightful pulp. Or, better yet…

She placed her hand on his and gazed into his eyes with all the pent-up yearning of the past three years. "In fact," she said with a tight little smile, "I wish you would lose control again."

CHAPTER FIFTEEN

CONTROL. IT WASN'T EVEN some last vestige of control that had kept Ned from breaking every last bone in Harcroft's body. It had been nothing more than an animal instinct to protect what was his, to stay here, growling, hunkered down over the object of his desire in unthinking possession.

Desire? Hell, desire barely covered it. His hands tingled with the need to feel that visceral crunch of breaking bone. If Ned shut his eyes, he still saw that satisfying image of Harcroft lying bruised and bloody in the aftermath of his fury. It wasn't about reason or rationality; it was about that hot, unending rage that had filled Ned when he'd stepped into the corridor and seen that bastard—that pretentious, arrogant bastard—with his hands on Kate.

Everything had ceased to exist but the roar in his ears, and the next thing he realized, he'd latched his hands around the bastard's throat. He flexed his fingers even now, but he could not shake off that murderous hatred. Harcroft had placed his hands on Kate.

He turned to her. Her breathing was only now beginning to even out; her hands were trembling. She hadn't shaken one bit when that bastard was manhandling her; she hadn't even betrayed the slightest tremor. She'd been

as strong and unyielding as a stone cliff battered by the
ocean's rage. And perhaps that was why he'd held on to
his civility by the bare thread that remained—because
she had been strong enough not to lose control. And if
she could maintain her cool demeanor…well, he could,
too.

He didn't know what to say to her, and so he reached
out and took her hands in his. Her bones seemed so
damned thin, so impossibly fragile. He could feel, now,
the aftereffects of that frightening episode. Her hands
were cold. Her eyes, when he looked down into them,
were wide, as if just beyond Ned's shoulder she could see
the vista of what might have been. She let out a shaky
breath—one, then another, and Ned looked down, away
from her fear. If he let himself see it any longer, he *would*
lose control. He would leave now and hunt Harcroft down.
God knows what he might do if he actually caught him.
Ned felt capable of any violence.

"Are you well?" He knew the question was stupid even
as he asked it.

Still, she nodded.

Looking down had been a mistake, too. Because now
he was caught by the veins in her wrist, that thin spider-
tracery that formed a network. He could feel her pulse
slamming against his fingertips. And there, at the edge
of the lace of her cuff… Oh, God.

Every scrap of discipline kindled into heat. He slid her
sleeve up her arm.

He had no words for the inchoate rage that welled up,
hot and bitter, in his stomach. He had no label to put to
the emotion that filled him in that devastating instant.

Because there, tracing up her delicate skin, were the un-mistakable red marks that Harcroft's fingers had left on her. They were branded deep into her skin. The imprints were bright red for now; in a few hours' time, they would purple and bruise.

That bastard had hurt his wife.

He looked up into Kate's eyes. He couldn't think what to say, how to apologize. He'd been enforcing an artificial distance between them because he feared if he spent much more time in her intoxicating presence, he'd succumb to complete savagery.

He'd been right. Language deserted him. There was no room for words in his mind; just that limitless, unspeak-able rage. He held her hand—gently, even though every muscle in his body screamed to contract.

And then, as if to tempt his anger, he saw the im-pression the wall had made against her cheek—the red-on-white mark where that bastard had slammed her into the plaster, the tiny scratch where the rough surface had drawn a bead of blood.

"I take it all back." He could not clench his hand around hers, could not even squeeze his hand. He had to stay in control. "I am going to kill him."

It wouldn't make it better, though. Nothing he did *now* would heal that cut, would undo the pain she had felt. She'd needed him, and once again, he had been gone, thinking of *himself* when he ought to have been think-ing of her. He'd vowed that he would find a way to be a good husband not two days ago, and already he was forsworn.

Worse, whatever semblance of civility he had, he

needed just to keep from crushing her hand. All his dark wants, all his savage desires—they were welling up in him now. A gentleman would walk away until he gained control—but the last thing Kate deserved after her bravery was solitude.

"I am going to kill him," Ned repeated, "just as soon as I work up the fortitude to let go of your hand."

"Don't," Kate said. And for a second that word, too, was meaningless—that silly implication that Harcroft's life ought to be spared. She could not have meant anything so vapid.

But she said it again. "Don't let go. Hold me." And she looked up at him with those luminous eyes, eyes that betrayed all the fear she had not let Harcroft see. It was, Ned realized, her strength that made her vulnerable. She'd claimed she was weak, but in almost every way she was the strongest person he had ever met. And she needed him now.

And so he didn't let go. He wanted to clasp her to him, wanted to squeeze her hand until the anger ran out of him. Instead, he pressed her fingers lightly between his palms, willing the hot rage in him to flow out of his hands, to warm the fears that echoed in her eyes. He moved his hand in circles until her hand curled in his, until her shoulders relaxed. As if that spare motion could lift away the pain she'd felt.

And when that scant comfort couldn't take the past five minutes away—when she looked up at him, her eyes still wide with the unspoken horror of what she'd just experienced—Ned turned her hand in his, exposing her wrist and those damned angry red marks. He leaned in and placed a kiss over them.

She smelled like a summer bower in full bloom. He lingered over that inch of fragile skin and let his breath heat her.

No, he wasn't going to leave her to assuage his own desire to beat Harcroft's face in, however pleasant the prospect might seem. He was going to stay here, where he belonged. And not just because she needed him, but because he was too damned weak to do anything but take in the scent of her, taste the sweetness of her wrist against his lips.

He could not take her memories away; he could not eradicate her bruises. He'd failed her enough for one day. But now, when she'd used up her strength, he would stand here while she needed him.

"I'm here," he murmured against her skin. "If you need me, I am here."

She stepped toward him, and he put his arm around her. She was cold all over; her shoulders were trembling in the aftermath of her fear. He wrapped his other arm around her and felt her press against him.

"Not as if you needed me," he breathed into her neck. "You were—you *are*—marvelous. When I left for China, it was a mistake. I'm not doing it again. Not if the Queen herself asks me." He rubbed his hands up her shoulders, and then down them again.

"I know." Her breath warmed the fabric of his shirt. She turned and laid her head on his shoulder; her hair tickled his nose. But still, he held the warm miracle of her against him.

"I know," she repeated. And then, slowly, she tilted her head up to look at him. Her eyes were a solemn gray, and they tugged at some tender spot just inside his breastbone. She laid her hands against his chest.

"You hurt me," she whispered. "When you left."

"I'm sorry."

"There was a time I wanted to hurt you back. I wanted you to suffer. I wanted you to feel as awful as I felt. I wanted you to ache the way I did."

He shook his head, wordless, not knowing what to say, not knowing how to apologize to her for all the mistakes he'd made. He didn't know how to prove to her that he would make it up to her. "You said once—that our marriage would dry up and blow away, with one good gust of wind. I'll do what it takes to make it take root again, Kate."

But she surprised him again. "I'm sorry," she whispered. "Now I just want you." And then, impossibly, she went on her tiptoes and placed her mouth against his.

It wasn't an angry kiss or a frightened kiss or a kiss intended to seduce him. It was just Kate's kiss, pure and simple. It was the taste of her, given freely; the feel of her lips, warm and soft. It was her body in his arms, light and fragile and vulnerable, and yet strong and unbending all at the same time.

He wanted to be strong for her, and yet unbidden, it became Ned's kiss, too, an outpouring of all those words he could not find, all that emotion he could not express. When his hands touched her shoulders, she understood that it meant she could rely upon him. When she opened her mouth to him, when their tongues touched, it was because she wanted him. And when she melted against him, it was the trust he'd hoped for.

She tilted her head back, and he kissed his way down the delicate swell of her throat. She leaned against his hand, trusting he would not let her fall. This time, he wouldn't. He *wanted* her—needed her with a palpable desire.

She must have felt the restraint in the tightness of his shoulders because she raised her head to his. "How many times do I have to tell you, Ned? Let me inside your control."

She ran her fingers down his form, slipped her hands inside his coat. It was so unspeakably intimate, that gesture, a sign of sweet possession.

"What control?" he growled.

Because with her touch trailing down his ribs, there was none left, not even the bare semblance of civility he'd been struggling to maintain. Not with her hands undoing his waistcoat, her fingers dancing down his abdomen. Not with his mouth on her neck, nor the sweet swells of her breasts soft against his touch. The lacy edge of her bodice was in the way; he tugged it back, revealing the muslin of her shift. He could see the dark rose circle of her nipple through the fabric. Every last sinful fantasy flitted up in his mind and screamed to be made reality.

"What control?" he whispered again, and he fastened his mouth around her breast. Fantasy and reality merged; she was responsive and willing in his arms. The hard nub of her nipple tasted sweet, even through the sheer material of her shift. She gasped, and his fevered imagination could never have manufactured the hard choking sound of her desire, the feel of her body.

He should *think*. He should stop. But instead, he kissed his way up her neck. His thumb found her wet nipple. A thousand desires flooded him; he circled it back and forth, feeling her own want build up. She was gasping. And then he leaned down and gathered her skirts in his hands. Lace and starched petticoats foiled his approach for the barest seconds; then he found the muslin of her drawers. He reached inside to the place between her legs.

She was wet and silky, as hot as he'd ever hoped. He tasted her mouth as his fingers found that spot. He'd learned her last night. Now he knew just where to touch her, knew just how to flick his fingers along her sensitive flesh.

Dimly he recalled that he should…that he was supposed to… What was he supposed to do? Any consideration beyond this—this hot need for her—seemed immaterial. There was nothing but his want. His hands fell to her waist. His groin pressed into her pelvis. It felt wonderful against his erection. She felt so damned good.

It wasn't enough. It could never be enough, not with this distance between them. He wanted her in every way possible.

But there were consequences. There were considerations. He knew there were, even if his mind could not recall what they were.

When he pulled away, however, her hands fell to the placket of his breeches. He could feel himself twitch against the rough fabric. She undid his breeches, and then her fingers were warm against the length of him. He might have come right then, from her touch. He didn't. Instead, he gritted his teeth and slid his fingers against her. It didn't take much to imagine plunging into that warmth, to imagine those legs of hers around his waist. Her fingers brushed the head of his penis.

"Damn," he swore. "If you keep doing that, I'll—"

"Do it." Her words were a taunt, a dare to shed the last vestiges of his discipline. And when she ran her finger down the length of his erection, he did. He growled, wordless, and lifted her against the wall. He didn't think; instead, his hands held her steady.

She wrapped her legs around him, and then, with one motion, he sank inside her. Gravity pulled her down his cock, settling her around him. The slick friction of her was glorious. He leaned down and found the tip of her nipple again. She was joined to him. He pulled out and stroked back in, and she shuddered.

Yes. This was what he'd wanted, what he'd needed. This slick wetness. This unthinking bliss. This spiraling, thrusting want, their bodies coupled. He'd needed this damned burn, painfully pleasurable, a satisfaction that raged from his balls all the way to his hands, clasping her to the wall.

Her body tensed around his. She was his fully; he was inside her, taking every last stroke he'd denied himself.

When she came, he felt the heat of it like the opening of an oven. He pumped inside of her again, and again, and again, until he was shooting all of himself inside her. Until he was sated and weak and barely able to hold even her slight weight against the wall.

Breath returned first.

Then followed the scream of his muscles, aching after that physical exertion.

Sanity was longer in coming. She was looking up at him, smoothing away the sweat on his forehead, a faint smile playing across her lips. Her legs were wrapped around him; he was still embedded in her, his cock too sensitive, aware of the pulse deep in her body. Perhaps that beat was in him. He couldn't tell any longer.

And they were in the thrice-be-damned hallway, for God's sake, where anyone could see them. What the hell had he been thinking?

He hadn't. He hadn't even waited to take her to bed like a civilized man.

"Damn me."

That shy smile spread across her face, lighting it up. "If I had known that it would be like this, I would have goaded Harcroft to manhandle me years ago."

God truly *had* damned Ned. He'd ignored everything— his concerns for her well-being, his control. Rage had transformed into desire. He'd not had one thought in his head but taking his pleasure of her.

Then again, she hadn't seemed to mind. Quite the contrary. He shook his head, trying to make sense of it all. Slowly, he disengaged from her. He lowered her to the floor with all the gentleness that he could muster.

She did up his breeches, her hands steady. She bit her lip in concentration as she worked, and an unbidden flush of affection hit him. He'd always thought his wife a striking woman. How had he not noticed before now how *adorable* she was?

She looked up at him, smiling. "Well, Mr. Carhart.

You've embarked on a love affair with your wife. Now what do you intend to do?"

Run away. His first thought, unworthy as all his baser impulses usually were.

No. Kate was right. There was no taking back what he'd done to her these past minutes. There was no withholding from her this dark, ravenous side of himself.

And there were many, many worse things than having a wife who enjoyed his body as much as he enjoyed hers.

So she'd breached all his defenses, all but the last one. She thought he was strong. She thought he was warm as summer, and didn't understand that he'd merely reached apogee. He had the distinct sensation of hanging weightless in air.

It didn't matter. He'd suffered winter before. He'd make his way through that as well when it came again. If she needed to believe him strong, he'd be strong for her, no matter what the seasons brought. She didn't need to know what plagued him.

And so he mirrored the slow laziness of her smile. "Well, my lady. The first thing I suggest is that we call for a bath."

CHAPTER SIXTEEN

"A BATH?" KATE ECHOED incredulously. Her body still throbbed, satiated. And yet she hadn't had enough.

"Trust me." He smiled at her. "You want a bath."

"Oh." She suddenly realized how sweaty, how sticky she was. Not romantic in the least. Was he trying to say—

"Oh, don't stiffen up." He took her hand. "I want to *give* you a bath. Trust me."

"I do trust you." Kate hadn't realized it was the truth until the words came out of her mouth. But she did—she could taste it in her mouth, a warm taste as volatile as brandy and twice as heady.

His eyes widened slightly. He lifted his hand to her cheek, oh so slowly. "Of course you do." His voice sounded deeper than usual. It seemed to resonate through her bones. "I told you that you would."

"You can make all the jokes you like, Ned, but I see through you."

It was nothing—a trick of the light, perhaps, or a waft of the air. For a second, she thought the pupils of his eyes contracted to dark pinpoints, and all that heat turned to ice. The sensation passed so quickly, though, that she must have been mistaken.

"Of course." His voice was a warm caress. "It's all a

part of my diabolical plan. I confess it now. Do you realize I've never really seen you unclothed?"

"What? But—" She stopped, remembering the darkness of their wedding night.

He shrugged. "Poor lighting. Unfortunate night rails, fortunately brought up to your knees, true, but never removed all the way. But no. You've seen more of me than I've seen of you. I intend to remedy that."

She hadn't seen enough of him. And with the fire of lust banked for the present, she could see that his humor had returned, that quirk to his mouth. He was easy again.

"If we call for a bath midday, won't the servants guess that we've been…"

She paused, delicately searching for words again.

"Rutting," he pronounced helpfully. "Swiving. Engaging in intercourse, naturally, although that has a rather proper feel about it. I don't suppose you can call it 'engaging in intercourse' when it's done up against a wall. Tupping, perhaps."

So many words. So many ways to try it. "What word would you use?"

"I'd say I've been having my way with you. And since I know you'll ask, I'm not done—you're heading upstairs and removing every stitch of clothing. Now."

"But everyone will know—"

"Kate." He set his hand on her wrist. "Ring for a bath."

She managed it without breaking into a blush. She even managed to ascend the stairs without running, even though she could feel his eyes on her. *I've never seen you unclothed.* True, perhaps, in the strictest sense. But he'd seen down to the core of her barest vulnerabilities. He knew everything—her hidden fears, her secret needs. She knew only the substance of his desire. She could still feel his body pressed against hers, could feel him with the unflinching memory that skin possessed.

She'd seen him without clothing, but she wasn't sure she had ever seen him naked.

The servants filled the bath with ewer after ewer of steaming water. Her maid fussed around, setting out soap and towels, crushing petals and pouring oils into the water, preparing a rinse of elderflower tea and willowbark for her hair. The woman glanced once at Ned, who watched the proceedings from a chair, but she made no mention of his presence.

When the woman came up behind Kate and set her hands on the laces of her gown, though, Ned spoke. "I'll take it from here," he said, his tone calm, as if it were an everyday occurrence that he undressed his wife for her bath. "You may leave."

The servants were too well-trained to smile knowingly. But Kate's maid sent a glance to Ned and, without a flicker of emotion crossing her face, walked to the chest of drawers and removed another stack of towels. As if they might spill water all over the place. And how that would happen… Kate's cheeks heated. The maid set these next to the original set and then left the room, closing the door behind her.

"Does that blush go all the way down?" Ned walked up to her. His finger traced the meaning of his words—the pink, flushed skin of her neckline, vanishing into the lace at her bodice.

She heated further. "I—oh—"

"Nothing to be done now," he said. "They all believe we're indulging our carnal desires. If we don't do anything, they'll talk of that, too. We might as well make the best of this."

He set his hands on her shoulders and turned her gently around. She felt his hands on her laces. She'd been dressed and undressed thousands of times in her life. She'd felt her maids' hands tug on those crisscrossed ties too many times to count. But they'd never been his hands—big, strong, warm, caressing…yanking?

"Ned, what are you doing back there?"

"They're stuck." He sounded confused. "I just pulled this one bit here, and then it knotted, and now this part over here is all tangled. Is this some sort of cruel joke?"

She frowned and peered over her shoulder to see what he was talking about. Then she bit back a smile. "I suppose, in a manner of speaking. Women call that cruel joke a bow."

"I disapprove. What on earth is wrong with buttons?"

"Laces allow a gown to fit the form more closely. Don't pull so hard. You're just going to tangle them more."

There was a longer pause, followed by another tug.

"Ned, do I need to call my maid back in?"

"I can take off my wife's gown without help, thank you. Ah, there! These bits are looped together. Cleverly designed to foil a husband's hands. I see how it is. I'll have to have a discussion with your dressmaker."

Kate felt her gown loosen around her. His hands were

gentle, going up to her shoulders and settling there. "Next time," she said through a grin, "I shall ask my maid to leave the instruction booklet next to the towels. I see why you preferred the wall. No removal of clothing necessary."

It was probably the least efficient undressing Kate had ever undergone. But there was something sweet in all his fumbling. The hesitance with which he eased the muslin off her shoulders warmed her heart. The touch of his hands tingled against her skin as he gently disengaged her arms from her sleeves. The cool air that flowed over her as he gently slid the gown to her waist brought her arms out in gooseflesh.

Then there was the coarse mutter when he'd got the gown off her.

"Christ. There's another damned set of laces on your corset."

"Actually, there are two of them, interlacing. You wanted to see me naked, Ned."

"You're the one who donned all this clothing in the first place. I never realized it, but fashion was clearly invented to encourage celibacy. Admit it: these were invented to bedevil a man in the throes of lust."

"I think it's more about creating a silhouette that is pleasing to the male eye."

"What's wrong with your silhouette?" He attacked her corset laces with perhaps more enthusiasm than finesse, but eventually the strings loosened and the garment came off.

Kate took a deep breath, filling her lungs. "I have a confession to make, Ned. And it's terrible. No, not terrible—it's *awful*." She felt his hands come to a stand-still on her. They rested against her waist for a second, pressing as if to hold her upright.

He moved around her and took her hands. His eyes were clear and guileless. "What is it? Is it about Lady Harcroft?"

She squeezed his hands back. "No." She looked up into his eyes and licked her lips. She dropped her voice, and he leaned in to hear her. "After our walk this morning," she confessed, "I went back up to my room. And I put on four petticoats."

He laughed, and his hands contracted around hers. "That *is* bad. But I see buttons. There is hope, after all."

There *was* hope. If she and Ned could find this enjoyment together, after all the mistakes in their past, they might solve the problems with Louisa. They might grow to trust one another, maybe even love one another. In ten years, they would laugh about these times.

He managed her petticoats with some semblance of grace. And when he'd removed the last one—when she was stripped to her shift—he knelt before her. She reached out and set her hands in his hair. It was disheveled—she'd made it so, she realized, grasping his head to hers in that frenzied coupling downstairs. It was soft to her touch, and still too long. He took the hem of her shift in his hands and then, as he stood, stripped it off her.

Finally, she was naked before him. He held her last muslin undergarment balled up in his hands and looked at her. He just looked, his eyes traveling from her legs up her waist, to her breasts. She felt her nipples point under his gaze.

He made a motion with his finger. "Would you…" He paused and swallowed. "Would you turn around?"

She did. He hissed as she did so. His hand fell on her shoulder. "What's this?"

His fingers rubbed a sore spot. "Harcroft threw me against the doorframe in the hallway."

He made no response. Instead, he pressed his hand over that spot, as if he could simply warm the bruise away. His hands skimmed down her back, cupped her buttocks. They came to rest, once again, on her hips. "What are *these?*"

She glanced down her own body. There, on either side of her hips, was a faint red mark. She knew where she'd got those without even thinking. She could still feel his hands there, pressing her, holding her, as he'd thrust into her. "That's where you held me downstairs."

"Oh, God. Kate. I'm sorry. I'm no better than Harcroft, doing you injury when—"

"Don't be ridiculous. It didn't hurt. And if you think that I shall let you treat me as if I'm made of glass, you're mistaken. You told me I was strong. Well, don't see bruises when you look at me. See *me.*"

He looked in her eyes and then nodded once, jerkily.

For all that controlled power in his movement—for all the strength of the arms that had held her up against the wall—he was still gentle. He turned from her and took off his own coat, and then his waistcoat. He folded up the cuffs of his sleeves, matter-of-factly, as if he didn't realize the effect that glimpse of wrist—masculine and strong, with that gold fuzz of hair—would have on her.

He turned back, and whatever emotion had gripped him earlier, he'd banished it. At least, Kate could not see it on his features any longer. He walked to her and then lifted her in his arms. She fit there, falling against him. And then he walked her to the bath and laid her gently in.

She hissed as the hot water enveloped her. Lilac-scented steam swirled about her. Next to her, he dipped a cloth in the water and then rubbed a bit of soap into it. The bar released a powerful scent, complex and unexplainable. It smelled of cultivated gardens and civilized walks; simultaneously, it reminded her of flowers in a riot across a field, not hedged in or clipped into compliance.

He really did intend to give her a bath. The rough fabric of the washcloth rubbed against her neck, over and over. He massaged her over and over, her shoulders, her back. She could feel his ministrations down her spine. Her every muscle loosened, soaking in the heat of the bath and the pleasure of his touch. And then he was washing her breasts, the undersides in sweeps of the cloth, the nipples with tender touches.

He focused on her arms with as much care as he had her breasts. He pulled her foot from the tub and covered it in suds, massaging the worries from her; then the other foot. And then his cloth dipped under the water and his hands went up her legs, slowly but surely, past her calves, her knees. Her thighs parted for him, and the cloth dipped between her legs.

There. Yes, there. She was still sensitive for him. He

would touch her more. He would join her here in the copper tub—don't ask where, there was no room for him.

"Ned?"

He pulled the pins from her hair in answer and dipped a pitcher into the water. His hands shielded her face from the splash as he poured the heated liquid over her head. His fingers found her scalp. There should have been no touch more intimate than that of his fingers between her legs, but somehow this was it—the feel of his hands rubbing her scalp, finding the tension she'd stored there and releasing it into the water. Another splash, as he rinsed her off.

She blinked the water from her eyes and looked at him.

He was watching her with a startling intensity.

"Thank you," she whispered. She felt not just clean, but free, unbowed by any of the worries that had plagued her in recent weeks. "Thank you, Ned."

"You're quite welcome."

She stood, and water cascaded down her shoulders. His attention was riveted on her. He stared at her, as if she were Venus arisen from the sea—as if she were one of those paintings where Venus had dry hair that curled beguilingly, not wet, bedraggled strings.

He didn't seem to notice the difference.

He took a towel from the stack and set it around her shoulders as she climbed out of the bath. He dabbed her hair to dampness, and then knelt before her. The towel brushed against her thighs and she let out a low moan.

At that sound, he looked up into her eyes. It was as if a current passed between them. She felt hotter, more liquid in his gaze. Without taking his eyes from her, he leaned forward. He licked his lips. And then he planted a kiss between her legs. It was tender at first, a mere touch of his lips. Then his tongue parted her folds. His hands came to her hips. She was melting beneath him; his tongue slipped back and forth, tasting her own liquid. She shut her eyes, but that only intensified the sensation, the feel of dark waters rising about her, enfolding her in their warm embrace.

He'd already robbed her muscles of their tension. With this, he seemed to steal all the remaining frustration from her nerves. She could feel it all building inside her, sweet, undeniably sweet—and then it crashed down on her, and she shuddered against him. Her muscles ceased to work. She could not hold herself upright.

It didn't matter. He was holding her now. She wasn't sure when he'd stood; clearly sometime after he'd brought her to ecstasy. His hand slipped down to find hers, and then he was leading her out of the room and into her own bedchamber.

The sun was setting, casting rays of red light against her skin. He led her to her bed, and then, deliberately, slowly, he pulled his shirt over his head. His muscles rippled as he removed the fabric. Still, he'd not said a word.

He didn't need to.

He removed his boots and stockings, and then pulled his breeches down. He was erect; when he leaned down over her, his mouth questing for hers, she found his member. He was hard; she squeezed, and he pulsed in her hand.

She pulled away from his kiss. "Let me inside, Ned."

His pupils dilated. He didn't say anything, but he leaned against her, pushing her into the mattress. One hand captured her wrist, holding her there. He spread her legs and then she felt his hand guiding his member to her sex.

Her body welcomed his. She gave a quiet gasp at that feel—so new, and yet so familiar. He was stretching her out. Her hips rose to his. She was sensitive still, so sensitive; with his member inside her, that delicious ache began once more.

Her hands clenched the bedcovers uselessly.

And then he looked into her eyes and thrust forward. His fingers clenched around her wrist. His mouth gritted; not in pain, but in the onslaught of pleasure. She wrapped her legs around him, pulling him in.

There was nothing between them but the smooth slide in and out, the friction, the heat that built between them. She had no control over her body, nothing in her head except the feel of his skin against hers, the grind of his pelvis, the pleasure building once again.

He reached his climax first; his thrusts grew stronger; his fingernails bit into her wrist. He let out a hiss between his teeth, and the hot rush that filled her, the sure knowledge that she had given him the pleasure he gave her, was all she needed. She clamped around him. And then she was spasming around him again—insanely, perfectly, completely his.

NED COULD NOT FIND WORDS afterward. None of them seemed right; they didn't seem to fit the intimacy they'd just shared. Any words he could imagine would only emphasize what he'd given her—and what he'd hidden behind that tender display.

But then, Kate didn't know what he hadn't said. She turned against him, her hand falling on his naked hip. "You were right." Her words were soft against the silence, but still he prickled, inhaling cool air. She trusted him. Her breath, warm against the hollow of his throat, bespoke security. She cinched her arm around his waist, unconsciously molding herself against him. That posture, that welcome confidence, had to be genuine.

"You knew about Louisa," she said quietly.

"Perhaps I should have said something to you." He traced his finger idly down her shoulder. Easier than looking in her eyes.

"But why did you not *do* something more about it?"

For a second, Ned's heart froze. He should have, he realized. Should have intervened, offered to take the matter off her hands. He should have insisted—

"After all," she continued, "when I was younger, every time it seemed to me I had hit upon something interesting to accomplish, my father always found someone else to do it for me. It made me think that I was supposed to be some helpless creature. An accomplished lady is one who plays the pianoforte, who speaks six languages. Who can converse with her dinner partners on Byron and Shakespeare. Accomplished ladies aren't allowed to accomplish anything of value."

"Ah." Ned felt a restless sense of familiarity at those words. Truth be told, most gentlemen didn't accomplish anything, either. She hadn't wanted him to take the burden from her, after all. She wanted a challenge. He knew what that felt like.

He hadn't realized women longed for the same things men did.

"Now you know the truth," he told her. "You've saved a woman from her husband."

Her hair brushed his chest as she shook her head. "No," she contradicted.

He was about to tell her that Lady Harcroft *would* be safe when she spoke again.

"I've saved seven."

"Pardon?"

"Do you recall the circumstances under which we first met?"

"We encountered each other in the servants' quarters at a ball." In point of fact, Ned had followed her in—not alone, accompanied by Gareth and Jenny. "You never did tell me what you were doing there, except to feed me some story about needing to help an old nursemaid."

The story hadn't explained everything. But then, he'd been so wrapped up in his own problems he'd accepted her tale without question.

She sat up, her eyes sparkling. "Oh, that much was true. It just wasn't the full truth. You see, when I was sixteen, I discovered that my old nursemaid had broken a limb. A duke's daughter is allowed at least to bring baskets of jellies to her dependents—and so I did. In the course of the visit, however, I discovered that her husband had caused the accident. It wasn't the first time."

For all the dire seriousness of the subject matter, she

was warming to the conversation. As she spoke, she gesticulated with her hands.

"That first one was easy," she continued. "I just arranged for passage across the Atlantic with a bank draft waiting for her on the other side. Now she owns a bakery in some odd place in America—Boston, I think."

She took the injuries seriously, Ned knew. But that light in her eyes was about more than the seriousness of the injury. How much of herself had she been hiding? His chest felt tight and uncomfortable. There was more than a twinge of jealousy mixed in with his feelings of astonished respect. When she had been sixteen, she'd been saving women from violence, unbeknownst to her father.

And what had Ned been doing?

Wagering on horses. Weathering the aftermaths of his first bouts of drinking.

"Louisa," Kate said, "is the seventh one I've spirited away. She's the first lord's wife, though. And she has *definitely* been the hardest." She looked over at him. "You're—you're not going to insist that I stop, are you?"

Ned shook his head.

"I love my father," she said, "and he adores me. But he thinks of me as his little poppet, a delicate thing to be shielded from all difficulty. My mother trained me to throw parties and perform gracious acts of charity. I love them, but these last years, I've been glad to have the excuse to remain here. In Kent, they would never have let me do so much."

There was a wistful quality to her voice, and Ned was

reminded again of what he'd thought earlier. She was lonely. She hadn't had any true family—or at least, not anyone who knew the truth of her. She leaned against him. "Oh, parts of this will be so much *easier,* now that I know you approve. Do you know what I've had to do to get the funds for my bank drafts?"

Ned shook his head again.

"I've had to go shopping. I have an account with several dressmakers. I purchase extravagant gowns. They write up the bill with twice the amount, and then slip me the rest in bank notes. I am *famous* in the *ton* for my shopping."

Harcroft had remarked as much. And now that Ned thought the matter through, he had never seen his wife wear the same gown. "Woe is you," he said dryly. "I can tell you absolutely despise that."

"Oh, yes. It's a winning proposition for me in more than one regard. After all these years of silence, it feels extraordinarily freeing to talk of it."

She trusted him. It was precisely what he wanted. After all, he'd vowed to make things right with her. He was doing it.

So why did her warm hands feel like ice against his heart?

She trusts me only because she doesn't know the truth.

He wanted to get out of bed and walk away. At a minimum, he wanted to turn from her, to give her the ridge of his spine. He'd gotten precisely what he wanted. And now he wanted her to take it back.

"Now, what do we do about Louisa?" she asked. Her

voice was growing lazy with sleep. And that simple word—*we*—left Ned biting his lip.

That certainty in her voice, that confidence in her breathing, the evenness of every inhalation—it was all because he'd fooled her. He'd made her believe he was strong and capable, the sort of powerful man who might face down rampaging horses and raving husbands alike. She believed in him, and the weight of her belief sat upon his shoulders.

She didn't know the truth. She didn't know that every few years, winter came upon him, replacing the warmth of summer. That all her trust was reposed in a man who might crumble.

Yet he hadn't crumbled the last time the darkness had come. For *years* he'd fooled people into believing that he was strong and capable. For years, they'd believed him. And so long as he kept his mouth shut—so long as he just put one foot in front of the other in the morning—well, nobody would ever need to know.

Least of all Kate.

"We'll see her in the morning. Everything will work out—just you see." It was more a promise to himself than a vow he could make to her. He would take care of her. He wouldn't ever let her fall. She didn't need to know about Ned's own idiotic problems.

She didn't find his reassurances ironic. She seemed, in fact, to take his strength for granted, a trust that warmed him almost as much as it left the palms of his hands cold. His promise seemed to settle into his skin. No; when faced with this sweet trust, winter wouldn't matter. He simply wouldn't let it.

CHAPTER SEVENTEEN

As much as Kate wished to spend her time exclusively with her husband, when morning dawned, her responsibilities overwhelmed her. They were going to have to do something about Louisa. Now that the earl was aware that Kate was involved, the matter had become a thousand times more dangerous.

Kate and Ned made certain that Harcroft was not lurking nearby, then they started off. Kate splashed across a cold stream, holding on to her husband's arm. They crept across fields, avoiding country roads. They didn't dare be spotted on their way to the cottage where Louisa was staying.

When they were ushered inside, Kate explained the problem. "Louisa, your husband believes I had something to do with your disappearance."

"So what does that mean?" Louisa shook her head. "I'm not going back. I'm not letting him have his son, either."

"No. Of course not," Ned said.

"But it does mean that this situation is no longer tenable," Kate finished. "It never has been. You have to either decide to leave England, or you must confront your husband and find a way to wrest your freedom—and your son's—from his grasp."

Louisa simply looked at Kate before shaking her head. "Unlikely. I'm *his*. I married him. He controls my funds. And besides…" She sighed. "If he looks at me that way, I might just crawl back to him. I did it once before." There was a grim edge to her speech.

Kate set her hand on her friend's shoulder. "I know it's not easy. But you're going to have to do something."

"I can shoot him," Louisa offered hopefully. "Isn't that ridiculous?" Her voice shook. "I can't imagine looking him in the eyes and telling him *no,* but I can see myself shooting him." Her voice dropped. "I can see myself shooting him very easily."

"Perhaps we might consider solutions that do not lead to your subsequent hanging," Kate suggested.

Ned flicked a glance at Kate. She had no notion what he intended. The hardest part of her hobby had always been convincing the women in question to act. She didn't understand why it was so hard to make the decision to leave a violent husband. A man who was willing to break bones didn't deserve much consideration, in Kate's opinion. And yet there was this vacillation. She tried not to let it irritate her.

Sometimes it still did.

Louisa pulled her knees up to her chest and hugged them to her, as if making herself smaller would shrink her problems. "It's easy for you to tell me to make a choice," she said. "But when I try to think of the future, my head just hurts. I can't face it."

Kate exhaled in exasperation. "But you shall have to do so."

Louisa set her fingers to her temples and didn't respond.

"You know what?" Ned's voice rang out, doubling Kate's annoyance. "Did I ever tell you about my experience with Captain Adams in China?"

At those words, Louisa looked up, and Kate pressed her lips together. This hardly seemed the place to exchange anecdotes. They needed to plan, to *think,* to charge forward. They had little enough time as it was. Kate turned toward her husband, and her brows drew down.

But at least Louisa had uncurled from her little ball, as if once the tension was released, she could sit straight again.

"No," she said softly. "You didn't. I've heard almost nothing about your journey. What was China like? Was it foreign? Exotic?"

Ned rested one hand easily on his knee and leaned back. He looked toward Louisa, as if she were the only person in the room, and Kate felt her annoyance grow.

"It was frustrating," he replied. "Very frustrating. I arrived, thinking my mission would take me maybe a month or two. But when I first got to the Eastern hemisphere, hostilities had broken out. The ship I was on rerouted, so as to find a safe place to land. It took me months just to make my way to Hong Kong. But I'd promised Gareth I would investigate the opium situation in China. And I was bound and determined to go forward, war or no war, hostilities or no hostilities. After all, I hadn't traveled halfway round the globe, just to be fobbed off with secondhand accounts. I wanted to see the British action in China, and I wanted to see it personally."

Kate tapped her foot, one hand on her hip.

Ned put his hands behind his head and looked up. "The man I needed to talk to was Captain Adams. He'd been appointed as a liaison to all the silly, foolish second sons and aimless aristocrats who'd been shipped out East for no reason other than that nobody wanted us back in England. I suspect he despised us all. He took one look at me and knew precisely what to make of me."

"He thought you were someone he had to respect, as the heir to a marquess?" Kate asked. "The sort of person who could solve problems decisively?"

Ned cast a glance at her, that smile on his face, but ignored her. "Absolutely not. He thought I was useless, and that I would prove to be a headache."

"Well. I hope he learned his lesson, judging you so quickly," Kate said. "But back to Louisa…"

Ned shrugged. "He was right. I went to his office day after day, requesting that he allow me aboard one of the ships they were sending down to the mouth of the Pearl River, to observe what was happening. At first, he said no. Then I began to wear into the thin veneer of his patience, at which point he said, 'Definitely not.' After about three weeks of my constant badgering, it turned into, 'My God, man, don't you frivolous idiots have the brains to see I have real work to do? Stop pestering me.'"

"But then he gave in," Kate predicted. "As for Louisa…"

Ned smiled more broadly. "No. He didn't. It took another week to turn into 'Mr. Carhart, as God is my witness, if you set foot in my office one more time, you will regret it for the rest of your life.'"

At this point, Kate noticed that Louisa had begun to lean forward, her eyes alight. And when Ned paused contemplatively, she let out a little gasp. "Oh, don't stop there. Did you? Set foot in his office, I mean."

"Of course I did. I was scared out of my wits, too. I had promised Gareth I'd not leave until I had personally seen what was happening. And so the next morning, I presented myself once more. By that time, I wasn't really sure why I continued to march into his office. I surely did not expect to meet with success. I had all the feeling of throwing myself against a brick wall, violently, repeatedly, for no other reason than there were no other brick walls available. It was pure foolishness. Only idiots and madmen continue to better themselves in the face of persistent failure, and by that time, I was certain I was both."

There was a certain gentle humor in his retelling, a glint in his eye, and out of the corner of her eye, Kate could see Louisa smile. Ned had always had this skill, even when she'd first met him—this ability to say something funny and unassuming, to set someone at ease, to bring out the light in shadowed eyes.

He'd been sweet. Over the years of his marriage, that sweetness had been given more substance than she'd guessed.

"So? What happened?" Louisa asked.

"He clapped eyes on me. And this time, he didn't say one word. Instead, he rang a little bell on his desk."

Kate was leaning forward as much as Louisa, now. "And then?"

"And then, eight soldiers marched in. They must have

been lying in wait for the moment. They grabbed me by the arms and legs."

"Didn't you fight?"

"I tried. But there were eight of them and one of me. If I'd had as many arms as a squid, I'd still have been at a distinct disadvantage. Especially at close quarters. In any event, they lifted me off the ground and carried me like a sack of potatoes. And the only thing the captain said was this—'Dunk him.'"

"Oh, no." Louisa covered her mouth in sympathy. "Did they toss you in a lake?"

"I can tell you've spent no time around soldiers, if a lake is the worst you can imagine. That would have been very kind, in comparison with what actually happened. You see, the garrison had built these privies. And it was so wet there, that… Well, in any event, the waste eventually collected in these massive holes in the ground. They were foul, disgusting swamps."

"Oh, dear God." The words escaped Kate's mouth.

Ned smiled at her, his cheerful tone at odds with the filthy scene he set. "So in I went. It was quite possibly the most humiliating moment of my life. It was disgusting and degrading, and I do not have the words to describe how impossibly awful it was. I couldn't even scream in protest, because that would have required me to open my mouth. I have never felt quite so helpless in my life as I did at that moment."

The two women stared at him in shock.

"You realize," Ned said in a low voice, "that if this story ever gets out, I will be a laughingstock. I am trusting you ladies with my deepest, most shameful secret.

You must never tell another soul. I know I can count on you."

Louisa nodded, and in that instant, Kate's breath stopped wildly. Somehow he'd managed to calm her friend's fears. He'd managed to make her smile. And now he was subtly making her feel that she was important, trustworthy. Somehow he'd known that she'd had so much taken from her that she couldn't possibly give anything back. Her husband didn't need to beat his chest or roar. He didn't need to make arrogant demands. He just needed to smile and make Louisa laugh. Now Kate's heart stung just a bit.

"So," Louisa asked, "what did you do?"

"What would you have done? I took a bath." He grinned. "A *long* bath. Then I got in a little boat and I tooled around and I thought. There's something extraordinarily valuable about having someone do their worst. If you survive it, they can't truly touch you again. There's nothing they can do to bring you down. And Adams— well, he'd done his worst. He couldn't kill me. My cousin would investigate my death and make his life miserable if he did. He'd had me thrown in the privy on the assumption that I'd be too humiliated to admit it to anyone once I got home. He believed I would simply make up some rubbish for a report and leave him alone." Ned leaned back in his chair. "He believed wrong. The next morning I got dressed. I went down to his office one last time. And then…" Ned smiled, stood. He walked over to Louisa and bent down, so that he was level with her.

"Then I looked in his eyes, just like this." He fixed Louisa with a look. "I smiled, just like this. And I leaned forward and I said, 'Captain Adams, I believe I'll be on the next boat to the river.'"

Kate watched him in breathless agony.

Ned straightened. "He looked at me. He looked at that damned bell. And then he looked back at me. It was as if he'd bullied me as far as he could. Once he realized I could outlast him, that was that. From there on out, he actually proved quite helpful."

At those last words, Louisa looked away. "Oh, Ned. I know what you're trying to say. But I can't. I can't testify in court. I can't petition for a divorce. I can't even imagine looking Harcroft in the eyes."

"You can't right now. I needed that time on the boat, Louisa. I burned my skin crimson that day, sitting on that boat and thinking. I needed that time, because if I'd seen him right after coming from the privy, I would have flinched from him, and that would have been the end of it all. I needed to know what I *wanted*." He flashed Louisa a grin. "You can't know what to do, until you know what you want. What *do* you want?"

"I want my baby to be safe." Louisa's arms curled about her, and Kate bit her lip. "I want him to take his father's place as earl one day. I want him to believe that love and affection are typical, and violence a mere aberration."

Ned tapped his lips. "So, for instance, escaping to America and obscuring your identity might cloud his chances at taking his seat."

Louisa nodded. "I want to stay here with my family." She glanced at Kate. "And my friends. And I don't want my husband to ever, *ever* threaten me again."

"There," Ned said. "Was that so hard, then? To want?"

"But I don't dare want *all* of that, Mr. Carhart. It's impossible."

Ned glanced at his nails, as if in boredom. "A minor detail," he announced airily. "My wife has been performing the impossible for years, and this time around, she has me to help her. We'll find out how to get you much of that. It might take some time, but we'll manage it."

Oh, he was impossible himself. Impossibly attractive—and impossibly heartwarming, to say such things of her.

"The first step," she said, "is to keep you safe. And to that end, we need to distract Harcroft. We'll need to direct his attention elsewhere."

Ned nodded. "We should let him think we're desperate. That we'll make mistakes. That we're running off somewhere—perhaps rushing to your side." He looked over at Kate. "What say you to going to London? I have some unfinished business there in any event."

"And what am I to do there?" Kate asked.

Ned gave her a slow grin. *"We,"* he said with emphasis, "are going to drive Harcroft mad."

As they walked back to the house, Ned felt Kate's eyes on him. His little story had undoubtedly piqued her curiosity. Unfortunately. She'd not been distracted by her own worries the way Louisa had, and no doubt she'd noticed that there were holes in his tale.

"That," she finally said, "was very brave of you. To

take your embarrassment and use it to make Louisa feel comfortable."

"Hmm," Ned said, looking away. "More like foolhardiness."

"You told us that story with such a smile on your face, as if it were all some sort of joke. But I get the impression there was more to it than you disclosed. What really happened?"

"It was basically as I laid it out." Precisely as he'd said, except so much more.

By the small puff of air she expelled, she knew it, too.

"Oh, very well. If you must know." He rubbed one hand against his wrist. "I left out this—they didn't just throw me in the sump. They bound me, wrists and ankles, and blindfolded me. I didn't know where we were going, what they had planned. When they threw me into what was essentially a lake of human waste, I had no notion what was coming. The liquid closed over my head, and trussed up as I was, I couldn't swim. I couldn't do much more than wriggle futilely." He'd woken up for months afterward, with that memory of bonds cutting his flesh. Thankfully, his mind seemed to have expelled the worst of the memory.

"How did they dare?" She looked at him in shock. "How did you escape?"

"They'd tied a rope to my feet. After about a minute, they just dragged me out, and I came, flopping like a fish. They intended to humiliate me, not hurt me. I have never felt so helpless in my life."

She was looking at him with something akin to pity. Christ. He didn't want her to feel *sorry* for him.

"Don't look at me like that." The words came out rather more sharply than he'd intended. "It was quite possibly the best thing that could have happened to me. I spent a great deal of time out on the ocean, in that boat. Under that sun. It didn't just burn away my skin. It burned away my most timid parts. I needed to look that part of myself in the eye and reject it. The experience built substance."

More than he would ever tell her. She didn't need to know precisely *how* weak he'd been at the time—and how close he'd come to crumpling. All she needed to know was that he'd survived.

"What sort of substance?" she asked.

"The sort that brought me home to you," he replied shortly. "The sort that made me brave enough to venture into naval battles and opium dens alike."

"The kind that made you sleep in bitter cold?" she asked.

He nodded, jerkily, and she subsided into a frown.

He had no wish to tell her the entirety of what had transpired out there on the lake. She didn't need to know how close he'd come, how *dark* that final darkness had truly been. She'd seen enough for her to understand what had happened to him without understanding precisely what sort of person it had happened to.

He'd tamed his dragon. He wouldn't leave Kate. And that was all she needed to know.

CHAPTER EIGHTEEN

SOME THINGS truly hadn't changed in the years since Ned had left London. One of those things was the dimly lit gaming hall that stood in a disreputable portion of town. From the doorway, Ned could hear the crack of dice bouncing on green baize. Smoke permeated the air of the room, so thick he could imagine it spilling out into the night air and meeting the fog bank in a swirl of cloud.

He'd spent much of the day traveling back to town, but this particular encounter with the gaming tables could not be put off.

His quarry—five fellows who no doubt called themselves *gentlemen*—sat in a corner, clutching cards. They might well have been playing loo again. The only thing that had changed in the intervening years was that while Ned had been growing muscle, his erstwhile friends had gone to fat.

Any other man in his position might have challenged them to a duel. But there was little honor in slaying a quintet of oversize drunkards, and besides, Ned's method of dealing with the problem promised to be more amusing. Real heroes, after all, tamed their dragons.

Ned stepped into the room. As he made his way around tables littered with jugs of cheap wine, he fingered the silky bit of fabric he'd purloined earlier. They didn't see him approach, so caught up were they in their game. They didn't even catch his shadow—multifaceted, from the many lamps—falling across their table.

It *was* loo, and by the pile of papers on the table, play was deep.

Once, Ned had been as oblivious as these men. He had been so desperate to drown his past in spirits that he had tried to wager away his future on the deal of a card. Thank God he had stopped.

Lord Ellison—a onetime friend of his—crowed in triumph as he laid his final card. "I win!" he gloated. The others murmured congratulations. Another man shook his head in disgust—and then stopped, seeing Ned. He peered at him through eyes made bleary with spirits.

"Carhart?" Alfred Dennis asked slowly. "Is that you? I heard you had returned." He blinked a few times, as if trying to make sense of Ned's appearance. One rusty mental process must not have been entirely dissolved in alcohol, because he brightened. "I say, are you joining us?"

He reached for a chair and made an attempt to pull it up to the table.

"Come on, Carhart!" Ellison said. "It's been ages since we last had a good time together. You're feeling up for a little wager, aren't you?"

Neither seemed to have the tiniest inkling that they might have done something wrong. Another reason Ned couldn't duel them: It would be like slaying pond slime. Algae never understood when it gave offense.

Ned straddled the chair. "Actually," he said, "I'm here to collect on a wager."

"Which one?" Ellison asked. "Dennis—no, Port-Morton, you can still stand. Fetch the book."

One of the men from the back began to heave to his feet on wavering legs.

"No need," Ned said. "This wager is quite famous." Ned set the fabric he'd been carrying on the table. It was a fine specimen of work—roses embroidered on pink silk with satin ties.

"Carhart," Dennis said, "is that a *garter* you laid on the table?"

The five men stared at him, lips pursed together in identical expressions of dismay. No, not identical; they turned different colors, ranging from a pale green—that was Port-Morton—to Ellison's bright red.

"That's the wager," Ned said equably. "Any man who seduces Lady Kathleen Carhart and delivers an undergarment as proof collects five thousand pounds."

Dennis stared at the embroidered cloth. He stared at it for ten full seconds, in dull incomprehension. Finally, he looked up, his eyebrows a mass of confusion. "Carhart," the man finally said, "you can't seduce your own wife."

Ned raised one eyebrow. "Oh? I'm dreadfully sorry to hear that, Dennis. How *difficult* that must be for you. I would say it was not very hard…but then, given your admission, perhaps that's the problem, eh?" Ned shrugged apologetically. "You might be doing it wrong. There are physicians who can help with that, you realize."

Even pond scum recognized when its masculinity was challenged. In fact, it was probably the *only* thing pond scum recognized. Dennis flushed and shook his head.

"I have no notion what you're talking about. No need for physicians here." The man hunched, though, as if to protect his groin. "I suppose a man could seduce anyone's wife. Including his own. All I meant was, it's no *fun* if *you* do it."

"No fun?" Ned shook his head ruefully. "You are *definitely* doing it wrong."

Catcalls rose up at that, and Dennis turned an even brighter red.

"You don't *need* five thousand pounds, Carhart," Port-Morton put in. "What are you going to do with it, anyway?"

Ned shrugged. "I don't know. Likely I'll buy my wife something pretty."

"Jewels?" Ellison asked. "As if she were a *mistress?* Good God, Carhart. What a waste. What a phenomenal waste."

"Ellison," Ned said, "I hate to repeat myself—but you are probably doing it wrong, too. And that, gentlemen, is why you all lost. And why, after three years away, I still won. Close the book on this one. The wager's over and done."

They stared up at him still, their eyes wide and unbelieving.

Ned let the smile on his face widen, and he leaned in. "Close the books, or next time it will cost you all a great deal more than money."

Ellison shook his head, stupid to the end, and gestured next to him. "At least play a hand, give us a chance to win it back."

Ned shook his head. "I have my wife to get home to."

LONDON HAD BEEN a dizzying mixture of good and bad and confusing for Kate. The gossip about she and her husband had run high the first few days they had arrived, in no small part due to some stunt Ned had pulled at a gaming hell. But the discussion had been romantic—and it had served only to carry tales of how they spent their time to Harcroft's ears. And oh, how those tales must have confused him. All of society was talking about how the couple had inquired into passage to France, particularly departing from Dover. Mr. Carhart had then shown a less than subtle interest in minute happenings in Ipswich.

There had been a hundred misdirections.

After the third day of it, Kate's head pounded. After the fourth day, her entire body ached. Today, a week after they had begun their campaign of confusion, she had seen Harcroft for the first time. He had been in attendance at a party last evening. He'd seen Kate—and had glowered at her across the crowded room before turning away with a smirk.

Smirks, of course, were Harcroft's peculiar speciality. If self-satisfied expressions had been coins, Harcroft would have generated enough currency to personally sustain the commerce of the entirety of the kingdom of Sardinia. One more shouldn't have mattered. But this one had got under Kate's skin. It stayed there, after she and Ned had left the glittering lights of the party behind them. She felt that unease even more now, the back-and-forth swaying of the carriage buffeting her to the point of nausea.

"He's planning something," she said aloud.

She didn't need to say who *he* was. Next to her, Ned

was a warm, solid mass. Their carriage rounded a corner and she lurched against him. He didn't move, as if he were somehow strong enough to be immune to the effects of inertia.

"He's started a proceeding in Chancery," Ned said. "He has been quite secretive about it, of course. But I've managed to dredge up a few pieces of information. That, coupled with some comments he made to me when he believed I was in sympathy with him…" Ned sighed; she felt it in the movement of his chest against her shoulder, and she stared ahead into the darkness.

"Well, what does he intend?"

"This is speculation, mind. These sorts of proceedings are usually kept in the strictest of confidence. For reasons that will soon be obvious."

"What is it, then?"

"I believe he's filed a petition in Chancery to have Louisa declared a lunatic." Kate gasped. "He said something about this to me before. At the time, I dismissed it as a token of his emotional overset. If his petition is successful, she won't be able to testify—not for a divorce, nor in a criminal suit for spousal cruelty."

Kate felt a chill creep into her, something colder even than the oncoming winter. "He means to flush her out, like a partridge. She'll have to come to Chancery just to testify on her own behalf. If she doesn't…"

"She'll be held incompetent." Ned set his hand on her knee. "Incompetents have no freedom. He'll be able to lock her up. Any measures he takes after that, however stringent, will be seen as attempts to cure—or at least subdue—her mental infirmity. If he is made a trustee over her in lunacy, he'll have even more control over her than a husband has over a wife."

Kate put her fingers to her temples. "He's tired of chasing down our little leads, and so he's begun to attack instead. Well. That makes our course of action clear."

"We need to communicate with Lady Harcroft, and ascertain her wishes," Ned said.

"That." Kate tapped her fingers to her temples. "And we might consider a little bit of an attack ourselves. I think we should talk to Chancery about his claim of lunacy." She smiled, tightly. "Testify on Louisa's behalf. And perhaps, I think, we should give the Chancellor some other petitions to consider."

"Harcroft has some other plan, too," Ned said. "I haven't determined what it is yet, but don't you worry. I'll keep you safe—you and Lady Harcroft both."

She nodded solemnly. "And who shall look out for you?"

He snorted, half amusement, half appalled consternation. "I didn't realize I needed someone to look out for me."

The Earl of Harcroft had proved vengeful, spiteful and not above using violence to get his way. Kate didn't imagine the man spared much love for Ned—not after Ned had hurled him bodily across the hall.

"Of course you do." Her hand slipped to his knee.

She had not realized that the knee could tense so. Yet his did, lifting underneath her hand as if he were unconsciously flexing his feet at her words. His breathing stopped.

"I'm not going to be a burden to you," he growled out.

"A burden? Who said you would be a burden? I just want to help you."

"I don't want to be helped. I don't *need* to be helped." She could imagine the stubborn set of his chin as he spoke.

Slowly Kate pulled her hand away. She swallowed back the hurt that encompassed her. She'd thought he was different—that he saw beyond the delicacy of her appearance. That he saw her as strong enough to be trusted.

But of course. He'd taken her a week before, but since that first evening, he'd not spent the night with her again. Instead, he'd made his bed alone in that murderous cold. It was a silent way of pushing her away. He liked her well enough for a few hours, but not enough to trust with his secrets. Not even with something so simple as his sleep.

He took her hand. "No. This is not about you. You have to understand."

But rather than explaining, he stopped again. Kate waited, wishing for patience.

He let out a breath. "You're so *strong*. You can't imagine."

She wanted to pull away from him, wanted to curl about the hurt in herself. Instead, she drew in another measured breath. "I can try."

He blew out a breath and shifted uncomfortably. "Sometimes—this *thing* happens to me." He seemed to think that description adequate, because he sat slouched in the carriage next to her.

Heaven save her from uncommunicative men. "*Thing* is not a very specific word," she prodded.

"It's not a very specific…*thing*, you understand. I've never found words for it. It's not exactly like madness, you see."

She hadn't really been expecting him to answer—just to provide more obfuscation. But what he'd said well and truly shocked her into silence. If it wasn't *exactly* like madness, how close did it come? His elbow jostled her, and she realized he'd removed his hat from his head and held it against his chest.

"I asked a physician," he told his hat. "And so I know that much. It's not madness. It's madness if you can't control what you do or say, or if you're unaware of reality. I'm always aware of reality, when it happens. And I'm entirely in control of my own actions. All the time. I can do whatever I want."

What he wanted was to sleep in the freezing cold, shutting her out.

"I can do whatever I want," Ned repeated slowly. "I just… Sometimes I don't want."

"What don't you want?" The carriage turned; as it did, Kate pressed full against him again.

She felt the shrug of his shoulders. "When it starts, I don't even want to get up in the morning. When I was nineteen, it came for the first time. I stayed in bed for weeks. My mother thought I was ill, but the physician could find nothing wrong with me. I just didn't want to get up."

"That doesn't sound like a *thing*."

"It's easier if I think about it as something separate. The alternative is that *I* am that thing. That every few years, *I* wake up one morning and I decide to act as if

I'm a different person. No, Kate. I'd rather think of those times as if they were a brief, bitter winter. As if it were something outside me. I can't explain it, except to say that I'm not mad and you shouldn't ever have to worry about it."

"Not *worry* about it? But—"

He raised his gloved hand to cover her lips. "No. Don't make me into some sort of wounded creature, one that you need to tend to wellness. There's nothing to heal here, Kate, no dragon for you to slay. There's nothing but a beast that I've already managed to tame. It raises its head occasionally. In the past, it tried to defeat me. But it won't. Not ever again. I don't need help. I don't *like* help—it makes me want to do even less."

"But—"

"It's *nothing*." His hand hit the side of the carriage for emphasis, and the carriage rumbled to a stop. It took Kate a few moments to realize they were stopping not because of that ill-timed rap, but because the carriage had arrived at their London townhome.

Ned reached over and grasped the door handle, holding it in place to preserve that brief space of privacy. The door rattled, and then, as the servants realized it had been blocked from the inside, stood still.

"You don't have to worry," he repeated. "I don't stay in bed any longer, when it comes. I'm prepared for it now. I practice for those mornings when I can't bear to get up, because I know they'll come again. I practice by doing things I don't want to do."

"Such as…"

"Such as running three miles in the morning, and

when I don't think I can possibly manage it, running three more. Like sleeping with the windows open, without a fire." He met her gaze. "Occasionally, abstaining from intercourse when I desperately desire you. I make myself strong enough so that those times don't matter."

"That seems…" Kate trailed off, groping for a word. Odd? Inexplicable? Extremely cold? Nothing seemed to fit, and so she raised her chin. "That seems like something you should have told me about."

She could have helped. She could have done something. The inkling of a plan started to assert itself.

In answer, he let go of the latch and pushed the door open. A footman greeted them; Ned turned his head, and like that, his tension disappeared into a wicked grin.

"Well," he said flippantly, "I have much more fun making you laugh. Don't you think?"

He stepped down; she stared out the doorway of the carriage in disbelief. He hadn't—he really *couldn't* have packed away the conversation as if it hadn't happened. Kate stood so rapidly, she almost struck her head against the roof of the carriage. "Ned, you—you…"

Her words sputtered out into cold silence. Exhaling, she gathered her skirts and stumbled to the door of the carriage. But he hadn't left her; he'd taken the footman's place, and as she stood at the edge of the steps, he held out his hand to help her alight. His fingers were warm, even through both their gloves.

"I'm *good* at jokes," he said to her, his voice so quiet she strained to hear it even above the velvet silence of the night. "When we married, I was excellent at playing the buffoon. After all, it's better to have your sins chalked up to tomfoolery than it is to have everyone realize that you occasionally succumb to this cloying thing that is not quite madness." He grinned again, and that expression was so at odds with the seriousness of his tone that Kate shook her head.

His arm came about her as they walked up the steps.

"But—"

"I didn't tell you, Kate, because I didn't want you to know. I won't have you looking at me and seeing weakness. I don't need anyone to feed me gruel and wipe my chin. Besides, the more people know, the more real it seems."

The last seemed like such a superstitious thing to say. Kate frowned at her husband. But he wasn't looking at her. Instead, he swept through the front door, as if he could guide the conversation as easily as if he were leading her about a dance floor. He was shunting her aside again. It was a different sort of abandonment, compared with traipsing off to China, but it was an abandonment nonetheless. It was a denial of what their marriage could be, of what *she* could be to *him,* if only he would let her.

If he thought she could not even hear the truth, he didn't really trust her at all.

Kate locked her knees and braced her slippers against the floor, and he stopped.

"No." Bare denial was all she had.

A second footman paused behind her, in the act of reaching for her wraps.

"My lady?" A hint of bewilderment touched his voice.

"No," Kate repeated, her tone subdued, "we won't be needing your services any longer tonight."

Ned didn't contradict her. Instead, he leaned against the drawing room door and watched as the footmen departed. After they were alone, he pushed off the wall and wandered into the parlor. A low fire flickered in the grate, but gave off barely a glow. Ned made no move to take a candelabra with him, or to light the oil lamps.

It would be a mistake to think he was pushing her away. No; he was holding her as close as he dared. But she wanted him to dare more. Kate held her breath and waited.

He seemed nothing but a silhouette to her, his back lit by the gleaming lamp in the hall beyond. She almost couldn't fit his features to the shape of his profile; the sharp line of his nose, the stubborn jut of his chin. The silence seemed smoky with possibility.

"Well?" he finally said. "I thought you wanted to pose some questions. Is there anything you should like to know?"

"I thought you didn't want to answer me."

"I don't." His breath hissed out, a faint approximation of a chuckle. "So I'll do it. Lovely how that works, isn't it?"

There were a thousand things she might have asked him. When did this "thing" come? How had it started? Was there anything to be done about it, besides accept his suffering? But in the darkness and the silence, nothing mattered except one small detail.

"Will you not let me help because you think I'm not

capable of it? Because you think I'll break if you lean on me?"

He shook his head. "Kate," he said quietly, "you are the most indomitable woman I know."

"Don't lie to me."

"Really. If you were tossed in a den of lions, you would order them to sweep the bones of the lambs they'd devoured for breakfast out into the refuse pile—and they would not dare disobey. If you were abandoned in a wilderness, you'd rebuild ancient Rome, from the humblest fountain to all its marble halls. And you'd do it using your bare hands, and perhaps a pocketknife for assistance."

"I have no interest in being left in the wilderness, Ned. If I'm as capable as you keep saying, why don't you trust me to help?"

For a moment, he didn't respond. And now the silence preyed upon her, resurrecting old doubts, older hurts.

He'd been lying. All those fine words about lions and Rome and indomitability—they'd been tales, spun to comfort her.

Kate didn't want comfort, and she didn't particularly care for lies. Not now.

"Ah," he finally said in tones of amusement. "I suppose...I suppose that some of it is what jealousy looks like."

"Jealousy?"

"I told you men were beasts. Do you want to know how unworthy I really am?" He turned to her quietly; she took a step back. Her backside hit a sharp edge—her hands splayed out behind her onto polished wood. She'd bumped a table, just above her hips in height.

"Jealousy? But—"

He straightened and moved toward her. She could not see his features, but his shoulders were held rigidly as he walked. He seemed a tall blaze of smoldering emotion. And he was coming closer. She swallowed.

"Calm and control come so easily to you. Even when you're most upset, you're always in control." Those words, from another man, might have sounded harsh and embittered. From Ned, they felt like a caress.

Kate leaned back against the table. It wiggled lightly, and she heard some ceramic object—a vase set upon it, perhaps—rock, but there was no escape from his intensity. She folded her arms about herself, but the gesture offered scant protection.

"I'm jealous," he continued, "of the way that you let nothing stop you—not fear, not even marauding, brutish husbands. If *you'd* found yourself bebothered by some odd *thing,* you'd never stay in bed. You would face it calmly and matter-of-factly, and then simply vanquish it with a shake of your head. If *you* wanted to prove yourself, you'd never have run off to China to do it." His fingers brushed her cheek.

He was towering over her now, the heat of his thighs radiating into her legs.

"I'm jealous," he whispered, "of every breath that enters your lungs through your lips." He was so close, she could almost taste his words, wafting to her on the wind. "It's utterly unfair that you should be so self-possessed, when I am desperate to possess you for my own."

Kate's breath sucked in. "That… Actually, that can be arranged."

He set his hands on her hips. "How many petticoats are you wearing tonight?"

"Five."

He leaned down to her. "I hate them all." He held her, his hands clamped about her waist, his body canting over hers.

"Take them off," she suggested.

His fingers cut into her flesh through all five of her hated, useless petticoats. Then he lifted her a few inches into the air and deposited her atop the polished table behind her. It creaked as she settled onto it, but subsided into silence. "No," he said. "It would take too long. I'll get used to the jealousy."

He pressed against her, his body hard and demanding. He parted her legs, his hands sliding up to her knees. She felt a momentary breeze against her thighs—and then he stepped into that space. His fingers slipped upward. She couldn't see his hands to anticipate where they would fall. The touch on her thigh came as a tickling surprise. He leaned down and nuzzled her ear. Oh, yes, the ear; sensation blossomed and she let him possess her.

How long they stood there, his hand caressing her leg beneath her skirts, his lips nibbling the curve of her ear, she did not know. But when his hand slipped up her leg, he found the slickness of her desire. He slid across her sensitive flesh. *Yes. Touch me there.* Kate bit back a shaky moan; he let out a shuddering breath.

She reached up for a taste of him. Her skin ached to brush against his; her mouth found his in the dark. That long kiss transformed into a fumble, his hands against hers, racing to undo the buttons of his breeches. He leaned over her, adjusting her legs—and then he filled her, thick and hot.

She stretched around him. This wasn't self-possession; it wasn't any sort of possession at all. Instead, it was an admission, a deep-seated requirement, as if the circling of his hips had become as necessary as breath.

He rocked into her, slowly, steadily. The table creaked under her weight and his thrusts. He kissed her throat, up to her chin. His kisses came in time with each thrust. His breath was on her lips, as if she were his air; his tongue met hers, as if she were the only taste he desired.

He was holding himself back from release; she could feel it in the tensing muscles of his shoulder through his coat, in the exquisite control as he took her. Beads of sweat slid down his face. She could feel what waited in the burn of her own body, in the delicious coiling of pleasure in her center. She lifted her hips to his, and pleasure enveloped her, starting in her slippered toes and thundering through her as relentlessly as an autumn squall.

His thrusts came harder, filling her with sweetness as she reached for ecstasy. Her world shuddered; a great crashing noise sounded in climax.

And then he grasped her hips. He didn't cry out, didn't so much as let a moan escape him. The only evidence of his passing pleasure was the clutch of his hands on her.

After what he'd done to her—in the drawing room, with the hallway wide open for anyone to see, she realized—his own release seemed curiously restrained. And she realized as he pulled away, adjusting his clothing, it *had* been restrained. Because for all Ned's talk of self-possession, *he* had been the one to possess her. He'd been the one to give her pleasure. And even in the throes of ecstasy, he'd maintained control.

Ah, she thought dazedly, *I am the one who is jealous.* She wanted all of him, without reservation. But that greedy urge passed as the pounding of her blood faded. For a long while they stared at each other, breathing heavily. Then he took a step—an oddly crunching step—and swore.

"Damn," he said quietly. "Whose brilliant idea was it to decorate these tables—these lovely tables, set at such a perfect height—with vases?"

Kate glanced down in confusion. It took her a moment to understand what those tiny shards were, glinting in the dim light. That final crashing noise she had heard as she reached ecstasy had not been a product of her fevered imagination.

She couldn't help herself. Despite the unquiet misgivings inside her, she started laughing. She pulled Ned close and buried her face in his shirt. He was sweating; so was she. It was a warm autumn evening; she was still wearing those five hated petticoats, and his heart thumped in rapid time with her own, through every layer of their clothing. His hand patted the damp hair on her head.

"Next time," she said, "remove the petticoats. Please."

She could feel his cheek press into a smile next to hers.

It wasn't possession. It was still some damnable form of inequity, where she let him have all of her, and he held himself back. She could cry about it. She could accuse him of poor sportsmanship.

But what good would that do? She'd take what she could get, and fight for the rest as best she could.

She let out a long breath, exhaling her fears away. "With glass strewn underfoot, I see we have only one option."

"Oh?"

It hurt to smile, but she did it anyway. His arm snaked around her waist.

"Have you seen how thin my slippers are?" she whispered in his ear. "With all this danger about, you'll have to carry me to bed."

CHAPTER NINETEEN

BY THE NEXT AFTERNOON, the glass had long been swept away. But as Kate left her house, she felt a chill prickle up her neck, as if danger itself were still present. She had one silk-slippered foot upon the carriage steps, one kid-gloved hand on her footman's shoulder.

There was a man standing on the pavement, not three yards behind her. He was dressed in the blue uniform of a metropolitan police officer; the cuffs of his jacket were frayed at the edges. He watched her, and as she halted, he walked toward her.

"Are you Mrs. Carhart?" he asked. As he spoke, he shifted his truncheon from one hand to the other. He didn't look as if he planned to use it. His gaze dropped down her form—not in sexual interest, but in wariness.

Kate turned from the carriage that awaited her. She drew herself up to her full height—which, compared to the man who approached her, seemed nowhere near full enough. Still, in her experience, officers and servants alike were more likely to speak with respect if they knew precisely with whom they were speaking. Short as she was, the yards of lace at the hem of her gown would make the man think twice. Lace was dear; more importantly, it was a symbol that she was the sort of woman who could purchase such a thing and wear it, even on something so mundane as a morning call. Police officers did not often mix with ladies.

"Officer," she said sternly, "I am more properly addressed as—"

"Yes or no will do, ma'am."

Kate touched the pearls at her neck. "Yes, but I am La—"

He interrupted her again before she could finish.

"Well, then. I have a warrant sworn out for your arrest, and you're to come with me."

All those yards of lace stopped feeling like armor. Instead, she felt nakedly vulnerable. "My arrest?" No. She wasn't going to flutter like a useless sparrow. She balled her fists. "See here, Officer." She glanced at his jacket collar, where his designation was marked. "Officer 12-Q, what do you mean by ordering my arrest?"

Officer 12-Q took another step forward. "Didn't," he explained. "The warrant's signed by Magistrate Fang. I don't order anything—I just execute it. If you'll excuse the witticism."

She stared at him blankly.

"I just execute it," he repeated. "*Execute*. See? Heh. Heh." Despite that odd chuckle, Officer 12-Q had not even broached a smile yet.

Kate let her blank stare take on a chilly component.

"I suppose," the officer allowed slowly, "it would be less amusing to you, what with your having to stand trial and all."

"Stand trial! On what charges? And when?"

The man came forward, and Kate stepped backward. Beside her, her footman winced. No doubt he was trying to figure out precisely how far his loyalty to his employer stretched.

"Oh, come," 12-Q was saying. "Fine lady like you doesn't want to resist the metropolitan police. As for when—right now. Why do you suppose I was sent to fetch you? Justice waits for no man. Or woman. Particularly not when justice is administered by Magistrate Fang. He doesn't like staying after his time."

"But I have an appointment to take tea." Kate set one foot in the carriage, and her footman backed away from her slightly. Her voice was significantly steadier than her nerves. "Are you intimating that instead, I must undertake a tedious journey to—to—"

"The police court at Queen Square, ma'am." He fingered his collar. "It's what the Q stands for."

"So I must travel to Queen Square, hear a set of trumped-up charges and stand trial? But I shall be quite late. I pride myself on my punctuality."

Officer 12-Q shrugged and reached for her arm. "If you plead guilty first, there's no need to stand for trial. Trial's only if you wish to establish your innocence." His hand closed around her elbow—firm, but not harsh.

Kate glared at him. "Thank you. That is most helpful."

"Of course," he continued, "six months in gaol will likely delay your arrival, as well."

"Six months!" Kate was no longer even able to pretend at equanimity. "You must be joking. What on earth are they charging me with?"

A ghost of a smile played across 12-Q's face. "Fang tends toward lenience with women, he does. Six months is if he's feeling kind—and given the lord who brought the charge, he's unlike to do so."

Of course it was Harcroft. She had guessed it from the first. But what would he claim she had done? It could have been anything from theft to murder. At the least, she had the luxury of knowing that whatever it was he claimed she did, she was innocent. Now all she had to do was prove it.

She turned to the footman, who gave her a pained shake of the head, one she translated as *I like my wages very well, but not enough to leap upon an officer of the police force. Please do not expect it.* She sighed.

"You need to fetch my husband," she said. "He's off at Chancery. Tell him I've been brought to Queen Square. And that I need him. *Now.*"

The officer yawned at this interplay and shrugged as the footman turned and dashed away. "Will you come now, or must I bind you and carry you down the street?"

Kate raised her chin and went.

NED CHARGED INTO THE STUFFY ROOM where the police court was held.

He'd convinced himself, on the mad dash over to Queen Square, that the footman's garbled tale held little relation to the truth. If Kate had been required to make her way into the somber, grubby office lodged in Westminster, surely it was because she had been set upon by some cutpurse. She was there to testify, and nothing more—

But no. As he entered, a sergeant of the police stretched his arm out and grabbed Ned's wrist. He gave a little twist as he did so—some police trick—and Ned stumbled, one knee stiking the ground, his arm wrenching.

The officer was one of only a few occupants—a red-faced drunkard lay snoring across one bench, a woman and her children, all clad in matching shades of brown, took up another. A handful of officers, all in uniform blue, waited. If Ned had wanted, he might have picked out individual scents: five different bouquets of unwashedness. He didn't want, and so he held his breath and looked forward.

Kate stood at the front of the room, beautiful, her hair slightly disheveled. She held her head high. He couldn't see her face; instead, she was looking at the magistrate. The man sat—if you could call that disreputable slouch "sitting"—in a rumpled coat and trousers, his sole nod to respectability being a white powdered wig that lay somewhat askew on his head.

Directly across from her, standing just before the bench, was the Earl of Harcroft.

Harcroft had engineered this, then. Ned had known he had some other plan. He just hadn't expected to find his wife charged with some crime before a magistrate.

Kate tossed her head, and something about that ungraceful movement drew Ned's eyes to her hands. Her wrists were bound.

"What have you to say to the charges?" the magistrate asked. By his tone of voice, he was bored with the proceedings already.

"I can have little to say, Your Worship, seeing as how I haven't heard them." Kate's voice was strong—as always, she betrayed no weakness.

"Haven't heard them?" The magistrate looked puzzled. "But how can that be?"

"You haven't read them to me, Your Worship."

The magistrate cast Kate a baleful look, as if it were somehow her fault that his court had to pause for such futile things as the reading of charges. In an elaborate gesture, the man swooped a pair of spectacles off the bench and balanced them on his nose. He held a piece of paper in front of him at arm's length. "There," he said. "Abduction."

He ripped the glasses off and peered at Kate again. "*Now* what have you to say to the charges?"

"Abduction of whom, Your Worship?"

A longer pause, and the magistrate's lips thinned. "I am accustomed," he said in a commanding voice, "to people knowing with whom they have absconded." He glared at Kate.

She shrugged her shoulders helplessly.

Slowly, he picked up his spectacles, and once again set them on the bridge of his nose. He read the paper more carefully. "Ah, yes. I recall now. Abduction of this fine lord's wife." Off came the glasses again. But instead of glaring at Kate, he glanced at Harcroft.

"How odd," he said. "Abduction of a wife? By another woman? I have only ever seen the case brought against other men." He glanced back at Kate.

"But there is nothing in the law preventing its application to a woman, is there?" Harcroft spoke for the first time, his voice soothing. "You heard the evidence for the warrant, Your Worship. Must I repeat it all now, or can we dispense with the formalities?"

"He claimed to have evidence that I forcibly abducted his wife?" Kate said. "He's lying."

"Abduction by persuasion, at a minimum." Harcroft didn't look at Kate as he spoke. "A wife, of course, has no power to consent to leave her husband without his permission."

Ned looked down at the hand still restraining him, and then slowly, gingerly, he pulled his sleeve from the sergeant's grasp. He'd never given it much thought, but what Harcroft said was likely true. And if that was the case…Harcroft might in fact have hit on a crime Kate had actually committed.

"Wait!" Ned called from the back. "I'm her husband!"

The magistrate took Ned in. He gave him one long, pitying look, and then shook his head in dismissal. He turned back to Kate. "Well? Did you do it?"

"How can you even charge her?" Ned demanded. "She's my wife. Whatever she's done—whatever you *think* she's done—should I not be charged with responsibility for it, as her husband?"

The judge fixed Ned with a pointed stare.

"That is, I should be charged with responsibility, Your Worship," Ned appended belatedly.

"Mr. Carhart, I presume," the magistrate said. "This is not the proper way to present an argument to the bench." He looked around the room. "Having heard the evidence in this case, I hereby find that—"

"Your Worship," Ned said, "which of these individuals—" he spread his arm to encompass the courtroom stuffed with sorry specimens of humanity "—is sitting on the jury?"

"Jury?" The magistrate frowned. "Jury? There isn't time this afternoon for a trial by jury." He glared at Kate. "You didn't say you wanted a jury. In fact, you can't have one. Not unless the amount involved is over forty shillings."

"The Countess of Harcroft is likely worth more," Ned said. "Your Worship."

Harcroft glanced at him through slitted eyes, but did not contradict.

The magistrate sighed and set his glasses back on his nose, looking at Ned in the back of the room. "You appear to be a gentleman."

"I *am* a gentleman. I'm the heir presumptive to the Marquess of Blakely."

A crease formed in the magistrate's brow, and he peered once at Harcroft. "But you said—that is, I thought Mrs. Carhart—"

"My wife is *Lady* Kathleen Carhart. The prosecutor did disclose that she is the Duke of Ware's daughter, did he not? This is not a suit that you can dispose of in such a summary fashion."

As Ned spoke, the magistrate looked to Harcroft again, his lips thinning. Ned could imagine how this particular case had evolved. Harcroft had indeed tried to take the upper hand. No doubt he'd impressed the judge with his title. Perhaps he'd even attempted to purchase the outcome with a few well-placed bank notes. But even the most corrupt magistrate would balk at sending a duke's daughter to gaol for money.

Under Ned's scrutiny, this particular magistrate straightened his wig and shuffled the papers on his bench. "Perhaps a fine," he said to Harcroft. "You'll be satisfied with a fine—a few shillings?"

"The Countess of Harcroft," the earl said, with a cutting look at Ned, "is worth a great deal more than a few shillings. That woman has my wife. I want her back. No, Your Worship—I must insist on pressing charges. Trial will proceed."

The magistrate pressed his hand to his forehead for a few seconds before he spoke. "This court," he muttered, "has decided to reject the first argument put forward by Mr. Carhart. The accused in this case must remain Mrs.— that is, *Lady* Kathleen Carhart."

His Worship, Ned thought grimly, was hiding his guilt behind an excess of formality.

"On what grounds, Your Worship?"

"By the evidence I have heard, the events in question occurred when you were absent from the country. We no longer live in times so benighted that we imagine a husband is responsible for everything a wife does. You are free of indictment."

"I don't want to be free," Ned protested. "In fact, I want you to let her go and charge me instead."

"Facts, Mr. Carhart, are facts. Wants are wants. The law does not allow me to substitute one for the other, no matter how keen the wanting might be." The magistrate drew himself up as he spoke. *Law* hadn't seemed to matter much to him before he discovered that Kate was the daughter of a duke. "Mr. Carhart also suggested that Lady Kathleen be tried by jury."

Harcroft smiled at Ned. "I am perfectly happy to put the evidence I've obtained before a jury," he said with an aggressive lift of his chin. "I should love to have one sworn in, right at this instant."

"Right now?" The magistrate looked vaguely ill. "But it is almost three in the afternoon."

"What has that to do with anything?" Harcroft demanded.

"This court closes at three." The magistrate glanced at Harcroft, astounded. "We don't stay after hours, my lord. Not—not for anything."

Harcroft stared ahead, his jaw working. "Very well. Toss her in the cells. We'll finish this in the morning."

"The cells!" Kate said.

"Lady Kathleen," Ned said quietly, "will not be seeing the inside of the cells. Surely Your Worship recognizes that a gentleman such as myself can be trusted to return her for trial tomorrow." He stared the magistrate full in the eyes, letting his threat sink in. If a duke and a marquess were to turn their attention on a puny little police magistrate, the man would be stripped of his seat on the bench before he had a chance to pronounce sentence.

"Ah. Yes." The magistrate glanced warily from Ned to Harcroft, and licked his lips.

An earl could cost him his seat, as well. Ned would have felt sorry for the magistrate, except that he'd agreed to go along with this travesty in the first place.

"I release the prisoner into her husband's care for tomorrow's trial," the man finally said. "We'll start at eleven. Sharp."

NED FELT HOLLOW ON THE carriage ride home. He'd known Harcroft was planning something. He just hadn't guessed *what*. He should have known. He should have done something. But now Kate was threatened, and all his fine plans to prove himself tangled up in his mind.

"Are you sure," Kate asked dryly, seated across from him, "that we can't just slay this dragon?"

"Ha." Ned shook his head wistfully. "I think there are a handful of swords somewhere in Gareth's home. Maybe stored in the attic?"

It was an enchanting thought, that—sneaking into Harcroft's house in the dark of night, swathed in a black cloak, sword in hand. With nobody to prosecute the case on the morrow, Kate would be sent home.

It would be lovely, up until the moment when Harcroft was discovered dead in his home. At which point the municipal police wouldn't need to look far to discover a person who had both an interest in his demise, and an inconvenient bloody sword wrapped in a black cloak.

As if Kate knew the path down which his thoughts had drifted, as if she'd trodden silently down the hallway of his imagination, sword in hand, she sighed. "Drat." The carriage rolled up to the house and she shook her head as the door opened.

She disappeared into the night, and Ned stared after her. She'd meant the crack about dragons as a joke, as a way to defuse the tense, despairing energy that ran between them. But to him, it felt like more. Dragon or no, she was in need of a hero. And lo, here sat Ned, in the carriage still. He fought the urge to rush into the servants' quarters in search of long kitchen knives. Some knight he made.

Damn it.

As names went, "Harcroft" didn't even have a particularly villainous ring to it. It sounded respectable. Stodgy, even. And the threat—imprisonment—wasn't even the sort of thing that could be slain. Not by typically heroic means. The heroes in the stories had it *easy*. A week ago Ned had been trying to figure out how to win Louisa's freedom. Now he was fighting for his wife's. His entire quest had started off-kilter, and it had only skewed with the passage of time.

Ned pushed himself out of the carriage. "You know," he said, catching up to her at the door, "If I killed *Gareth,* we could forestall this whole affair, too. I'd be the Marquess of Blakely. And you, as my wife, could only be charged in the House of Lords."

"Well. There's a thought. And so convenient, since the swords are stored in his attics." Her lips quirked up.

And the sight of that tentative smile—the first he'd seen since she'd been taken to Queen Square—was exactly what Ned needed. Enough with the analogies. Enough with the panic. Kate didn't need the sort of hero that slew her enemies. That was the easy kind of heroism— the stab-and-vanquish sort. Any idiot with a sword or a kitchen knife could engage in the appropriate hacking motions. No. At this moment Kate needed a *real* hero. The kind that would put a smile on her face today, and bring her victory tomorrow.

Ned could be that sort of hero.

She walked into the parlor and sat on the silk-cushioned

sofa, her silhouette illuminated by the firelight. She turned to look into it, presenting him with her back.

Her back seemed as good a place as any to start. The thin, tense line of her stance made a miserable curve.

He set his hands on her shoulders. The silk of her gown seemed cool to his touch as he slid his hands down; he could feel the ridges of whalebone beneath, stiff lines against his hand. She was wearing a small corset, one that fit neatly under her breasts, clasping her ribs. The chances of his being able to remove it seemed as dim as the lighting in the room.

But above that garment, he could still massage away the hard knots of worry that had collected in her shoulders. He took them on, one by one, letting his fingers speak the reassurance that his voice could not. And once her shoulders had loosened, he noticed how tight her lower back seemed, just at the edges of her corset.

There was only one way to defeat Harcroft on the morrow. Oh, it was possible that Harcroft's information wasn't sound, that the testimony he'd collected—and the gravity of his charge—would leave the jury unconvinced. But Ned wasn't willing to accept a mere possibility of her release. After all, she was charged with a crime, and however good her intentions, she *had* committed it. He'd gambled enough in his youth; Ned was not going to merely toss the metaphorical dice again and pray for the best.

He pressed his palms into the heated curves of her waist and made gentle circles there, over and over, until those muscles, too, had relaxed.

By contrast, he was all on edge. Kate could tell the

entire truth of her story—that Louisa had come willingly, that she'd been beaten by her husband—but so long as Louisa was absent, it was Kate's word against Harcroft's.

She had relaxed a little more under his touch, but she was still stiff. Her hands were still clenched at her sides, her fingernails biting into the palms of her hand.

There was the possibility of countering Harcroft's claims with charges of their own. Assault on Kate, assault on Louisa herself. But every charge Ned could imagine would require Kate to explain the circumstances that had brought them about. She would have to admit her guilt. No, there had to be another way out of this. Something that would leave Kate unquestionably free.

He took her hands. They were still cold and trembled slightly. He flattened her delicate fingers between his, and then pressed his thumb along her palm. *Trust me. Trust me.* He coaxed the tension from every finger, squeezing them in his grip, working his way up the muscles of her forearm.

She had leaned back as he rubbed her arms, her body molding against his. Holding her as closely as he was, he couldn't help but brush his arms against her chest. And as he did, he couldn't help but notice that her nipples had grown hard and tense. And so he massaged them, too.

He made little circles with his fingers about her breasts, radiating from the center on out. She let out a sound, halfway between a sigh and a sob, as he did so. And when that did not relieve the tension in those tight buds— when she turned around and straddled him, her petticoats covering his legs, her thighs clasping his, her body sweet against his—well. Only a cad would have left her in such a state.

Only a cad would have removed his hands, would have kept his mouth from finding her breasts beneath that gown. Only a cad would have pushed her hands away as they undid the fall of his breeches. And only a true villain would have ignored the rising tide of lust that came up between them.

She slid on top of him; he clasped her waist tightly. She leaned her forehead against his. Their breath mingled, then their bodies. Ned could have let everything go in that first half a minute. He might have rolled her beneath him and held her tight, until he emptied all his fears inside her. But her hands clenched tight on his shoulders. For her, this was more than release. It was reassurance, proof that even the courts of the land could not make her into a small powerless thing.

She was a heated breath of air about him, a warm clasp around his member. Her hands pinned him in place. Only a cad would have taken that control from her.

Tonight, Ned was determined to be her hero.

And so he was.

CHAPTER TWENTY

RELEASE HAD NEVER SEEMED quite so relieving to Kate. After they had finished, after he'd kissed her and withdrawn from her and rearranged her skirts, he pulled her back onto his lap. She sat there, her cheek pressed against his, his arms clasped about her. Somehow, that act, primal and real, had jolted something loose inside her. She could *think* again, could face the prospect of an uncertain tomorrow.

"What do we do?" She whispered the words into his hair.

His hands splayed on her backside, caressing her still.

"We need to tell Gareth," Ned said. "Send for him immediately, in fact. We'll need to have our marquess here, to press our advantage." He smiled slightly. "I shall enjoy using my cousin as a figurehead."

A thousand doubts clamored up in Kate's mind. "But—"

"Jenny was already suspicious of Harcroft, I think. And after the role they have played in this, they deserve to know. I would like them to hear it from you."

"They don't *like* me," Kate said in a small voice.

"They don't know you. They don't know anything

about you. Don't you think, Kate, that it's time you told someone besides me?"

She'd been hiding this side of herself for so long, she couldn't respond at first. She *wanted* to, wanted someone else to know what she'd done—and she didn't want to, all at the same time. If they rejected her for the person she wasn't, it was almost as if it didn't sting.

"Gareth respects people who get things done. He'll take your side of things. Just tell him honestly what you've done, and what has transpired."

Laid out logically like that, the thought was actually a relief. After all these weeks, she could finally tell someone besides Ned the truth—about Louisa, and about herself. It had been a confining secret. Perhaps it was best that it was about to be blown apart. She might have allies again. She nodded in agreement.

"And," Ned continued, "I'll need to get Louisa. We need to prove she went of her own accord, and she's the only one who can convince the jury of that."

Those words froze Kate. "But Harcroft will demand she return to him."

"We can shield her from him for a little while yet. Gareth is a marquess. He has no legal claim on her, but in the public's eye, if he places her under his protection, people will start to *think*. And the more Harcroft rages, the more society will see him for what he truly is."

"That's not what I meant. You've seen the state Louisa is in. What could she do? She won't testify against Harcroft. She can't even sit up straight when she thinks of confronting him. How can I ask her to speak on my behalf with him sitting there in the courtroom?"

"She'll testify." Ned's voice went dark. "She's strong. And I can convince her to give Harcroft a taste of his own medicine. I must get going if I'm to fetch her. It's past dark, and she's still twenty miles away."

"Going?" Kate felt a cold flush wash through her. "Fetch her? You're leaving now?" The words tumbled out before she had a chance to think them through. She knew rationally that he didn't need to be by her side. But tonight of all nights, she wanted to be held. She wanted to know he was close. She desperately desired to know that she hadn't been abandoned. It had, after all, happened before. "I wish you wouldn't."

He pulled back from her and met her gaze gravely. His eyes seemed impossibly dark in the night, and yet warm, like the charred remains of a log in the fire. "You know Louisa wouldn't trust a hired man who arrived on her step. Hell, I wouldn't trust anyone enough to send him, either. It has to be me."

"I know." Kate shook her head. "I *know*. But…" It was foolish to think herself safe when wrapped in his arms, not with danger threatening her so. And with her trial pending in the morning, it would be downright idiotic to suggest going herself, however much she wanted to.

She felt irrational, foolish and mulishly idiotic. Just not so much that she would actually say so.

He must have understood, because he smiled and tipped her chin so that her lips were inches from his.

"Kate," he said. "I'm not leaving you. I am merely willing to forgo a great deal of sleep in the next few hours. This time, I *am* going to slay your dragons and leave them for dead. You can count on me."

Trust him. He lifted her off him and then stood, adjusting his clothing. Something in Kate's stomach jarred loose.

A great deal had changed since his return to England. She had thought trust was an evanescent thing, impossible to cabin. But whatever the stuff that their marriage was made of, it was not some dry and weightless thing any longer. It had taken root inside her, and it wasn't going to blow away.

"Ned."

He turned back toward her again, his face wary.

"Be safe," she said.

A smile spread across his face, as if she'd given him an unexpected gift.

She wrapped her arms around her waist. It was as if she could feel his hands against her skin, even as he stood yards away. He looked up at her and grinned one last time. She memorized that expression, every last line of it. The memory of his smile was as good as an embrace, even as he walked away.

THE SHEPHERD'S COTTAGE where Louisa was staying was three hours' hard ride from London on a good night. This night, Ned realized, wasn't good. It was desperately dark out; only a sliver of moon lit the way, and even that pale lantern shone fitfully behind ragged, breathy clouds. Tiny, icy spicules of rain cut into Ned's face as he rode out of the stables.

His mare's hooves clopped dully, muffled by the rain. The streetlamps edging the cobbled roads of London cast globes of light, dividing the world into stark regions of harsh yellow and impossible shadow. But after half an hour, as he urged his horse on, even that dim illumination faded into nothingness behind him. The moon slipped closer to the horizon. He could make out nothing about him but the dim moonlit track, two muddy wheel-ruts carved through dying autumn grass. It rustled in the wind, rattling in the rain. His horse fell into a relentless canter; the wind rushed by his face, cold and numbing. It didn't matter. There was no direction but forward; no possibility except success.

It seemed Ned had been riding for an eternity, suspended in night air. The horse's rhythm pounded into his flesh, until he was nothing more than the fall of hooves against mud, and the whip of the wind about him. One hour faded into two, then crept up on three. The rain stopped; the wind did not.

He came to the point where the track turned off toward Berkswift and entered the woods. During daylight hours, the grove seemed nothing more than a scraggly copse of trees. Now he could feel the change in the night air immediately as the horse entered those shadows. The musky scent of earth grew thicker; the air felt colder when he drew it into his lungs.

The foliage had never seemed particularly dense in the sun. But the black leaves filtered out all but the most persistent light—and that came through in dark, waving blotches, shadows chasing each other across the uneven forest floor as the branches overhead moved in the wind.

His mount shied and skittered, throwing her head in fear of those moon-tossed shadows. Ned patted the animal's neck in a fashion that he hoped was soothing. There wasn't much time to cater to equine sensibilities in his schedule. And while he'd chosen the animal for the speed and sureness of her footing, with these shadows about, she was almost as skittish as Champion.

A quarter-mile into the forest, an owl hooted. For one heart-stopping second, Ned felt his horse's muscles tense in panic. He reached forward to give the animal another soothing pat, but before his gloved fingers landed, the animal let out a frightened cry. She reared up, and before Ned could regain his balance, she broke into a teeth-jolting gallop.

Ned sawed uselessly on the reins. The heavy leather strings cut into his gloves, but the mare had grabbed the bit between her teeth and was too frightened to pay the least attention. She stampeded along the unlit path, her sides heaving in terror. Branches crashed into Ned's cheeks, little whippy things that left stinging lashes across his face.

"Hush," he tried. And then, "Quiet." Not that the horse could hear any of Ned's attempts to calm her, not over the cacophony of breaking branches.

"Stop!" he finally shouted.

As if the mare heard this command, her forward motion checked. It happened too fast for Ned to react, and yet it seemed to occur so slowly, he could see every leaf on the tree in front of him. There was a cracking noise; Ned felt a sudden sense of drunken vertigo as inertia slapped him against his mount's neck. The beast stumbled. There wasn't time to move as his mare fell, but still, Ned tried to kick free. His boot caught in the stirrup—he swung wildly—and the ground rushed up to slam into him. The next instant after that, the horse was rolling on him. Ned's leg twisted underneath that crushing weight. He pulled away; his leg wrenched.

He pulled again, and his leg finally came free. He scrambled away, backward, his elbows digging into the cold mulch underneath him. It was over. He'd survived. His lungs burned and he fell back on the cold ground, expelling the breath he seemed to have been holding.

He was light-headed. He lay, a thousand little twigs poking his spine. He was a mass of cuts and bruises. Just beyond him, his horse let out one last panicked whinny before surging to its feet.

Ned felt a momentary flit of pleasure that whatever had caused the fall had done no permanent damage to his mount. But before he could clamber to his feet and rescue the reins, his mare raced off again. He heard her hoofbeats echoing into the distance.

Oh, yes. The evening had wanted just that.

This was not yet a total disaster. The beast was familiar with the area; he'd ridden her to Berkswift before. She'd go there now—and Ned would perforce need to walk behind. It would take him longer on foot, but he was no more than five miles distant at this point. Once his heart slowed down—once his breath ceased slamming into his lungs—he'd follow after. The schedule… He would make it work. Walking would mean delay, but there were more horses and a carriage at Berkswift. He would have needed them, in any event, to bring Louisa and her infant home. He'd be back in London hours before eleven in the morning. It was a delay, but it was *only* a delay. Just an unfortunate setback, not a catastrophe.

Ned took another deep, calming lungful of air. With that breath, he came to a very odd realization—his leg hurt. He noticed it as an intellectual curiosity before he truly felt the pain. And then it hurt like *hell*.

He vaguely recalled the twist of his hip as he'd fallen, the slam of his horse's weight atop him. Now, with every last respiration, it felt as if his lungs were taking in acid in place of oxygen. It was a sharp pain, like a thousand shards of glass all stabbing his ankle with vicious glee. Beneath that, there was a dull, persistent throb, a pressure where his leg seemed to swell against his thick riding boot.

Deeper than any of the coruscating sparks of hurt, lay an exceedingly bad feeling in his gut. This was not good. It was so not good that he couldn't even bring himself to think of what had occurred. He could only act.

His gloves had shredded when he hit the rocky earth. Slowly, he pushed himself to his knees. His breath caught against his ribs. From his knees, he pushed himself upright onto one foot. His ankle dissolved into a fire of pain from even that tiny amount of weight.

"Holy Christ," he swore aloud.

Blasphemy didn't make the pain any better. It sure as hell didn't make the truth any more palatable.

He didn't want to admit it, didn't want to take off his damned boot to feel the telltale fracture. But he knew with a sick, sure certainty, knew it with the grinding pattern of pain he felt, pressing his foot into the ground.

Somewhere in that fall, he'd broken his leg.

The black despair that seeped into him was all too familiar. At least *this* time he actually had a reason to feel it. It felt like little tearing claws, that sure knowledge that he'd failed, that he'd made Kate another promise he couldn't keep. He'd thought he was good enough. He'd imagined he could do anything. But that had been sheer pride. Reality now stripped him of his arrogance.

Failure settled about him like a lead cloak. He wasn't good enough. Wasn't strong enough. He was an idiot to have allowed Kate to rely on him, and now she—and Louisa—were going to pay the price of depending upon someone who was fool enough to think he could be a hero.

At that moment, Ned should have given up. Any reasonable man would have done so. He *wanted* to give up, to simply declare this task impossible so that he wouldn't have to stagger through the pain that awaited.

But then, this wasn't the worst thing to happen to Ned.

He shut his eyes. A privy, a dunking, a boat on the ocean. In some ways he felt he'd left a part of himself there on the water. The sun on that boat had scoured away so many of Ned's illusions, all except one—when you needed to live, you kept on going, no matter how impossible the future seemed. And you didn't stop.

Kate didn't need a hero who could slay dragons. At the moment, she needed one who could stand up and walk.

And so Ned took the fear and pain yammering in his head and set them to the side.

"If I can do this," he said aloud. "I can do anything."

It could have been worse. Compared to that moment in the boat at sea, when his own will had betrayed him, a little thing like a broken leg was a picnic in the park, complete with beribboned basket. It was a baby dragon, belching tepid puffs of flameless smoke.

Ned didn't want to stand—but then, he'd practiced doing what he didn't want to do for a good long while. His leg hurt. Good thing he'd practiced pushing through physical pain before. When he shifted his weight, his breath hissed in.

On its own, he doubted his ankle could have supported him. But the stiff leather of his riding boot was as good as a cast. Well. He thought it would do. It was going to have to.

Before he put his full weight on it, however, he felt around the forest floor.

"Damn," he said aloud, as if talking to himself would make the pain leach away. "I encountered enough branches on my way down. There has to be one here." The leaves rustled around him in grim appreciation of the joke. He found a suitable piece a few feet away. It was crooked, and the bark rasped roughly against his skin. But it was long enough to lean on, and strong enough not to snap if he put his full weight on it.

He was going to make it to Berkswift.

One step was agony. Two steps sent shooting pains up his leg. Three… The pain didn't get better as he went along; it got worse. It invaded his bones, his tendons; the strain of holding himself upright tested muscles he'd rarely used.

If he could do *this*, he could do *anything*.

He would never again need to flinch when he thought of his early years. He could win, step by step, yard by yard. Ned kept going. The first mile gave way to the second. The second, more slowly, gave way to the third. The third turned into a bone-jarring, fatiguing crawl uphill, where even the thought of success couldn't drive him on. By the fourth mile, the pain had deranged him enough that he imagined the sound of bone grinding against bone with every step.

He reached the top of the hill, much relieved. There was the fence of the old goat pasture where Champion was kept. Ned paused and grabbed for the rail. It supported his weight better than the battered branch he'd been using. He shut his eyes, and tried to remember if the fence wound all the way to the stables. It did—but unless he crossed into the pasture, he'd be diverted an extra half mile. If he could just cross this final acre, he might finally be within shouting distance of the house.

Climbing over the stile into the pasture was even harder than struggling uphill. He slipped on the last rung of the descent, and his bad leg slammed into the ground on the other side. His hands grabbed the splintered wood of the fence rail, just as his limb twisted underneath him. He barely kept from toppling over. Instead, he grasped the post and breathed in.

He could do this.

He could do this.

And perhaps the only reason he was muttering that he could do this in the gray of near dawn was that he couldn't. The world swayed dizzily about him, even as he clung to the fence. He had no notion of balance any longer. He wasn't sure which direction was forward. His mind was fuzzing around the edges, everything turning to uniform gray with the pain.

He wasn't capable of taking another step. It really couldn't get any worse.

And then, in the darkness of the night, he heard a sound. The stamping of hooves. A challenge, from an animal frightened because its sleep had been interrupted.

Stay away, that noise proclaimed. *I am a dangerous stallion.*

CHAPTER TWENTY-ONE

KATE COUNTED close to a hundred unfamiliar faces in the courtroom just before eleven the next morning. Word of the trial must have spread overnight. Perhaps the drunkard had not been so drunk. Or more likely, the sergeants who had been on duty the previous day had boasted of the coming spectacle.

Most of the people in the room Kate could identify only by function. The back two rows were taken up by men, pencils at the ready. Gossip-columnists, caricature artists, no doubt all determined that *his* version of the most sensational trial to grace the police magistrate's bench would appear in the evening paper. No doubt they would reach their verdict before the magistrate's gavel even took up the matter.

Kate sat for them, properly polite, her spine straight, her stance relaxed. Nobody would write that she was in tears, or that she'd broken down under the weight of the matter. No doubt there was another set of wagers running about her in the gentlemen's betting books, and she'd not give those idiots the satisfaction of showing fear.

Besides that, in the front rows sat several people she knew very well.

The Marquess of Blakely and his wife sat on the left. Lord Blakely watched Kate intently. He was not frowning at her—which was a good start. He was peering at her, as if there were something to see.

He sat close to his wife, both of them meticulously dressed in sober attire. But their faces told the story of a sleepless, troubled night.

For once, Kate knew precisely how Lord and Lady Blakely felt.

In the police courts, Harcroft himself was the one who had to prosecute the case. Even with the jury and the crowded courtroom, she could not count on him to tell the truth. In fact, with half of London guaranteed to learn of this through the gossip rags, it was rather a given that he would lie. Despite—or perhaps because of—that, Harcroft looked as if he had slept the sleep of the innocent. If Kate hadn't already hated him, she would have despised him now.

Beyond that first row sat a smattering of people Kate knew quite well—Lady Bettony, Lord Worthington—and some she knew by sight and name only, from one of the million *ton* parties.

If they'd cleared away the oaken magistrate's bench and thrown in an orchestra, this courtroom could have been mistaken for a ball.

But of all the hundred souls packed into this room, not one of them was her husband. She glanced toward the entrance for the seventeenth time. When she did so, she held her chin high, as if she were a lady expecting a morning call.

But, of course, she was. Where was Ned? He'd been riding alone at night. Anything could have happened to him. He might have broken his neck, could have been set upon by footpads. If she'd been thinking clearly the previous evening, she would have insisted that someone accompany him. As if Ned would have brooked any *assistance*.

Kate met Lord Blakely's eyes across the crowded courtroom again. And for a second, it was as if all of her greatest fears were coming true. He looked at her, and she could imagine what he was thinking. He was castigating her for not telling him, cursing her for letting him waste his time, shaming her for those days of silence while he searched. He could not be thinking kindly of her.

To her surprise, he gave her one simple nod.

The magistrate entered. A jury was sworn. But instead of looking somber at the prospect of deciding her fate, the men exchanged tight smiles, as if to celebrate their luck, to be deciding one of the most talked-of affairs in all of London. Their apparent glee didn't make Kate feel better about the likelihood of justice.

And then Harcroft began to speak. In the weeks since his wife's disappearance, Harcroft had actually done an incredible job of scouring up information—better than Kate had expected. He had brought witnesses—the York-shire nursemaid's husband, who brought along the note sent from the agency Kate had used to find her.

Then there was testimony from the stagecoach workers, who testified that Kate had met the nursemaid upon her arrival in London; a statement from one of her grooms, who'd conveyed Kate and an infant in a carriage to Berk-swift. Finally, there was a seamstress who'd testified about parcels ordered by Lady Harcroft, but delivered on Kate's orders to Kate's house.

Kate had done her best to hide her traces, but once the eye of suspicion had fallen on her, her tracks were indelibly marked. She'd have been convinced of her own guilt, given that evidence.

And by the eyes of the jurors, they agreed with that assessment. After the first fifteen minutes of testimony, not one of them would meet her gaze. They had already come to a decision. She could not even blame them. She *was* guilty. She *had* stolen Harcroft's wife. She'd just done it for a very good reason.

With that tide of evidence damning her, there was almost no reason for her to speak. Still, it was half eleven when the magistrate motioned Kate forward.

Magistrate Fang eyed her uneasily. He could not *want* a lady convicted, but Kate knew how suspicious the evidence seemed. That he appeared nervous was a good sign—he would be looking for ways to interpret the evidence he'd heard to exonerate her, to avoid any difficulties her father or her cousin might cause.

Finally, he sighed and began questioning her. "Lady Kathleen, did you hire Mrs. Watson as a nursemaid?"

Nothing but the truth would do. "Yes, Your Worship."

He bit his lip and looked about, still looking for an escape. "And did you do so because you had a child of your own?" he asked hopefully.

"No, Your Worship."

More silence. Magistrate Fang rubbed his wig. "Perhaps it was a sister you were assisting?"

"I have no sisters," Kate answered.

"A favored servant?"

"No."

He had just stripped Kate of any possible legitimate reason for hiring the woman. The magistrate almost pouted, and then folded his arms on the bench. "For whom, then, did you hire the nursemaid?"

With Ned absent, Kate's only choice was to tell the truth. The question was how much of it she would have to tell before he arrived. Kate shook her head in confusion. "For Louisa, of course. Lady Harcroft. I thought we had already established that, Your Worship."

A soft susurrus of surprise spread through the courtroom at those words.

The magistrate frowned. "And where is the nursemaid at present?"

Kate gave him a sunny smile. "I imagine she is with Lady Harcroft, although it has been some time since I last saw either of them."

The jurors had lifted their heads at Kate's cheerful words. She was not cringing or ducking her head. She was speaking in a pleasant tone. In short, she was not speaking as if she were a guilty woman. Kate was waltzing precariously close to the edge of the cliff. Still, she forced herself to look Harcroft in the eyes and smile.

He looked away first. A tiny victory, that, but it seemed as if an extra ray of sunshine cut through the gloom in Queen Square.

"Where," the magistrate asked her, "is Lady Harcroft?"

"Oh, I couldn't *possibly* say," Kate replied.

Another murmur from the crowd, this one louder.

"You can't say, or you won't?" Harcroft moved toward

her. She didn't have to pretend to shrink from him. Standing above her, tall as he was, he seemed dark and menacing. Precisely how she wanted everyone to remember him.

"Lady Kathleen," he growled, "must I remind you that you've pledged yourself to tell the *whole* truth?"

Kate looked up, widening her eyes in pretend innocence. "Why, I am telling the truth! I truly *can't* say. I believe Lady Harcroft is in transit at this moment." At least, she hoped she was—unless something terribly untoward had happened to Ned. "Of course, as she's not with me in London, and I've not had a post from her, I can't say for sure."

Harcroft folded his arms and glared at her. "If you hired her nursemaid and abducted her, you know her whereabouts. Divulge them, Lady Kathleen."

"She's in a carriage." Kate smiled brightly. "Or— maybe she is not. It is so hard to say. If I could see her now, surely I could say where she was."

He frowned at that bit of stupidity. "The prisoner," he said tightly, "is mocking the honor of this court—of *you,* Your Worship, in front of all of London. *Demand* that she tell where my wife is. Demand it now."

The magistrate reached for a handkerchief and dabbed at the sweat that trickled down his forehead. "Lady Kathleen?" he asked faintly.

At those words, the courtroom doors opened on the far edge of the crowd. As they did, a blast of midmorning sun spilled into the room. Dust motes sparkled in the sudden light, suspended in air. Then two figures, dark silhouettes against that sunlight, appeared. Kate went breathless with hope.

They moved into the room. Ned was in front. He moved slowly, deliberately placing each foot, as if every step had meaning. He paused, resting one hand on the bench.

That incandescent warmth she felt, seeing him for the first time that morning, was barely marred by the utter filth of his attire. Her husband was dirty, missing a cravat, and his trousers were ripped at the knee. Louisa came up beside him. In stark contrast to Ned's ragged clothing, she wore a dove-gray traveling dress, its edges trimmed in falls of black lace. She seemed poised, as she never had before in her husband's company.

One of the earnest young reporters in the back row lifted his head at the draft of air—but he only glared at the entering company before bending back down to scribble on his paper.

"Lady Kathleen?" the magistrate asked. "Are you saying you can't tell me where Lady Harcroft's wife is?"

Kate smiled sunnily. "No, Your Worship. *Now* I can."

Harcroft leaned toward Kate, his fingers curled, as if he could claw the knowledge from her. He was so intent on Kate that he did not hear the footsteps behind him, proceeding up the aisle.

"Is it necessary for me to do so, Your Worship?" Kate asked.

"It would be advisable," Magistrate Fang said dryly.

Kate raised her hand gracefully. "She's right there," she said, pointing at Louisa.

Half the room stood, all at once. The judge banged his gavel to no avail a first time, and then louder. But it was only when he shouted a threat to have them all carried away that everyone subsided in their seats. In comparison with that roar, the silence that followed was so absolute Kate could hear the scritch of the reporters' pencils against foolscap.

As for Harcroft… A thousand emotions seemed to flit across his face. Fear. Triumph. Concern. And then, as Louisa did not move forward down the aisle toward him, a hint of anger. He drew himself up.

A week ago, Louisa had curled into a ball, thinking of the possibility of confronting her husband. Kate could see Ned place his hand on Louisa's shoulder. Louisa didn't flinch.

Harcroft strode down the aisle toward her. When he was a few feet in front of her, he reached for her. But Louisa looked up. She squared her shoulders. And then without the slightest trace of uncertainty, she met his eyes.

Kate wanted to cheer. The earl stopped where he was.

"Where have you been?" He glanced about, as if searching for a hidden spring gun.

"Don't you recall?" Louisa gave a little laugh. "I'd made plans to go to Paris. I was shopping."

The moment of silence stretched in the courtroom, as hair-raisingly electric as the second before lightning struck. Kate could feel that energy, the back of her neck tingling in awareness.

"Shopping?" Harcroft repeated weakly. *"Shopping?"*

"Oh, yes. You don't suppose I would leave for another reason, now, do you?"

Louisa gazed at him.

He was the first to look away. He looked to the back of the room—at the cadre of reporters, their pencils poised to record every word he spoke. Kate could see the visible calculation in his face. Harcroft was beloved of society. *Everyone* thought he was perfect. He could no more announce his true thoughts to this room than he could fly.

"Ah." He rubbed his head. "Shopping. Perhaps you forgot to mention." His voice took on a darker tone. "I'll see you home, then."

"Oh, I'm not going with you, Harcroft. Not today."

Every person in the room turned avariciously to Harcroft, waiting to see his reaction to that impertinence.

Harcroft whirled to face the magistrate.

"You see? Lady Kathleen has persuaded my wife to refuse me already. Clap her in chains!"

"Oh, Harcroft," Louisa said with a sigh. "Do be rational. I made the decision not to accompany you home on my own. Do you really suppose I would be *happy* that you tried to toss my dearest friend into gaol, simply because you couldn't remember my traveling plans?"

He looked dumbstruck. "I—"

"Your Worship," Louisa continued. "The only person who is keeping me from my husband is…my husband. If anyone is to be clapped in chains, I suggest it be him."

The spectators broke out in laughter. And as Harcroft

realized it was directed at him, his countenance darkened. He took two steps down the aisle toward Louisa.

"What are you going to do, Harcroft? Force me?" Louisa laughed as she spoke. Kate knew exactly how hard it must have been for her to do that. "In front of all these people? No, *darling*. I'll come home when you deliver a suitable apology. For *everything* you have done."

The earl's hands fisted at his sides. His jaw twitched in a murderous, violent anger. Kate saw his eyes sweep across the entire crowd.

"Well, my lord," said the magistrate hopefully. "Shall we call this all's well that ends well?"

Harcroft turned to look at the man. "I suppose this proceeding is over, Your Worship." His eyes fell on Kate. "But it's not over. Not until I've delivered the apology my wife deserves."

AFTER THE MAGISTRATE BANGED his gavel and pronounced the court in recess again, pandemonium broke out. Ned barely managed to remain standing, buffeted as he was on all sides by the intrepid young men from the gossip rags. They dashed pell-mell through the door, nearly tripping over Ned's feet in their haste to deliver the story.

Harcroft took one long look at Louisa, and then marched down the aisle toward her. Louisa didn't cringe, even though he stalked up to her stiff-legged. She didn't look away. They'd practiced that in the carriage—although, under the circumstances, Ned hadn't managed to project even a tiny portion of the menace that Harcroft had. Oddly enough, it hadn't been the pain that had posed the greatest difficulty. He'd gone somewhere beyond hurt, to a world where pain no longer had any meaning. It was the problem of keeping himself firmly in the present that had proved a challenge.

And he had to be in the present now. Harcroft reached for his wife. Ned wasn't sure what the earl intended, but Ned had promised Louisa her husband wouldn't touch her. Before he could grab her arm, Ned interposed his own body between them in a graceless, lurching motion. He intercepted Harcroft's outstretched arm with a handshake.

"Get out of my way, Carhart," Harcroft said through the gritted teeth of his false smile.

"Your wife has a pistol in her reticule," Ned responded quietly. "If you touch her, she'll shoot you."

Harcroft glanced behind Ned. "Death threats," he finally said. "How quaint." He cast his wife another, more vicious look. "Enjoy your freedom," he hissed. "I hear there are excellent sanitariums in Switzerland."

At those words, Ned felt an inappropriate cheer. So he *had* guessed correctly—Harcroft had filed a petition in lunacy in the courts of Chancery. Not really a cause for rejoicing, but at least they'd been correct about that much. Good thing they'd managed to confuse *that* suit, at least. But cheer was a mistake. With happiness came feeling; with feeling came the urge to beat his head against a wall until he passed out and could feel pain no more. Harcroft simply glared one last time, and then stalked out of the room.

The real reason Ned had made it all this way—the real reason he'd suffered these past hours—was coming slowly down the aisle. Kate looked wonderful—small and delicate, and yet strong and indomitable. The sort of woman who might take on magistrates and madmen alike, and never blink in surprise when they crumpled at her feet.

She approached, and he wanted to fold her into an embrace. He would have, were it not for the certainty that if he let go of the back of the bench he was clutching, he would fall forward onto his face.

She stopped before him, smiling shyly. He could appreciate the beauty of that smile, even through the gray haze of pain that enveloped him.

"You," she said, "look both wonderful and awful at the same time."

"Do you like the attire? I have always dreamed of setting a new fashion in road-weary gentlemen's attire. I call this particular knot in my cravat 'The Incompetent.'"

She shook her head in puzzlement. "What cravat?"

"Precisely."

She laughed. Good to know he could still make her do that, even under these circumstances. "Turn for me," she suggested, "and let me get the full sense of the fashion."

"Oh, no. I'm already spinning," he informed her solemnly. And he was. The room inscribed a lazy orbit around him. He could track the path of her face, trekking across the sky like a moon on a cloudless night.

Louisa took Ned's elbow. "Kate, there is something you need to know."

Kate glanced at Ned again, and a hint of worry flashed

across her brow. "You look as if you're about to fall down."

No. Not that. He'd proven…he'd proven…he'd proven something fairly clever and intelligent, and as soon as the room stopped whirling about, he would let her know what it was.

"Here," Kate was saying. She took his other elbow, and then she and Louisa were guiding him toward a chair. He landed in a heavy thud that jarred his leg.

"You've been up all night," Kate was saying. "You're tired. And your trousers are ripped. Did you take a spill on the road?"

"I think he must have sprained his ankle," Louisa said. "He limps."

They were talking about him as if he were not there. In another world, another place, that would have bothered him. But Ned felt curiously as if he were not quite present. It was quite clever of them to sense that.

Kate sat down next to him.

"Sprained your ankle?" she was saying. "What on earth were you doing standing on it just now? Was this some attempt to prove some idiotic masculine point?" Her fingers against his neck were far more gentle than her words.

He thought about explaining that he hadn't *sprained* his *ankle,* but somehow he did not think she would find the truth more palatable.

"If I can do this," he told her seriously, "I can do anything. And if I can do anything—"

Then he never, ever had to worry about finding himself on a little rowboat in the ocean again.

But she didn't know the whole of that story. "Well, you can't do *everything*," she said, as if reason and logic mattered. "You can't walk on a sprained ankle. Thick skull." She was smoothing his hair against his brow. Before he could protest that he obviously *could,* she patted his head. "I won't let you."

She was smiling. He was supposed to smile back. He couldn't quite make his lips do more than curl in a wretched little half grimace.

"What is it?" she asked. "Here. We need to get you home, to a physician. Blakely, you'll have to help."

"No," Ned protested. "No—I don't need any help. Not from Gareth."

"Ned," Jenny was saying, "do you want me to—"

"Not you, *especially* not from you, Jenny. I can do it myself."

"He's been this recalcitrant the entire morning," Louisa said. "I don't even understand how he managed to walk inside."

"Riding boot is long and stiff enough that it makes a decent splint." Ned shut his eyes. It didn't make the pain any better. "And this isn't about me and my stupid little broken leg. That will heal. We need to see to Lady Harcroft first."

"Broken leg?" Kate's voice was dangerous in his ears. "What do you mean, *broken leg?* I thought you had a sprain."

"Oh," Ned said uncomfortably. "Did I say that?"

He had.

He wasn't sure how he got to the carriage. On the ride home, Kate fussed over him, her breath hissing in with every turn of the carriage as if she were the one feeling the pain. As if he were some damned weakling, to cry out at every little hurt that came his way.

He was already floating on a fog of pain so pervasive, a little gentle rocking had no meaning. As they alighted, Kate went to his side. He didn't need support. If he could do this, he could do *anything*. He was clinging to that thought, he knew, because the alternative was to faint like a girl.

If he could finish this—see Lady Harcroft safe, get Kate home, placate his cousin's worries and solve the universal problems of poverty and war, while he was at it—well, *then* he would know he was good enough.

"Kate," he growled as she tried to get her shoulder under his arm to offer support, "let me do it."

"Blakely." Kate's voice seemed very far away. "Help."

"I don't need help," Ned insisted. It seemed like a very reasonable statement as he made it. "I can do it on my own. I can stand on my own two feet."

But there were hands on his back, arms around him, grabbing him, lifting him from his feet and threatening his last hold on consciousness.

"No," he protested weakly, "put me down."

"Don't be an idiot, Ned."

They were the last words he heard, and he wasn't even sure who uttered them.

CHAPTER TWENTY-TWO

"I FEEL LIKE AN IDIOT."

Kate stopped in the hallway. She stood just outside her own parlor, and yet she suddenly felt like an intruder in her own home. It wasn't the words that arrested her; it was the fact that they'd been spoken by Lord Blakely, who had always struck her as the opposite of an idiot. Intimidatingly intelligent, in fact.

Stopping was not a good idea. In the past few hours, her duties as a hostess had carried her forward. After the relief she'd felt at the end of her trial, she could have collapsed. Instead, she'd settled Louisa in a suite of rooms with her baby and left Lord and Lady Blakely in the parlor. Ned had not been conscious when the physician had come, cut away his boot, and pronounced his diagnosis. So Kate had been there as well.

She hadn't had time to stop. Kate had come to convey the news to Lord and Lady Blakely, who were waiting patiently for word of him. She hadn't come to overhear their conversation. She surely hadn't come to lean against the wall, fatigue threatening to overwhelm her. But now that she'd halted, she couldn't quite make herself move again.

"Well. You aren't the only one." That wry, tired voice belonged to Lady Blakely.

Lord and Lady Blakely had always struck Kate as rather a conundrum. Lord Blakely seemed cold; he always looked to be watching everyone and finding fault. She'd had the impression that he had at first considered whether Kate was a potential human being—and once he'd answered the question in the negative, had ignored her thereafter.

Lady Blakely, on the other hand, had tried to encourage Kate into friendship at first. And perhaps at second and third. It was Kate who had turned away from her.

"She didn't like you," Lord Blakely said shortly. "I assumed she had to be ten kinds of a useless fool."

Kate felt a flush go through her. They were talking about *her*. No doubt they thought they were having a private conversation, even if it was being held in her parlor. She needed to clear her throat, or trip over the door as she came into the room. At the very least, she could do them the courtesy of coughing very, *very* loudly.

But she didn't. Instead, she held her breath.

"People don't have to like me," Lady Blakely said with amusement. "You didn't, at first."

"That's calumny." A longer pause. "If we'd known, if she had felt she could come to us, none of this would have happened. Ned's leg. Being charged with a crime—in a police court, of all places, and God above, will the gossip rags go on about that. Jenny, she's a *Carhart*. I'm responsible for her. And I let this happen. All because I let myself be fooled into thinking she was precisely as she seemed on the surface."

Kate had spent most of her life having people dismiss her because of the way she looked. Even put in these stark terms, the hidden approval in those words shook her. She'd sent Blakely the letter, telling him everything she'd done. And now it was too late to take it back.

"She's not quite as useless as she seems, is she? I do recall *someone* might have said something along those lines.…"

"Don't gloat," Blakely huffed. "It doesn't help."

"Does this help?"

No answer. Kate hardly wanted to be the source of marital strife. She peered into the room. Lord and Lady Blakely sat next to each other on the divan; the marquess had turned to his wife, and his head rested against her shoulder. Her hands ruffled his hair gently. The couple looked upset, tired and altogether miserable. Nobody would have looked at them and imagined them *happy*.

And yet still it hurt to watch that easy intimacy, to see that comfortable sharing of burdens. It was almost a physical pain she felt, stabbing into her. So this was what a happy marriage looked like, even under circumstances that were far from happy. This was what it really meant— not that they never suffered, but that when they did, they shared their burdens.

Does this help? Three words she could never imagine saying to Ned—not without him freezing and walking out of the room. With a broken leg, no less. *This* was what she wanted—this trust from her husband. And while she could rely on him, he'd told her in no uncertain terms that he didn't want her close enough to offer assistance.

Kate crept from the room, not quite understanding what she'd just witnessed, or why it had shaken her so. She knew only that if she entered, the tired mass of burdens she carried might overwhelm her.

If you fall, Ned had once told her, *I will catch you.*

She now knew precisely how true this was. He was strong, powerful and *reliable*—so much that she might lean on him for support, not even realizing as she did so that he was walking on a broken leg.

This feeling that she might throw herself backward and he would catch her, no matter the consequences—this blind and unhesitating *trust*—this was what love really looked like. Love was courage. It was shyness made gregarious, softness rendered strong. It was all her secret vulnerabilities trusted to him, and transmuted into hidden strength.

But there was pain in that realization. That moment of intimacy she'd witnessed between the marquess and his wife burned in her mind. Lord Blakely had had no compunction about leaning on his lady.

Ned knew all her weaknesses, her biggest fears. He'd stood straight when her legs buckled. He'd whispered strength when she most needed to hear it. But the one thing he hadn't done was let her give strength to him in return.

He had told Louisa once to think of what she wanted. Kate knew what she would say if he asked her that same question now. She wanted *him*. She wanted him to believe that she was as strong as he'd once told her she was. She wanted his trust. She wanted his love. She wanted to nurture her hopes for her marriage without fear that he might hurt her again.

The world had forced her into practicality enough. She didn't want to be practical about her husband.

Kate squared her shoulders and went to find him. As she'd suspected, the physician had set and splinted his leg. The door to his room was open a crack, and from the sound of silence within, he was alone once more. She pushed it wide and stepped through.

He'd woken at some point. He must not have heard her enter, though, because he did not turn to her.

He sat on the bed, his leg stretched out in front of him. He looked as if he chose to sit there not because he was an invalid, but as a matter of prerogative. He might have been presiding over a meeting, the way he sat, ramrod straight. Even now, with nobody watching, he did not let a hint of weakness show. Kate felt suddenly weary on his behalf.

But instead of letting the emotion show, she simply tapped on the wall beside her. He looked up, and now that she was peering into his eyes, she could see the hints of emotion. There was that slight widening of his eyes when he saw her. His lips compressed, not in anger, but in pain, as he shifted his legs as if he were going to—

"Ned," Kate said in as oppressive a tone of voice as she could manage, "you are not going to stand up to greet me. That would be *extremely* foolish."

He paused, on the verge of swinging his legs over the edge of the bed. "Um," he replied.

She sighed. "And let me guess. You refused all laudanum."

As he was gritting his teeth in pain, instead of smiling

in the dreamy wonder the drug would provide, she didn't need him to answer.

"It's cold in here," she said. "Do you want me to—"

"No."

Oh, yes. That. She always managed to forget it.

"On the physician's orders, you'll be confined to crutches for months. You might as well be comfortable. Can I bring you…some tea? A book?"

He glanced at her once more. "No."

"Can I sit with you, then, and keep you company? Isn't there something I can do for you?"

He smiled. "Nothing, Kate. No need to bother yourself."

Kate stepped toward him. He was smiling, but his words were as much a betrayal as ever. When he'd been half dead on his feet, he'd insisted he didn't need any help. Some of that, no doubt, had been a masculine, irrational response to overwhelming pain. But now that he was himself again, he was doing the same. He was just doing it more politely.

"Ned, you're going to be limited for weeks. Months, perhaps. You might as well let me care for you, just a little."

He didn't say anything. His shoulders stiffened, though, and he leaned forward just an inch.

"You *were* planning on staying in bed today, weren't you?"

Still no response. No *verbal* response, that was, and the lack of meek assent on his part was as a denial. She waited until he finally looked up at her.

"But there's Harcroft," he said.

Just those words, and she understood what he meant. If she let herself think of what Harcroft could do, her own skin crawled.

"If I can stop him," he said quietly, "I can do *anything*."

"But you can't," Kate said quietly. She sat in the chair by his bedside and reached for his hand. "You *can't* do anything you wish. You certainly can't do everything. There's nothing wrong with that. I can respect you, even if your bones knit at a human pace. I can trust you even if you can't get out of bed to catch me."

He turned his palm down before she could take his hand. "That's not it."

"It's not?"

"It's not that I believe I must heal unnaturally quickly. It's that… It's that…"

"It's that you don't want me to help you."

His head shot up at that, and a flare entered his eyes. "I don't *need* help." He spoke through gritted teeth. "I don't ever intend to be a burden on you, Kate."

"You're not a burden, Ned." She rested her hand lightly on his shoulder.

He looked away for a second. "Do you want to know why I don't accept help? Why I can't accept your charity, however kindly you mean it? It's the same reason I sleep in the cold. Why I pitch hay, instead of having servants do it for me. It's because I don't dare allow myself common weaknesses."

"I don't want you to be weak. I just want—"

"You want to wrap me up in cotton batting, so I can't

get hurt. Do you want to know what happened in China, Kate?"

"I thought—"

"Do you want to know what *really* happened in China, after they pulled me out of the privy? I nearly killed myself."

"An accident—"

"No. When I confronted Captain Adams in China, I wasn't just desperate. I was fighting for every last scrap of determination that I could find, but weighted down by a black despair."

She stared at him.

He spoke quietly. "You don't know what I mean, when I speak of black despair. You think that is just hyperbole. After Captain Adams tossed me into the swamp, the feeling only intensified. I washed three times. It didn't help. I couldn't get the stink from my mind, no matter how raw I rubbed my skin."

Ned was staring at a spot on the wall, his hands gripped on his knees. "He'd won. And there was no escaping the fact that he was right—that I was a useless excuse for a man, sent off because nobody at home needed me any longer."

"You know that's not true."

He glanced at her once, and then looked away. "At first, I thought only to get myself to water. As if I could become clean again by proximity. And so I found a dinghy and rowed out into the ocean." He sighed. "Funny how I felt so trapped, with nothing about me."

"Accidents happen at sea." Kate took another step toward him, reached out her hand. But he sent her another quelling look, and her fingers curled up. "You were upset. You can't blame yourself."

"Don't run from it, Kate." His voice was dark, quiet. It echoed in the room. "You want me to trust you? You want to understand what I mean when I talk of darkness? Then listen to this. I had a pistol with me. And I held it to my temple."

She couldn't answer. She couldn't even swallow the gasp of horror that escaped her.

"I was this close to pulling the trigger—and it wasn't hope or comfort or help from anyone else that drew me back. It was simply that when faced with the stark choice between life and death, I discovered that I wanted to live. *Truly* live, not just stumble through life from point to point, waiting to be plunged into darkness again. So don't you dare feel sorry for me. I survived."

She grappled for words. "I don't think you're weak because you had a lapse—"

His eyes blazed. "No. I'm not. I'm here because I made myself *strong*. Because I knew if I intended to go on, I had to stop feeling as if I was a burden to everyone around me. If you want to know who I am, if you want to understand why I do what I do, then you need to comprehend that some part of me has never left that boat. And for me, the choice of whether to live the life I want is as simple as believing that I *can* do this all, without ever being a burden on anyone again."

"It's not *pity* when I offer to make you comfortable. It's not an apology if I hurt for you when you tell me you've suffered. You aren't weak if you let me care for you."

"No," he said in a clipped tone. "You're quite right. It's

none of those things. But it is also not something I allow myself."

And on those words he turned away. It wounded her, that dismissal. Strength, her husband could discuss. But for all that he'd promised to be worthy of *her* trust, he'd never once made a covenant to trust Kate in return.

She'd run up against the rock wall of this need of his—this need to be strong, no matter how much it hurt her—often enough that she knew how immovable it was. All she could do was bruise herself slamming against it, and her spirit ached enough as it was. And now she'd managed to uncover the *why* of it. The cold, hard truth that made him who he was. She knew enough to know that he *wouldn't* change.

It would have been too simple to say she was hurt by the knowledge. "Hurt" sounded like a mere pain in her mind, a onetime twinge that flared up and would ebb away. What she felt was not so sharp as pain, but much more pervasive. Every inch of her skin ached to lean close to him, to pull his head toward her and smooth his brow. Every fiber of her being wanted to give him comfort, to tell him that he was strong, that he didn't need to *do* this to himself. It wasn't hurt she felt. It was worse. It was all the hopes that she'd nourished without evidence all these years turning to disappointment inside her.

She stepped forward until she stood over him. Ever since he returned, he'd been towering over her. Now, trapped on the bed as he was, she loomed over him. The darkness of her shadow, cast in the afternoon light, crossed his face as she stepped forward.

She wanted to yell at him. She wanted to grab him by

the shoulders. If he hadn't broken his leg, she might even have done it.

It wouldn't have done any good.

"I don't mean to hurt you," he said.

No. He never had. "Of course not," she replied as calmly as she could manage. "You just need to…to protect yourself first. I do understand, Ned."

She just wished she didn't. She shut her eyes to stave off the salt prickle of tears. She wished she were impractical enough to threaten to run away. But this was what marriage meant: that even though she'd entered into another pretense with him, she would stay. She would learn to stop asking to become a part of his life. She would pretend that his refusal to trust her didn't hurt. It was another disguise, one as cloying as the one he'd penetrated. And one a thousand times more painful. Because in *this* masquerade, she had to pretend that his distance didn't hurt her. Even though it would, every single day.

He reached out and touched her, even now giving her strength that he would not accept in return.

She closed her eyes and let the feeling of loss run through her. His fingers were still on her elbow, strong and warm and steady. That steadiness ached now, and that gentle circling of his fingers against her seemed to sting some deep place inside of her.

Before the hurt could build up, she took her arm gently from his grasp and left.

CHAPTER TWENTY-THREE

FAT FLAKES OF EARLY SNOW were falling around the stores on Bond Street, but once they hit the ground, they melted into the slushy pavement. Kate remembered the little shop all too well; she'd visited it once, in that hectic flurry that followed her wedding. The night rail she'd purchased there, filmy and gauzy and full of hope, now sat in a chest of drawers in her room. She had used it only the once, a mere handful of days ago. It hadn't worked as she'd intended it. And now it seemed a token of the dreams she'd once possessed: translucent and insubstantial. It wouldn't have survived even a good hard rain.

The shop had placed bolts of fabric in the narrow window to advertise its wares. Behind the spread of silks and satins, some cheaper goods were laid out for the less privileged customers—thick, serviceable cottons and warm wools in sober colors. But the front of the display was taken up with colorful bolts of watered silk, satin, creamy muslin and fine striped cambric. Ribbons and lace and a welter of buttons were laid out in an eye-catching formation.

Kate's eye was not caught by any of them. She brushed off the snow that had collected on her shoulders. In this weather, looking at all that filmy fabric just made her feel cold.

Before Ned had come back to England, she'd believed the feelings she'd harbored about him would simply dissipate over time. Now she wished they could. It was the marriages that *could* blow away that she envied. As if the people mired in them might simply close their eyes and puff and, like a dandelion, their wishes would be carried on the wind.

This thinking was rather too maudlin for Kate. She'd intended to go shopping; she was a duke's daughter, and a wealthy gentleman's wife. Everyone who was anyone—who'd read the gossip columns that were even now being distributed by dirty-faced postboys—would be watching her now. She was *shopping,* after all. She and Louisa would be famous for that for years.

And while she might wish things were different with Ned… Well. There was no use sobbing over what could not be. And so shopping she would go. Anywhere, that is, but here. She had no need for any more night rails.

Kate had just tipped up her nose and was on the verge of stalking past, in search of a really, truly incredible bonnet, when she felt something pull at her. She looked in the window of the shop more closely, at one of the bolts that her eyes had passed over before.

The fabric was not silky. It was not sheer. It was not the sort of fabric that a lady would use for a night rail. It was the sort of thing that a servant might order. Serviceable. Practical. *Warm*.

It had been a mistake to overlook that one. Hope tugged at her still, faint but unmistakable.

It wasn't time for boots or bonnets.

No, she needed to purchase a night rail, after all.

THAT EVENING NED LAY IN BED, the cold of the room swirling around him. The predicament before him was impossible. For the moment Louisa was safe, but her husband still had a legal right to her. There would come a time when Harcroft might stand in court and simply demand that his wife be returned to him. They might be able to refuse, on grounds of cruelty, but no court in England would let Louisa keep her child.

The unscalable wall that was the law was as good a distraction as any from the pain in his leg, and an even better distraction from his conversation with Kate that afternoon. He hadn't wanted to tell her. But then, after all that they'd been through, she deserved to know who he truly was—and why he couldn't let himself slip, not even one little bit. The cold of the room helped with that.

He would rather think about Louisa. As little as he relished the prospect, he might call Harcroft out—death would solve all of Louisa's problems. Except he wasn't a particularly good shot, and fencing on a broken leg was simply out of the question. Besides, Ned didn't think he could murder the man in cold blood, no matter what the bastard had done.

As for his other plan… He'd planned to draw Harcroft out himself, but how was that possible now?

In the midst of these thoughts, the door that connected Ned's room to Kate's swung inward on silent hinges. He didn't hear it; it was only the movement of air that alerted him to her presence. He clumsily lurched onto his elbows. A warm breath wafted to him from her room.

Or maybe the warmth came from Kate herself. She had donned a night rail that trailed thick fabric, covering her hands, curling up to her neck. Far more demure than the flimsy scrap of material she'd put on before, and yet the tableau still struck him straight through to his gut. He forgot everything—the persistent, throbbing ache in his leg, the cramping worry that had taken over his mind.

Lit by moonlight, she seemed like some ethereal creature, scarcely touching her feet to the floor.

He swallowed. "Kate." The word trailed off into nothingness. He didn't know what to say to her.

She wanted to *help* him. It seemed such a reasonable thing for her to ask. From some other man, she would have had instant acquiescence.

But then, she'd married him. And he had nothing but a complex prickle of requirements that she had to negotiate. If he could not rely on himself, the only assurance he could offer her was the certainty of his failure. He'd failed before; he wouldn't do so again. If he gave in to her demands, if he let himself grow soft…well, he'd barely be able to trust himself. He needed to be strong, not just for himself, but for her.

She held up one finger. "Shh," she admonished. "Don't say anything."

And maybe she was right. Anything they said would disrupt this moment in the moonlight. It would break whatever spell ensorcelled him now. Words would only bring them back to reality.

She floated toward him. She was even walking silently, as if she were some unearthly spirit visiting him, rather than a woman composed of flesh and blood. The only sound she made coming forward was a gentle swish of fabric, coupled with the quiet exhalation of her breath.

His own breath had stopped long ago. How, then, was his heart still thudding so monstrously?

Maybe this was the solution, then. To let their marriage lapse into this unreal thing by moonlight. No hard questions. No difficult thoughts.

She came up beside him and he turned on the bed to face her. The act caused his leg to twinge. Even the most ethereal of spirits could not hold off reality for long. Pounding rhythm did not, at this moment, appeal to him. Drat.

"I have a gift for you." Her voice was low.

And oh, if he'd been able to get up on his knees, if he'd been able to grab hold of her and bring her beneath him, he would have had a gift for her, too. It was the only sort of gift he could imagine giving her, the silent caress of his body.

She lifted the thick material of her wool gown two inches, and set her foot on the bed next to him. He leaned forward, to trace a finger down her ankle—but caught up short. A discordant note sounded in the sylphlike fantasy he seemed to be having. She wasn't bare-footed like the pixie he'd imagined her to be. He glanced up at her in puzzlement.

"Stockings," she explained. "*Thick* stockings."

Her voice wasn't low and spiritual; it was bright and cheerful. That tone sounded a second discordant note. He stared at her covered foot for just a moment too long, trying to reconcile his thoughts about ghosts and ethereal spirits with the undeniable oddness of warm, woolen stockings.

"Um," he finally managed to say. "Stockings are the

gift? Why are *you* wearing them?" He glanced dubiously at her tiny feet. "I don't think they would fit me."

She looked down at him and tilted his head up. "They're for me. Like the night rail. So I can sleep with you in the cold."

Something painful wrenched inside him. "Oh, Kate. There's no need—"

She covered his mouth with her fingers. "You seem to be operating on the belief that when I tell you I want to help, that I want to swaddle you up so you can't move and do everything for you. That's not what it means, Ned. I want to help *you*. And if what you need is to make sure you feel strong, I will help you feel strong. If you need me to set you an impossible task just so you can complete it before breakfast, send me the word, and I'll find you a dragon to tame. 'Help' need not be an empty, cloying affair. Sometimes…it really can help." She sat down on the bed next to him and took his hand. "You don't have to do everything alone anymore, Ned. Let me walk with you."

His head buzzed. He felt it like a tickle in the back of his throat. It filled him, those words, and he couldn't even say why or how or with what. He pressed their entangled fingers to his forehead, as if he could push the burn of emotion away. She was not a sprite, then, come in moonlight to tiptoe away at dawn, but a woman—one better than he could have imagined. And she wasn't going to leave.

He didn't have to be alone. He didn't have to leave

some part of himself stuck out there, still on that sea. Maybe he didn't have to fear himself any longer.

It seemed a foreign concept, odder than anything he'd ever experienced. And still he didn't know what to say in response. In place of speech, he kissed her hand. When she didn't draw away, he drew her down next to him and put his arms around her. Even the touch of his lips to hers seemed like an importunity; and besides, he would have to draw back from her to do it. He would have to pull his head from where it rested against her shoulder, and if he did that, she might see there was something suspiciously like moisture in his eyes. She could no doubt tell that his breath was already ragged.

But maybe she knew. And maybe she held him so closely, stroking his shoulder, because he didn't have to be alone any longer, not even in this final discovery of her. When his breath stopped racking his body, when he let out one last shaky exhale against her collarbone, he realized she'd been right. He was stronger for having her, not weaker. They lay next to each other, exchanging careful caresses. The comfort overwhelmed him.

"Do you know what it means, to help me?" He finally spoke against the edge of her collar. He was drifting off to sleep; his eyes would not stay open.

"Of course I do." She sounded amused. And then she leaned forward. He could feel the bed shift under her weight, the heat of her against his face. Then she kissed his eyelids slowly. "It means I love you."

"Oh."

So that's what love looked like—not some stifling,

too-careful creature, who wanted to cut his meat into digestible pieces for him. It was something bigger, more robust. He ought to say something in return, he knew, but she was still running her hands across him, and for the first time in longer than he knew, he felt safe. *Not* alone.

He drifted off to sleep.

When he awoke in the morning, she was still with him, a solid, warm presence. Overnight, all of the nonsense, all of his fears, the sheer impossibility of their situation seemed to have become manageable. He knew precisely what they needed to do about Harcroft, and now he finally knew how to do it.

For a long while, he watched her, afraid to disturb her rest. When her eyes finally fluttered open and met his, a slow smile spread across her face. She didn't say anything. She didn't need to.

Some things were even harder than walking a handful of miles on a broken leg. But then, Ned had gotten quite good at doing things he didn't want to do. He looked his wife in the eye.

"Kate," he said softly. He took a deep breath and held her hand, for courage. "I am going to need your help."

LONDON SOCIETY often constructed rumors out of nothing but glances, and gossip from little more than a few wrinkles on a gown. So it was no surprise when Ned discovered that everyone had taken an avaricious interest in the matter between Harcroft and his wife. Everyone knew that Louisa was staying with the Carharts—and speculation as to the reason ran rampant.

The most likely possibility listed in the betting books, was the one Louisa had announced in the courtroom—she was angry with her husband for putting her dearest friend in jeopardy of life and limb. But there were other theories.

Kate sorted the gossip papers into little stacks on the breakfast table. "Feminine pique," she murmured. "Feminine pique. Masculine bravado. Feminine pique." She looked up at him. "That makes three for feminine pique."

"And nobody," Ned said dryly, "has noticed there are double petitions filed in Chancery, on the subject of madness?"

Kate shook her head. "These things are kept quiet, you know. And besides, the petitions weren't posted in a ballroom or penned in a betting book. The *ton* is substantially less likely to notice them."

Ned smiled and felt a grim sense of satisfaction. Everyone knew there were only three ways to end a marriage. Divorce—but Harcroft would retain all rights to his son, and so the result was unacceptable. Annulment—but it would be impossible to prove nonconsummation, particularly given aforementioned son. And there was death, but nobody had the stomach to kill the man.

And with Harcroft's suit pending in Chancery—a suit that claimed Louisa was mentally incompetent—her ability to testify even in divorce proceedings might be cast into doubt. If he had her declared a lunatic, his victory over her would be complete. He would not only be her husband, but her guardian, the trustee of all her care.

For the first time in days, Ned smiled.

Everyone *knew* there were only three ways for a marriage to come to an end.

Everyone was wrong. And tonight, Harcroft was going to discover it.

CHAPTER TWENTY-FOUR

KATE WAS NOT ENTIRELY SURE of their ability to succeed when they arrived at the musicale. Her role for the evening had been set out and discussed, time and again. She was to keep Harcroft away from Louisa for as long as she could, and make him as angry as possible in the process.

This objective turned into a dance—one in which the steps were constantly thwarted by the other members of the *ton,* who hoped that Lord and Lady Harcroft would strike public sparks. Kate led Louisa from one room on a pretext; minutes later, Harcroft followed. On one of their stops, Kate caught a glimpse of the Lord Chancellor, decked out in his full regalia. The gold-embroidered stripes on the sleeves of his robes glittered in the shining lights.

He turned when he saw Kate and Louisa enter the room, but it wasn't yet time for Kate to make their introductions. Besides, the Chancellor was Ned's bailiwick. She ushered Louisa from that room quickly.

It was only when Harcroft began to show signs of distress—a tight line drawn across his forehead, and his hands clenching in his gloves—that Kate brought Louisa to the last refuge.

With everyone in the music hall and the adjoining

rooms, the ballroom was dark and deserted. In the corner, a screen had been set up; behind it, a door led to the servants' quarters. The two women hurried across the room. Kate left Louisa behind the screen and turned to face the entry.

She heard the door open behind her.

It took Harcroft a few seconds to find her shape in the darkness. She saw his silhouette in the doorway. He stared at her and shook his head. Finally, he started toward her, footsteps slapping in percussive rhythm across the floor.

"And what have we here?" Harcroft sounded tired. "Why, it's Kathleen Carhart. Are you proud of yourself? Do you wake every morning, delighting in the knowledge that you bested me? Your success won't last long."

"What sort of nonsense is this, Harcroft?" Kate did not let her voice drop. She could hear her response echoing throughout the hall, around the parquet dance floor. She hoped their words carried far enough. "Bested you?" The door to the servants' quarters *was* behind that screen, she reminded herself. He couldn't see behind it—and Kate still had not heard that door close behind Louisa. She would just have to trust that this would all work out.

"So you're playing the innocent." He stepped forward again. "You've made a mockery of my marriage, and all in the name of…shopping. You made the sacred frivolous. You've stolen from me."

He advanced on her. Slowly she backed away from him. Her back hit the ballroom wall distressingly quickly.

"Harcroft, I think you might need to sit down. Rest a bit."

He grabbed for her wrist and twisted it.

"Don't do that." Kate spoke calmly, although she could feel her pulse beat threadily in his grip. Nobody could see her; at best, she had to hope that someone would hear what was happening. "Harcroft. Let go of my wrist. You don't need to resort to violence. Not again. We can resolve this rationally."

"I don't believe I hit you hard enough last time."

He raised his fist; Kate ducked. She pulled her wrist from his grasp, and his hand hit the wall behind her.

"Be careful—you might hurt yourself," she suggested, and the glint in her eyes made the suggestion less kind than her solicitous tone suggested. "Harcroft…"

He whirled around swiftly. "Goddamn you," he spat out. Before she could react, he set his hands against her shoulders and shoved, pushing her off balance at an odd angle. The hard wood floor smacked against her backside with bruising force; her head missed the wall by inches. He dropped to his knees and leaned over her, pinning her shoulder to the floor.

Kate smiled up at him in sheer relief. Thank God; she'd goaded him into showing his true nature. She'd won. They'd won.

For the first time since they'd come into the room, Kate didn't pitch her voice to carry. This, after all, she didn't want overheard. "In the stories," Kate whispered, "the heroine slays the dragon."

A puzzled frown lit his face.

"She lops off his head and brings it to the villagers. And they build a bonfire, and everyone celebrates because darkness has been banished from the land."

"Dragons?" Harcroft snarled. "Dragons? What the hell are dragons doing in this conversation?" He raised his hand. In another second, his fist would smash into her face. Pinned as she was against the parquet floor, there was no escape. She ought to have been frightened. Her heart should have been hammering, but instead, all she felt was a heady sense of absolute victory. He couldn't hurt her. She smiled up at him; his eyes narrowed.

"True heroes," she told him, "tame their dragons."

"Harcroft." The voice came from behind him. "You'd better stop."

Harcroft turned, his hand arrested in midair.

It was Ned. He'd been waiting in the servants' corridor. He came forward now, limping carefully, his crutches tapping sharply against the parquet.

"How many times must I tell you?" Ned's voice was quiet. "Get your hands off my wife. Now."

Harcroft didn't move.

"Careful, Harcroft. You don't want to do anything you'll regret."

"Regret?" Harcroft let out a shaky breath. "Regret? You of all people know—what have I to regret? It's not *me*." His hands tightened, digging into Kate's shoulder. "I— If I had my wife back, it wouldn't be like this."

"Oh? You've never hit Louisa, then?"

"By accident." The words were hoarse. "Never on purpose. It wasn't my fault. Not truly."

"It wasn't your fault?"

"You know how it is. I get so angry—*she* makes me so angry. I can't let it go. She *makes* me do it, damn it. They all do. I can't stop it."

Ned smiled. "You can't stop it, Harcroft. But I can."

"Unlikely. You can't even walk properly."

Ned took another limping step toward them. Even wounded as he obviously was, he towered over Harcroft. And then he knelt *down* on the ground. "I don't need to." His voice was quiet. His hand found Kate's, curling around hers, replacing the cold of the ballroom with that tiny spot of warmth.

"What? What do you mean?"

Ned glanced behind him. "Are you satisfied, *Lord Chancellor?*"

Harcroft's head whipped around. "Lord Chancellor? Lord Chancellor? Lyndhurst is here?"

From behind the screen came two gentlemen. One, a short bespectacled man, pressed his lips together. He was dressed in sober brown—the physician, Kate guessed. The other man she'd seen earlier in his full ceremonial garb. In the darkness, the gold stripes on the Lord Chancellor's robe had faded to ochre.

"Lord Chancellor." Harcroft stared up at him in disbelief and scrabbled to his feet. "I— That is, what are you doing here? I thought—"

"I'm evaluating whether we need to call an inquiry in lunacy."

Harcroft glanced around. "But…but my wife is elsewhere. Why would you need to be here?"

"Because I've had two petitions brought. One by you, against your wife. And one by your wife, against you. By your own admission, these last few minutes, you pose a physical danger to those around you. One you are incapable of controlling."

"But—"

The bespectacled man leaned forward. "There's evidence of hallucinations, too. A potential cause. That talk of dragons."

"This can't be right. I took a first in Cambridge—"

"It *does* happen sometimes. Especially to intelligent men. And there's so much this might explain, such as bringing that odd suit against your wife's friend simply because you forgot that she went abroad. Did you truly forget, Lord Harcroft, or did you have another, more dangerous illusion?"

"But—"

"You'll be evaluated fairly," the Lord Chancellor promised. "The evidence will be considered by a jury of your peers. Your rights will be considered. We'll do only what's best for you. And if you are found incompetent, we'll appoint a trustee to oversee your properties."

"A trustee? You're joking. You would give someone complete legal control over my destiny? Doubtless you think to lodge that responsibility in Carhart, here. This has all been a plot from the beginning, an attempt to get me to give up—"

"No." The word was softly spoken. But as Louisa stepped from behind the screen, her back was straight and her shoulders unbowed. "I had rather thought they would appoint me." She looked at him—simply looked— and Harcroft's mouth dropped open, no doubt tracing through all the implications.

A husband had control over his wife—every husband, that was, except one who had been declared incompetent by the courts. In that case, he controlled nothing. And his trustee…why, she might control everything.

Harcroft sat back on his heels. His eyes fluttered shut, and he put his head in his hands. He'd lost. He'd well and truly lost now.

After all that Harcroft had done, it should have been impossible to feel sorry for him. And yet Kate did, not because he deserved any such emotion from her. But perhaps because he so plainly didn't. For a second he sat there, almost despairing. Then he stood, stiffly.

He brushed his coat into place and looked over at his wife. For one second, he seemed the old Harcroft again, the Harcroft that everyone always saw—full of charm and grace, doing nothing wrong. He was the man who took firsts at Cambridge, who never missed a point in fencing. He looked one last time at Louisa.

"Louisa," he said, all confident assurance. "You've always known I loved you. You wouldn't do this to me."

"I want the very best for you," she replied. "I hear there are excellent sanitariums in Switzerland."

Harcroft's eyes pinched closed, as if she'd spoken the final benediction over his grave. And then, oh so carefully, he adjusted his coat.

"My lord," the physician said, "we'll have to take you into custody before the inquiry."

Harcroft inclined his head and walked from the room.

Kate scrambled to her knees. Ned took her hand in his. She wasn't sure if he helped her to her feet, after that difficult ordeal, or if she helped him, with his limp.

Perhaps there wasn't any difference any longer.

"HERE WE ARE," Ned said gaily. "We've arrived."

"Yes," Kate replied from her somewhat uncomfortable seat on the carriage, "but *where* have we arrived? You're the one who directed the coachman, and I have been forced to wear this uncomfortable thing about my eyes."

"It's called a blindfold," her husband told her, which was not helpful in the slightest. "Here. I'll help you alight." She reached out her hand blindly, searching for his.

His hand took hers, steady and strong even though he was leaning on crutches all the while.

They'd left the hubbub of London behind them. In the distance, she smelled burning leaves. The air was chilly, but not cold. Cattle lowed.

"Have you taken me to a farm?" she guessed.

"Good guess." His hand found the small of her back. "But no." He turned her. The bulk of his body radiated heat behind her. "You can take off your blindfold now."

Kate raised her hands to her eyes and eased the cloth off her head.

She was facing a house—a large country house, gray but not uninviting. The grass around her was still damp with morning dew; little wisps of mist rose up around them, restricting her view. She thought there were trees off in the distance, but she couldn't be sure through the fog. She could see nothing through the windows—no light, no movement.

"It's an empty house," she said in confusion.

"Correct," her husband replied. "But also completely

wrong. It's *your* empty house." His arm came around her and he stared ahead.

Kate waited for an explanation, but he just looked ahead of him with a faint half smile on his face. "Very well, Ned. What am I supposed to do with an empty house?"

"As it happens," he said, "I had a windfall of five thousand pounds. I promised the gentlemen of London to spend it on something for you. There's a bit of attached land—not much, but enough for a garden."

He didn't say anything more, and so she turned around, looking. Behind her stood an empty paddock and barn. "Don't tell me this is for Champion."

Beyond the wooden structure, a lake was barely visible through the mist.

"No." Ned grinned. "Haven't you guessed, then? Maybe you should see the property."

Nothing came to mind as she walked the perimeter of the paddock. He followed behind her, his steps uneven. They came to the shore of the small lake, and rocks crunched underfoot.

"I confess. I still don't understand."

Ned had been wearing a satchel the entire journey. He slipped it from his shoulders and fumbled the buckle open. "Here. Take this out."

Kate glanced inside. Sitting on top of a pile of sandwiches wrapped in paper was a pistol—the same pistol she'd stolen from Ned and given to Louisa. She glanced up at him again, but he only motioned once more.

She reached in and took it. The metal was hard against her gloves.

"Over the years," he told her, "you've done a great deal of good. You've helped people. And you've done it so silently, so quietly that half the *ton* has never even glanced beyond your face to see who you truly are inside. You've hidden yourself away."

"I— But if people *knew*…"

"Not everyone needs to know," he said quietly. "But more than me and Gareth and Jenny. Some of your friends. Your parents."

She sucked in a breath. "But my father— He'll—"

She'd had a thousand reasons to keep silent about what she'd done, and they all bombarded her now. He'd take work from her. He'd dismiss what she'd done.

But, no. He couldn't do that any longer. If Ned approved, her father couldn't change a thing. And so Kate examined the worst possibility of all—if he knew that she wasn't the fragile daughter he believed her to be, he might not care for her any longer.

"Whatever it is you fear," he said gently, "take it and toss it away."

She drew in a shaky breath.

"I mean that literally," he said. "Because you're holding my fears, too—that pistol and I have been through a great deal together. Throw it as far as you can."

The gun felt heavier in her hands. She looked up at Ned once more, and then slowly hefted the weapon. It seemed too weighty to just toss away, and yet too light to contain all her fears. Still, she heaved it.

It flew in a sailing arc over the water. For one brief second, it caught the morning sun. It glinted. And then the waters closed around it with a splash.

She felt immensely lighter.

"Now," Ned said, "you have someplace to bring the women who need your help, which is rather better than a shepherd's cottage. I thought you might show your parents the house, when they come down to London next Season."

Kate swallowed. She turned around in a slow circle, looking at the house with new eyes. It was no manor house, but it was large enough for the purpose. It was not just a house; it was a statement of hope. It was a promise that he would not turn away in disgust if she proved strong. It was an invitation for her to let the people she cared about see how brilliantly she could shine.

"You know," Ned said, "once they get over their surprise, they'll be proud. I promise."

"How did you know?" she asked, her voice shaky. "How did you know what I wanted, before I even wanted it?"

"That's easy," he said, sliding his arms about her. "It's because I love you."

EPILOGUE

Six months later

AFTER A LONG WINTER, the trees were finally sporting apple-green leaves. The dark mulch of the fields was broken up by new growth snaking up through the soil. After an arduous fight in Chancery, one that had been as short as it was only by dint of the pressure applied by the Marquess of Blakely, Louisa had finally won. As if to make up for those months of worry, spring had burst upon the scene.

As painful as those months had been, they had been bearable for Kate because Ned had been with her. Kate was walking outside, arm-in-arm with her husband, and smiling. Twenty yards distant—just outside the paddock where Champion had once resided—Jenny and Louisa sat on a rug. Beside them, their children played. With the coming of spring, Jeremy had suddenly decided it was time to scoot in earnest. Jenny's daughter, the older, larger, much more vocal Rosa, was delighted to have a new playmate, one who would undoubtedly do her bidding.

"Did I ever tell you," Ned mused, "how Champion saved me on the night I broke my leg?"

"No. How?"

"I was clinging to the fence rail, sure I couldn't take

another step forward without falling on my face. I had convinced myself it was impossible for me to move. Then, Champion being Champion, he charged."

"What? Is that why you had him sent away?"

Ned smiled. "Yes, although not for the reason you imagine. You see, I thought I couldn't have walked any farther, but as I wanted to live, I discovered I could move. It was a good thing to know."

He paused and plucked a dandelion from the grass. "I wanted him to improve because I wanted to believe anything could happen—that if Champion could redeem himself, so could I. But what I really needed to do was realize that I was already saved. And what Champion truly needed was not the weight of my expectations, but someone who would give him no chores, have no expectations of him except that he eat hay." Ned smiled at Kate. "From what I've heard from the vicar we pensioned off a few years ago, being around a pair of old nanny goats—no other horses, no threatening humans—has been good for Champion."

Only her husband would worry about the comfort of a horse that had threatened him. Kate smiled. "Aren't you a little disappointed, to have tamed all your dragons? Whatever will you do with your afternoons?"

He smiled, and his arm came around Kate's waist, pulling her close. "A confession," he whispered in her ear. "With you beside me, all dragons are tame."

"You don't feel that you need a struggle, that you need something to prove yourself?"

He shrugged. Kate knew there were still moments when he'd resorted to sheer physical exercise to regulate some of his emotions. There had been a month in the middle of winter when she'd come to understand precisely what he'd meant when he'd described his bouts with darkness. But they had both known that it was a finite thing, that it would leave. And it hadn't been as bad as Kate had feared.

"I think," Ned said quietly, "I've come to the point where I trust myself enough not to need the proof. I see no need to seek out another challenge."

"Oh." Kate suppressed a small, secret smile, and let only a note of timorous wistfulness creep into her voice. The ground was soft under her feet, and she waited until they were out from under the limbs of the trees before continuing. "That's too bad."

"Are you trying to rid yourself of me?" He was joking, by that tone. "Send me off to China again? Or India?"

"Oh, no. That would be very inconvenient. You see, I was thinking that in another…oh, seven months, I'll be presenting you with a very lovely challenge indeed. I was rather hoping you would want this one."

Ned stopped dead and turned to her. A low smile lit his face. "Ah," he said, a hint of a quaver in his voice. For a moment, he didn't say anything more. But their arms were linked, and Kate could feel a tremor run through him. She'd felt the same way once she'd realized she was expecting. Fear. Exultation. And one silent scream, halfway between "I'm not ready!" and "It's about time."

Ned looked off into the distance and coughed before turning back to her. "We ought to name her Iphigenia."

"Isn't that overly formal?"

"Iphigenia," he repeated, as if the name were the most

reasonable one in the world. "We could call her 'Figgy' for short."

Kate choked on her laughter, relieved that he wasn't serious. "She would hate us forever."

"Yes, well. You're the one who insisted we needed to add difficulty to our life. How better to accomplish that than to guarantee from the start that our daughter can't even pronounce her own name?"

"Ned, if you name our daughter Iphigenia, I will…I will…"

"You," Ned said with an assured sparkle in his eye, "will love me just as much as ever. But maybe you are right. How's Hatshepsut?"

"Hatshep*what?*"

"Egyptian is all the rage right now. No?"

"Decidedly not." Kate smiled at him. "Try again."

"Vertiline? Permelia?"

"Where are you getting these names? Why is it that they all seem to have eighteen syllables?"

"I know the one. Obraya."

"That is not a name."

He waggled his eyebrows at her. "Can you be sure?"

"Goose."

He frowned. "Well, at least that one's short, but I think she won't appreciate the connotations. Isn't that a little pejorative?"

Kate burst into laughter. "Stop. You have to stop." When she finally was able to breathe again, she shook her head at him. "What's wrong with your mother's name? Have you some objection to Lily?"

"I suppose not," Ned said. "This is why I love you.

Always practical." He reached out and took her waist and drew her closer.

No. Not always. Not when he held her this close, not when his lips brushed her cheek once, her jaw a second time.

"And what if it's a boy?" Kate asked.

He leaned over to brush a third kiss on her forehead. "Then, my love, he is really going to hate being called Lily."

* * * * *

AUTHOR'S NOTE

Kate's trial takes place without an indictment being presented to a grand jury. This is mostly because that step in the process would be boring to read about and boring to write about. In 1842, that step would have been necessary. I've taken the liberty of bending time a little in this regard; in 1849 legislation was passed that allowed police magistrates to certify that indictments could proceed to trial without being presented to a grand jury.

In early Victorian England, summary trials (that is, trials without a jury) could come before police magistrates under some circumstances (certain petty, nonviolent crimes). In many instances, particularly for the lower classes, magistrates sat as judges of fact over other crimes, too, so long as the parties agreed that no jury was necessary. It's not always clear that the parties under those circumstances consented to the lack of jury; in some cases, they may not even have known they were entitled to a jury. Kate's first abortive trial, interrupted by Ned, is one such. Both the speed and the apparent laxity of the courtroom depicted here are in keeping with the few accounts I've read of such proceedings.

Harcroft's statements to the magistrate as to the elements and legality of abduction of a wife by persuasion were drawn (with little alteration) from Blackstone's

Commentaries on the Laws of England—presumably the source of our hypothetical Harcroft's cribbed notes, anyway. Magistrate Fang was borrowed from Charles Dickens's *Oliver Twist*.

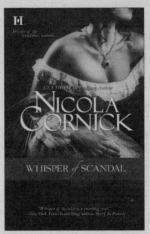